HOME SICK

British-Italian Silvia Saunders has an MA in Creative and Life Writing from Goldsmiths, University of London. Her debut novel, *Homesick*, won the Comedy Women in Print Unpublished Prize 2023. Originally from Nuneaton, birthplace of George Eliot, Silvia is ashamed to admit that she hasn't read a single one of Eliot's books – not even the skinny ones like *Silas Marner*.

She lives in East London with her boyfriend and all her books.

SILVIA SAUNDERS

HOME SICK

HarperCollins*Publishers*

HarperCollins*Publishers* Ltd
1 London Bridge Street,
London SE1 9GF

www.harpercollins.co.uk

HarperCollins*Publishers*
Macken House,
39/40 Mayor Street Upper,
Dublin 1
D01 C9W8

First published by HarperCollins*Publishers* 2025
1

A catalogue record for this book is available from the British Library

ISBN: 978-0-00-866701-6 (HB)
ISBN: 978-0-00-874283-6 (TPB)

This novel is entirely a work of fiction.
The names, characters and incidents portrayed in it are
the work of the author's imagination. Any resemblance to
actual persons, living or dead, events or localities is
entirely coincidental.

Typeset in Adobe Garamond Pro by
Palimpsest Book Production Ltd, Falkirk, Stirlingshire

Printed and Bound in the UK using 100% Renewable Electricity
at CPI Group (UK) Ltd

MIX
Paper | Supporting
responsible forestry
FSC
www.fsc.org   FSC™ C007454

This book contains FSC™ certified paper and other controlled sources
to ensure responsible forest management.

For more information visit: www.harpercollins.co.uk/green

Per mamma. Per tutto.

And for anyone who struggles with their mental health.
There's brightness ahead. Hold on.

PART I

Autumn

1

I become an heiress overnight.

This is a huge shock. I am twenty-five and a librarian and have never had a savings account.

My mum calls and says, 'There's some money. I think we should buy you a flat.'

I say, 'What money?'

She says, 'You know when dad died there was a payout?'

I don't know this at all, but I say, 'Yeah?'

'Well, I think it's time for you to have it. I kept moving it from place to place back when you could still make good interest that way, and now it's a lot more than it was initially.'

'How much more?'

She tells me a number that sounds obscene. My mum doesn't work anymore, and I feel as though what should really be happening is she should be paying off her own mortgage, then travelling the world. I don't say anything for a while.

'Mara?'

'Mmm?'

'You'll have to take the lead on this. But I'm very serious. It's what he would have wanted us to do with the money.'

2

For the last year, I have been living with a childhood friend, in a small, damp Hackney flat which is out of my budget and, as a result of this cohabitation, I don't think I can confidently describe us as friends anymore. Lewis doesn't seem to have been that keen on me since the start of us living together, but now it's getting harder for him to hide.

'Are we keeping these flowers forever?' he says, pointing at a vase of lilies he received from work last week. 'No, I'm just curious. If I didn't say anything, would you just leave them there to rot?'

He has been on a work trip somewhere in Sweden for a few days, and his moods are always nastier when he's back from one of these things.

'They're yours, though?' I try. 'I didn't want to assume you were finished with them?'

'They fucking stink, Mara.'

I keep stirring my tea. He cooks smoked fish nearly every single evening, the smell of which permeates the sofa and the curtains and the bed linen, and he has never made a single phone call to our landlady when there's been a problem in the flat, and he point-blank refuses to wash up cutlery as it *makes him feel weird*. I don't feel able to bring any of this stuff up, because he has such a high-flying job and I do not. Whenever he gets home from work and I am on the sofa, watching one of my shows, I know what he thinks. Even his viewing habits are intellectual. He favours gritty documentaries about the way we live now, Scandi noir, the news. I favour the *Real Housewives* franchise, sitcoms, MTV.

Nobody touches the lilies that evening, and they're still there when we both go to work the next morning.

3

I have a boyfriend called Tom. He is a newly qualified teacher and is working at an academy in Croydon, where the children are all taller than him. He works long hours like my housemate, and I often don't get to see him on weeknights anymore. He's from Birmingham. We met at university there. We have been together for five years and in London for only one of those, and he's suddenly homesick. Though his accent was never particularly strong, he has started spending his weekends back at home and when he calls me, drunk and happy with the friends he has known since he was tiny, he sounds like Ozzy Osbourne.

4

I invite my friend Noor round for a McDonald's, and she actually agrees to come. She's recently moved back into her mum's house in Bow, and though it obviously makes financial sense for her, it does mean I see a lot less of Noor than I did before. Whenever I ask to hang out, she says things like, 'Come to me! It's only half an hour if you make your connections!' But it always seems to be me that has to make the connections.

Get us a big mac meal, she texts now. *Large. Nana milkshake.*

I do as I'm told, even though the McDonald's is literally right next to the station exit, and she could have brought the food nice and hot for us on her way, instead of it sitting on the side next to my housemate's lilies, getting colder and soggier by the minute.

Just getting some ciggies! Be with you in 5!

The off-licence is also right next to the McDonald's. I think that I should say something about this when she arrives, but she pushes into my living room with a full skit about one of the girls she works with, and she does the girl's posh home counties accent to a T, and then it seems petty to ruin her high by telling her that it was definitely her turn to get the food. She drops a nail polish for me onto the coffee table. It's a denim-effect one she's stolen from the samples at the beauty counter she works at. I thaw at this gesture.

'Wouldn't suit me,' she says. 'Bit tacky.'

5

I go into an estate agent's on a Tuesday after work. It is one of the more famous ones where they give you glass bottles of sparkling water and all wear the exact same navy blue suit from Next. Three members of staff flock to me at once.

'Selling?'

'Buying?'

'Browsing?'

'I think I'm trying to buy a flat?' I say.

'Amazing! Well, you're in the right place,' the shortest of the trio says, leading me by the small of my back – which feels inappropriately intimate – to a plush seating area. He sits opposite me and beams, without saying anything further.

I guess it's my turn to talk. 'I've come into a bit of money and I'd like to see what it would get me.'

'Lucky girl!' he says. 'Wow! The dream! What's your secret?'

'My dad died.'

He scrunches his face up in imitation of compassion. 'He'd be so proud of you. Such a big step for someone so young.'

I'm ninety percent sure the estate agent is at least five years younger than me. 'Mmm.'

'So, talk me through. What's the checklist? Budget? Area? Just you? You and partner? One-bed? Two-bed?'

I tell him the budget. It feels like the easiest question to answer for now.

'Okay, a healthy deposit,' he says, misunderstanding me.

'No, that's the whole sum.' I am confused.

'What sort of mortgage are we looking at?'

'I was hoping I wouldn't need to get a mortgage?'

The estate agent does a nasty laugh. 'Oh, sweetheart.'

6

The library I work at is in Homerton. Mid-sized, not terribly well frequented. Close to a Co-op and a few decent cafés for my lunch breaks. A walkable commute, which is a real luxury in this city. My boss, Derek, is overfamiliar. Never quite steps fully over the line, but always has one toe dangerously close to it. Whenever we get book deliveries, he sits on the counter in front of me, bum crack peeking over the top of his leather-belted chinos, and reads whole opening paragraphs out to me, gauging my reaction. Sometimes, when I can't sleep, Tom will read me a Raymond Carver story, a tiny two or three page one, and those are the moments I love him most. When Derek reads to me it's as though he's breathing on the back of my neck, or rubbing himself against me.

We have a book delivery today. It's a box of manga for the anime section, thankfully. Not something Derek can really read from. Not one to miss the chance for one-on-one time, though, he invites me for a *catch-up*. This is what he likes to call my line management meetings.

I traipse after him into the staffroom, and he closes the door behind us.

'So,' he smiles. 'I do so love to hear your stories. What's new with you?'

I try to at least pretend to keep it professional. 'Well. I've noticed a higher uptake with the treasure hunt worksheets now we've put them by the door.'

'And Tim?'

Derek heard me crying on the phone to Noor a couple of weeks ago about Tom's recent mood swings, and has been unable to drop the topic since.

'He's fine.'

'Still a bit weepy? I did feel for you the other day, I really did. Call me old-fashioned, but I think the man should always be the stronger one. It's not right for him to lean so heavily on you.'

I don't say anything for a moment, just sort of grimace.

'Poor thing. Maybe he's just one of those Eeyore types.'

'Mmm.'

'I wanted to say, I know I'm technically your boss, but I do think of us as friends.' He pauses, waiting for a reaction. I don't give him one. 'If you ever need to let off some steam, be the needy one for once, I'm here. We could get a drink. No shop talk. Just two pals.'

'Derek, thanks for this. I have quite a lot of cataloguing to do before lunch, though, if that's everything?' I have stood up.

'Yes. Such a brave girl.'

I manage to pin Tom down for a date night. Somehow, I have found myself needing to romance my own boyfriend. I book us tickets to a West End show and we go to Burger & Lobster beforehand.

Tom says, over and over again, 'It's actually good up town, isn't it? You forget.'

We order a lobster each and put on the novelty plastic bibs. I instantly regret my choice of restaurant. It's all so jovial and forced, and Tom looks a little mad, grinning with his bib on and saying that we should come to Soho more often, every night, even, why not?

'Babe,' I say, before the food arrives. 'I've got something to tell you.'

His eyes go wide behind his specs. He wears those see-through round ones that everyone our age has now. When we first met, he still wore the basic rectangular ones from Specsavers, two pairs for £49.

I want to soothe him, tell him that it's a nice thing, something to be excited about. The problem is that I don't know if he will think it's a nice thing at all.

I blurt it out. I don't want to have a lobster in front of me when I'm saying it. 'I'm going to buy a flat, babe. Apparently there's a big chunk of money from my dad, and my mum wants me to use it to buy a flat. It doesn't need to affect you, but obviously it would mean that we could live in it together, and you could stop paying rent, and that might take some of the strain off, and you could look for a different school to work at, a less stressful one, or maybe even take a few months off if you wanted, or—'

He's gone a bit white. I can almost see his brain whirring. A waitress places a bowl of lemon water in between me and Tom.

'Hope you're hungry!' she says.

Tom seems unable to verbalise anything about the news I've just shared. Once the waitress has backed away, he manages some platitudes like, 'Wow!' and, 'That's the last thing I expected you to say!'

We watch *Les Mis*, which, honestly, might have been my most stupid decision to date. Tom doesn't sleep over, and doesn't invite me to sleep at his either. We hug outside the tube station, and I watch his little back disappear underground.

8

Having realised that the money my mum is giving me – fortune though it is – would realistically get me only a garage or a canal boat, I organise a phone call with a mortgage advisor. I shut myself in my bedroom and put on *First Dates* on catch-up, so my housemate won't hear me if he comes home. It all feels very real now. I'm not just thinking about buying a flat, I might actually really be buying a flat.

The phone rings. Six on the dot, as promised. It's a woman called either Janet or Jeanette, I don't quite catch it, and she is stern and doesn't have a very good bedside manner. She asks me questions about my spending and my salary and my relationship status. She just wants a *Single* or *In a relationship*, not an, *I've been with my boyfriend for a large part of my twenties and I assumed he was The One but he's been acting very out of character lately and I don't think I can depend on him to stick around for this next phase of my life.* I'm embarrassed to tell her about my regular outgoings. They seem frivolous and silly. Why do I get a *New Yorker* subscription when I never find the time to read them? Why do I pay £45 a month for my phone when phone calls and texting give me anxiety? Why do I actually pay for my own Netflix account? Nobody does that, do they? Everyone but me has someone they can steal a log-in from. I lie about how much I spend on booze and takeaways. I downplay my monthly underwear and skincare purchases. I tell Janet/Jeanette that all the things I buy now are negotiable, and that I could give them all up tomorrow if I had to. I find myself agreeing to a forty-year mortgage, which boosts my total budget by about a third. I thought my library job paid pretty well, but Janet/Jeanette is less than impressed. I promise to bring it up with Derek at our next *catch-up*.

9

My housemate starts seeing a girl and cheers up a bit. He wants to chat again in the evenings, he asks my advice, we pore over her texts together.

One of them reads, *Sure, dinner works for me. We can cook together next week?*

We dissect this one for quite some time.

'It's Tuesday,' he says. 'Why next week? There are still six nights left of the week we're already in. That's such a long wait.'

He is lying on the brown leather sofa that neither of us like. I have been granted the red armchair, which is slightly more comfortable. He sat down first, leaving the good seat for me. This feels like a step in the right direction.

'Look, I think this is good,' I say. 'Cooking together is really intimate. And she clearly trusts you not to be a creep if she's willing to start the evening in a house?'

He breathes out, his stomach pushing at the buttons of his work shirt, which he still hasn't taken off, even though it's nine o'clock. I have been in my pyjamas since six, like usual. 'I suppose,' he says. 'No kisses though. I always put kisses to her.'

'I've told you not to do that,' I say. 'It's too much.'

'How many dates until you sleep with someone?' he says.

'Me in particular, or people at large?'

'You. How long did you wait to sleep with Tom?'

The truth is that Tom pursued me doggedly at the start, passed me little notes in class, made up excuses to see me at any opportunity. We weren't even strictly friends. We just sat next to each other in a D. H. Lawrence module for a year. Something switched on a night out in Reflex. We bumped into each other, drunk, and began dancing together in a jokey way, until suddenly it wasn't jokey anymore. We went home together that night and have been together since. So the answer to my housemate's question could either be *one day* or *one year*.

'I can't really remember,' I say. 'It's best not to compare anyway. Every couple is different.'

'This will be our sixth date,' he says. He sighs and I get a whiff of his dinner mackerel. 'We kiss super passionately. The attraction is definitely there from both sides. It's just something seems to be holding her back.'

I feel accused of something. Like he's trying to blame this on me, my presence in the flat maybe, or me being a woman.

'I probably shouldn't say this,' he says. 'But I've invested a lot in this relationship already.'

I don't like where this is going.

'I've taken her to some *really* nice places,' he says.

'Lewis,' I warn.

'I'm not saying I *deserve* anything. It's just a bit questionable from her to accept all these dinners and things if she doesn't have the right intentions.'

I measure my words carefully before speaking. 'She might still be working out what her intentions are herself. That's allowed, you know.'

I sense him closing off from me again.

'Look, I'm going to suggest she come over at the weekend. Could you maybe go to Tom's?'

'It depends if he's in London or Birmingham,' I say.

The look Lewis gives me then is so withering that I get up from the red armchair and say, 'I'll go and call him now. See what his plans are.'

I don't call Tom. It's still early enough that he'll be marking books and fretting and probably won't even have had his dinner yet. I sit on my bed and scroll through Rightmove. One day soon I won't be in this toxic flat anymore. One day soon I will hang my own photos on my own walls and sit on my own sofa which I will have chosen myself, and my boyfriend will be his old self again and Noor will be more open to visiting regularly, and there'll be fresh flowers from Columbia Road Market in a vintage vase on my dining table, and I'll have nice linen bedding which I won't have to wash with Lewis's Calvin Kleins, and I'll be happy and a grown-up and things will start to make sense.

10

My first house viewing is revelatory. I meet a man with a one-syllable
name a few streets away from the library. He's in a navy blue, shiny
suit and has on really long, pointy, black lace-ups. I can't stop staring
at them and wondering where his foot reaches inside.

'Mara!' he says. 'So this is your first ever viewing, I'm told?'

I nod, and shake his outstretched hand.

'You're in luck, because the search may already be over!'

I have come alone, but have promised to send my mum photos
and videos of every corner of the flat. It's a mid-height new-build,
second floor, with balcony. In the photos it looked airy and bright.
I follow the estate agent. It takes him five goes to unlock the front
door. Inside the actual flat, there is stuff everywhere. Piles of clothes,
empty cardboard boxes, bulging bin bags, the contents of which seem
to be actual rubbish. It smells musty – much like my existing abode
– and there's a cat slinking from room to room, leaving little black
hairs in its wake.

'As you can see,' he says, 'it's been very well loved and looked
after. Two young professionals, just had a baby, moving to Brighton.'

I hope he won't be following me around for the whole viewing.
It's that same uncomfortable feeling you get when you go into a
small boutique and the owner asks what you're looking for and you
weren't really looking for anything, and they watch you browse the
rails, all erect and hopeful, their livelihood depending on lots of
people just like you liking what they see.

'So?' the agent says.

I haven't moved from my spot on the welcome mat.

'Nice,' I say.

'Knew you'd love it.' He starts to walk me from room to room.
The extent of his knowledge seems to be just naming each space.

'Kitchen,' he says.

'Bathroom.'

'Master.'

'Living area.'

'Spare room slash nursery,' he says, winking at me.

We have done the whole flat in thirty seconds.

'Any questions?' he says.

I shake my head. 'I think I have everything I need,' I say.

I text my mum on my walk home. *Didn't have time to take any photos.*

11

I know I should be extra careful with my money for the next few months, that every pound counts. That said, when Noor calls and asks whether I want to go to Sketch for an Instagrammable dinner date with her, I agree immediately. I meet her in Central after work so we can get new outfits from Zara. We haven't done something outside the house, just us two, for ages.

She tries on five different pairs of faux leather trousers, and looks great in all of them. I try on a couple of block-colour jumpsuits and look like a child in both of them. The legs pool around my ankles, no matter how much I hitch them up or fiddle with the waistline.

'Show me, show me!' Noor calls from the changing room next to mine.

I don't want to, but being shy is not in the spirit of things. I edge sheepishly behind her curtain.

She makes a *pfff* sound and says, 'They should be sued for the length of the trouser legs in here. What human woman has legs that long?'

I am cheered by this show of camaraderie, and happily spend the next forty minutes advising Noor on Victoriana blouses to match her new trousers. It is seven o'clock by the time she has finalised her outfit. Our reservation is at seven thirty.

'What am I going to wear?' I say, looking down at my work outfit: a bobbly black roll-neck and wool checked trousers.

'That?' Noor says, slicking red lipstick over the red lipstick she already has on.

'Noor.'

'Okay, look.' She looks around. Seemingly at random, she picks up a pair of electric-blue leather boots. They have a thin six-inch heel and are completely impractical. They are also beautiful and the clock is ticking and she knows what she's doing.

They are eighty pounds. Noor's whole outfit only comes to fifty and she'll definitely get loads of wear out of both items. This always happens when we go shopping together. She has a way of sweeping me along with her. The day we met, we ran into each other – quite literally – in the corridor of our halls of residence. I had a box of books in my hands, she had a bottle of gin in hers. She ushered me straight into her room and poured me a shot in an egg cup. It was as though she'd picked me. She seemed like such a woman of the world that I couldn't believe she would willingly move from London to Birmingham for three years. I was dazzled by her. I still am.

She bats her eyelashes at the cashier and is granted permission to get changed into her new clothes in the changing rooms. In there, she pulls out her make-up bag and does us both a perfect smoky eye in under five minutes. I put on my new boots and shove my loafers into the paper Zara bag. The boots instantly rub my bunions.

'Come on,' Noor says, yanking my arm, 'we're going to be late.'

Sketch is a pink marshmallow dream. Everyone in there is gorgeous or young or both. I feel a bit mad in my work clothes and tottery heels, while Noor looks entirely at ease, like her parents own the place. Speaking of which, I wonder whether this might be an appropriate evening and an appropriate location to share my news with Noor.

I am distracted by Noor ordering for us: a wanky cocktail each and frogs' legs to share.

I sip my drink slowly, while Noor tells me about a guy that keeps coming into her department store and asking for samples.

'It's no skin off my nose,' she says. 'But this man is never, ever going to buy anything. I must've given him about a litre of face cream by now. For free. Gratis. I admire the audacity, to be honest.'

'Noor,' I say. 'Something big has happened.'

She pales. 'Oh babe,' she says. 'That prick.'

'No, it's not – It's a nice thing.'

'Oh?' She seems genuinely surprised that something nice could have happened to me.

'I'm buying a flat.'

She can't hide her instinctive reaction. I see it written all over her face. She wants to say, *How, when you have such a shit job? How can you do that, if I can't?* She takes a long drink and composes herself. 'A flat?' she says. 'Where?'

'Here. I don't know exactly the area yet, but it'll be in London somewhere. My mum is helping, of course. A lot. It's my inheritance, really.' I want to apologise for my fortune. I want to remind her of my dead dad.

'Wow,' she says. 'Well cheers to that!' She waves the waitress over and orders us another drink each.

I am careful with my main and order the cheapest thing at £22, which is some form of tartare, while Noor throws all caution to the wind and orders langoustine. I manage to dissuade her from dessert by making a vague comment about how unforgiving leather trousers can be after a big meal. I feel terrible about this, but I feel worse about our impending bill. When it arrives, the total comes to £140.

I gasp and say, 'Noor! We'll have to scrub the pots!'

She doesn't laugh.

Though Noor has definitely ordered more than I have, we split it 50/50. What with new boots and gin brambles, I have spent over a hundred and fifty pounds on a weeknight dinner, which I haven't enjoyed, and which I can't even flaunt on social media, in case Tom or Lewis or my mum sees.

12

Tom comes to the next viewing with me. It's a converted fire station, which I feel excited about seeing. Though it's significantly over budget, I have it on good authority that there's some wiggle room. Tom's quiet on the bus, keeps checking his work emails. I squeeze his hand every few minutes, and he offers me weak half-smiles. I glimpse the same name in his inbox repeatedly. If he were in a chirpier mood, I might tease him about this. I know Emma is just his teaching assistant, but we always used to pretend to have jealous rages about innocent relationships. It was a sort of skit we'd do. *Love his big sack, do you?* he'd say, when I thanked the DHL guy for a delivery. *Why don't you marry her?* I'd hiss at him, if he held a door open for an elderly woman. It was funny because we loved each other so much, it seemed unthinkable that we'd fancy anyone else.

'So you said it's a one-bed?' he manages.

'Yes!' I say. 'Which is plenty, unless you want to start sleeping in separate rooms!'

This is not the right thing to say, and I wish I could just be more chill, not come off so needy, when I know he's the one who needs more at the moment.

He gives me a placatory laugh. I am winded. We get off the bus and, a few streets down, we see the block. There is a small, noisy crowd outside the main entrance. I see a flash of blue suit, and realise that all these people are here for the same reason as me.

'Are you serious?' I mutter.

I want Tom to say something encouraging, or even to suggest we sack the viewing off completely and go for brunch somewhere. There was a time, not too long ago, that he'd have told me I was too good to compete, that I deserved a flat that was exclusive with me, that put me first, that appreciated the opportunity to have an owner like me. Today, he looks genuinely scared about the task ahead.

'Okay?' I whisper.

He nods.

'Mara!' Blue Suit calls.

'Sorry we're late!' I call. 'This is Tom. My boyfriend.'

Blue Suit doesn't give a fuck about Tom or who he is to me. He just wants to herd us all inside. It's a lot less guided of an event, this time. We are each handed a pamphlet and left to our own devices. I count six other groups of people. One man has a measuring tape. A woman in a tan skirt suit is describing each feature to somebody on the phone. There is a pregnant woman, someone else in their fifties. I don't belong in this building, and am enormously out of my depth. While I enter and exit each room, Tom stands immobile in front of the living-room window, gazing out at the busy road below. I take a couple of photos, for show, and when the agent asks if I have any questions, the only thing I can think to say is, 'What's the biggest supermarket nearby?'

13

After the fire station, I vow to go to all future viewings alone. In just one week, I see another four flats. One is a basement conversion and so dark that I struggle to put one foot in front of the other. The next is a converted attic, and, even at my modest height, I have to duck in eighty percent of the space. The third one I'm shown is a full fifty grand over budget. The final one, which I see at eight in the morning on a Sunday, is directly on top of Whitechapel overground station. Its windows rattle every time a train goes past, which is often.

'So much potential,' the agent says, grinning wildly at me, while he steadies himself on the table after a particularly vibration-heavy train passes.

'I don't know. I think the noise would drive me mad,' I say, inching towards the door.

'Oh, you'd be surprised! You get used to it and then you can't sleep without it.'

An ambulance shrieks past as he says this. I'm unable to hide a wince.

14

Derek suggests we have our next *catch-up* at the pub, after work. Unable to think of a fictional prior engagement fast enough, I agree. I don't really know if I'm allowed to say no. In a bid to get wear out of my extravagant purchase, I have on my electric- blue boots behind the counter. When I get up to switch the computer off and follow Derek out of the door, he does a wolf whistle.

'Yes, queen,' he says, unforgivably.

We go to The Adam and Eve, which is in walking distance, and Derek orders us a bottle of white, without consulting me.

I'm thirsty, so I drink. He makes a good show of talking about our actual jobs for the first half an hour. I start to wonder whether it really is just a work thing.

Then he says, 'Tell me something nobody else knows about you.'

Though it sounds like a joke, I know enough about Derek now to know that it's not a joke. His cheeks are rosy from the wine and the warmth of the pub. I have no idea how old he is. He could be thirty, he could be forty-five. He is looking at me eagerly.

'What sort of thing?' I say, popping a crisp in my mouth. He wants something saucy, a secret that'll bond us together. I'm not willing to give him that. Not for free, anyway.

'Something I wouldn't expect from you. Something shocking,' he says. He is leaning across the table now.

'I don't always wash my hands after I pee.'

He throws his head back with glee. 'Even in the library?'

'Especially in the library. Your turn.'

He places his hands palm-down on either side of his wine glass, bracing himself. I can see wiry black hairs on some of his fingers. They're uneven. Some have a whole clump, some have none.

'I once did stuff with a cousin,' he says, his answer coming quickly. 'Not full sex, but.'

'A first cousin?'

23

He nods. 'Consensual, obviously. She initiated it, actually.'

I down the rest of my glass of wine. 'Derek. You're a lot.'

He has the decency to look a bit embarrassed. 'Shall I get us another one?' he says, nodding at the nearly empty bottle.

'Sure. Why not?'

It's still seven o'clock and there's only Lewis waiting for me at home. I know he treasures the nights that he doesn't find me sitting on the sofa when he gets in from work. Total freedom to fry his salmon fillet and read *The Economist* in peace. His love interest still hasn't spent the night, and the energy in our house is charged. Any time apart is good for us both, I think. Before we lived together, we used to do everything as a double act, talking relentlessly, laughing so hard that we threatened to be sick. Now, when I ask if he wants to go to the pub or for a walk with me, he says, 'Why? I can just see you at the flat.'

I go to the loo and don't wash my hands.

Predictably, Derek says, 'I hope you washed your hands this time!' when I sit back down.

It doesn't escape my notice that the second bottle he's bought is a cheaper one. I pour myself a glass. I have a fleeting thought about Tom. He hasn't called me yet, so he doesn't know I'm here. I'll tell him. We don't have secrets. Well, I don't anyway. There was a time when he'd be healthily jealous about this, would want to know all the details, might threaten to *have a word*. I'm not sure what his stance would be now.

I tell Derek about my flat hunt. He is visibly impressed, and this buoys me along. The truth is, the search is not as exciting as I assumed it'd be. I drink and I fill Derek in on some of the shitholes I've been seeing both online and in real life.

'It's mad,' I say. 'I've noticed that if you up your budget even by twenty thousand, you get loads more for your money. The quality jumps up *a lot*.'

Derek looks pensive. 'Couldn't you just get a bigger mortgage?'

'I don't get paid enough, Derek.'

'I wonder if I could tweak a few things on your contract,' he says. 'Or write a letter about how much overtime you regularly do.'

I look at him, incredulous. 'You don't have the power to do that. Do you?'

He winks at me. 'I've done it for other people.'

I'm not sure how willing I am to accept a favour from Derek and be in his debt. That said, I have something on him too. He lives in the same world as me. He must know that he shouldn't be taking his underling to drinks outside of the workplace, framed as a line management meeting. It would be nice just to see what I could get for twenty grand more.

15

A man called Max or Mark or Matt takes me around Hackney in his jaunty red Citroën C3, talking incessantly. Kiss FM is on, and in the small gaps in conversation, he hums along to all the songs.

'I'd like to put an offer on this one myself,' he says. 'Truly. It's an absolute gem of a place. Just you wait.'

My hopes are modest. I haven't brought anyone along, and this time I haven't even told my mum about the viewing. My new stance is: speak up only once I can picture myself living somewhere. Until then, it's all on me.

'So why are the owners selling if it's so nice?' I say, goading him.

'Sad story, actually. It's a really nice young couple, and the guy's mum got very ill, very quickly, so they're moving in with her in Aberystwyth. Don't know how long they'll be there, so unlucky for them, and very lucky for you.'

I join him in humming along to the radio.

The flat in question is opposite the big Sainsbury's in Dalston. Max/Mark/Matt looks coquettishly over his shoulder at me, as he leads me to an unassuming gate. He knows what he's doing with the fob, buzzes us right in, and swaggers his way over to a very shiny black door.

'Wait for it,' he says.

'I'm already excited that we're the only ones here,' I say.

He pushes the door open with the palm of his hand, and steps out of the way to allow me in first.

'Oh,' I breathe.

It's split-level, exposed brick everywhere, with an industrial spiral staircase leading to the second floor. Big factory windows let in indecent amounts of natural light, and the owners have clearly spent a lot of time and money on tasteful vintage furniture.

'Told you,' I hear from behind me.

It's like being on an episode of *Grand Designs*. I'm half-expecting

Kevin McCloud to jump out from behind the Smeg. I don't ask anything useful, don't take any photos, don't call my mum, don't make any notes. I don't need to do any of that. I can picture myself in this space, would love this to be my home, and really, that's the only thing that matters.

That same evening, behind my closed bedroom door, sitting under the ever-expanding damp patch, I call Max/Mark/Matt and ask him what I need to do next.

'They're asking for final and best offers,' he says. 'This isn't a time for playing games. If you want it, you'll have to go in all guns blazing.'

I tell him my very top end number.

'Can you add anything at all?' he says. 'Couple of extra grand? Might make all the difference.'

He is talking as though it's a fiver. He is pulling me along with him. 'Sure,' I say. 'Add on two grand.'

'Good luck,' he says. 'Will leave this with them and be in touch as soon as I hear anything.'

16

I go out with Noor. We get so drunk I can't remember either of our names. When I check my online banking the next morning, I see that I have spent £85 on drinks. I am so ashamed, I spend the whole day shut in my bedroom. I don't move from my bed until long after the smell of Lewis's dinner tuna steak has drifted through the flat. I venture out only to quietly vomit, with the tap running, and to gingerly brush my teeth for whole minutes.

17

Tom's mum invites us to her sixtieth. Tom's dad planned her a surprise party, but, when he inevitably told her about it, she asked him to cancel. Her stance is that sixty is nothing to make a fuss about and she just wants a few people over for a takeaway and a couple of tinnies.

'You don't have to come,' Tom says to me. He sees my wounded look, and corrects himself, 'If you don't feel like it.'

'Of course I feel like it. Do you not want me there?'

'Babe,' he says. 'Come on.'

So on the Friday, we meet at Euston and take the 17:52 to Birmingham. He's rushed from school and is still in his little suit. The sight of him all dressed up like a grown-up makes me want to cry.

'You look nice,' I say.

He gives me a kiss. A real one. He has quite a small mouth, and I used to tease him that he never fully opened it when he kissed me, so over the years he's learned to widen it and poke his tongue in slightly. It's a particularly wet mouth too, which I've always found strangely comforting.

'Have we got time to get some cans and snacks?' he asks.

That he's thinking about snacks is a really good sign.

'Sounds good!' I say, a bit too loudly.

'Wait here with the bags,' he says, and gives me another mouth-kiss.

I beam under the departure boards, especially when I see him come back, laden down with stuff. He proudly presents me with a mini bottle of the pinot grigio I like, and wags his finger when I ask to see what else he's bought.

On the train, he moves down the carriages, right to the last one. This usually annoys me. Not today. He finds us two seats next to each other, and helps me put my bags on the storage shelf.

'Are we facing the right way?' he says.

'Well yes, babe. The train's not going to drive through the station, is it?' I feel able to tease him today.

He does a belly laugh.

Though I know his joy is down to Birmingham rather than me, it doesn't detract from my pleasure in witnessing it. He doesn't put his earphones in, doesn't take any books out of his bag to mark. He looks at me, hands me treats – a bag of Kettle Chips, a pot of hummus, a tub of miniature millionaire shortbreads, paper cups pillaged from the coffee station, a packet of gummy bears – and once he's relieved himself of all his loot, he strokes the inside of my palm. We whisper bitchy comments about the people in our carriage, take the piss out of a couple who are having a barely concealed fight, both of us in on the same joke again.

His mum meets us outside the station and drives us back to Tom's childhood home. She seems especially chirpy, even considering the fact that it's her birthday weekend.

'You look so smart, bab,' she says to Tom, grinning at him over her shoulder.

'Eyes on the road, love,' he says.

'Have I told you how proud of you we are?' she says.

'Me too,' I chime in. 'So proud.'

'And how are you doing, Mara, hun? It goes without saying that you look smart too. You always do.'

'Not too shabby,' I say. 'My housemate has just started seeing someone new, so he's being a lot nicer to me.' I don't know why this is the one headline I've chosen to share with my boyfriend's mum.

'Such a jumped-up little prick. Never liked the sound of him.'

'He can be okay!' I don't know why I say this either. Lewis has turned into someone who is very rarely okay to be around, and he doesn't deserve to be defended.

At Tom's parents', we're offered Tom's childhood bedroom, as usual. All his old posters are still Blu-Tacked to the pale blue walls, a shrine to the teen Tom: a bikini-clad Kelly Brook, a grubby Aston Villa scarf, The Streets' *A Grand Don't Come for Free* album cover, blown up and printed on a home LaserJet.

'Out?' he asks, the minute I've put my bag down on the floor.

'Oh, I thought you might want to be with your parents tonight?'

'Alright, yeah! You're right,' he says, easily convinced. 'I'll see if the lads want to come here then. Is that okay?'

'Of course. Anything you want.' I mean it.

Within the hour, four of Tom's oldest friends are crammed into the front room, along with me, Tom, Tom's parents, his nan, and his sister, Sarah. We're all drinking cold lagers and half-watching *Gogglebox*. Tom is somehow involved in three conversations, simultaneously. I keep surreptitiously checking my emails to see if there's anything from Max/Mark/Matt.

Tom tells a story about one of the kids he's taken under his wing. One by one, everyone in the room stops talking and tunes in to what Tom's saying.

'He's got this severe stutter and his confidence is at rock bottom,' he says. 'He's got this nice group of mates, though, and they all accept him as he is – honestly, kids these days are so much sounder than when we were kids – but he just won't speak up in class. I thought initially that maybe he was shy in front of adults, but that's not it, because he'll happily speak to me alone after the lesson's over. Then I noticed that his demeanour would change whenever this girl, Amina, was close by.'

There is a collective *oooh* from the group. Tom has them captive.

'Exactly. So, in a discreet way, I asked to see him after school for a couple of minutes – said I wanted to discuss something about his homework – and I asked if there was anyone that made him feel as though he couldn't express himself freely. And he was blushing and lowering his face and stuff, and it was so obvious, but I waited and didn't push, and eventually he said, *I get very nervous when Amina's there. She's so smart and it's nothing to do with anything she's done, I just don't want to say anything stupid.* Tale as old as time. So I said to him, *Look, mate, I hope you know that that can happen to any of us, regardless of whether we have a stutter. It used to happen to me whenever I'd try to speak to this one girl. And that girl eventually became my girlfriend.'*

I get a little frisson of pleasure when he says this. When we were first getting to know each other, there were occasions when Tom could barely get his words out.

'So what did he say to that?' Tom's mum says, leaning in.

'He said, *Sir, leave off. It's not what you're insinuating it is. I just really respect her as a person and want her to respect me.*'

31

'Bloody 'ell,' Sarah says. 'Kids now are intense, aren't they?'

I could listen to Tom talk about his students all night. He hasn't shared this story with me before now. Often, when we talk at the end of the day, I get a, *Fine*, or a, *Busy*, when I ask about work. I certainly never get these one-man shows.

18

In his single bed in his childhood bedroom in Birmingham, Tom touches my shoulder. Light is bleeding through the thin curtains. It's very early morning and we've been asleep for a couple of hours. Though it's a soft touch, it's loaded, and I know exactly what it means. He's touching me because he wants to touch me more, wants to touch me everywhere. I offer up my face for one of his wet little kisses.

'I love you,' he whispers.

'I love you.' I stroke his cheek with my whole hand. 'I had a nice night with you.'

'I had a nice night too. Really nice.'

His hand has moved to one of my breasts and is encasing it, kneading it gently.

'We have a whole day today. What would you like to do?' I say.

'We can go into town,' he says, squeezing. 'We can go out for breakfast. We can go for a walk with my mum and dad.' Squeeze. 'James invited us to the pub.' Squeeze.

'Any of that sounds good,' I say, pushing my hand down the front of his boxers. 'We can do all four things.'

'Yes,' he says, closing his eyes and exhaling. 'Yes, we can.'

He's hard in my hand, full. He pushes the fabric of his underwear down, out of the way, threads his legs through, releasing himself from the constraints of the cotton. He does the same for me, with my underwear. What follows is one of our favourite, most-used routines. Mutual masturbation for a couple of minutes, Tom going down on me for long enough for me to get out of my thoughts, and then about fifteen minutes of quiet, loving sex, looking into each other's eyes. It still feels good, if predictable. He's always taken the time to make sure that I'm having fun. He knows my trigger words, my trigger moves. He knows how I like to finish with his fingers in my mouth. He knows that I like him to carry on for a little while, even after we're both done. We start to drift off with our legs still tangled up together.

'I wish you were this happy all the time,' I say, into his ear.

He doesn't respond. I don't know if he's heard me.

19

After a dreamy Saturday, Sunday morning is a completely different story. I wake up to a frantic Tom. He is sitting at the little desk in the corner of the bedroom – a desk that still has football trophies and his Year Eleven yearbook on it – marking books. His head is down, his neck bent at an unnatural angle, cup of tea by his elbow.

'Morning,' I say.

'Mmm,' he says. 'Hi.'

'You been up for long?'

'Couple of hours.'

I pick up my phone from the bedside table. It's 07:47.

'You okay?' I say, nervously.

'Just have a lot to get done,' he says. 'And these books won't mark themselves.'

He's on edge all day, even when we sit down with his whole family for Sunday lunch, and his mum's made his favourite roast beef and there are Bloody Marys for our hangovers and everyone is being jovial. He keeps looking at his emails on his phone, and so do I. There's still nothing from the estate agent, and there's nothing I can do about that. For every new email Tom gets, though, he has to walk out of the room and check something upstairs or make a quick phone call to Emma, his teaching assistant. His mum is visibly concerned.

When he leaves the room just as the trifle's been brought out, Tom's mum says, 'I'm starting to get a bit worried.' She looks at me.

I can't tell her the truth – that I've been worried for months. 'Sundays are hard for everyone,' I say, and hate myself.

On the train back to London, there are no snacks and there are no tinnies and there are no laughs. It's like this every time. He's so happy for those two days, but then even more miserable than before when he gets back to the place where he actually lives. The trip doesn't seem worth it. Maybe it is for him, though. We separate at Euston. He is looking at his phone as he walks away from me.

20

When I get back to the flat, it's clear that Lewis has his new squeeze over. I can hear him giggling in the front room. The sound makes me feel funny. I try to close the front door quietly behind me. I don't want to be invited to meet her. The only time Lewis is nice to me is when there are other people around. I don't need him to be nice to me right now. I want to be invisible. I get inside my bedroom – thankfully it's the closest room to the entrance – and drop my overnight bag onto the carpet. Sinking onto the bed, I flip my laptop open and log in to my emails. There it is, right at the top, even though it's a Sunday. The email I've been waiting for.

I've been outbid. Max/Mike/Mart is really sorry. It was a great flat and there was a lot of interest. It's not personal. In the end, the sellers had to go for the highest offer. Not to worry, though, because Mark/Mop/Milk has a whole host of other really exciting prospects that he can't wait to show me! One of them is mine, he's sure of it!

From the front room there is a joyous squeal. 'Stop it, silly! Get *off!*' The new squeeze is not responsible for this display of playfulness; it's Lewis's voice.

21

Work, avoid Derek. Home, avoid Lewis. Flat viewings five nights a week. A station pasty or Boots sandwich for dinner. Two episodes of *It's Always Sunny* in bed. Fall asleep with my laptop still on my lap. Wake up to a text from Tom that says something like, *Sorrrrrrrrrrry I've been swamped with lesson plans!*

Start the whole cycle again.

22

The female estate agents tend to have two-syllable names. Kelly, Sharon, Janice, Michelle, Lauren. They wear neat little skirt suits or structured dresses from Karen Millen or Jaeger in jewel tones. They call me *hun*. They laugh a lot. They drive fast, have loveable, useless boyfriends, complain about them at length. They are always in their early twenties, and favour Clapham, Balham and Putney as neighbourhoods for themselves, while still totally getting the appeal of *trendy Hackney*. They try to have conspiratorial conversations with me about my lifestyle. *Well, you've just got to have a gym within a mile, haven't you? I can see you're into your fitness. There are some lush cafés in the area – great for hot-desking. Ooh, there's a precious little indie cinema a few streets away. I bet you just love your films, don't you?*

The one called Sharon adopts me as her personal project. At our first meeting, in the lobby of the agency, she asks me what my non-negotiables are, handing me a bottle of sparkling water I haven't asked for.

'Well, I'd like to be first floor or above. For safety. And light, you know.'

'Noted,' she says, taking the sparkling water back to unscrew the cap for me. She hands it back, grinning. 'You can't trust anyone in this city. First floor or above it is.'

'I like period conversions,' I say. 'I know they're very popular, but I just think it's important to like the look of the building I go into every evening.'

'One hundred percent.'

'A window in the bathroom?' This is the one detail my mum is insisting I should insist on.

She laughs, a lot. 'Aw, bless ya.'

'I'm serious. If I'm not going to be able to afford any outdoor space, I at least want to be able to dry my clothes with a window open.'

'Oh my god, you're so right. I never even thought of that. Sure, sure. What else?'

'Dalston, Homerton, Hackney Central area,' I say. I take a sip of the sparkling water. 'And not too far from a station. I don't drive, and don't plan to any time soon.'

Sharon shakes her head and her tight blonde bun barely moves. 'You *are* good. Environmental warrior! I couldn't do without my Audi.'

'And please don't show me anything above my budget. It's a firm budget,' I say.

Sharon winks at me. 'Okay, boss.'

23

Sharon calls me on a Wednesday afternoon while I'm in the library, helping a patron log in to one of the desktop computers.

'Sorry, Derek,' I say, waving him over. 'Could you finish helping this gentleman, please? I have to take this.'

Derek is all too happy to make his way over to me, all too happy to squeeze my shoulder, all too happy to help. I pop outside to answer the phone.

'Hi,' I say. 'Have you found me something?'

'Have I ever! I've got three *gorgeous* properties to show you. Could you get here in the next fifteen minutes?'

It's two thirty. 'Not really,' I say. 'It's a Wednesday afternoon. I could be there in about . . . four hours?'

Sharon tuts. 'Uff, they might be snapped up by then, but okay. See you at the agency?'

'Sure,' I say.

I make my way back inside. Seeing me, Derek waves. *Put your feet up!* he mouths.

After work, I get a bus to the agency. Sharon is pacing up and down outside it, dressed in turquoise. Her hair is poker straight and she is wearing very pointy, very matronly patent slingbacks.

'Finally!' she says, spotting me.

It's six thirty-five.

'You would've kicked yourself if you'd missed these!' she says, bundling me into her car.

The first one she shows me is in Bow, not far from where Noor and her mum live. This is an area I specifically don't want to live in. The flat is fine, nice even, but it's an oddly proportioned two-bed. Both bedrooms are tiny, with barely enough room for any furniture apart from the bed. The bathroom, on the other hand, has enough room to comfortably fit a three-piece suite.

'I feel as though this would make much more sense as a one-bed,' I dare to say.

'Do you never have guests?' Sharon says. 'No friends? No plans to start a family?'

The second flat is a basement flat with not only a windowless bathroom, but also a windowless kitchen.

'No,' I say, when she looks at me expectantly, smile on her face.

The third flat is a new-build in Highbury and Islington. It's on the thirteenth floor and, to be fair to Sharon, it does have a small balcony. I venture out onto it. There is a sort of cage on all three sides.

When I point this out, Sharon says, 'Well, you did say you wanted to feel safe?'

24

Sharon calls me on Thursday morning, Friday morning and Friday afternoon. I pick up her sixth call. Having been burnt, I ask more questions before agreeing to any viewings.

'Where *exactly* is this house?'

'Lordship Lane. So cute. You're going to love it.'

I type *Lordship Lane* into the search bar on my work computer. Dulwich. My commute would take me one hour and twenty minutes each way.

'Sharon,' I say. 'I feel like you're not really listening to me.'

'Look, I've been doing this for a long time. I know that sometimes the buyer just doesn't know what they want until they see it.'

'I feel like I do know what I want, though.'

Sharon takes a sharp inhale, as though something exciting has been dropped onto her desk. 'Hun, this is fate. This absolute gem has *just this second* come back on the market.'

'Is it local?'

'Extremely. E9, just like you asked.'

'Period?'

'Oh, yes. Victorian conversion. And two-bed.'

Derek is coming towards me with a stack of Mills & Boons.

'Alright, send me a link.'

Sharon is fast, if nothing else. The email comes through within seconds.

Property Description

At a swoon-worthy 1,089 sq ft, we are thrilled to offer to the market this handsome Victorian house, located a stone's throw from Victoria Park. The property offers a stunningly bright and airy living space, recently refurbished to a high standard by the current owner.

With an ample entrance hallway, this beautiful house boasts a bay-fronted reception and a roomy modern fitted kitchen with double doors onto the covetable patio. On the first floor, there are two generous double bedrooms and a large family bathroom.

Victoria Park, which recently benefitted from a £12m update, is practically in the back garden. Queen Elizabeth Olympic Park is also nearby, making this the perfect forever home for a young family with children or dogs.

I text Sharon: *I finish in an hour. Meet me outside Homerton library.*

For this viewing, Sharon is decked out in a pinstriped jumpsuit and ankle boots.

'You look nice,' I say, conscious of my very casual-Friday attire of jeans and a mustard cardigan.

She looks me up and down, but doesn't seem able to find anything positive to comment on. 'I was a buyer for Harrods before this. Did I tell you that?'

We walk to the property. It takes just over ten minutes. This is good. It's on a quiet, tree-lined street. Also very good. Every house in the terrace is neat and well-looked-after, and I start to feel quite excited. I try not to talk too much. Sharon babbles about nearby schools, the distance from my workplace, the civilised neighbours. She stops in front of a mid-terrace house, brown brick, aquamarine door, large bay window, potted bay tree on the doorstep.

'This one?' I ask.

She nods.

'This whole house?'

She laughs. 'Yep! I couldn't believe it either.'

'This can't be in budget,' I say.

'Oh, but it is. Ten grand under, even.' She is extremely pleased with herself. 'They must be anxious to sell.'

This seems unthinkable. I take a few steps back to take in the whole façade. I imagine rolling out of bed and being so close to work. I would have time to eat breakfast at home. I picture myself stopping off for coffee on my way to the library. Tom could sit in the kitchen, marking books, while I potter around him. Even Noor would visit me if I lived in this house. Sharon is struggling to get the key in the door. She's really shoving it in. Her bun is coming loose with the force of her exertions. I take a picture to send to my mum. Sharon's pinstriped back is in the bottom right-hand corner of the shot. This is the sort of place that would make my dad proud, a family investment, a real first home.

'For goodness' sake,' Sharon is muttering, looking through a leather folder full of keys. 'Which one is it?' She makes a quick phone call and manages to find the right key, insert it, and push through the front door, shoulder first. 'Come on!' she calls. 'Before I buy it myself!'

I follow her inside. As promised, it's bright and the entrance is ample. Lined up in a little row, there are two pairs of tiny yellow wellies next to two much bigger pairs of green wellies. The fact that the house is clearly owned by an outdoorsy family is heartening. To help me with this image, I see a framed photo of the four of them, larking around on a British-looking beach, smiles stretching across their faces. Next up, the kitchen is indeed roomy and modern, the patio covetable. I picture being able to sunbathe in London, somewhere private. I text my mum: *This one is looking very promising.*

She texts back: *That's so great! Send me lots of pics!*

Sharon is switching on lights as we pass from room to room, but the house is already luminous, and pleasingly clean. The bedrooms are both a great size, and I get carried away, imagining who I could invite to stay over. I start to formulate the conversation I'd have with Tom. *Your friends can come every weekend if they want to. Invite your parents, your sister. Everyone's welcome!*

The tour ends, and Sharon stands smugly by the door, hands on hips. Though she manages to refrain from saying *See?* out loud, her body language says exactly that. I concede a smile.

'Yes, well done. This is really more than I even hoped for,' I say. 'I'm sure I'll be in touch before the end of the day.'

25

Sharon calls me while I'm still walking home. I answer. I've already had a conversation with my mum, and we've agreed that haste is of the essence on this occasion. I don't need to reflect. The house is perfect.

'Hi,' I say. 'I think I've got good news for you.'

Sharon is quiet on the other end of the phone. She's told me more than once that I'm her *pickiest client*, and I guess she must be in shock that I've finally found The One.

'I'd like to offer them asking price,' I say. I relish the moment. I'll remember this forever.

Sharon clears her throat. 'So that'd be nine hundred and fifty thousand, then?'

'Sorry?'

'Asking price is just under a million.'

'You said it was ten grand under my budget?'

'So. The thing is. There was a misunderstanding.'

'What misunderstanding?'

I wait. She says nothing. For someone who loves to talk as much as Sharon does, this is quite the novelty.

'You literally said it was in my price range,' I say, trying and failing to keep my voice calm. 'I asked you whether you were sure that it was in my price range, and you said that yes, it was definitely in my price range. What is there to misunderstand?' My breathing is laboured. I want to kill her.

She breathes out, and when she speaks again her voice is chipper, jaunty. 'I looked at the wrong figures.' She says it fast. 'That's all. I was looking at the ex-council flat we have for sale on the same road.'

'So not the family home I've just fallen in love with, then, no?'

'I'm happy to show you this other property? We could go right now?'

'Fucksake, Sharon. My mum booked a train ticket to come and

45

see the house tomorrow. What am I going to tell her? That the estate agent – someone who's meant to be trained to know how much a property is worth – didn't put two and two together, and realise that it was a bit weird that her client who until now only seemed able to permit herself a canal boat could suddenly afford a whole house?'

'Mara, you're looking at this in the wrong way. I'm on your side.'

'Sharon, I'm hanging up now.'

I block Sharon's number after that. She tries to call me from various other numbers and I block all of those too.

26

My mum comes to visit anyway. Rugby – where I grew up and where she still lives – to Euston takes just under an hour on the fast train, but I still feel guilty. She says that we should have the weekend off from flat hunting. She books a hotel just off Hyde Park and suggests that we both stay there. I'm more than happy to oblige. I'm tired.

'Is there anything in particular you'd like to see or do?' I ask her once we're checked in.

'The only thing I care about seeing is right here in this room,' she says.

'What, the minibar?'

'No. You.'

When my mum says this, I burst instantly into tears.

'Oh, love.'

She doesn't ask me to explain why I'm crying. She just reaches up and puts her arms around my neck. She's shorter than me, so I have to rest my cheek on the crown of her head. It's funny to still feel like a child when I'm so much physically bigger than my mother.

We go for a wanky lunch at a small plates place called Hands or Feet or Legs or something, and my mum tells me to order for both of us. We eat fresh, unadorned food: huge hunks of burrata, slices of thin bresaola and a tiny bowl of cacio e pepe. I ask the handsome waiter to bring us a glass of natural orange wine each, and my mum makes appreciative noises as she sips it and I tell her that it's meant to be one of the only types of alcohol that doesn't give you a hangover. Though she says she likes it, she asks for a lager when the waiter comes back around.

'Should I invite Tom to join us for a drink later?' I ask.

'I think it should be just us girls today,' my mum says. 'I have a feeling we have a lot to catch up on.'

This makes me want to cry too.

My mum sees the expression on my face and raises her eyebrows. 'Oh dear,' she says. 'We really do have a lot to catch up on.'

We have beef carpaccio, and a jacket potato with sour cream on it, and some gnocchi with sage and butter, and I tell my mum vague stories about Tom's behaviour over the last couple of months.

'What does his mum think?'

'That he should move home,' I say. 'She'd never say it out loud, but it's obvious. Everyone in his life wants him to get out of London. They think it's London's fault.'

'And what do you think?' She says this softly, passing me a piece of bread that she's used to mop up the sagey butter.

'I think that he hasn't given it a proper chance.' My voice is angry, even though I'm doing my best to keep it measured and calm. I don't want my mum to know how much this is all affecting me.

'But, darling, you do know that this probably has nothing to do with you?'

I don't know that. I don't know that at all. I feel as though, in Tom's eyes, me and London are inextricably linked now, that the hate he feels for this city is starting to bleed into the love he has for me.

'Mmm.'

'Mara, look at me.'

I do as I'm told.

'You can't help him with this decision. If his heart is telling him to go back to Birmingham, then that's what he'll end up doing. It might not be tomorrow, or next week, or even next year, but when someone feels that pull to go home, trust me, they will.'

My chest hurts. I want so much to be able to disagree with her, to tell her that she couldn't be more wrong, that it's just a moment that will pass, that all it'll take is for Tom to really throw himself into his new life, and that actually, maybe me buying this flat will be just what he's been needing all along. But I can't say any of that.

I wave the waiter over and ask him to bring us a cheese board. My heart is already beating fast with all the cold cuts and dairy we've eaten, but I need more.

27

One of the agents at Sharon's agency manages to get through to me on the Monday after my mum leaves. It must be the only phone left in the office that I haven't blocked yet.

'Yes?' I say. 'What?'

'Oh, hi! Maria! I'm getting in touch because we've got the *most* perfect property for you.'

I roll my eyes at the *Jane Eyre* poster on the wall facing me.

'It's a one-bed. A *big* one-bed. Lovely Victorian terrace. Local. Window in the bathroom, close to the overground.'

So someone in the office has actually made a note of what I want. I don't say anything.

'There's a fair bit of interest, but I'd love for you to see it first?'

'Send me a link,' I sigh. 'I could meet you on my lunch break.'

The email pings through while I'm still on the phone. I click on the ad and scroll through the photos. The price is in big bold font at the top and is a tiny bit higher than I'd like, but not one million pounds. The pictures are really fucking nice.

I keep all emotion out of my voice when I say, 'Can you do twelve thirty?'

I know the road the house is on. It's got a strong, no-nonsense name. It's tree-lined and there's a doctor's surgery halfway down it.

I tell Derek I'm popping out to buy lunch.

'Get us a Twirl!' he shouts at my departing back. 'Or one of those Lindor bars if they've got them!'

A guy called Guy shows me the flat. He has shiny black hair and a mole in the middle of his chin. He keeps calling me Maria, and I don't correct him.

Guy gets the key in the door on his first try, which makes me instantly respect him. He knows the answers to all my questions too. As we climb the stairs to the first floor, he tells me that the ground floor flat is owned by an older gentleman who's been there for years, and the top floor flat is a young couple who rent. He knows about ground rent and how the freehold is shared and what sort of council tax I could expect to be paying and whether or not the sellers are in a chain. He leaves gaps for me to think, and doesn't talk unless I ask him something specific.

In the doorway of the flat he says, 'I'll leave you to explore,' and discreetly steps out onto the landing.

It's a little kitsch inside. There are pink gingham curtains and a purple feature wall and a framed painting of a pug in a tutu. The kitchen is a little tight, and the appliances look well loved, if I'm being generous. The front room is big but set up in a strange way, the sofa and armchair pointing away from the two windows, the focal point a large TV fixed to the wall above the fireplace. There's a draught and I notice that the panes in the windows are all single glazed and rattling slightly in their frames. I shiver as I move into the bedroom. The bed's unmade, the sheets crumpled in a pile at the bottom where the owner has clearly jumped up in a hurry. Late probably. Like I always am. A pile of denim is on a rattan chair in the corner, a large potted monstera plant next to it, looking wilted and pathetic. These details endear me to the owner. I wonder whether we could be friends in a different life. Or even in this one.

I step closer to the bedside table – a cheap white IKEA one. There's a photo of two girls about my age, arms draped around each other's shoulders. They're dressed in sequins, a feather boa shared between them. They're laughing; they look happy. I'm relieved to see that there are books in here. A lot of them in short piles on the floor and on a wooden shelf behind the door. Titles I recognise and appreciate, both classics and contemporary. The owner has good taste.

I go into the bathroom next. It's the only room left. There's visible mildew and it's colder than the other spaces. There's a bath with a shower extension, and there are bottles of every description lined along the edge of it. Shampoos, body wash, conditioner, hair masks, scrubs, face wash. Everything is on display. It reminds me of Noor and her hundreds of beauty products stolen from work. Guy hasn't mentioned who lives here, but I know in my gut that it's one of the women from the photograph and that she lives alone. I think she must have a pretty nice life. There's a lurch in my stomach, a weird feeling. I'm very conscious of the saliva in my mouth.

I go back out to Guy. He's scrolling on his phone and doesn't immediately look up at me.

'All done?' he says, his eyes still down.

'I think so.'

'Nice, right?'

'Mmm,' I say.

Guy is very good. He pockets his phone and motions for me to go down the stairs before him.

'I guess you have to head back to work now?' he says. 'You'll let me know if you're interested?'

'I'll be in touch, yeah.' I give him a little half-wave.

He nods and flashes a small smile.

'Oh!' I say, as an afterthought. 'I'd like to deal with you. If I do end up being interested. Not Sharon.'

'Of course.'

I stop off at the Co-op and buy Derek a Twirl and a Lindor bar.

28

Tom sends me a text which says, *You can sleep over tonight if you want? Only have two lesson plans to do.*

I jump at the chance. I haven't seen him in over a week. I send Lewis a text to say I won't be home tonight.

Lewis replies, *Aw okay! No probs!*

I know it's no probs. I know he's ecstatic at the prospect.

I start the long journey to Tom's shared flat. One of his housemates will let me in if I beat him there. It'd be one thing if he'd chosen to bunk with friends, but he lives with strangers – a vegan vet and a pastry chef from Surrey. Our separate houses were meant to be for convenience. It seemed to make logistical sense for Tom to live in Croydon near his school, and for me to live in Hackney near my library. Even so, I have suggested on multiple occasions that we could live at a halfway point together. Tom's stance is that there's no rush, life can be long, and there will be plenty of time for us to cohabit.

Sherry, the vet, opens the door to me. She's in an Adidas tracksuit and rubber slides. She has a mug of fruit tea in her free hand.

'Mara! Long time!' she says.

Though she's only being friendly, it sounds like an accusation.

'Busy term for him, I'm sure you've noticed.' My tone is defensive, and I'm embarrassed. I've only been here two seconds and I'm already showing Tom's housemate all my tender bits.

Sherry leads me through to the kitchen.

'Kettle's just boiled. Want something?'

I nod my consent.

'One of these okay?' She holds up a turmeric teabag.

'Sure.'

I don't like turmeric tea.

'So what's new with you?' I ask, politely. I'm in her house, after all. From what I've gathered, Sherry veers between two distinct states. She's either monotone or incredibly chatty.

'Oh god,' she says, leaning back against the counter. 'I've had such a day. We had this Dalmatian in, and he'd been constipated for days, his owner was beside herself, so I had to keep telling her over and over, leave him with me, he's in good hands, come on now, off you go, he won't settle while you're still in the room, and she was crying and couldn't catch her breath and, basically, she got herself into such a state that she passed out on the floor. A minute passes and I've done everything you're meant to do, I've lifted her legs up and unbuttoned the top of her blouse, and nothing. So I've had to call an ambulance, and I've got this Dalmatian crying now too because his owner's on the ground, and the manager comes in to ask what's going on, and he's like – Sherry, what have you done? As though it's my fault that this woman's passed out and the dog is weeping. Honestly. So he goes, well have you called an ambulance? Like I'm an idiot. So I go, yeah I've called an ambulance, obviously I've called a bloody ambulance, and he goes, don't swear in front of the patients, and I'm gesturing at this woman on the floor and opening my eyes all wide like, seriously, do you think this woman here with spit coming out the side of her mouth is arsed about me saying the word *bloody*? I don't think so, pal. So between us we put her in the recovery position, and by the time the ambulance has arrived she's already coming to, and you can just see that the paramedics are annoyed at having to come out for this, but I couldn't not call them, what if she had a condition? So everyone calms down and this is, what, an hour later, so I'm late for all the rest of my appointments, but I finally manage to do an X-ray on the Dalmatian, and he's got about thirty-five socks in his stomach, and it's just one of those days, you know. But over now!' She beams at me, shrugs. 'You?'

I sip some of the bright yellow tea and wince. 'Nothing compared to that, but – I don't know if Tom mentioned anything – I'm trying to buy a flat, and I think I might have found one I really like today.'

Sherry is smiling manically. 'Oh my god! A flat!'

'Well, hopefully.'

'So Tom'll be moving out then?' She doesn't wait for an answer. 'I'd love to buy a flat, but I'll never be in a position to. Not on my wages. What do you do again?'

I blush and try to cover as much of my face as I can with the mug. 'Librarian.'

'How have you wangled that!' She reaches out and touches my wrist.

'With a lot of help.'

She sighs. 'It's the only way for our generation, isn't it? I'm one of four though, so I don't stand a chance. Will be renting forever.'

I look around the kitchen. It's visibly clean and everything is in its place, but it has that sort of vague baked-cheese smell that all shared houses seem to have. Not for the first time, I feel guilty.

I hear a key in the front door and know that Tom's home. I turn and grin at him over my shoulder. He's laden down with tote bags, his laptop case and his little Eastpak backpack hanging off one shoulder. His top button is undone and his tie is wonky. His whole look screams newly qualified teacher.

'Sherry, Mara,' he says, giving Sherry a nod and me a dry kiss on the cheek. 'Both okay?'

'Some of us better than others,' Sherry says, winking at me.

'Oh? Who pulled the short straw?' Tom says.

I would like to talk to him about this privately.

'Mine was decent,' I say. I look pointedly at Sherry. 'Sherry's less so. Tell him about the Dalmatian.'

Sherry needs no further encouragement, and starts the whole story from scratch, as Tom slowly unloads all his loot onto the kitchen table. I make him a cup of tea the way he likes it, mid to dark beige with one and a half sugars. He looks so tired.

He keeps saying, 'No!' at all the most dramatic parts of Sherry's story, and I feel very warmly towards him for this. Though she's a nice enough girl, she's not a born storyteller.

'Wanna go through?' Tom says to me, in a break in Sherry's spiel. 'I won't be long.'

I nod, and traipse into Tom's bedroom, so different from his room in Birmingham. There are absolutely no signs of his personality in here, neither his teen nor his adult one. It looks almost exactly the same as when he moved in a year ago. It could be anyone's room. I perch on the end of his bed and wait for him.

He appears after a couple of minutes.

'Sorry about that,' he says. 'Sometimes I feel like I need to make more effort with them than I do.'

I smile and pat the spot next to me on the bed. He sits. His head

54

flops to the side and I catch it with my shoulder. I reach my hand up to stroke his cheek with the backs of my fingers and I mumble little platitudes. 'You're doing so well,' and, 'It won't always be like this.'

I don't notice that he's crying at first. Not until he starts making noise.

'Hey,' I say, pulling away so that I can look at him. 'Hey.'

He doesn't speak. I don't think he can.

'Baby,' I say. We don't call each other *baby*, we never have. But I'm not saying it in the romantic sense, I'm saying it because I feel like his mum. 'Please.' *Please* is a really fucking stupid thing for me to say. Though I know this, I'm also desperate for him to stop. My heart is pounding and I feel sick. I've only seen him cry once before, and that was when his grandad died, and it sounded nothing like this. He's wailing, and I'm nervous that Sherry will be able to hear.

'Don't cry,' I say. Another stupid thing. 'What's happened?'

He has inched away from me now and is lying face up, his knees slowly travelling further and further up his body. He's curling into a little ball. I think I'm in shock, because I stop saying anything, just stare at him. Do I need to call someone? Do I need to leave the room? All I feel able to do is cry with him. So that is what I do. We stay there, both in tears, for what seems like forever.

29

After we both stop crying, we lie side by side, on top of the duvet, not touching. We eventually fall asleep like this, and in the morning it feels like a fever dream, something that would be tacky to bring up in the cold light of day. Tom doesn't mention it again. I don't feel like I can, either. It's his choice to make, not mine. We are overly friendly with each other, say *Sorry* when we graze past each other on the way to the shared bathroom.

In the kitchen, over rushed toast, I say, 'Feel okay about your lessons today?'

He says, 'Yes, thank you. Should be fine.'

A few seconds pass. We're both nodding softly.

Then he comes to and says, 'Got a busy day ahead yourself?'

I say, 'Nothing out of the ordinary. Nothing out of the norm.'

I don't recall ever having used the word *norm* in my life.

When we part ways at the overground station, he gives me a lingering, wet kiss and holds on for a long time. When I pull away, he grabs me again and holds my gaze. 'Have a good day,' he says. 'I *love* you.'

Before going into the library, I call Guy. I make an offer on the flat.

30

Noor convinces me to go and get my nails done with her. Apparently there's this place in Bow that does Shellac for £15. You can't argue with that, so I don't try to. It's not an activity that I particularly enjoy. My main gripe with it is that I don't see why they insist on trimming your cuticles off. It sets my teeth on edge. And they always file the nails just a little too sharply for my taste. It's not about the activity, though, it's about the company.

Noor's in a weird mood.

'Hard week?' I ask, once we've chosen our colours. I've gone for a mint green and Noor's having her signature beige.

'Well, I asked for a fifteen percent pay rise at work.'

'Oh?'

'And they said they'll think about it.'

I wait. 'That's good, though, right? They clearly value you.'

'What is there to reflect on? That's what I'd like to know. I do the work of two people for the price of one. Ever since Janine went on maternity I've been covering for her and I do literally double the amount of work I did this time last year. They're lucky I'm not asking for a hundred percent pay rise, the ungrateful pricks.'

'They haven't said no yet.'

'I should quit.' She raises her left hand to investigate the nails. 'Shorter, please.'

'Maybe just wait and see what they say before doing anything drastic?'

'It shouldn't even fall to me to ask. They should see how hard I work.'

I snort. I can't help it. 'Come on, Noor, be serious.'

She looks at me, curls one side of her mouth up, like, Oh *you're* going to give me advice on this?

'I'm just saying,' I wince as the nail technician slips with the nail file. 'It's a business. If they can get away with paying you less, then they will.'

'When did you last get a pay rise?' She's on the verge of snapping, I can see it on her face.

She knows the answer to this question. She's so fucking annoying sometimes. It's not enough that I'm out here in the sticks so that an underpaid woman can chop my cuticles off. Now I have to defend the fact that I haven't ever been brave enough to question what I myself earn. 'I've never had one.'

Noor lifts both eyebrows in mock surprise. 'And you're okay with that?'

'I won't always be on the same pay. But for now, it's fine. It's a small library and the work is simple enough and it suits me. And – more importantly – I believe in the service we provide. Okay? Money isn't everything.'

Noor's eyes look ready to pop out of her face.

'What?' I say. I know what.

'Nothing. It's just a nice position to be in.'

'What is?' I'm goading her.

'To be able to not care how much you're paid.'

I exhale. It's extremely embarrassing that we're having this conversation in front of two women who are being paid £15 for an hour of their time, when the going rate for this service is at least £30 anywhere else in London. Especially when they probably only get a small percentage of that for themselves. Neither of us says anything for a few minutes.

I can't let her have the last word, though. 'I obviously care how much I'm paid, Noor, that was a stupid thing to say,' I mutter. 'I was just saying that I'd rather economise in certain areas of my life and have a job which doesn't make me want to be dead.'

She stares at me, incredulous. 'Can you hear yourself? Your mum is buying you a fucking flat?'

I feel my face flushing. 'Can you stop?' I hiss.

'Oh sorry, is your privilege uncomfortable to confront head-on?'

I pinch the bridge of my nose with my free hand. 'This is all new to me,' I say. 'A few weeks ago, I was in the exact same position as you. I don't know what you want me to say.'

Noor barks a laugh. 'Look at you. It's not that deep.' She leans back in her seat. 'Your face is fuchsia. Relax. Let's just change the subject.'

After that, we have some disjointed, stiff conversation on a whole host of surface-level subjects: what happened in last week's *Made in Chelsea*, a mutual acquaintance's recent wedding photos, Noor's mum's latest culinary experiments. The whole time we're talking I can feel the two nail technicians glancing at each other, waiting for me and Noor to get back into the juicy stuff.

'Still up for lunch?' Noor says, when we leave with our shiny new manicures.

She's trying to be nice in her own way. We don't usually snap at each other like this, and it's weird to feel as though I don't want to share such a big thing with her. But the truth is, she's not able to detach herself from what me buying a flat means for her personally. She can't talk about it with me in a neutral way, and maybe I shouldn't expect her to.

'Think I might just head back actually,' I say. 'If that's alright?' I look down at my hands. The polish on one of my thumbnails is slightly wonky, and I know that this will bother me until it grows out.

'I could probably do with an afternoon alone myself.'

We nod at each other.

'Hey,' I say. 'I hope you get your pay rise.'

'Yeah. I hope you find your flat.'

31

Guy calls me on Monday morning.

'Sorry,' I say. 'Just gimme a—' I push through into the work loos. I'm alone. 'Okay, hi.'

'Maria. Hi.'

'Do you have some news for me?' I brace myself for the punch of disappointment, his consolatory words.

'I do.' His tone gives nothing away. 'I put forward your offer, and the seller thought about it long and hard over the weekend.'

'Right.'

'And she was hoping for slightly more than you wanted to pay.'

'Okay.'

'But she likes that you're chain-free, and I told her what a nice girl you are.'

'Yes.'

'And she'd like to accept.'

'What? She said yes?'

'She said yes.'

'Oh my god.' I look from left to right, agog. I wish there were someone here to share this with. I want my mum. 'So I can have the flat?'

'Yes, you can. It's all yours.' I can hear the smile in Guy's voice.

'Thank you. This is the best news ever. Really.'

'You're very welcome. Congratulations, Maria.'

'So, what now?'

'Now there's a little bit of paperwork and a fair bit of patience. But don't worry about that just yet. Enjoy this moment. You're going to be a homeowner.'

32

There is a huge amount of paperwork and a huge amount of patience involved in buying a flat.

My mum comes to London for the day so she can see it. Although she's said a hundred times that she trusts my instincts, I feel as though I need her permission to proceed. I still FaceTime her before buying a new winter coat.

I meet her at Euston, and we take a long, slow bus east. She won't stop talking about her next-door neighbour's new extension, and I am unable to offer any satisfactory comment on the matter. *What if she doesn't like it?* is stuck in a loop in my head. We get off at Homerton Terrace and she squeezes my hand.

'So you're one hundred percent sold on this area, then?' she says, nodding at a singed wheelie bin. 'I always quite liked Chelsea.'

I elbow her.

'It's a joke, Mara. You look so serious.'

'Well this does feel very serious,' I say. I have a lump in my throat. I want to say to my mum that we can back out at any moment, that she can spend the money on something else, something less demanding. Or save it. We could save it for another ten years, and I could have it once I feel like more of a real person.

'Mara.' She's stopped walking and has grabbed hold of both my hands. 'This is a very exciting time. I couldn't be happier that we're doing this, and I wouldn't want to do anything else with this money. Do you understand that?'

I nod, a small child's nod.

It's a five-minute walk to the flat, and we chat about things that have nothing to do with the purchase we're making. I tell my mum about Derek, leaving out the worst bits; I tell her about Noor, leaving out the worst bits; and I tell her about Tom, leaving out any bad bits whatsoever.

As we approach the row of houses, I see Guy, suited and booted, hopping from one foot to the other. My mum and I wave at him, and he beams.

'Maria!' he says. 'Maria's mum!'

My mum looks at him with real disdain. 'Who's Maria, please?' she says. 'She's called Mara. And I'm Rachel.'

Guy pales. 'Oh,' he says. 'I'm so sorry about that.'

As we follow him into the house, my mum mutters, 'Maria, Maria's mum. Bloody joker.'

The whole house is quiet. I can't tell if anybody in the other flats is home. I watch my mum as she looks around the stairwell. It needs a refresh. The wooden floors must have been painted white a very long time ago. Now they are sort of beige, brown in places, splintering in the middle where shoes have trod time and time again. The smell is a tiny bit damp, closed – you can tell it doesn't get much air circulation. My mum's face is blank. Guy is silent after being chastised. He unlocks the door of the flat, pushes it open and steps back so that we can enter.

My mum usually asks hundreds of questions. Today, she is very quiet. I see her touch a couple of the walls, peer behind a curtain, open the fridge door, all the while seemingly deep in thought. It's earlier in the day than my first viewing and the rooms are brighter. The owner's recently done a load of laundry and her clothes are drying on a contraption above the bath. I stand in the doorway for a minute. There are dark jeans, some very wet t-shirts, and tens of tiny lace bras and thongs: in fluorescent pinks, pastel yellows, bright whites.

She's made her bed with a checked beige duvet cover and the hoover is out in the corner – a clunky old Henry. I wonder whether she's had someone over.

I meet my mum in the living room. She's sitting on the sofa, one leg crossed over the other.

'Do you think we could fit a three-seater in through that door?' she says.

'So you like it?'

'Let's talk once we get rid of that donkey outside.'

'Mum!' I sit down next to her. 'He's not even a bad one.'

'If we're going to help him with his commission, the least he can do is learn your name. It's not hard.'

My overriding feeling is one of relief. I want to say lots of things. My mum's opinion means more than anything, and I've seen so many flats at this point, I've been starting to doubt my own judgement.

'Mara,' my mum says, pointedly, once we're back in the hallway. 'Go and get us a coffee from that place over the road. I want to have a word with Gus.'

I'm happy that she's going to talk to him one-on-one without me. I'm happy to feel like a child today. As I cross the road, I glance over my shoulder and see the blinds in the downstairs window move slightly. I raise my hand to acknowledge the face that appears for less than a second. The blinds fall back into place.

PART II

Spring

33

It's three months later when I get the keys. Guy calls me and tells me I can come to the agency any time after nine thirty. I text Derek to say that I've been sick and won't be making it in to work. I am outside the agency at 09:25.

It's a disappointingly uneventful affair. Guy isn't even there, so I have to deal with bloody Sharon.

She simpers. 'I thought we'd never get you sorted, but we made it!'

I hold out my hand and smile. 'Yep.'

'Sometimes you just have to adjust your expectations.'

'I didn't adjust my expectations. I bought a flat I actually like. Can I just?' I open and close my palm, angling for the keys she's yet to give me.

'Eager to get in there, I bet. Few things,' she says. She's loving this. 'The previous owner left a couple of bits for you – a big mirror, the Sheila Maid. She says if you don't want them, she can arrange to have them picked up. And if you could just sign here to say I've given you the keys.'

She still hasn't relinquished them to me. I nod furiously and motion for her to hand me the bit of paper. I scrawl my name and snatch the keys from her grip.

'You have a great day, Sharon. Tell Guy I said thank you for everything. He'll have to come round for a cup of tea once I'm settled in.'

I leave the agency in the knowledge that I am the owner of a flat that I can go into at any time. I walk very slowly in the direction of the house, even though I shouldn't linger so close to work when I'm meant to be at home ill. All this time spent waiting for this moment, and now I want to put it off. Though I should probably call my mum or Tom, I don't want to share this with anyone else.

Lewis has texted me: *Good luck! Now you can leave your stuff anywhere you want!* and the sticky-out-tongue emoji.

There's nothing to say to that. I push my earphones into my ears and put on a HAIM song: 'Days Are Gone'. It's not a particularly significant song for me, but I feel as though I should mark the occasion by having something playing as I walk into my first home. In theory this song will remind me of this day every time I hear it.

I round the corner and there it is, in front of me. My flat. I breathe out. There's an elderly woman litter-picking on the forecourt and I beam at her as I approach.

'Can I help you?' she says.

'Hi! Nice to meet you.'

She looks at me blankly.

'I'm moving in today,' I say.

'Haven't got much stuff, have you?'

I'm only carrying an overnight bag, my pillow, and a sleeping bag. I'm going to Uber the rest of my stuff round later in the day. I've been keeping it at Noor's mum's place, where I've also been staying for the last week. Tom put me up the week before that. The two of them kept taking it in turns to host me. By the end of the five weeks that I was in between houses, I couldn't be sure how welcome I was in either of their places.

'I'm a minimalist!' I say to the woman.

It smells different inside the house, sort of marshy. I stand still at the bottom of the stairs for a few seconds before starting the climb up to my own entrance. Tom says he can't stay over on my first night because he's doing an assembly on FGM in the morning, which he's been stressing about for the last two weeks. I actually don't mind. This feels private.

I pause by the door to the top floor flat, directly opposite my own. Their paintwork is brighter than the rest of the hallway, like it's been refreshed more recently than the other areas. I have the stupid, fleeting thought that it must be nice to have stairs inside your flat, even if they only lead to the flat itself and not to a second floor.

When I hear the click of the lock, I know that it's me and my flat. Nobody else. Just us. Inside, I'm caught off guard by how empty it is. There is nothing surplus at all. It's just a blank space with the shadows of the objects that used to fill it.

I walk in and out of the four rooms: kitchen first, then living room, bedroom, bathroom. The bedroom is the bleakest of all. I hadn't noticed when the old owner's bed was still there that one of the walls was dirty beige, dingier than the other three, a feature wall of some description. Retracing my steps, I settle in the living room. It's funny to me that there are curtains in here, now that there's nothing else. I push them further open, trying to encourage more light to come in. At a loss, I sit down cross-legged on the floor, my meek little possessions by my feet.

I type *cheapest energy supplier london* into Google on my phone. I get started.

34

With about three-quarters of my to-do list for the day checked off, I order a pizza. A big one with goat's cheese and honey on it. When it arrives, I play the HAIM song on a loop and eat greedily, sitting on the knotty carpet.

I don't have the Wi-Fi set up yet, so when I've finished eating, I have nothing to do. It's starting to get dark. I roll my sleeping bag out and place the pillow flat at the top: my bed. The noise from the traffic outside is shockingly loud.

I text Noor, *Traffic right outside my window quite loud . . . Might have made a terrible investment?*

She replies, faux-jauntily, *I'm sure it's great!*

Though I understand that she might have nuanced feelings about this stage of my life, I do wish she could push them to the side, at least for my first night.

I FaceTime my mum, who I know has much less nuanced feelings about us buying this flat.

'My baby! In her own house!' she answers. 'Wow, is that your four-poster bed?'

I wave my phone this way and that, showing her the few things that I've brought into the space. 'I haven't worked out how to put the heating on yet.'

'Come on, you donkey. Show your mother.'

I swivel the camera round to face the thermostat and she calls out suggestions that I've already tried. It's just nice to talk to her, so I go through the motions of trying everything she comes out with.

'Google it?' she says after a while.

'Yeah,' I say. 'I'll put a jumper on for now. It's not urgent.' In my hand, I bring her over to the mantelpiece. 'There you are, look. Pride of place.' I show her a framed photo of her laughing her head off in her tartan pyjamas from about five years ago.

'Oh lovely. Such a flattering one, thanks.' She's smiling through the screen. 'Alright, my love. Go and enjoy this moment. Have you had your dinner?'

I nod. 'Enough for the two of us. Have you?'

'Going to have a boiled egg.'

'Soz Oliver Twist.'

'Spent all my grocery money on a flat in London, didn't I?'

'Mum.' I don't like these jokes.

'Oh, lighten up. I'm having a glass of bubbly too, don't worry.' She holds up a coupe, brimming with champagne.

After I hang up, inspired, I go to the corner shop and get a bottle of the cheapest Prosecco for myself. It's a happy night.

35

It's wild to me that I'm still expected to go to work when there's so much to do in the flat. I write endless to-do lists on my walk to the library, compare swatches of mildly different white paints on my lunch break, hurry back home at the end of the day to clean and organise my few possessions. It's been ten days before I register that Tom hasn't come round yet.

Want to come sofa shopping at the weekend? I text him.

God yes! he replies.

I grin at this. I wonder whether sometimes with Tom all he needs in order to thrive are precise offers and instructions. He performs the worst in situations where the possibilities are endless, like in the supermarket or when faced with a six-page menu. A month or so ago, in the Tesco Express near his flat, I held up a packet of chicken kievs and a quiche and asked him to choose. He stood there for a full three minutes just looking from one to the other. He looked so stressed that I told him to leave it and I ordered us a chippy.

36

I meet Tom outside Habitat. He looks like a little husband. Smart trousers, denim shirt buttoned to the top, suede trainers, a smile.

'You look like a little husband,' I say, kissing his mouth.

He laughs and says, 'Yes.'

We walk around the ground floor of the shop and I point out things I like, mostly mid-century-ish bits. He's shy at first, agreeing with everything I say. Once we go up to the next floor – the bedroom department – he's grown in confidence and wanders off on his own.

'Mara!' he calls. 'What about this?'

He's standing next to a blue velvet armchair with high scrolled arms.

'For the bedroom?' he says, as I join him.

I stroke the material. 'Yeah? You like this fabric?'

'I do actually.' He sits on it.

'You know we'd end up just piling our clothes on it if it was in the bedroom. Could be cute as a feature chair in the front room?' I take a photo of him reclining with his eyes closed. 'It suits you.'

'Could it be my personal sofa?'

'What, you don't want to cosy up to me on a little loveseat?' I push my lower lip out in a pout.

He pulls me down to sit on his lap and I brim over with glee.

'I want to cosy up with you everywhere,' he mutters into my ear.

I can feel that he's hardened a little in his smart trousers. 'Hello,' I say. 'That's nice. You like this chair this much?'

Tom is properly engaged, not just going through the motions. He helps me choose a bed frame and a round dining table and a big mirror to go over the fireplace. He offers to buy the mirror for me. 'For when I'm not there and you need something to remind you how beautiful you are,' he says.

We go for lunch at Leon and eat fish finger sandwiches, then go to Heal's and look at lots of beautiful furniture I can't afford.

'Shall we see what's on at the Odeon?' Tom says, once we've seen enough chairs to furnish the whole of Buckingham Palace.

37

There's a note under my door when we get back to the flat. We're giggly. We shared a pocket-sized bottle of vodka in the cinema, passing it back and forth, wincing with every sip.

Tom says, 'You've got a police summons.'

It's not a funny or clever joke, and this makes me laugh even more. I pick it up.

'Shhh,' he says. 'They might be able to hear you opening it.'

We make a show of tiptoeing into the bedroom and pulling the door closed behind us. The note is in an A6 envelope with *FAO Mara* written on it in blue-biro cursive.

'Where's my name?' Tom says. 'I'm here too. Rude.'

Even though he's messing around, this is a nice thing to hear him say.

I put my finger to my lips before using it to tear open the envelope. Inside, there's a lot of writing. Immediately, it doesn't seem funny at all. I have a horrible gut feeling that I might be about to be told off for something.

Dear Mara,
I am quite concerned about your actions of last week. I noticed on three separate occasions that the front door was left on the latch, or even, in one case, AJAR. I'm sure I don't have to tell you what a safety risk this poses. I understand – from having seen various vans over the last few days – that you may be having work done in your flat and be accepting deliveries, and this would explain the lax attitude to locking the front door. I do take this into account. However, this area – though largely gentrified – is still not particularly safe, and an opportunistic burglar would not care about the reasons behind the easy access to the house, they would simply seize the chance as they found it.

I have been very worried about this and ask you to please bear the safety of not only yourself, but your neighbours, in mind as you proceed with any further work in your flat. I trust that this will not happen again. If you need any guidance on how the locks work on the front door, do not hesitate to knock for me, and I will be more than happy to demonstrate. I am often home during the day.

All best,

Jerry (ground floor + basement flat)

P.S. Welcome to your new home! I hope you'll be very happy here.

I shove it into Tom's hand for him to read, my eyes wide with horror.

38

When I run into one of my upstairs neighbours for the first time, I have an enormous cold sore. This is not ideal, and I keep trying to hide it by placing my chin in one of my hands, in a sort of pensive pose. It's a man about the same age as me. He's wearing expensive-looking stiff denim and bright white trainers, and has a tote bag full of fresh vegetables on his shoulder. He has just come inside and smells of fresh air.

'Oh, hey!' he says.

'Oh, hey!' I echo. I am on my way out to the bins, and am not in expensive-looking stiff denim or bright white trainers, but in grey leggings with a hole in the crotch and some Polish wool slippers.

He grins. 'You must be our new neighbour.'

'You must be mine.' I hold out my hand, very aware of my exposed lip. 'I'm Mara.'

He shakes it. His grip is quite loose, and I don't blame him. 'Baz.'

I wonder what it's short for. He doesn't look like a Barry. 'It's funny,' I say. 'You'd think we'd run into each other all the time, what with having the same front door and stuff, but I've been here nearly three weeks now and you're the first person I've actually seen.'

He laughs, graciously. 'Well, we both work pretty long hours. Me and my girlfriend, I mean. Adele. She's on a shoot at the minute, actually. She'll be back tomorrow. And Jerry,' he nods at the door we're standing next to, 'keeps himself to himself. For the most part.'

I'm tempted to broach the subject of the note, but it feels too risky when we're standing right outside Jerry's flat. I smile instead.

'Well, it was great meeting you. Hopefully I'll run into Adele soon too.' Chin back in hand. 'And Jerry.'

39

Lewis sends me a text which says, *Hey Mara! My mum is curious about your new place! Could you send a video over for me to show her?*

I stare at this message for a long time. The very last thing I want to do, now that I'm in this new Lewis-free space, is share anything about it with Lewis or his mum.

An hour or so later, I reply. *Bit of a mess atm lol! Very much a building site . . . Would rather show it in its best light in a few weeks. Love to your mum.*

40

My mattress arrives and my quality of life instantly improves. I still sleep on the floor – the bed frame appears to be stuck in the warehouse, despite my many passive-aggressive emails to Habitat – but having a few inches between my back and the ground makes all the difference.

I get curtains, and it's lovely. They're blackout curtains and it's hugely relaxing to draw them closed every evening at eight and nest down. Tom hates the dark, so I have to leave a tiny crack open whenever he sleeps over. He doesn't sleep over that often.

I join a community gym around the corner and start going there two to three times a week. This makes me feel better about myself, my community, and the fact that I often don't hear from Tom until bedtime.

I meet Adele. She is beautiful with shiny blonde curls that she pins away from her face in clever ways. She wears bright lipsticks with no other make-up, and looks ready for the catwalk even first thing in the morning. She is a head taller than me, and when I see her and Baz one afternoon, coming up the forecourt, hand in hand, I realise that she is also a head taller than him. She is friendly too, which makes it difficult to be suspicious of her, and offers me use of their tools, spare paint, and a wanky bottle of wine as a 'late housewarming gift'.

I learn how to regulate the heating and I do a successful load of laundry and manage to roast a chicken in the unfamiliar oven.

Now that my internet is set up, I get really into *Parks and Recreation*, watching up to six episodes per sitting.

41

Noor vows to start coming over at least once a fortnight, and keeps her promise, at least for the first go. We sit cross-legged on the floor, eating duck chow mein out of foil containers and flicking through her new dating profile. I help her choose the best pictures of herself: a variety of action shots and pensive still lifes. I've never had cause to download a dating app for myself, so the novelty of it is exhilarating. Each time she gets a match, I squeal with glee. She's historically gone through phases of trying very hard to meet someone, followed by phases of hating all men, so she is much less excited than me. She entrusts me with sole custody of her phone each time she pops downstairs to smoke. I am giddy with the amount of appealing men there seem to be on offer. I swipe right on a personal trainer, a banker, a PhD student, a bartender, a DJ, someone I sort of recognise from uni, one of Tom's colleagues, a guy with face tattoos, someone five years younger than us, someone ten years older than us, slim guys, chunky guys, tall, short, of all ethnicities, ones with skateboards under their arms, ones posing with classic books, ones with pints in their hands, one with a baby on his shoulders. By ten o'clock I've organised three dates for her, two of which she agrees to actually go on.

42

I oversleep and have to get dressed for work with my eyes still half-closed. I have the promise of a hangover brewing, and, because I'm running so late, have to forgo my coffee. I have some post in my pigeonhole, so grab it as I run out the door. I shove it all into my bag and speed walk to the library. Derek takes a parental stance with me.

'Late night?' he says, miming the guzzling of a pint.

'A little. Nothing crazy. Just had my friend over.'

'Still waiting for my invite, aren't I!' he says.

'Ha,' I say.

'No, seriously, though. I'm happy to hear that you're having some girly time. It's good to be surrounded by women.'

'Yeah,' I say, backing away and running upstairs to the staffroom.

I switch on the kettle and rub my temples. As I wait for it to boil, I remember my post and sort through it. Bill, bill, bank statement, handwritten note.

Fuck.

I can't face it in my current state, so I push it back inside my bag and concentrate on making my coffee. There's a man who's started coming into the library twice a day to stare at me from across the room. I've told Derek, and now, whenever it happens, Derek rushes over to stand next to me with his arms crossed, and this is somehow worse than the original problem.

Starey Man doesn't make an appearance on this particular day, and there aren't too many other visitors either. My favourite kind are the elderly patrons who come in to use the desktop computers. There are only two of those today, though, and I'm grateful for that. One wants to check his Ancestry profile and is quite content to be left to his own devices. The other one tells me her grandson has signed her up for weekly artisanal veg boxes and, though the first few were free and that was quite nice, the company have started charging her £50 a month, and half the time it's all just courgettes and how many courgettes can one woman eat? And she just wants to speak to a bloody person on the bloody phone so she can cancel the subscription, but they make it so bloody hard, it's like you have to have an IT degree to even log on to the website.

I get through the day with the help of lots of black coffee, an empty white baguette at lunchtime, and Derek's near-constant quips of how my bloodstream must be made up mostly of pinot noir.

43

Mara,
To say that I was horrified last night to find the front door unlocked on NUMEROUS occasions, would be a huge understatement. I thought my last letter was clear and fair, and yet the safety of yourself and your neighbours appears to continue not to concern you very much at all.

I know I won't have to remind you that were we to be burgled while the front door was unlocked, we would NOT be covered by our home insurance. I keep my bikes in the hallway, and each of these is worth quite a significant sum. Our post is also often stored on the sideboard by the door, leaving us open to identity theft.

I noticed a rogue rose sticking out of my front garden last week – a possible sign of someone scoping our property out or marking it out to an accomplice as an easy target. Have you seen any suspicious activity in the forecourt lately?

Please do double lock EVERY time you leave and enter the house. All it takes is a few minutes for your computer, TV, jewellery etc. to be taken from you forever.

Regards,
Jerry (ground floor + basement flat)

44

I send a photo of the letter to Noor.

WTF, she texts back.

That's you and your bloody fags, I reply.

Are you taking the piss? Is he? I was literally sat on the stoop, smoking. Somebody would have had to step over me to break into your house.

Do we think this man is a bit mental? What's all this stuff with the rose about?

Just ignore him. He probably thinks he owns the whole place. It's your flat, you can do whatever you want. He's not your landlord!

Yeah . . .

On my return from work, I scan the forecourt to make sure Jerry isn't around, and when I lock the front door behind me, I make a point of doing it noisily. I rush up the stairs, lest he come out and confront me. Once inside, I think it best to stay inside. I watch six episodes of *Parks and Rec* and fall asleep on my mattress on the floor.

45

I wake with a start. The window panes are rattling in their frames. I can hear a wailing. I rub the sleep from my eyes and sit up. I strain to hear it again, but it appears to have stopped. It sounded like a baby crying, but I don't think there are any babies in this row of houses. I've already started drifting off when the noise starts up again, this time more prolonged and much louder. The windows vibrate. My bedside glass of water shakes, the water rippling inside. I get up and peer through the curtains, looking for a fox. All is still. I am confused. Another bout of the wailing, which seems to be coming from above my head. I look up. The wailing turns into something slightly more intelligible.

'*Yesyesyesyesyes.*'

Oh. I sit back down on the mattress. It's just Adele being thrown around. Or Baz. I don't claim to know their dynamic.

'*Fuckfuckfuckfuck.*'

I feel like a voyeur, but it's out of my hands. I couldn't block them out if I wanted to. The rattling redoubles.

'*Fuuuuuuuuuuuuuuuuuuuuuuuuuuck.*'

A pause of a few seconds.

'*Thank you.*'

46

Starey Man finally says something to me. He approaches me on a Wednesday morning, his eyes firmly on my chest, hidden though it is under a high-necked blouse. He opens his mouth, sticks out his tongue and wets his bottom lip before speaking. I wince.

'Where are the large print murder mysteries?' he says. 'That's what I like.'

I point to the far right corner. 'Just over there. You can't miss them.'

There is a very visible sign which says: *Large print: thriller.*

'I'd like you to show me, please.'

I see Derek dawdling not far from the section in question.

'You see that man over there? He's the library manager. He can help you.'

'No,' Starey Man says. 'You.'

'Okay, no problem at all,' I say, through gritted teeth. 'Just this way, then.'

I walk the twenty metres it takes to get from one side of the library to the other, my nemesis in tow. I drop him off in front of his large print thrillers display.

'There you are.' I start to back away.

'Which one do you recommend, darling?'

I tut, inadvertently. 'It's not really my—'

Derek finally notices us. 'All okay here? Mara, I think there's a phone call for you. Urgent.'

I smile gratefully and hurry over to the safety of the main desk.

I can hear Starey Man saying, 'Mara. What a pretty name.'

47

My bed frame arrives on a Saturday lunchtime in nine separate cardboard boxes, and I'm so excited that I call Tom and ask him to come over.

'I need to bring some books to mark, though?' he says.

'Of course. Bring anything you want.'

In preparation, I shave my legs and paint my toenails red and put on my best leggings.

When Tom arrives, he is weighed down with bags of books. He has his normal Eastpak bag, his satchel thing that he carries his laptop in, a Sainsbury's carrier, an Aldi carrier, and a Tesco bag for life.

'Poor love,' I say, taking two of the bags off him as he stumbles inside. 'You definitely don't want to retrain as a manual labourer of some description? You're going to help me put this bed together for free. It doesn't seem right.'

'I'm looking forward to it. Will be nice to make my mark on the place. Okay if I do a few of these first, though?' He points at some of the exercise books, struggling to escape from the hold of the supermarket plastic bags.

I know he won't relax or enjoy himself if he doesn't make a dent in his work. 'Babe, obviously. I'll make us a bit of food. Act as if I'm not here.'

I leave him at the makeshift desk – it's my dressing table without the mirror yet attached – and go through to the kitchen to make an elaborate pasta bake. I put my earphones in and listen to a podcast about the Yorkshire Ripper.

True to his word, by the time the food is ready, he's done twenty books and looks three times more chilled than when he arrived. He says that he can do the rest tomorrow. We eat perched on the edge of the mattress, and we talk about lots of things that have nothing to do with either of our jobs.

Between the two of us, it takes three and a half hours to assemble the bed. I have to sheepishly knock twice at Adele and Baz's – once to borrow their power drill and once to ask for some antiseptic when I slip with the screwdriver.

When we finish, we stand back to admire our work, then, wordlessly, pick up one side of the mattress each and lift it on top of the frame.

'Our bed,' Tom says, beaming.

'Yes,' I say.

We make it up with some new linen bedsheets and get inside. Though it's still early, we stay there until morning, chatting and kissing. It is pure joy.

48

Tom decides to stay over two nights in a row, which is virtually unheard of. His blues start up at around four o'clock. We've just started washing up after our roast. I bought us a rotisserie chicken, and Tom made his crispy roast potatoes and a really good stuffing, and we shared a bottle of Chablis, and he seemed happy, at least for the duration of the meal.

Now, he keeps saying, 'The real secret is to bash the potatoes around in the tin.' He says this maybe five, six separate times.

In these situations, I'm careful. His mood is precarious and it doesn't take much to completely push him over the edge. So I keep agreeing and saying, 'Your best ones yet.'

He's soaking the dishes in a sink full of greasy, soapy water. Though I hate when he does the dishes like this, this is in no way the time to criticise, so I gratefully accept the clean items as he passes them to me, and I rub them dry with the tea towel, ignoring the suds still clinging to the forks and plates and glasses.

He turns off the tap and excuses himself to go to the bathroom. He still seems kind of alright at this point. I wait for him in my spot by the sink, tapping my foot to the Motown that's playing softly from my laptop. Two songs. Three. Four. They're shorter than modern songs, but it's still a long time for him to be in the loo.

'Tom?' I call.

No answer.

I wander into the hallway and see that the bathroom door is slightly open.

'Tom?' I'm close enough now to see his outline through the mottled glass. He's sitting on the floor, his back against the bathtub. 'Babe?'

He's peering at his phone and looks entirely out of it. I sit down next to him.

'What's happened?'

He hands me his phone and says, 'I'm just setting my alarm for tomorrow.'

He's set three separate alarms: *05:05, 05:10, 05:15.* I think I can see the problem.

'Okay, so,' I say, softly. 'Why do you think you need to get up at five? Even factoring in the slightly longer commute from here, that seems quite generous.'

'I still have twenty books to mark, and we have briefing at eight.' His voice is small, wavering, frightened.

I take his limp hand. 'Tell me what we can do to make it feel more manageable? Would you feel better if you marked some more books now? It's still early.'

He shakes his head.

'Do you want to go back to your flat so you're a bit closer? I could come too. You could go on your own. Whatever you want.'

The last thing I want is for him to go off on his own in this state, but I want him to feel like he can choose that if he needs to.

'I can't face public transport,' he says, sadly. His head has flopped down.

'Uber?'

'That's just stupid, though. I can't get an Uber all the way to Croydon.'

Something in his voice makes me think that he's already considered this as a viable option.

'Why is it stupid? It's not stupid if it'll make you feel better.'

'I don't know,' he says. 'I don't know what to do.'

My heart is racing and somehow also beating in slow motion. 'Do you want me to leave you for ten minutes?' I can't think of anything else to suggest.

'It doesn't matter.'

I say, 'Wait here,' as though he's going to go anywhere when he's seemingly fixed to the floor.

I go back to the kitchen and finish the washing-up, taking some deep breaths. Then I switch the music off and put the kettle on. I brew us a camomile each and take them through to the bathroom. He's managed to get off the floor and is now perched on the edge of the bath. I join him. He accepts the camomile. I could hand him anything right now and he'd accept it.

'Here's what we're going to do,' I say, with an authority I don't feel. 'We're going to sit and drink these, quietly. I'm not going to ask you anything or suggest anything. We're just going to sit. And then we're going to mark ten books, and then you're going to set your alarms for a more reasonable time, and then we'll watch something mindless and go to bed. Okay?'

'Okay,' he says. He lifts the mug to his mouth, then lowers it again without taking a sip. 'I'm sorry.'

'Hey, no. There's nothing to be sorry about.'

'This was meant to be a happy weekend.'

'It has been.'

'But I'm spoiling it. I always spoil it.'

I shake my head, over and over. He has started to cry a little. I pull his precious head towards me and crush it into my chest.

49

Tom wakes me in the night, nudging my side with his elbow.

'What's that?' he whispers.

It takes me a few moments to get my bearings. 'What's what?'

'That noise.'

I strain to hear the noise he's referring to. I can faintly make out some disembodied voices.

'A telly?' I say.

'But it's like two in the morning.'

The sound is admittedly louder than I first realised. 'It's okay,' I say. 'I'm sure someone's just popped it on for a bit because they can't sleep or something.'

Tom is agitated. He's jerking his legs around under the covers. He's taking the disturbance personally.

'Is it always like this? I've never noticed it before.'

'Well, if we've never noticed it before, then it's probably a one-off,' I say. 'I bet other people in the house hear us sometimes.'

'Not this late at night,' he says, kicking the covers off himself completely.

'Babe,' I say. 'Come on.'

The talking turns to music, a short jingle maybe. Or an advert. Tom's eyes are scrunched up tightly. He's breathing heavily.

'I need a good night's sleep,' he says. 'That's all I needed tonight. Just a solid eight hours.'

'Okay, and you can still have that. If we just relax again, you'll fall back to sleep in no time.' I lean over and nuzzle my face into his neck. It's sticky, clammy. He's sweating.

He rolls away from me. 'Sorry, Mara, I just.'

'It's fine.' These rejections always hurt. 'I'm right here if you need me, though.'

I am on high alert and completely wide awake now, ready for the day. I lie as still as I can, not wanting to set Tom off again. Minutes pass. The TV seems to get even louder. It must be a talk show of some description, because it's the same monotonous male voice, which drones on and on and on. Every now and then it stops and I hold my breath, but without fail it always starts back up again.

I go to the bathroom some time in the very early morning, just for a break. I discreetly look at my phone when I get back to bed and see that it's 04:14. Tom is rigid and obviously still awake. I dare not speak to him. I must fall asleep eventually, because I wake up alone when my alarm goes off at 06:45.

I have a text from Tom. *Well at least I got my early start!*

The flat is deadly silent.

50

Tom doesn't come round for a long time after that.

51

I finally meet Jerry. It's not on the forecourt or in the hallway or the front steps or any other communal space. I'm in the corner shop closest to the flat, buying tampons and eggs.

'Mara,' I hear.

I turn around and see an elderly man with jet-black hair. At first glance, he is smartly dressed, but as I look a bit closer I see that his suit jacket has a hole under the armpit and his shirt collar is a little grubby.

'Yes?' I say. It runs through my mind that this must be Jerry.

'Good to finally meet you in person,' the man says. 'I've heard you clomping around, but only seen you from afar.'

He is holding a box of matches, a loaf of white sliced bread and a half-pint of full-fat cow's milk. I'm put out that he still hasn't acknowledged who he is and that he's staring at me as intently as he is. It's all a bit off balance. I don't speak, waiting.

'I've been wanting to run into you,' he says, after a time. 'We should talk about the guttering.'

'Sorry,' I say. I feel bothered. I don't like the way he's looking me up and down, assessing me. It feels quite invasive, considering I have sanitary products under my arm. 'Are you my downstairs neighbour, then?'

His face changes instantly, clouding over. 'Well, yes,' he stutters. 'Jerry Bates, MPhil. I've been in the house since 1949.'

I beam, a big fake smile. 'Mara Lynch, BA. Been in the house for a number of weeks now.'

He doesn't laugh, doesn't react at all.

I change tack. 'I've been very thorough with the door locking,' I say. 'After that initial hiccup.'

'Well, like I said,' he says. 'It's for the safety of all of us. Not just me. I don't know where you were living before this, but this isn't the safest neighbourhood in the world, even now. Used to be a lot worse, of course.'

I want to go now. 'Okay,' I say. 'Lesson learned. I'd better go pay for these.'

'If you'd like to share your mobile number, I think that'd be good. I'll no doubt need to get in contact again, and it's quicker than writing a note and waiting for you to read it.'

Oh god. I realise that there's no way out of giving him my details, at the exact same moment as I realise with a sinking heart that we'll more than likely have to walk back to the house together immediately after this exchange.

'Sure,' I say. 'Shall we finish our shopping and meet up outside in a minute?'

He nods. 'That sounds fair.'

I pay for my items and stand outside the shop, vibrating slightly with unease. I keep taking my phone from my pocket and checking the time. Though I have nowhere else to be, this delay is still annoying.

Jerry comes outside around ten minutes later. He is carrying three plastic bags full of stuff. Printed on the carriers are the words *Have a nice day!* He's done his bloody weekly shop. I'm suspicious of anyone who does big shops in tiny stores like this one. It makes no sense. He has a car.

'Hi,' I say, hopping from foot to foot. 'Ready?' I try to keep any sarcasm out of my voice. I wish I could start the whole interaction again. No matter what my instincts are screaming at me, this man is someone I should probably have on my side.

'Yes. Let's go.'

We walk mostly in silence, with Jerry pointing out landmarks every now and then.

'That postbox is a bit of a worry,' he says, gesturing to the postbox closest to our house with his elbow. 'I've had a few things not end up at their destination when I've used it in the past. I'd use the one next to the post office, if I were you.'

'Right,' I say.

We stop.

'See that?' Jerry says.

I look this way and that, at a loss. He nudges the pavement with the toe of his shoe.

'This slab,' he says. 'It didn't used to look like this.' He waits for a reaction, which doesn't come, and continues. 'It was a real hazard.

One of the corners stuck right up. Risked your life every time you walked over it. But the problem around here, unfortunately, is that nobody wants to take responsibility for anything. I took it upon myself in the end. Few months of emailing and the council came out to fix it. You have to really persevere in Hackney.'

Finally inside, I watch him double lock the front door. As he does this, he looks at me over his shoulder. 'See?' he says. 'Just like that.'

'Yes,' I say. 'Thanks. I think I've got it.'

He has piled his shopping by his feet, and he pushes against the door with the palm of his hand, once, twice, three times.

'Do you want to pass me your phone, then?' I ask. 'I'll pop my number in.'

He hands it over, and I'm surprised to see that it's the latest iPhone, a much better model than my own. I tap my phone number in and type *Mara L (Upstairs)*. Now he can contact me whenever he wants. I don't ask for his number in return. I'm sure that he'll text me before too long anyway. I inch away.

'Wait,' he says.

'Yeah?'

'You have a partner? I think I've seen a man around.'

'That'll be Tom. My boyfriend. But don't worry. He only comes round once a week or so.' I don't know why I'm disclosing this. Like Noor said, this man is not my landlord.

'And he knows about the door?'

'As in to lock it?' I say. 'I come down with him when he leaves. I always lock up. I haven't got round to getting him a key cut yet. I'll do that soon.'

'You trust him with a key?' he says.

'My boyfriend? Yes. I trust him with a key.' This conversation is really taking a turn. All I want is to be safely in my own flat, away from this line of questioning.

'If you're sure.'

52

My mum comes to stay for a few nights. We go furniture shopping. I find a mid-century flea market in Stoke Newington and we have a whale of a time, looking at all the teak. She treats me to a side table, a set of drawers and a floor lamp. I lug the drawers along, stopping every few metres to put them down and lean against them, catching my breath. She carries the other two items effortlessly under each of her arms.

We run into Jerry just outside the front door. He looks flustered. He has a big plastic crate in his arms, full of loose papers. I assume he's on his way to the car, because he has a car key dangling in between two of his fingers.

'Hello,' my mum says, cheerfully.

'And you are?' Jerry says.

My mum pulls a face. 'My name's Rachel, mate. What's yours?'

Jerry doesn't appear to want to give this information up. 'You're Mara's . . .?'

'Yes, I'm Mara's,' my mum says.

'She's my mum,' I offer. 'She's here for a visit. Mum, this is my downstairs neighbour, Jerry.'

'An honour,' my mum says. 'This garden yours, then, I presume?' She nods at the scrubby patch of grass in front of the house. Right in the middle of it, there's a tall stack of plastic crates, much like the one Jerry is holding right now. It's been there for at least as long as I've been living in the house. My mum's going to get him back for his rude introduction, I can tell. I've told her all about the notes, so she's already decided he's a prick.

'Oh yes,' Jerry says, proudly.

'Be good if you moved all that,' she says. 'Looks pretty scruffy, and it's the first thing Mara sees when she comes home. You know. These things matter. Anyway. We've got to get these bits inside. See you.'

I follow my mum into the house wordlessly.

Once the front door is safely between us and him, I hiss, *'Mum.'*

'What? I've met men like him before. You've got to be stern with them right from the start, or they'll think they can walk all over you.'

'But he's been here for longer than I've been alive.'

'So what? You're here now, and you have as much right to ask him for stuff as he has to ask you for stuff.' She runs up the stairs with the lamp and the little table then comes back down to help me with the drawers. 'This is your home, baby. Never forget that.'

53

I have to tell Starey Man to leave the library when I see him smear tuna mayonnaise from his sandwich into the front cover of *Murder on the Orient Express*. Rather than seem at all embarrassed, he looks thrilled at having the chance to speak to me.

'It's a dirty protest,' he says, through a throaty laugh. 'It's Christie's worst one and I don't know why everyone loves it so much.'

'If you don't like it,' I say, 'don't borrow it. There's really no need to vandalise public property.' My tone is stern.

'What if I wanted an excuse to be told off?' he says.

My skin prickles.

He licks his lips and says, '*And Then There Were None* is my favourite. You do know what it used to be called?'

Rather than engaging any further, I say, 'I think we'll have to put a month-long ban on your library card. Please don't come in for a bit.'

Derek notices me talking to Starey Man and hurries over to join us, arms swinging. 'Everything under control here?' he says.

'Very much so,' Starey Man says. 'This young lady was just putting me in my place.'

'It's a shame that there's been a reason for her to have to do that. What appears to be the issue?'

'Derek,' I say. 'I've sorted it, it's fine.'

Starey Man is grinning. This extra attention is a real treat for him.

'What are your thoughts on *Murder on the Orient Express?*' he asks, directing the question at Derek.

'A classic,' Derek says.

Fucksake.

'This is the problem with your generation,' Starey Man says.

I'm offended that he would assume that me and Derek are the same generation.

'Go on.' Derek is giving Starey Man an indulgent smile.

I realise in that moment that there's truly no reason for me to be standing there anymore, so I leave to go and sit back behind the desk. I serve two people before Derek finally waves Starey Man off.

'Quite an interesting guy really,' Derek says, taking the seat next to mine. 'Misunderstood, you know.'

54

Baz and Adele have people round that evening. I know this because I hear the front door opening and closing about twenty times in the space of an hour. I hear heavy footsteps coming up and down the stairs, both the ones below me and the ones above. Someone in a pair of heels, someone in a sturdier shoe, someone in a backless mule which slaps against the floorboards. I hear some techno, then some Bee Gees, then some Spice Girls, then some TLC, then some Sbtrkt, then some Todd Terje, then some Madonna. From the amount of times I hear the same nasally voice going past my door, I guess that there is one lone smoker in the group. She seems to be having a protracted telephone fight with her partner, who doesn't think she should have come round to Baz and Adele's tonight when they clearly have so much to sort out in their relationship. There's a pizza delivery, then a delivery of something a bit more hardcore, which involves someone going and meeting another person on the street corner. Someone runs out for more booze. They play four Duffy songs in a row, and everyone sings along. There's dancing.

A couple of people leave at around three, and the others linger for another hour or so. Once everyone who doesn't live in the house has left, there are quieter, more quotidian sounds. The toilet flushing. Slippered feet. A charger being plugged in. Baz and Adele have some frenetic, moany sex which never seems to culminate in an orgasm for either of them, then they must fall asleep, because all I hear is my own breathing. I'm crying, actually. It's six in the morning, and my alarm is about to go off.

55

I go to Tom's. He's hosting a dinner party for some of his colleagues. I think this is very encouraging indeed. It shows that he's willing to make some connections, put down some London roots.

He says, with confidence, 'We should make cannelloni.'

'Great idea,' I say. 'Spinach and ricotta?'

He hesitates. This might be the question that pushes him over the edge. 'Yes,' he says. 'Yeah.'

I pick up the ingredients on my way over to his house. His pastry chef housemate, Eulan, has offered to bake a treacle tart for dessert, so thankfully that takes that decision out of our hands.

Tom is standing in the middle of the kitchen when I get there. He has a bottle of gin in one hand and a bottle of vodka in the other. Sherry is sitting at the table, scrolling on her phone.

'How's the prep going?' I say, dropping the Tesco bags onto the counter. 'Hey, Sherry.'

'Mmm,' Sherry says.

'I was thinking, we could either do G&Ts, or Moscow mules?' Tom says.

'Both!' I say.

Tom beams. 'Yes.'

He's invited his teaching assistant, Emma, and two other newly qualified teachers. They arrive en masse, while me and Tom are mixing garlic into a huge knob of butter to rub into a baguette. The kitchen is pungent, and Sherry is still sitting in her spot at the kitchen table, scrolling, nose screwed up.

'Eyyyyyy,' everyone calls to each other, Tom the loudest of them all. They proceed to sing a little ditty about their school, getting louder and louder until they burst into another, 'Eyyyyyy.'

I am surprised by this. It gives off football team vibes. I guess I thought they might all just be tired and glum, not jaunty and well dressed like this little crowd in front of me now. The girls are wearing

Zara, the man is wearing ARKET. It's my first time meeting Emma. I'd pictured her to be dowdy – ironic considering the stereotypes linked to my own profession – and am on the back foot to see that she's anything but. She's curvy and has big brown doe eyes accentuated with moody eyeshadow. Her long dark hair is in a complicated French pleat that wraps around one side of her head. I can't help but feel inferior to anyone who knows how to do fun things to their hair. I can't even do a convincing ponytail. My hair tonight is air-dried and loose and probably already a little frizzy, considering how hot this house is. Emma and the other girl both hug Tom, and I get a horrible belly-twinge of jealousy to think of how much more time they get to spend with him than I do. I don't even know all of their names yet, while they know exactly who I am, and probably have insider information on our relationship.

Sherry has perked up, and is looking around the room with mild curiosity. I'm introduced to the man, Curtis, an Irish geography teacher with a dirty laugh.

He says, 'Mara, man! So nice to meet Tom's good lady finally. I'd move cities for a girl like you myself.'

This is the worst possible thing he could say. Tom and I do our utmost to avoid eye contact with each other.

I laugh, and say, 'He moved for the job opportunities too,' quietly.

Curtis does what can only be described as a guffaw, and says, 'What? Are there no schools in Birmingham?'

'Shall I grab you a drink, mate?' Tom says, squeezing Curtis's shoulder. 'IPA?'

'He's a top lad,' Curtis says to me, after Tom moves away. 'Everyone at school loves him. The kids all think he's cool as fuck.'

I resent the fact that Curtis thinks he needs to divulge things like this to me about my own boyfriend. I know he's a *top lad*.

'Hard work, though?' I say. 'Your job.'

Curtis exhales noisily. 'You're telling me. I feel like the walking fucking dead. I'm constantly counting down to the next half-term. Eighteen working days, if you're interested.'

'You think you'll stick with it?' I say.

'God yeah. What else am I gonna do?'

This strikes me as an odd thing to say. Life can be long and, like me, Curtis appears to only be in his twenties.

Tom comes back with a couple of cans of beer. He hands one to Curtis and one to me. I nod my thanks.

'You and Grace come together, yeah?' Tom says to Curtis, doing an exaggerated wink.

'Ha,' Curtis says. 'We might've done.'

'Oh, are you two—?' I say.

'*Big* time,' Tom says. '*Big* time.' He's talking in a weird voice that doesn't suit him.

'Ah, she's class. I'd be lucky to have her. It just maybe wasn't the smartest decision ever at this stage of my career,' Curtis says. 'Such a cliché as well.'

I have another one of those belly-twinges. I don't like the idea of Curtis and Grace being close. It means that there's a culture of new teachers getting together; it means that it's the sort of environment which fosters flirtations and flings. I think of these young, attractive people all thrown into the deep end together, feeling the same stress, the same small joys. It's sexy somehow. I glance at Emma again. She's talking to Sherry, who's starting to warm up. I can see how Emma could be a comforting presence to have in your classroom, a great person to have in your corner. It wouldn't take much. A couple of days staying late after school, nobody left except her and Tom. She could offer to help him with his lesson plans, they might go to the pub to celebrate the end of a long week, get tipsy, get carried away. Tom's house is so close to the school. Does it seem like Emma and Sherry have met before? Sherry's laughing loudly now, bent over double. Does Sherry like Emma more than she likes me? Does Tom?

I sip from my can of beer, try to steady my nerves. She's just his colleague. I need to chill out. Curtis is asking me something about my job.

'Sorry?' I say.

'I was just saying, are there many young people that work in your library?'

I picture Derek and his low-slung trousers. 'No, not really. I think I'm the youngest.'

'Ah, I don't know what I'd do without these lot. It's fucking crucial to have people you can vent to at work.'

I used to be able to vent to Tom. He used to vent to me.

Eventually, we all sit down around the table. It's a tight squeeze, elbows are touching. I try not to dwell on the seating plan. I'm next to Eulan and Curtis on one side of the table; opposite us, Tom is next to the three girls, and entirely in his element. I smile at him, trying to regain some form of insider solidarity. He smiles back. He looks genuinely happy. I relax.

56

Tom gets drunker than I've seen him since our uni days. He keeps shouting, 'Club, club, club!'

His friends all think this is hilarious and pour him more drinks. I have no desire to go to a club. I was hoping to have a nice Saturday with Tom tomorrow, maybe go to Tottenham Court Road again to buy a few bits for the flat. I can already see that this is not going to be happening.

Tom stands on the sofa and does a vaguely problematic impression of their Jamaican Headteacher.

Eulan calls, 'Alright, mate. Get down now, I think.'

Emma is doing an indulgent little giggle, like, *Aw, what's he like!* I feel a bit panicked.

'Babe,' I call, trying to assert some power. 'I think you could be a better host from down here, maybe.' I do a laugh. It's not a particularly convincing one.

Grace takes a photo of Tom on her phone. We haven't had dessert yet, and I don't know why Eulan isn't suggesting it.

'Eulan,' I say. 'What about your tart? That might be nice for everyone.'

Tom shouts, 'Do you know who *is* a tart? Mrs fucking Freeman!'

Grace and Curtis nudge each other and share a smile.

Emma says, 'Ooh, you *are* bad.'

I have no idea who Mrs fucking Freeman is.

'Shall we go into town, then?' Tom shouts. 'Town? Everyone? Town?'

I hate it when he describes central London as *town*. It's him at his most provincial, which doesn't even make sense, because he comes from the second biggest city in England. I go into the kitchen and start to wash up.

As I'm wiping down the hob, Sherry comes in and says, 'They've decided on the pub. Are you going? Me and Eulan aren't.'

I really, really don't want to go to the pub. I am entirely sober, and jealous of all these in-jokes, and actually quite hurt that – even though he's verging on paralytic – Tom hasn't come to look for me. I think, very distinctly, *What am I doing here?*

'The pub?' I say. 'Great. Perfect. I'll grab my bag.'

Back in the living room, Grace and Emma are propping Tom up, offering him a shoulder each. Curtis is looking at his phone screen and narrating the Uber's journey to Tom's front door. I don't have to go. I could stay here, go to bed. I could go home. But no matter how shit the next part of this evening has the potential to be, I'm more worried about not being there with Tom in this state than anything else. His friends don't seem to see any issue with the fact that there's a bit of dribble at the side of Tom's mouth, and that his knees keep buckling beneath him, even with two adult women holding him up. I wonder whether they've seen him like this before. Maybe this is Tom's thing now. The funny little English teacher who doesn't know his own limits. Emma is reapplying lipstick with her free hand. She is entirely unfazed. Maybe he should be with someone like her, someone who isn't crippled with anxiety at the mere possibility of him embarrassing himself. Someone chill.

I text Noor: *At Tom's with his mates from work. We're about to go out, even though I think Tom may officially be passed out . . .*

Noor texts back: *Cute! Any girls there . . .?*

I text: *Yes, two. Both attractive. I really don't know why he asked me to be here. I feel quite miserable.*

Noor texts: *Oh babe.* Then two seconds later: *If I lived anywhere near there, I'd come and provide my solidarity.*

I don't think this is strictly true, but it still makes me feel a little less alone.

The UberXL arrives, and we all pile in.

Though he is easily the drunkest person in the group, Tom makes the executive decision on which pub we go to.

'Royal Albert! Royal Albert!' He taunts the driver. 'The only pub worth its bacon round these parts!'

The driver's sat nav was programmed for Effra Social, and he keeps trying to remind Tom of this, but in the end must find him too annoying to ignore because he obliges and pulls up in front of the Royal Albert. It looks more like a social club than a pub. Inside, it has low ceilings and bright lights and hard furniture, and three old men who look like they've been there since 1976.

'You're sure this is where you want to bring your friends?' I whisper to Tom.

'They love it!' Tom shouts.

Sure enough, Emma, Grace and Curtis are already at the bar, asking a disgruntled barmaid for pints of Guinness and losing their minds at the idea that they don't stock any Fever-Tree.

'Look!' Emma calls. 'I just asked for a Merlot!' She's holding up a mini bottle of wine, like the ones you get on a plane. 'So cute!'

Tom runs over to join her. He looks genuinely excited to see this very normal object. I am uncomfortable that they're finding so much joy in this particular place. I want to tell them that it's not a space meant for us, and that we're probably – definitely – pissing the regulars off. One of the old men is openly gawping. I am embarrassed, but nobody else is.

57

We stay in the Royal Albert until we're asked to leave. This happens much later than I want or expect. The staff are enormously patient and polite, and my party is not. Grace asks one of the old men for a piggyback, then drags Curtis into the women's loos, where they stay for twenty minutes. Tom tries to get behind the bar to pour his own drinks. Emma tells another one of the regulars that he'd look *so cute* with a ponytail, then proceeds to gather his hair off his neck and tie it up with her own velvet scrunchie. I sip a half Guinness slowly and quietly.

Once the inevitable has happened, and the barmaid has said, 'Okay now, I think that's your lot,' we all stand outside for a long time.

Emma asks whether I'll take a picture of them all, and I oblige, noticing how close she stands to Tom. I take a deliberately blurry photo. It's not lost on me that it looks like two couples out on a double date.

I'm granted the small mercy of Curtis saying, 'Shall we call it a night, then?'

Emma doesn't take the bait. She lingers, telling a story about one of the students in her and Tom's class. Tom laughs much more than the story merits, and Grace chimes in with stories of her own about the child.

Eventually, Curtis says, 'Mara looks pretty bored, girls. I think we should maybe wrap it up. It's not that fun for people who don't work in a school to hear this much stuff about working in a school.'

'Is that party over then, Tom?' Emma says.

'I think it might be, yeah,' I say, as forcefully as I can manage.

'What Mara says goes,' Tom says, and I could kill him. 'She's the big boss.'

All night I've gone along with him and his friends. This is literally the first opinion I've expressed, and now I'm being pushed into playing the role of bad guy.

Fuck it.

'Yeah, I have had enough actually. I'm tired, I've not been able to partake in any of your conversations and, even though Tom's one drink away from hospitalisation, everybody's acting like he's just being a huge laugh. It's fucked, and I want to go to bed.'

Tom does truly the worst possible thing he could do in this situation and tells me in a slurred, wonky voice to, 'Calm down.' He follows it up with, 'It's not that deep.' This is a phrase he's learned from the children he teaches, and is another thing that doesn't belong to him.

I screw up my whole face and bite my lower lip.

'He's just having fun,' Emma says, petulantly.

'Fun? You think it's fun for someone of Tom's stature to drink seventeen pints? You think it's fun that he couldn't tell you his own middle name right now?'

Tom says, 'Stephen,' proudly.

'Tom, I swear to god.' I rub my hand over my face. 'I'm going back. You do whatever the fuck you want.'

I walk away, feeling four sets of eyes on my back. I don't know the way, but have no intention of taking my phone out of my pocket to look at Google Maps.

58

I don't talk to Tom for a week after that night. I'm furious with him, and am quite happy for the break, until Day Eight, when it dawns on me that he hasn't spoken to me either. I truly don't know what he could possibly be angry with me about, and it only makes me angrier to think of all those days at work he's had with Emma and Grace and Curtis in his ear.

During my many solo evenings on the sofa, I dwell on the situation, and decide without a shadow of a doubt that Tom and Emma are sleeping together. Of course they are. I even start to think about who I could sleep with to get my own back. I have no viable options at work. I don't really have any male friends. I don't have any proper exes. The only men in my life aside from Tom are Derek, Jerry and Starey Man. I'm pretty sure Starey Man would be up for it, but I'd also like to be able to look at myself in the mirror after the fact.

When I get into bed that night, I hear loud coughing from downstairs. It goes on for a long time. Long enough for me to become concerned. I'm kept awake, first by the actual noise of it, and then by fretting about the severity of it. By my calculations, Jerry's kitchen is directly underneath my bedroom. I've worked this out because, sometimes, early in the morning, I hear a microwave ping or the washing machine whirring.

The coughing isn't accompanied by any sneezing, but occasionally I hear an, '*Oh dear,*' in between bouts.

The whole of the next day I think about going to knock on Jerry's door to check on him.

I can never quite bring myself to do it, though. I want to know that I've contemplated doing a nice thing, without actually having to do anything at all.

59

On Day Ten, Derek lets me go home early because he says I look peaky. I feel peaky. At the flat, a set of shelves I've ordered has arrived. Somebody has placed it in front of my pigeonhole. I look at the package for long minutes, trying to work out whether I have the energy to attempt to build them. I barely have the energy to make myself a cup of tea. I leave the shelves in the hallway and go upstairs.

I sit first on, and then inside, my bed and start reading a copy of a *Baby-Sitters Club* book I've taken from work in a fit of nostalgia. It's the one where Logan and Mary Anne start seeing each other, and something about their innocent flirting makes me want to cry.

I'm about halfway through when I hear a doorbell. I assume it's Baz and Adele's, but I don't hear the scampering footsteps above my head that usually accompany their doorbell ringing. And why would they be in on a weekday afternoon? It rings again. It can't be for Jerry, because he never has people over. It has to ring a third time for me to realise that it's my own bell. My first instinct is mild fear. The postman has already been and gone and I haven't ordered any food or invited Noor round. It can only possibly be a bad thing at my door. For a moment, I even wonder whether it's one of my neighbours complaining that I haven't taken my package upstairs yet. I get up very slowly and go through to the front of the flat, into the kitchen, cursing myself for leaving the light on. Whoever it is, they know that I'm in. I approach the window, and jump as the doorbell rings a fourth time.

Nah, I think. *Step away from my property.* I inch my head as far forward as it'll go, my face touching the glass. I see the top of a familiar head. The head that's more familiar to me than any other. It looks up and sees me in the window. The face is sheepish, apologetic, mine.

I go downstairs and let it in.

We don't talk. He pulls me upstairs, and into the bedroom, and we go to bed, my *Baby-Sitters Club* book trapped beneath our bodies.

Once we're sweaty and panting, Tom says quietly enough that I could miss it, 'I don't know what I'm doing, Mara.'

I could ask him to repeat himself, but I don't. I don't think that falling straight into the Tom-being-a-victim-of-circumstance routine will serve us today.

'Tom,' I say, in my normal voice, 'you really fucking embarrassed me the other week. I was just trying to look out for you and you made me out to be like your strict mum or something. I've been so angry with you, I could've murdered you.'

'I know you have.'

'I was trying to include myself in your life, and now all your mates think I'm a tit.'

'Nobody thinks you're a tit.'

'Okay.'

'They don't. They were all bladdered themselves.'

'Did you even miss me? Why didn't I hear from you for all this time?'

He starts to talk, and I cut him off.

'This isn't normal, Tom. Nice couples don't do this to each other.'

'I don't think I'm very well.'

This winds me. I don't want him to say this.

'I don't think I've been very well for a while.'

There's no need for him to repeat this sentiment when it must be clear by my face that it's already had the desired effect. We're still naked, one of his legs in between both of mine. I'm breathing very shallowly.

'I haven't told anyone except you.'

'Okay,' I say, through the tears that have already come.

'That's not true,' he says, reaching for my hand. 'I don't know why I said that. I have told someone else.'

'Emma?' I say, hating myself even as the word slips out.

'No.' Tom looks genuinely confused. 'I had to tell HR at work yesterday.'

'HR?' I say.

'I started shaking uncontrollably in front of my Year Nines in period six, and one of them ran off to get the Head.'

I let out a whimper. I feel like the worst girlfriend anyone's ever had. I've been sulking about a fight while Tom's been having an actual nervous breakdown.

He says one more thing, before descending into silence. 'HR told me that after the Easter break, I should take some time off. I've been signed off for a month.'

60

We decide together that he should stay here with me in the flat. It took Tom having a breakdown for him to agree to move in with me, but there we have it. I got what I wanted. There's no point in questioning the way in which it happened.

It's eerie to come home from work and find him there. He cooks. He cleans. He does the food shop and proudly shows me the contents of the fridge, beaming as though he went out and caught and prepared everything himself. He changes the bed twice a week. I don't know this version of Tom. This semblance of domestic life with him should excite me, I know that, but what it actually makes me feel is scared. It's like we're playing house. Two children shacked up together. When I text him during the day to see how he's doing, he replies exclusively in emojis. If I pop home on my lunch break to eat with him, I find him either in the bath or meditating on the bedroom floor, legs crossed, palms facing upwards. I choose not to share with my mum that he's moved in. Though I don't think she'd have a problem with it in theory, I wonder whether in practice she'd be concerned about Tom's motivations. I don't tell Noor about it either, so, apart from Derek and the library users, I don't see anyone except Tom for three full weeks.

I start to lean into our cohabitation. It's such a novelty to have his full attention like this. He's so eager for news from the outside world that he hangs off my every word, laughing raucously at all my library anecdotes. He finally listens as I tell him about how scary I find Starey Man. I've tried to tell him about it on other occasions, but he always brushed it off.

'Do you want me to come and have a word?' he says, dead serious.

I look at him, like, *Tom, come on.*

'I mean it,' he says. 'It's not okay that he's making you feel weird about going into work.'

I nod. 'No, it's not okay, you're right.'

'And what's Derek's stance on the whole thing?'

I snort. 'The only thing more shit than being in a situation like that on your own, is being in a situation like that with Derek on your side.' I feel bad about the look on Tom's face, so try to backpedal a little. 'I just mean, I've got it under control. It's not as bad as I'm making out.' Now I'm just openly lying.

Tom lies down flat on his back, and exhales heavily. 'Mate, where have I been? I had absolutely no idea about any of this.'

'It's okay,' I say.

'But it's not. I'm meant to protect you from pricks like that. Or at the very least be there for you to vent to.' He leans up onto his elbows, then flops down again. 'I'm sorry, Mara. I don't know what else to say.'

I lean down from my seated position to lay a kiss on his little lips. He kisses me back, with real pressure.

'I missed you,' I say, into his open mouth.

61

I get a text from Jerry, which says: *Are the council aware that you're no longer a single-person household?*

PART III

Summer

62

There is an indoor picnic waiting for me when I get in from work. A tablecloth has been set out on the living-room floor, complete with fresh baguette, pâté, cured meats, soft cheeses, pork pies, mini Scotch eggs, strawberries, baby tomatoes, cucumber sticks, hummus, carrot batons, stuffed peppers, Kettle Chips, cream crackers, two flutes of champagne, and crockery I've never seen before.

Tom is sitting in the middle of it all, grinning.

'Hungry?' he says.

'Oh,' I breathe. 'This is so nice. On a Wednesday!'

He motions for me to join him on the makeshift picnic blanket. I haven't yet taken my shoes or bag off, but I fall into his little open arms and hold him tight.

'You like it?' he says, into my neck.

'So much,' I say, reaching over his shoulder and helping myself to a crisp. 'Mmm, spicy. I thought you didn't like these ones.'

'It doesn't matter. They're for you.'

I notice now that there's a sound playing. Crashing waves.

'What's this soundtrack, babe?' I ask, laughter in my voice.

'Ocean waves *slash* gentle breeze, ten-hour white noise playlist,' he says. 'I thought it'd be a good way to be in the moment and not fixate on the other noises in the house.'

I prickle at this. It seems like an accusation of sorts, but then I look at the spread he's put on and the effort he's made, and I'm happy to abandon the feeling. After all, he's right. We do sometimes allow both Jerry's and Baz and Adele's routines to destabilise our own. I sit back on my haunches and smile.

'Shall we eat?' I say.

Outside, the sun is blazing.

63

Baz and Adele's landlord sends someone round to sand their floor-boards back down to their original Victorian glory. Adele sends me lots of texts which say things like, *So sorry for the inconvenience!* and *Shouldn't be too much longer now, I think!* The main inconvenience this causes me is to remind me of how much work there still is to do on my own flat. The problem with any home improvements – as far as I can see, anyway – is that nothing costs less than a grand. And though a grand spent on your home never seems to equal a grand spent on yourself, it's still a thousand actual pounds. There is no spare money. Everything went on the deposit, and I'm still a librarian on librarian wages. So I don't get a professional painter-decorator in, I don't get quotes for my own floorboards, I stop browsing the Habitat website for furniture, and I ignore the growing mildew on the bathroom wall.

64

You finish at 8 tonight, right? Tom texts me.

Yep! Why?

No reason! Just looking forward to seeing you :)

It's such a luxury knowing that I get to see Tom every day. There is a great relief in the absence of planning and scheduling and carting big bags of clothes back and forth across London, inevitably leaving something crucial like underwear or a toothbrush in the wrong house. I always knew that if Tom could just give himself over to it, he'd like it, and now here we are, just as I'd hoped, and here Tom is, finding solace in living with his girlfriend.

'What you smiling about?' Derek says. 'Cheeky.'

At the end of the working day, I gather my things and head out. I think about taking a detour and going to Chatsworth Road to buy something special for dinner. I am all consumed with thoughts of artisan breads and organic ready meals, and don't see Tom right away.

'Hey, working girl!' he calls.

I do a double take. It's strange to see him out of context, dressed, in this place he's never come to before. It gives me a jolt, like that feeling you get when your mum comes to pick you up from a party in her dressing gown.

'Tom,' I say.

He's looking over the top of my head, at the entrance to the library. I can only assume he's looking for Starey Man. I hurry over to take Tom's arm, and lead him left, towards Chatsworth Road. He resists.

'Where is he, then?' he says.

'Tom, come on.' I feel suddenly quite unsure of what he might be capable of doing. 'Let's go, please.'

'I wonder if he wouldn't mind having a little chat?'

'Tom,' I say, more sternly now. 'There's really no need. It's not that bad.'

One of Tom's feet is tapping, faster and faster.

I take his face in both of my hands, force him to look at me. 'Hey,' I say. 'It's genuinely fine. I promise.'

His expression softens. 'Yeah?' he says. 'Because I really don't much fancy having a little chat with him at all.'

I narrow my eyes at him, teasing, willing him to laugh. He does, and then we're both laughing, clutching at each other with glee. I poke him in the side with my forefinger.

'Come on, Don Tommasino, let's go to the shop.'

65

We watch marathons of boxsets and films at the weekends. We work our way down to number thirty-three on *Empire*'s official list of *500 Greatest Movies*, without skipping any. We complete *The Wire* and *Peep Show* and half of *Mad Men*. We pause only for snacks and toilet breaks. The flat becomes our cocoon.

66

As the end of Tom's month off work draws near, he starts to panic. His face had begun to fill out a little. He was enjoying his food, cooking us big meals, ordering us elaborate takeaways. He loses his appetite, is still in bed when I leave the flat to go to work, and sometimes even when I get home at the end of the day. He becomes monosyllabic again. I stress about him constantly. I try not to let him see this.

'I can't go back,' he says to me, one night. 'I'm not ready.'

'Call HR,' I say. 'Tell them the truth. You would only be going back for the final term anyway. There's no point in rushing it out of some sense of duty.'

He shakes his head, helpless. 'I'll be letting everyone down.'

'Who gives a fuck?' I say. 'Your health comes before anything else.'

'What if I'm never ready to go back?' he says.

It's a very valid concern for him to have, one that I've had myself. There's every chance that this extended break will make him realise that he doesn't want to work at that school anymore. The advice that I've collated from the internet, though, is that it's wisest to tackle problems day by day, small task by small task. Today our only task is to get him to call HR.

67

I become very aware of Jerry's presence downstairs. This isn't always directly linked to the amount of noise he produces. Sometimes I can just feel him there. Other times I am truly amazed by how much din one single old man can make by himself. Tom comments on it as soon as I come through the door.

'Today he had two deliveries. I think one was books and one was a Tesco guy. He talked to them downstairs for fucking ages.'

Or, 'He didn't have his lunch until late today. The microwave only started going at about three.'

We learn Jerry's routines. Unusually for someone his age, he's a late riser. Tom often doesn't hear Jerry's toilet flush for the first time until after nine thirty in the morning. He also seems to go to bed seriously late. Mine and Tom's circadian rhythms are frequently disturbed by Jerry's radio starting up at unlikely times during the night. To balance this disturbance out, we learn to either put the fan or a rainforest white noise YouTube video on. My ears hum sometimes at work now, and I daydream of total silence. I can't remember the last time I could hear nothing but my own breathing. I become numb to the sound of traffic, sirens and people shouting in the street outside, but I can't find a way to switch off from the noises coming from inside my own house. They're all-pervading.

Two weeks into Tom's second month of living with me, Jerry's car disappears from the forecourt overnight. Since I've been staying here, I've never seen this happen before. We're ecstatic. We read in bed, have loud sex, sleep for nine hours. The next night, the car isn't there either. It's almost too much to take. We had tickets for the cinema, but we forget about them in order to have a quiet night in our little home. I realise it's the first time it's really felt like it's fully mine. I'm angry with Jerry for this. The worst thing about it is that he definitely has no idea how much power he has to affect our life. He only has noise from above – and me and Tom are always hyperaware of keeping it down – whereas we have two sets of sounds to contend with. A noisy neighbour sandwich, with us as the filling.

I worry about how much of his energy Tom is putting into tracking Jerry's movements. It's one of the only things that seems to rouse him from his stupor. He's endlessly fascinated by the ways in which Jerry spends his time.

'He hasn't gone out once today!' he says, once.

'Neither have you, babe,' I say, and instantly regret it.

I see that I've wounded him. He's quiet for the rest of the evening and doesn't even comment when Jerry's washing machine starts up after midnight that evening. It's so loud that it sounds like there are shoes in there, bashing round and round.

In the end, I'm the one who gets up out of bed and stands in the middle of the room.

'This is wild,' I say to nobody. 'This just can't be.'

Tom says, 'Yes, it's a joke.'

I'm happy that our disbelief has brought us back together. A team again.

'Well, what should I do?' It's the first time it's occurred to me that I could act at all.

'You could text him?'

I could do that, it's true. He certainly never hesitates to text me if I've done something he doesn't agree with.

'It's very late though,' I say.

'Exactly. Too late for him to be making this much noise right underneath our bedroom.'

This is a catalyst of sorts. Tom's right. This is not acceptable. I start to type. I type for a long time.

Hi Jerry. Sorry to text so late. I'd just like to flag up that Tom and I are being kept awake by your washing machine . . . It's extremely loud, and, due to the lack of noise insulation in the house, it sort of sounds like the washing machine is spinning in our bedroom. Going forward, we'd really appreciate it if you could just be more mindful of not doing laundry at night. During the day would be optimal, but as long as it's finished by 10pm that would also be acceptable. I understand if you can't stop it mid-cycle now, but thanks in advance for bearing this in mind in future. Best, Mara and Tom.

I show the message to Tom.

'What do you think?'

He hums. 'Take out the *sorry* and all the *just*s. You don't need to apologise for being alive.'

I nod and edit the text. I press send.

'Oh god,' I say. 'He's not going to like that.'

'Mara. We don't like this absolute racket either.'

I hear the ping of Jerry's phone through the floorboards, the ringtone much louder than it needs to be. I get back into bed and wait. The washing machine continues spinning. I hear a cough, then some shuffling.

Though not immediate, the washing machine does stop, and I'm sure it hasn't completed its full cycle. Tom and I look at each other with delight. He gives me a little high five.

'We did it,' he stage whispers.

'Yes.'

We lie perfectly still next to each other, a little sheepish, but triumphant. I don't make a sound, lest I be considered a hypocrite. We smile into the dark, gripping each other's hands.

68

Tom gets a phone call one Thursday lunchtime while I'm making us cheese toasties.

'Mara, help,' he says, passing me the still ringing phone. 'It's work. What do I do?'

'You should probably answer it?'

He widens his eyes at this suggestion.

'You're allowed to be at home,' I say. 'You've been signed off.'

He nods slowly and goes into the bedroom with his phone.

From my spot by the sink, I hear him say a tentative *'hello'*.

I'm nervous. I pause in my task to try and hear his side of the conversation.

I get snatches. A *'no, not yet,'* a *'definitely, that's a good idea,'* and finally, *'tell the kids I'm sorry and that I'll be back soon'*.

I switch the tap on so as to look busy. He has tears in his eyes when he comes back in. I dry my hands on a dish towel. It has the name of our university on it.

'What is it?' I say.

'She says I should go back to the GP.' He looks genuinely frightened.

'Okay.' I leave space for him to continue.

'Do you think I should?'

I chew my bottom lip. 'Well, you're not feeling very well, are you? And that's what the GP's there for.'

'What would I say, though?'

'You'd tell the truth. That you're struggling to do the things you used to find doable.'

One of the tears in his eyes spills over. It might be the first time I've explicitly said words to this effect out loud. Both of us have been reticent about calling the situation by its proper name, as though using the correct terminology might release the genie from the bottle. I haven't wanted to make it any more real than it already is.

I push. It's time. 'You're depressed, Tom. Aren't you?'

As I watch, his knees appear to buckle beneath him. He stumbles but doesn't fall, and makes a noise I'm not used to hearing adults make. My breath catches. He stays this way for long minutes, head cradled in his own hands, legs at an improbable angle. My poor little love. I am unable to move any closer to him.

All I can do is blink and say over and over, 'It's alright, you're alright.'

69

I try to convince Tom to invite some of his friends over for a drink. I have this idea that it might make him feel a little more connected to his normal life, might remind him that he used to make it work, that there were moments when he was quite happy.

'I don't know,' he says. 'Is it really appropriate?'

'Why wouldn't it be appropriate?'

'I'm meant to be ill.' He says the word *ill* more quietly than the other words.

I measure my response carefully. I frame it as a question. 'Do you think it's okay for you to maybe try to have some fun?'

He hums. 'Isn't that taking the piss, though?'

'Out of who?'

'My colleagues.'

He's being deadly serious so I do the same back. 'Do you actually think your colleagues begrudge you this time off? Please tell me you don't think that.'

Our whole conversation is questions in response to questions. We're two people fumbling around in the dark. The blind leading the blind.

'I'm still getting paid even though I'm not doing anything. It all feels a bit . . . leechy.'

Tom doesn't talk about money very often. If he has it, he shares it. If he doesn't have it, he gives the little that he does have to anyone he thinks may need it slightly more. He's generous to a fault, and I've always assumed that it comes from the fact that there was never much money in his house, growing up. I've found that the people who are least accustomed to having money are the ones who are most willing to give it up when the need arises. Even in his current state, he's made a point of offering me board more than once. This makes me incredibly uncomfortable, as any money talk always has. I put this down to the fact that, when I was little, I wasn't allowed to ask how much things cost. If I ever did, I'd get the stock response: *Not for you to worry about.* Tom doesn't know how much I earn, and I don't know how much Tom earns. Enough, I assume. I have no experience of sick pay. I couldn't say whether he's getting any less than he would in a non-depressed month. Regardless, we live in London, and he's still paying rent for his old flat. This is a weird tack for him to take, whichever way you look at it.

'You're not going to get better if you're not looking after yourself,' I say. 'Self-care includes having a nice time sometimes.'

'What about you?' he says, surprising me. 'You haven't seen your friends for a while.'

I scrunch my nose up, trying to hide my instinctive reaction.

'Where's Noor?' He's insistent.

'She's around.' I'm defensive.

'Invite her over. I wouldn't mind seeing her myself.'

This is the most surprising thing he's said so far. Tom and Noor have historically had a somewhat strained relationship. They're certainly not friends. When Tom and I first got together, Noor would often ask, 'But do you *fancy* him?' And in low, confidential tones, Tom would regularly ask, 'Why is Noor so *bossy?*'

I am cornered. We were talking about him, and now we're suddenly talking about me.

'Okay. I will,' I say. 'And why don't you ask Emma?' Because I feel off balance myself, I'm trying to throw him off balance too.

I catch the look of discomfort that clouds his face for a moment. I think I see him swallow.

'I don't know that Emma needs to see me like this,' he says.

So it's okay for me to see him like this, but his TA couldn't possibly be exposed to it. Does this make me feel special or like trash? It's hard to say.

Out loud I say, 'I'm sure she'd be pleasantly surprised by how well you're doing.'

He murmurs something noncommittal, and I realise with dismay that if I push even a tiny bit more, this intimate soirée will end up materialising for real. I have somehow managed to suggest that our first foray back into socialising should involve inviting round someone he doesn't particularly get on with, and someone I am acutely jealous

133

of. We could break this standoff so easily: one of us could laugh, or admit that it might not be the right time yet.

I reach for my phone and wait to see whether he'll reach for his. 'Tomorrow?' I say.

'Sure. Let's try for tomorrow.'

70

I buy a box of wine and stash it in the fridge. This is all the preparation we do. We've decided to order pizzas to try and make the evening as stress-free as possible, so as seven o'clock draws ever nearer, with nothing left to do, Tom and I buzz around each other, not settling to any activity, eventually sitting on the edge of the sofa, to look at our phones.

Emma arrives first. She texts Tom to tell him she's outside. I jump up to get the door. Though it is Tom's friend and now also Tom's house, I am still the host, and this has yet to be challenged.

Emma looks a little nervous on the front step, before I usher her inside. I want to get her up the stairs as soon as I can, want to avoid at all costs any run-ins with Jerry. The mood in the house is precarious as it is, and it wouldn't take much to throw the whole thing over. One wrong word from anyone and I think I would shut myself in my bedroom and refuse to come out.

'Wow,' Emma says, once we're safely inside the flat with the door closed behind us. 'This is great.'

Tom has stood up from his place on the sofa, and is nodding and smiling at neither of us in particular, just sort of into the room at large. I want to apologise for the still-barren living room, the bare walls. Instead, I am gracious. I know that Emma lives in a flat-share with people she doesn't love and that it is overpriced and doesn't warm up properly and is a long way from the school, rapidly turning her commute into the worst part of her day.

So I say, 'Thank you, Emma. I'm very lucky.' Then I add, to remind her that I have my struggles too, 'Lots of work still to do, but we'll get there.'

This *we* refers to me and my mum, but I am sure Emma will take it to mean me and Tom, and I am okay with this.

I have decided that I am going to make Emma my friend. Though thoughts of a staffroom affair have mostly left my mind, I still think it wise to get her on side. I vow to be charming and sweet and interested all evening.

I hold out my hand to take her jacket, and she misunderstands, haltingly giving me her own hand to shake. I laugh an inappropriate amount and then start to shuck her jacket off her shoulders myself.

She resists, confused, before saying, 'Oh. I think I'll keep it on if that's alright? It's sort of part of the outfit.'

That she is wearing an *outfit* to come to my unfinished flat and have drinks with me and my depressed boyfriend strikes me as unbearably comical. I find myself softly giggling, the sort of uncontrollable giggling I used to do in assemblies at school if someone made a funny noise with their hand and their armpit. Emma looks mildly alarmed. I wonder whether, in this nothingy time spent cooped up in the flat with Tom, I have completely unremembered all social cues.

Emma closes the gap between her and Tom to give him a hug. She is here for him, not me, and I don't know how I forgot that, even for a second. She is looking him up and down, smiling.

'Good to see you, Mr Atwood,' she says.

This is too much.

'Drinks?' I say. 'Wine for everyone? Wine.' I back out of the room before anyone can answer.

I spend a long time pouring the drinks. I both want Noor to get here, and also have no desire for her to come. Tom is chatty. I can hear him telling the story about how he ordered so much sushi the other week for his lunch that his order came with two sets of chopsticks. I am filled with tenderness for him in this moment. He is trying. He wants this to go well and he wants his friend to have a nice time, and that is terrible and brilliant all at once. Everything is so fucking fragile.

The doorbell rings and I do a little whoop out loud. This is for the benefit of Tom and Emma, to show them that I am in the party spirit, that I am accustomed to hosting. I don't know this overeager version of myself, and I am embarrassed. I go down to get Noor. Halfway down the stairs, I hear Jerry's door open. Even though I was hurrying, I stop in my tracks. I think about retreating quietly back upstairs, but if he's on his way out, he's going to run into Noor on the doorstep and I can't subject her to that on her own. I continue down the stairs.

136

I say, 'Hiya,' brightly, but Jerry doesn't hear me.

He's bent over in his doorway, fumbling around with a shoelace. I see the soft crown of his head, eerily white through his nest of wispy black hair. I can hear the doorbell go again, so I go to open the front door, and I let Noor in. She is wearing pink corduroy dungarees and Converse, and somehow doesn't look like a child.

'Alright,' she says. 'Glad you're still alive.' She hands me a bottle of tequila. 'I brought this in case it turned into a big party.'

I shudder. 'Thanks a lot.'

Noor raises a hand in greeting and I turn to see Jerry, both shoes safely on his feet, looking quizzically at us. He has an uncanny way of making me feel as though I have to justify myself for just living my life.

'Hi, Jerry,' I say. 'This is my friend Noor. We're going to order pizzas.' This is more information than I need to give.

He raises his eyebrows.

I shake the bottle of tequila from left to right. 'Take no notice of this. It's just going to be a quiet one.'

'Quite partial to a tequila myself,' he says.

'Ooh,' Noor says. 'Come up and join us if you want, party boy.'

I don't know what to do with my face.

Jerry does what can only be described as a chuckle. 'I've actually got to get to my physio appointment, but you never know. I can get quite stiff sometimes afterwards. Bit of tequila might help me to relax.'

'Well, you know where we are,' Noor says, and winks at him. 'If you're stiff.'

I lead Noor upstairs, yanking her the whole way.

As I'm pushing my way into the flat, still within Jerry's earshot, Noor says, 'I don't know what the problem is. He seems fine to me.'

'You're a bloody liberty, you know,' I hiss.

She laughs raucously, thoroughly enjoying herself. If nothing else, I'm glad that she doesn't seem to be holding a grudge about my temporary disappearance from her life.

Her expression changes when she sees Emma and Tom. I can't say precisely what it changes to. It just changes.

'Tom,' she says.

'Noor,' he says.

That's it. Nothing else happens.

After a few brief moments, I say the word, 'Ha.' I say, 'Nice to see that you remember each other's names.' Then, noticing Emma shifting from cute sandal to cute sandal, I say, 'Another name for you: Emma.'

Emma smiles graciously and does a weird little curtsy. I know that Noor will dissect this little curtsy with me at length once we get a chance to be alone together again.

'Ah,' Noor says, now, in front of us all, 'Tom's work wife.'

Again, I feel an overwhelming need to hit her, hurt her, shake her. She's trying to show solidarity in all the wrong ways. The only way I really want her to support me is quietly, with a shared glance or a kick in the shin under the table.

'I'll get you a wine,' I say. I'm a coward. I don't want to be in the room while Emma and Tom deal with this weird thing that Noor's just said.

I hum in the kitchen, snippets of a Biggie song. I try to embody carefreeness, lightness, joy. I feel heavy.

The three of them are laughing when I go back through. I start to laugh too.

I call for the pizzas. A margherita each for Tom and Emma, a goat's cheese and walnut for me, one with Parma ham and aubergines for Noor. We eat. We talk about surface-level stuff. A new sitcom, the extortionate price of council tax, an exhibition Emma went to see last weekend, dating apps, a recent change to Instagram's algorithm. Tom drinks quite a lot, and graduates quickly onto the bottle of tequila, which was meant to be a joke. His speech gets a little sloppy.

With two slices left on her plate, Noor excuses herself to go to the bathroom.

When she comes back, she says, 'Mara? Come out for a ciggie with me?'

Though framed as a question, I know it's an order. I smile at Emma, apologetically. She smiles back.

I go outside with my bristling friend. I lock the door behind us.

'Is this okay?' I say, before Noor has a chance to speak or light her cigarette. 'You seem a bit put out.'

'What's actually going on?' she says, eyes narrowed like a cartoon villain.

'With what?' I feign innocence.

'Has Tom had some sort of collapse?' she asks. 'And has he fucking moved in? Why is there so much of his shit in the flat? Like a whole life's worth? And what's this perverse thing with this Emma girl? Are we encouraging them to shag, or?'

I look over my shoulder, up at the living-room window. I'm nervous that they might hear us from inside. It's not unthinkable. The single glazing blocks out almost no noise at all. I realise it's my turn to talk.

'Do you actually want me to answer any of that?'

Noor is violently flicking at her lighter, trying to get purchase on it. 'Yes,' she says, through the side of her mouth that isn't holding the cigarette in place. 'Obviously yes. Answer all of it, please.' Her tone is gentler already.

'Okay. Yes. Tom has had some sort of collapse,' I say, keeping my mouth small. 'He hasn't been going to work and he's been staying here with me, and I've been trying to look after him. We've been in this little fetid bubble the whole time this has been going on, so I thought it might be healthy and maybe even fun to invite some of our friends over, and one of his friends is that very attractive woman upstairs. Okay? And one of my friends is you. So, please.'

Noor manages to light the fag, and inhales deeply before saying anything more. 'He looks terrible,' she says. 'Manic. I bet it's been stressful trying to sort him out.'

She hasn't expressly said that she's sorry about the situation, but this is as close as I'll get, and I'm grateful for some softness.

'Yeah,' I say, sitting down on the top step. 'It's been fucking painful and hard and fruitless, and I'm entirely out of my depth, to be honest.'

'I know what that's like,' Noor says, and this is completely the last thing I was expecting to hear. She sees my face. 'My mum.'

'Your mum has depression?'

'What? How do you not know that?'

'Because you've literally never told me before.'

'Oh. I guess I must have thought it was obvious.'

'Since when?' I want to reach out and make contact with Noor somehow, but can't think of a natural way to do it.

'Always. Well. Since I can remember. It's mostly under control.

139

Sometimes completely fine, sometimes horrible. That's why I moved back home. She's been having a particularly rough few months.'

'I thought you moved in to save money?'

'Not everything's about money, Mara.'

Though this petulant kick should be allowed, considering what she's just told me, I can't quite bring myself to let it slide. 'I wish you'd stop with this narrative about me being some sort of princess. We grew up the same way, me and you.'

Noor exhales a cloud of smoke in an ugly way, jutting her lower lip out like a bulldog and getting it all in her face. 'We did not grow up the same way. The fact that you think that is the most fucked up thing of all. Your dad did the noble thing and died. I'm sure he didn't want to, I'm sure he would've loved to still be here with you and your mum. Mine repeatedly chose to leave us. There was no pension, there was no being looked out for after he was gone. He was just gone, and we were left to our own devices and never had any help from anyone, and that is not the same thing.'

I knead my eyelids with the pads of my fingers.

'Look,' she says, puffing away furiously, 'we're not going to fight about this, but I do need to get it off my chest. You have every right to complain about stuff. Your boyfriend's not feeling very well, your neighbour's a bit weird, there's the old perv at your job. But please just read the room sometimes. Yeah?'

I run my tongue over my top set of teeth. It doesn't seem like a moment to defend myself. I wouldn't know how to. I've just been told off and I have a traitorous lump in my throat. I can't bear it that she thinks so poorly of me and understands so little about my intentions. Also, the line, *Your dad did the noble thing and died*, is playing on a loop in my head. I'm pretty sure that that was a terrible thing for her to say to me, but everything is off-kilter and I can't trust my own judgement out here on this step.

As we make our way back inside, I say, softly, almost under my breath, 'I wasn't even complaining.'

Noor turns sharply, and says, 'What?'

I say, 'Nothing.'

71

Over the course of the week, there is a flurry of post for Adele and Baz. Envelopes with our communal address handwritten on them in blue and black fountain pen. Thick, heavy stationery. Expensive. I assume it's one of their birthdays and feel a twinge of envy to think that they have this many friends who would take the time to buy cards and stamps and write personal messages and find a postbox, all just to wish them well.

One morning, on top of the stack on the doormat, there is a postcard. It's a photo of Adele in a white, floor-length satin slip and Baz in a beige linen suit. I pick it up. I see that they are holding flutes of champagne, and I recognise the building they're standing in front of as Hackney Town Hall. I flip the postcard over.

To the most perfect couple we know,
Thank you for letting us be a part of your special day. We had
so much fun! Adele, you looked stunning, and Baz . . . you
looked alright too! Wishing you the sweetest honeymoon, and a
life of joy and laughter together. Remember to never stop going
on dates – that's the real secret . . .
  All our love, Jan, Joel and baby Rufus xoxo

I let the postcard fall from my fingers. How can they have got married? When? How can I have not realised? How can me and Tom be struggling so much, just one floor below them, and Jerry be living his weird solitary life two floors below them, and all the while they've been this happy above us?

72

I leave a bottle of Prosecco outside Baz and Adele's door. I ask Tom whether he'd like to sign the note. He politely declines. He says they probably wouldn't know who he was.

73

I realise I don't fit into my everyday jeans anymore. Rather than question this too much, I just throw them away. I call the community gym and cancel my membership. I can't remember the last time I went.

74

Tom's mum rings me one morning while I'm at work. This is pretty much unheard of. The only other time I can remember this happening is when she called on the eve of his birthday one year to ask if I'd already bought the watch he'd been wanting or whether she could get it for him. It might have been the first birthday we'd had as a couple, because I'd only bought him some joke pyjamas and a book, and ended up feeling really stupid telling his mum that. I stare at her name on my screen for so long that it rings out.

'Derek, I'm just—' I say, already walking outside.

'Course, darling!' he calls. 'Whatever you need!'

He called me into the storage room upstairs for a *catch-up* a few days ago to ask me what was wrong. He said my *energy was off*. I didn't even try to deny it. I told him everything. He was actually pretty sympathetic.

Leaning against a low wall outside, I call Tom's mum back. She picks up immediately.

'Mara, thank god.'

'Is everything okay?' I say.

'You tell me, bab.'

I sigh into the phone. I'm careful. 'When did you last hear from Tom?'

'He hasn't picked his phone up in weeks. His texts are weird, and he's clearly not right, and I called Sherry this morning and she tells me he's not living there anymore.'

'He's with me. He has been for a while.'

'Right,' she says. 'And why is this the first I'm hearing of it? Should this not be a happy thing for him to share with his family?'

I naively thought he would've been in touch with them, at least with his mum. I'm as surprised as she is. 'The circumstances weren't necessarily happy, I guess.'

'And what does that mean?'

144

I don't know how much I'm allowed to say. 'Maybe it should come from him,' I try.

'Don't you dare,' Tom's mum says.

I cover my eyes with my spare hand and rub my temples with thumb and middle finger. 'He's not doing very well, to be honest. He's been signed off work.'

'What?' Tom's mum says this in a sort of long exhalation.

We talk for a few more minutes, and by the end of the call, Tom's mum has informed me that she's booked a train ticket and will be at the flat later today. I feel shellshocked when I hang up, as though I've betrayed Tom. We were trying to get things under control in our own way, and now the adults are involved.

75

Tom is absolutely furious with me, as though I had any say in the matter whatsoever.

'She doesn't need this stress,' he says. His hands are shaking as he pours hot water over a mint teabag.

'You don't think she's been stressed anyway?' I say. 'I didn't realise you weren't keeping in touch with them. You think she wouldn't notice that you'd dropped off the face of the earth?'

'Mara,' he warns.

'Well she's already on her way. I don't know what you want me to do about it. I think it'll be good for you.'

I think it'll be good for me too. A rest. Some advice.

She arrives with quite a large suitcase, and this is confusing. I assumed she would just be coming for one night. Within minutes, her presence fills the small space, making me feel surplus. She fusses. She kisses Tom, starts cooking a huge vegetable stew with ingredients presumably brought in the suitcase from Birmingham. She keeps putting the back of her hand to Tom's forehead, as though his illness might be a physical one. Tom reverts back to teenage boy and melts at everything his mum says to him. I wonder whether I should leave them alone together for a while.

I put on a load of laundry, just to keep busy.

'Tom likes Persil. Don't you, love?' Tom's mum says.

In dismay, I look down at the Ariel I'm pouring into the washing machine drum. Tom has never expressed any preference in detergents to me, or soaps, or food, or anything I buy, really. I don't comment. I don't think I'm required to.

'Right,' Tom's mum says. 'A walk.'

I raise my eyebrows. I think to myself, *Good luck with that one.*

Tom makes a little noise in the back of his throat. A sort of audible swallow.

'Come on. Just half an hour,' she says. 'It's lovely out.'

It's not lovely out. It's overcast and heavy. Going for a walk in this weather would worsen anyone's mood. Closing the washing machine door, I join them in the living room, hovering in the doorway.

I watch as Tom's shoulders travel up towards his ears. He's making himself small, hoping that she'll stop asking things of him. I know that that's what he's doing, because he does it to me too. I try not to feel insulted that Tom's mum has just arrived out of nowhere and is suggesting obvious things like hearty meals, fresh air and cold showers, as though I don't offer these self-care options up to him every single day. We're beyond all that. But then, this is new to her too. She's doing her best. I will him to give her the reaction she's after, any reaction, really.

He says, 'I'd rather not, Mum.'

She visibly slumps. She looks at me, pleading.

'Twenty minutes?' I say. I know that he'll say no to this too, but then at least he's turned us both down, and not just his mum.

'No thank you,' he says. 'I'm alright here.'

'Okay,' I say.

'Do you need some water? A herbal tea?' Tom's mum asks, desperate to provide him with something, desperate to move around in this enclosed space.

He says, generously, 'I could have a tea, I guess.'

'Great!' she says. 'I'll do you a nice camomile with some honey in it.'

I follow her back into the kitchen.

She says, with tears in her eyes, 'How has it got to this?'

She says, 'Do the school know he's this bad?'

She says, 'How could you have not called me?'

She says, 'My baby.'

She says, 'What are we going to do?'

She's not a quiet woman at the best of times. Here, at the worst of times, she's positively shouting. I don't know whether she's so overcome that she genuinely can't tell how loud she's being, or if she has just stopped caring. I rub at my cheeks with closed fists. I'm somehow the guilty party in all this, because I knew before she did, and have been unable to cure him by myself. Though this is completely unfair, I also see her reasoning. I felt guilty even before she arrived.

'Look,' I say. 'Do you maybe need to go for a walk by yourself? I can give you Tom's key. I don't know how useful it is for him to hear you in this state right now.'

She widens her eyes as though she's just been slapped.

'Don't you,' she breathes, '*dare* tell me what's useful for my son. I come here after weeks of complete radio silence and find him like this. A zombie. Of course I'm emotional. How else do you expect me to be? A robot? A wall of stone? I'm his *mother*.'

I shake my head. 'It wasn't a criticism. I just think we could all do with taking five. That's all I was saying.'

'Maybe you should go for a walk,' she says.

76

We fall into a routine of sorts. Tom's mum sets up a bed on the sofa and takes residence in the living room. She writes a checklist on a little blackboard she's bought, and Tom has to complete at least four out of the five things listed on it every day.

1. *Shower/bath*
2. *Go outside*
3. *Some form of exercise*
4. *Speak to someone who isn't me or Mara*
5. *Something fun!*

Tom responds well to this. He sometimes manages to do all five. He'll often choose to cook or pick a film for us all to watch as the fun thing for the day, and it makes the evenings pass less heavily than they have been. When I'm at work I have no idea what they're up to, and I don't ask. Sometimes he's flat when I come home, sometimes he's verging on jovial.

A few mornings in, when I creep back to the bedroom to get dressed after brushing my teeth, I find Tom sitting on the blue bedroom chair he helped me pick out. It's unusual for him to be up this early.

'You're awake,' I say.

He's smiling, looking out of the window. He says, 'Look.'

I go over and sit on his lap, follow his gaze. He puts an arm around me, and this is something from before, and so nice. It's a still morning, quiet.

'It's pretty,' I say.

'A Simpsons sky,' he says, proudly.

I kiss his cheek. I say, 'Yes. A Simpsons sky.'

77

During the second week of her stay, I get a notification from my online banking to tell me that £400 has been transferred into my account. The description next to the payment just says: *Board.*

I text Tom's mum: *What's this money for?? You're our guest!*

She replies: *Mara, it's a lot less than I'd be paying for a hotel. Please. I don't want to feel like I'm imposing.*

78

I start to quite look forward to my catch-ups with Derek. Feeling excluded from Tom and his mum's dynamic, and unable to turn to Noor, I tell Derek about the atmosphere in the flat, about how Tom's getting on, and how weird it is to be living with a parent again, especially when it's not my own. Derek asks how I'm feeling, how I'm coping, whether I need any help. This is touching to me. He genuinely seems to care. He's an unlikely ally, but I'll take anything I can get at this point.

79

Though we've warned her to steer clear of him, Tom's mum has a run-in with Jerry.

'Your neighbour,' she says, one evening when I come home from the library, 'is very rude.'

'Oh, I know,' I say. I don't need to ask her which one she's talking about.

'No, but like, extremely rude.'

'What did he do?'

'So this morning, I took it upon myself to clean those stairs out there. No offence, Mara, but they were terrible.'

'Yeah,' I say. 'They're a real dust trap.'

'So, I've extended the hoover as far as it can go, and I've got your door open behind me, and I've got Tom helping. And I hear the door open downstairs. And your man's bustling about, muttering to himself, and then I see him peer around the wall to see us. So I say *Morning!* and he doesn't say it back. He just goes, *Have you seen my magazines?* So I'm like, *What magazines?* And he says, *The ones I get delivered every week. They've not come, and they're always here by Wednesday.* So I go, *Sorry, mate. No idea. And if I did see them, I certainly wouldn't take them.* And, I don't know if it was my accent or what came over him, but he says, *Could I come inside and just check?* And I say, *Sorry, mate, check what exactly?* And he says, *Whether you've taken them in with your post accidentally.* Have you ever heard such nonsense? I said, *No, you bloody cannot.* And he looks over my shoulder at Tom and says, *Could I?* to Tom, as though he's going to get a different answer! The fucking nerve. I could've swung for him. I tell you what, bab, if those magazines come and I find them before he does, they're going directly into the recycling. You mark my word.'

80

We've stopped having regular sex. The conditions aren't really ideal, what with Tom's depression and his mum suddenly sleeping in the room next door. In fact, I can't remember if we've had sex once in the last month. Baz and Adele, however, are at it like proverbial rabbits. At any and all times of the day and night. I try to be understanding. It's their honeymoon phase, after all. Tom's mum finds the noises from upstairs so hilarious that she can't resist narrating their antics move by move.

'Early one today,' she says. 'Good for them. A quick and frantic start from Baz. They've gone for some traditional bed-based sex from what I can hear. And why not? Sounds like they're right on the edge there. Could be a real quickie. Ooh, what was that bump? He's knocking things over now, the stud.'

Tom made the mistake of laughing the first time she did it, so now she hams it up tenfold. Her favourite thing of all is how, whenever they finish, Adele always does that loud sigh and says, *'Thank you.'*

Now, as the noises draw to a close, Tom and his mum both say, 'Thank you' at the same time.

It's cute, I suppose. Anything that makes him laugh is fine by me.

81

Noor starts seeing someone. She doesn't tell me this, I find out through Instagram. Though it's not a post with the person actually in it, I can tell that the scene has been carefully orchestrated to show that she's out with someone. It's a photo of two pints of Guinness and a bowl of nuts on a pub table. She's tagged the pub: one in central London. A real old-geezer-type place, somewhere she'd never usually go. She doesn't drink Guinness and I'm pretty sure she won't eat nuts. I fight the urge to reply to the post. It's muscle memory, and it's unnatural for me not to comment on it. But I don't want to give her the satisfaction of reacting. There's a part of me that believes she's posted it just for me to see. She wants me to know that she's out on this date without having to speak to me. I really, really don't like her right now.

A couple of days later, she posts a photo of the night sky, with the caption, *Star crossed.*

That same evening, she puts up a picture of her mum's kitchen. The table is set for three and in the bottom left-hand corner of the shot there are a huge pair of oxblood Doc Martens boots. Much too big for either Noor or her mum. She captions it, *Tonight it's invite only!*

The day after that, she posts a moody selfie. She's kneeling up in her unmade bed, wearing a Run DMC t-shirt which is about six sizes too big.

Well done, I think, *Good for you.*

82

I ask Tom whether it would be okay for me to come for a run with him one evening. I want to be alone with him, and can think of no other way to do it. He looks doubtful, but agrees. His mum pretends not to be listening.

I find some old trainers that I don't remember buying and put on my house leggings and a loose t-shirt. We both do some half-hearted stretches in the hallway. As we go downstairs, I try to make small talk.

'What route do you usually take?' I ask.

He shrugs.

'Along the canal?' I ask.

He shrugs again. 'Could do.'

'Well,' I say, smiling. 'I want to do what you do. Let's just go on your normal route.'

He looks put out, and I feel self-conscious and also a little guilty. Maybe he likes his runs so much because it's time he gets to himself. Maybe I've intruded. We walk to the edge of the forecourt, and head in the direction of the library. We walk past the library. I wonder when we might start running. Tom's not talking, so I don't either.

We walk past the Adam and Eve, the good chippy, the Turkish barbers.

'Tom?' I say, after we've been walking for about twenty minutes.

'Yeah?' He looks at me blankly.

'When is it that you start running, usually?'

He looks away, and then back at me, as though he's just remembered something. 'Sorry,' he says. 'I don't know.'

'What do you mean?' I say, stopping.

'You want to do what I usually do?'

'Yeah?'

'Okay, well, what I usually do is this.' He turns back and starts walking towards home.

I follow him in silence. I have a feeling that I'm about to be shown something I'd rather not know. We walk nearly all the way home, but at the turning just before ours, he stops. He looks in my general direction, but not directly at me. We're in front of a tall block of council flats. He heads towards the communal bins. Just behind them, there's a metal bench, decorated with jagged, Tippexed love notes. He sits down on it. He puts one earphone in and closes his eyes. I take a seat next to him. He hands me the other earphone and I push it into my ear. He's listening to a Smiths song. We get through the whole album before he stands up.

Together, we make the short trip back to the flat. There doesn't seem to be any real reason to discuss what just happened. In the kitchen, Tom's mum is making chilli con carne. It smells rich and good and I realise with a jolt how hungry I am.

'Nice run?' she asks us, smiling widely.

'Great,' Tom and I say at the same time.

83

Jerry is standing in front of the house when I get home from work on Friday. He's bent at the waist, studying the front garden. I feel it's unfair for my weekend to have to start with an interaction with Jerry. I contemplate doing a lap of the block to avoid him, but he looks up and spots me.

'Hullo,' he calls. 'Come and see this.'

I can't really deny him this simple request, so I join him in his spot by the steps.

'Is this one of you upstairs?' he asks, pointing at a faint footprint in the mud.

'I don't know,' I say. 'I don't think so.'

'That's a tick there,' he says. 'If I'm not mistaken. Nike. Have any of you got Nike shoes?'

Mentally, I run through our footwear. Tom mostly wears Vans and his mum wears boots with little sensible heels and I'm usually in Converse. 'No,' I say. 'But we wouldn't be standing in your front garden anyway.'

'So it's not me and it's not any of you and it's not Baz or Adele,' he says.

I wonder whether I can leave now.

'The postman wears Doc Martens,' he says. 'And none of us have had any workmen round recently.'

There's nothing for me to say to this. 'Okay. Well, have a good weekend.'

I make a run for it in my non-Nike shoes.

84

Tom's work get in touch to ask him for an update. They want to know if he'll be back in September. They need to sort out his time-table. I've popped out to get a few groceries, so miss the actual phone call. I find out about it when I get back. Tom and his mum are absolutely fraught. Though he's friendly with the HR staff and I can only assume that they were gentle with him, the call destabilises him in a huge way. The three of us discuss it for a full evening.

At one point, after he's calmed down slightly, Tom's mum says, 'You could quit, you know. Then nobody will bother you about return dates and expectations, and you can put all your energy into just getting better.'

I don't think he should quit, but don't say this out loud. I thought the unspoken agreement was that we would do our very best to not influence Tom either way. I feel betrayed somehow.

I wait for Tom to tell his mum that quitting's out of the question. He's a lot of things, one of which is not very well, but I've never known him to be a quitter.

He says, 'Could I actually?' He's asking his mum for permission.

She comes closer to him, takes his chin in one of her hands. 'Course you can, bab. They don't own you.'

He's in a good mood after that. He asks whether we want to play Monopoly as his fun activity for the day. We say yes, obviously. He whoops each time me or his mum have to mortgage one of our properties, and after about an hour and a half, he wins.

In our bed that night, he reaches for my waist and pulls me into his body, curling himself around me. He whispers into my ear, so quietly it's almost just a breath, 'I love you more than anything.'

85

Tom's mum texts me the next day while I'm in the library. The text just says, *Call me?*

I go outside and press my thumb down on her name in my phonebook. She picks up after two rings.

She starts talking before I can say anything. She says, 'Mara, I have to go back to Birmingham and I think Tom should come with me.'

My heart quickens because I knew this was going to happen and I know that she's right. I say, 'Okay.'

She's his mum, and I'm just his girlfriend.

'Have you spoken to him about it?' I say.

'He's sitting next to me right now,' she says.

'Right. So when do you think you might go?'

'I think the sooner the better.'

'As in,' I say, sinking back against the wall, 'tomorrow?'

'As in now, love.'

I massage my eyelids with my thumb and middle finger.

'What about his old flat?' I say, clutching at straws.

'His old flat?' She sounds genuinely confused. 'We dealt with that ages ago.'

'Oh, right. That's good.' I start to chew on the inside of my bottom lip. 'Should I come home? I don't finish for another couple of hours.'

'I know you don't, love. I thought it'd be easier for him this way.'

'So I won't get to see him before you leave?' I have that feeling you get when the worst thing you can imagine is happening and all your brain is able to do is go, *Oh, it's happening.*

'I really think it's best if we don't do a big protracted goodbye.'

'It wouldn't have to be protracted,' I say.

'Mara,' she says. 'Please. This is very hard for me.'

I don't see how this could be harder for her than it is for me. She's the one who gets to look after him.

'Can I speak to him?' I say.

'Not at the minute, no.'

Panic sets in. I begin to walk. I think, if I can just keep this woman on the phone for ten more minutes, I can step in and Tom will see me and he'll realise that I'm his family too and he won't leave the flat and London and me.

'How long will he be in Birmingham for, though?' I say, my pace quickening. I feel like I already know the answer.

'I don't know. I can't think about timeframes right now and neither can he.'

I start to jog.

I say something stupid then, through my laboured breathing. I say, 'Does he still want to be my boyfriend?'

His mum exhales loudly. 'Mara. Love.'

I need her to stop saying my name like that. 'Can you just put him on?' It's wild to me that he could be sitting next to her as she says these life-altering things to me and not intervene. Surely he should be taking the phone from her and saying, *This is temporary. I'll be back in a few weeks and nothing will change between me and you.* But it's still his mum's breath that's sounding in my ear.

'I'm going to hang up now,' she says, not unkindly. 'We'll be in touch in a few days. Just give him some time to settle.'

The phone goes dead. I run. I run faster than I've run since school. A couple of cars beep their horns at me as I cross the road. I can barely see.

A faceless man shouts, 'Y'alright there, girl?' as I pass him.

My knees hurt. I don't have a plan. I guess I just hope that seeing me will do something to him, remind him of something, give him some hope, bring him back to me somehow. His mum can't make this decision on his behalf, and if it's his own decision then I want him to have to look at me as he makes it. If they haven't already packed, that will buy me a few extra minutes. But maybe they don't care about his stuff and will walk out empty-handed, leaving me with his t-shirts and toothbrush and boxers as a consolation prize.

When I can see the house, I speed up with the little energy I have left. My stomach and my chest tell me I'm too late. I pat my trousers and realise that my keys are in my bag and my bag is under the desk in the library. I stop and walk the last few metres, defeated. I ring my own doorbell. Once, twice, three times. I wait, my insides stinging. I press my thumb down hard, continuously. They've gone.

PART IV

Late Summer

86

Now that the flat is a one-person property again, it feels huge, like a completely different space. I buy a couple of new bits. Sheets. Expensive linen ones. An ironic cushion that says, *Queen of This Castle.*

Derek tricks me. At work, on Friday, just before we close, he asks, 'What you doing tonight, then?'

I exhale and say, 'Fuck all.'

That's when he says, 'Why don't we have a few bevs? I've got nothing on either. And it's been a long week.'

I look down at my work outfit. 'I'm not dressed for it.'

He's walking me home so I can get changed before I have the chance to formulate a reason why he can't.

Inside the flat, he touches walls, leans against doorways, sniffs a window frame at one point.

'Rotting,' he declares.

I pour us a glass of wine each, then perch awkwardly on the edge of my own sofa, unsure. He continues to move around the space, nodding and shaking his head.

Finally, he says, with gusto, 'This is really great. Well done.'

Though Derek's opinion should matter very little to me, I'm proud. He's an adult and he thinks I've done well. The flat really is great. I decide to lean into the role of host. The dynamic has shifted. Derek is in my space now, I dictate the rules. I talk knowledgeably about plastering, noise insulation, plumbing. I feel wise and independent.

'Good job you've got a friendly boss on side, ey?' he says, from his position by the living-room window.

'What do you mean?'

'The paperwork?' he reminds me. 'For the mortgage lender? If you're in such a nice flat, it's partly down to me. I helped you get into that higher bracket.' Though this is a weird thing for him to bring up, he's grinning, teasing.

When the wine is finished, we have shots of tequila and he asks me whether I'd like to go out-out. I can't think of when I last went into central London at night, so I say yes. He plays a-ha and the Bee Gees while I get changed in my bedroom with the door closed. I opt for some leather trousers I bought on a whim, even though they're quite constricting around the waist.

A song starts playing that I've never heard before: somebody just singing the word *no* over and over again. I find that I'm dancing around a little bit and that I feel okay. I'm probably already a bit drunk, but I also have a lightness in my body which hasn't been there for a long time. I'm young. I live in London. I have my own flat to come back to. I have a friend.

'Who sings this?' I call through to Derek.

'The Human Beinz,' he calls. 'Good, isn't it? I heard it on *The Office*.'

I go back into the front room in my little outfit, and Derek does a wolf whistle, which I'm happy to accept for once. I bow.

'Thank you, thank you.'

Derek gets us an Uber, and we go to a Be At One. Derek buys all the drinks. He encourages me to try complicated, colourful cocktails. He takes selfies of us, hugging and smiling. We dance. I wonder whether he might just be my best friend now.

At one point, while Derek's in the bathroom, a man approaches me. He's tall and wearing a nice coach jacket and has frosted tips in his hair, which is funny to me. He says, 'Hi,' and smiles.

I say, 'Hi,' back.

'Great trousers,' he says.

I actually laugh. I say, 'Bit tight, gotta be honest with you.'

'Think that's what I like about them, to be honest with you.'

I think to myself, *I'm flirting with a man.*

'Drink?' he says.

I hold up my tequila sunrise. 'Got one, but thank you.'

'The guy you're with. Is he——?'

'Friend,' I say. 'And boss, actually.'

Frosty does a low half-whistle. 'Is he protective or would he let you dance with me?'

'I can dance with whoever I want.'

When Derek gets back, I'm being twirled around to Whitney

Houston's 'Million Dollar Bill'. I'm nervous for a total of three seconds, until Derek wordlessly joins the routine. They take it in turns to spin me, and as I get dizzier and dizzier, I forget about Tom and his mum and Birmingham and my job prospects and Noor and all the other things that usually flood my brain.

87

I wake up on a sofa which isn't mine. It's smooth, hard leather, hot under the parts of me that have stayed stillest through the night. My head feels heavy on my neck and I'm scared to move it. I peel my eyes open, sticky with sleep. I'm very aware of my limbs. They feel the way they do when I've been lugging boxes of books around at work. Rough as I am, disoriented as I am, it's nice to be present in my body. I can see a pint of water on the glass coffee table in front of me. It takes me a good ten minutes to get the energy together to reach for it.

88

The rules of mine and Tom's exile are never expressly stated. I don't know if I'm meant to be leaving him alone. I don't know whether the ball is in his court, or mine, or his mum's. I don't know what to do for the best. I draft tens of texts to him.

Hi babe
Tom
Hey
I just want to say
I know I'm probably going to say the wrong thing but
I'm hurting too
I really wish you'd been brave enough to face me that day
Did your mum push you into this or was it your decision?
Are we even still together . . .?
How are you feeling?
Can I call you?
Do you maybe want to chat?
I miss you so much
Are you okay?
Are you sleeping?
I'll wait for you
Our song was playing in the Co-op earlier
Do you know how fucking angry I am?
Jerry's got the bloody shipping forecast on tonight
The bed feels empty without you
You left your lucky shirt here. I'm choosing to take that as a good sign.
Our toothbrushes are still touching in the pot
If you were here tonight we could order pizzas and watch Masterchef
Please
I'm sorry
Come home

I don't send any of them. Sometimes, while I have the messaging app open, he pops up as being *Online*, and I stare at that little word, hoping and believing that he's doing the same thing his end. That we're connected. On the sixth consecutive evening of doing this, I have the harsh realisation that what it really means is that he's texting somebody else, that he's not too sad to send word to other people in his life.

89

Three weeks pass with no contact. The whole situation is surreal. That afternoon – when I sat on my own doorstep, chest heaving with sobs, feeling as abandoned as I've ever felt – seems as though it happened to somebody else. The intensity of the sorrow mellows out. I find that it's impossible to constantly be as worried and disappointed as I was in those first few days. There are moments of respite. I temporarily forget. I laugh. I find things funny. I take pride in helping patrons at work. Whenever I experience this slight levity, it's tied up with acute guilt. I have no idea what state Tom is in. I have no clue what's going through his mind. At this point, I don't know if he even wants me in his life. And yet I can giggle at Derek doing an impression of Starey Man? It seems perverse.

90

There's a knock on my door on a Tuesday evening while I'm boiling water for pasta. It's odd to hear my individual door being rapped on, rather than the doorbell from downstairs, and my first thought is that it's Jerry wanting to complain about something. I look around the kitchen, panicked. I'm sure the light from my flat seeps under the door, and if there's someone standing on the landing they'll definitely be able to hear my music playing. There's no chance of pretending I'm not in. I stand still. There's another, lighter knock. I look down at my clothes. I'm wearing some of Tom's football shorts and a big, coffee-stained Stevie Nicks t-shirt. On my feet I'm wearing mismatched bed socks. I have hairy knees. There's no time to deal with any of this. I open the door slowly, peering round it gingerly, like a nervous old woman. What I find there is almost worse than Jerry. It's a fuchsia-lipped, smiling Adele, dressed impeccably in her little work outfit, chunky lace-ups on and hair scraped back into a sleek bun, a few blonde curls escaping around her face.

'Is this a bad time?' she says.

'Now? Not at all,' I say.

I notice she's clutching a bottle of red. I open the door wider.

'Sorry about my attire. I've had a bit of a day,' I say, pulling the drawstring on the shorts tight.

Adele laughs, generously. 'You should see what I look like once I'm safely inside my flat. You've got nothing on me.'

I'm not buying it, but it's sweet of her to say. I don't know where to lead her. The sofa has my duvet on it, and the dining table seems too formal. Helpfully, she walks herself into the kitchen.

'This is set out exactly like ours. How fun,' she's saying. 'Oh, I love this.' She points at the window seat. 'Does it open up?'

I nod.

'Oh, amazing. Hoover and suitcase storage, right?'

'Yes. And a million carrier bags.'

She does another generous laugh as she sets the bottle of wine down on the counter. 'So, look. You need to help me out.'

'Oh?'

'Baz is on this really intense detox, which I'm meant to be on as well, and it's boring as anything, and I just really need to drink half a bottle of wine with no judgement.'

Their weekly recycling bags are normally bulging with empty IPA and orange wine bottles. I haven't noticed any less clinking of late when they've taken the bags out for collection, but then I've been distracted.

'I guess I'll get us some glasses, then,' I say. I know I'd definitely rather drink a whole bottle of wine alone than share half a bottle with this perky individual, but that doesn't seem to be an option available to me.

Adele can talk. She tells me about her sister's new baby and her brother-in-law's reluctance to ever get up in the night to help. She tells me about Baz's work colleague who's going through dialysis. She tells me about these trainers she's had her eye on for the last month or two that she can't seem to take the leap with because they might just be *too* nice for everyday use. She tells me about her friend Zara who's going through a really hard breakup. She barely stops to take a breath.

'She's found herself having to start again from scratch, and it's not a position she ever imagined she'd be in. I keep reminding her of all the good stuff that comes from being single. You know, starfishing in bed, wearing your biggest pants every day, more time with your friends.'

I realise with sudden horror what Adele's trying to do. The same way I know everything that's going on with her and Baz just through proximity, she must know just as much about me and Tom. She's trying to help. She thinks I'm newly single. She's come round on a bloody charity mission.

91

Word from Tom arrives in an unexpected way. On a Saturday lunch-time, I open the fridge and see that there's nothing in there except half a withered cucumber and one sad-looking, solitary egg. I fancy a salmon bagel, so I shove my Converse on and head out. Halfway down the communal stairs, something catches my eye and makes me turn back. Next to my door, there is a slim package, leaning against the frame. Someone's brought it upstairs for me. My guess would be Adele. Certainly not Jerry. Even from this distance, I can see Tom's unmistakable spidery handwriting on it. I suddenly can't remember where I was going or what I needed to buy.

I shuffle straight back into the flat, parcel clutched to my chest, as though someone might snatch it from me. I tear at the brown paper, anxious to see what he's broken his silence to send me. I recognise the cover. It's a dog-eared copy of D. H. Lawrence's *Sons and Lovers,* the ugly Penguin Classics version, with the orange font and the picture of a swollen, pregnant, apron-clad belly, the one we both had back in uni. The cheapest option they stocked in Blackwell's. I am overwhelmed with nostalgia. I flip to the first page, and sure enough, there are all of Tom's notes. He would elbow me and point at what he'd written, trying at all costs to make me laugh. There's that first paragraph that we pulled apart over the course of three seminars:

THE BOTTOMS succeeded to 'Hell Row'. Hell Row was a block of thatched, bulging cottages that stood by the brookside on Greenhill Lane. There lived the colliers who worked in the little gin-pits two fields away. The brook ran under the alder trees, scarcely soiled by these small mines, whose coal was drawn to the surface by donkeys that plodded wearily in a circle round a gin. And all over the countryside were these same pits, some of which had been worked in the time of Charles II, the few colliers and the donkeys burrowing

*down like ants into the earth, making queer mounds and little
black places among the corn-fields and the meadows. And the
cottages of these coal-miners, in blocks and pairs here and there,
together with odd farms and homes of the stockingers, straying over
the parish, formed the village of Bestwood.*

In the margin, Tom has written: *Sounds like where I grew up!* I feel
pathetic with longing for him. I flick through the soft pages, looking
for more. The text is riddled with his notes. About halfway through,
at the top of page 211, he has written: *You look nice today! I like that
jumper :)* On page 302, *Lola's never worked a day in her life though,
right??* I haven't thought about Lola in years. She was this shockingly
beautiful girl who was in nearly all my English classes, and always
seemed to know the answers to everything. She spoke in a big booming
voice and was friends with all the tutors. I found her demeanour
intimidating, the way she was comfortable in every room, never
questioning her right to speak. When Tom picked up on the effect
Lola had on me, he took it upon himself to highlight all her flaws.
As I thumb through the paperback, I see her name on page after
page. *Give it a rest, Lola, mate. Lola LAWRENCE, am I right? Lola,
why don't you tell us what you thought about that, for once? We never
hear your opinion, Lola – it's such a shame you're so shy.* Even then,
before I belonged to him in any way, before my feelings were intrin-
sically linked to his, he still did everything he could to make me feel
good about myself. On the inside back cover, in the same pen as all
the other notes – so I know he hasn't added it in later – there is a
full page of my name. First and last. Over and over again, like in a
teenage girl's diary.

*Mara Lynch Mara Lynch Mara Lynch Mara Lynch Mara Lynch
Mara Lynch Mara Lynch Mara Lynch Mara Lynch Mara Lynch
Mara Lynch Mara Lynch Mara Lynch Mara Lynch Mara Lynch
Mara Lynch Mara Lynch Mara Lynch Mara Lynch Mara Lynch
Mara Lynch Mara Lynch Mara Lynch Mara Lynch Mara Lynch
Mara Lynch Mara Lynch Mara Lynch Mara Lynch Mara Lynch
Mara Lynch Mara Lynch Mara Lynch Mara Lynch Mara Lynch
Mara Lynch Mara Lynch Mara Lynch Mara Lynch Mara Lynch
Mara Lynch Mara Lynch Mara Lynch Mara Lynch Mara Lynch*

Mara Lynch Mara Lynch Mara Lynch Mara Lynch Mara Lynch
Mara Lynch Mara Lynch Mara Lynch Mara Lynch Mara Lynch
Mara Lynch Mara Lynch Mara Lynch Mara Lynch Mara Lynch
Mara Lynch Mara Lynch Mara Lynch Mara Lynch Mara Lynch
Mara Lynch Mara Lynch Mara Lynch Mara Lynch Mara Lynch
Mara Lynch Mara Lynch Mara Lynch Mara Lynch Mara Lynch
Mara Lynch Mara Lynch Mara Lynch Mara Lynch Mara Lynch
Mara Lynch Mara Lynch Mara Lynch Mara Lynch Mara Lynch
Mara Lynch Mara Lynch Mara Lynch Mara Lynch Mara Lynch
Mara Lynch Mara Lynch Mara Lynch Mara Lynch Mara Lynch
Mara Lynch Mara Lynch Mara Lynch Mara Lynch Mara Lynch
Mara Lynch Mara Lynch Mara Lynch Mara Lynch Mara Lynch
Mara Lynch Mara Lynch Mara Lynch Mara Lynch Mara Lynch
Mara Lynch Mara Lynch Mara Lynch Mara Lynch Mara Lynch
Mara Lynch Mara Lynch Mara Lynch Mara Lynch Mara Lynch
Mara Lynch Mara Lynch Mara Lynch Mara Lynch Mara Lynch
Mara Lynch Mara Lynch Mara Lynch Mara Lynch Mara Lynch
Mara Lynch Mara Lynch Mara Lynch Mara Lynch Mara Lynch
Mara Lynch Mara Lynch Mara Lynch Mara Lynch Mara Lynch
Mara Lynch Mara Lynch Mara Lynch Mara Lynch Mara Lynch
Mara Lynch Mara Lynch Mara Lynch Mara Lynch Mara Lynch
Mara Lynch Mara Lynch Mara Lynch Mara Lynch Mara Lynch
Mara Lynch Mara Lynch Mara Lynch Mara Lynch Mara Lynch
Mara Lynch Mara Lynch Mara Lynch Mara Lynch Mara Lynch
Mara Lynch Mara Lynch

92

I shake the book, shake the empty packaging, but there's nothing else. The whole message is the book. It isn't followed up with a text or a call, and each time I go to send Tom a message, his last *Online* time says early morning yesterday. I'm confused. I want to call Noor, but I can't do that. I don't want to bother my mum with this: she's too invested. I briefly contemplate reaching out to Derek.

Without actively deciding to do so, I'm on my way out of the flat again, but rather than heading down the stairs, I stall on the landing. I watch as my fist raps against Baz and Adele's door. I listen as the slapping of slippers draws closer. The wrong person answers the door, and I realise too late that I'm crying.

'Oh,' Baz says, eyes wide. 'Adele!' He calls over his shoulder. 'Are you okay?' he says to me.

I can't answer. I'm too embarrassed. We stand in silence for whole seconds. The book hangs limply in my left hand.

Adele appears behind him, wearing an outfit so chic I can't believe that it's really loungewear. She's in a peach velour jumpsuit, unzipped to just under her cleavage. Her hair is damp from the shower, and she still looks ready for an editorial campaign. I have made a grave error. I know that for sure as I gaze dumbly at this gorgeous couple.

'Baz,' Adele says. 'Do you think you could pop and get the dry cleaning, honey?'

'Course,' he says. He winks kindly at me as he goes past, still in his Adidas sliders. He's nothing if not discreet.

'Now, you,' Adele says, sweetly. 'Come inside and show me what you've got there.'

As out of sorts as I am, I can't help looking around me in wonder as I follow Adele into her home. There's built-in storage everywhere, so that the only things on display are things that Adele and Baz are presumably happy to look at. The floorboards are buffed and varnished to a glossy sheen and feel smooth under my socked feet. There's a fully stocked drinks cabinet in one corner of their living room and DJ decks in another. Their sofa is yellow, a colour I've never considered for my own space, but that makes this whole flat seem luminous and bright, even with the smaller windows.

I still haven't spoken.

'Is this a tea situation or a gin situation?' Adele says.

'Gin, I think,' I say, very quietly.

'Thought so.'

As nice as she's being, I've definitely overstepped here. I've given this woman absolutely no say in being my shoulder to cry on. I've ambushed her in her own house on a Saturday afternoon, and I don't know how to get back out of here. I'm already sitting on the yellow couch. I let myself sink back into the cushions. I could sleep. I tune into Adele's chatter.

'I actually wanted to knock for you when I saw that parcel,' she's saying. 'I had a feeling in my stomach that it was something from him. I could tell it wasn't just an Amazon order, you know. But at the end of the day, I think you had to open it alone and go through that by yourself. I'm so glad you've come to me now, though. Really, I am.'

She offers me a large glass tumbler, and I accept it. I wonder how she can be this open and friendly, what her agenda is. How does she have this much energy to spare for a relative stranger?

'Thank you,' I say. 'I'm sorry about this. I don't know what came over me. I didn't want to interrupt yours and Baz's weekend.'

Adele shakes her head, smiles. 'Don't be silly! I'd hate to think of you being stressed out down there, all on your own.'

All on my own.

I sip my drink. I see that Adele hasn't made herself one. I feel even worse. I've probably interrupted peak mating time. Despite this, I hand her *Sons and Lovers*. 'It's from our uni days,' I say. 'When we first met.'

She opens it carefully, leafing through with caution, as though it's a valuable antique.

'Oh,' she breathes, as she makes sense of what she's holding. 'Oh, this is so romantic.'

My heart does a little double-beat. 'Do you think?' I'm desperate to cling on to any positive interpretation of this gift. 'I thought maybe it was a way of closing the chapter.'

Adele snaps the book closed and presses it against her stomach. 'No! He wants you back. He wants to go back to the start.'

'Really?'

'Definitely.'

Looking around Adele and Baz's shared home, at their framed wedding photo, Adele's basal thermometer on the side table next to my G&T, their collection of books and records that, over time, have become communally owned, I feel more strongly than ever that the person I want all of this with is the boy who wrote those notes to me all those years ago. I want to build a life like Adele and Baz's with Tom. No matter how long it takes.

93

I'm playing the long game, and when you play the long game, the whole point is that there's no rush. The important thing is to do it right, not to do it fast. Back in my own cluttered flat, I opt against a phone call. I don't want to text him, either. The correct response to a piece of post is another piece of post. There's no urgency needed.

I pull a stool under my bookshelves, clamber onto it, and reach for a shoebox on the top shelf. Even in the time it's been nestled there, it's gathered a fair amount of dust, and I blow it off, rubbing my hand lovingly over the lid. I get down and, leaning against the radiator, open it. There's plenty to choose from.

Mine and Tom's love story, stored in this cardboard box: the receipts from our early dates, the boarding pass from our first holiday to Berlin, our Valentine's Day cards. There's the wrapper from the first condom we used, which we kept initially as a joke and later as an actual relic. There's the note Tom left me on my pillow after we had our first argument and he thought I was going to leave him. In the same scrawl that's all over *Sons and Lovers*, it says: *Whatever I did or said last night, I didn't mean anything by it. I only want you forever.* The fact that he'd unintentionally recreated the lyrics to Take That's 'Back for Good' was so funny to me that morning all those years ago that I instantly forgave him. I can't remember now what the argument had been about, even though it was obviously serious enough at the time for Tom to feel he had to win me back.

Here, folded neatly into quarters, is the sign he made when he surprised me at the airport. I smooth it open and see, in capitals: *WELCOME HOME MARA AND RACHEL!* I'd forgotten that my mum had been there too that day. She'd already booked a hire car for us, and a clueless Tom had come all the way to Gatwick on the train. He ended up coming home with us in the car, back to my mum's, and she laughed at him the whole way. 'What was your plan?' she'd asked him. 'You can't pick someone up from the airport without a car. What's the point in that?' But the point had been that he was desperate to see me, that even the extra few hours that it'd take me to get home from the airport seemed too long to wait, that he'd rather see me with my mum and be teased than spend even another minute apart.

I lose an hour to the box. In the end, I choose a failsafe item. Something that can't possibly be misinterpreted. It is a line of photo booth pictures of the two of us, taken on a day trip to Nottingham. Minutes before the photos were taken, I'd told Tom I was in love with him. He was so incredulous he demanded that we mark the occasion with photographic evidence to prove it really happened. It wasn't until we were sitting inside the booth that he remembered to say it back to me. With the strip in my hand, I find that I'm grinning. I'm right back in that moment with him, giddy with excitement. I flip it over and write today's date on the back. Under that, I add, *I love you now 1,000 x as much as I loved you on this day.* I find an envelope, a stamp, and lovingly write out his name and his mum's address.

94

I scroll through Noor's Instagram multiple times a day. There are ample updates. Things appear to be going well with her new guy. She's started sharing slices of his face. In one, a sliver of cheek, in another, nearly his whole chin. If I squint and look at a few of the pictures in one go, I can almost make out a whole man.

95

At work, I'm distracted. Derek keeps coming over and asking whether I've heard from Tom yet. It makes it impossible to think about anything else. The fourth time Derek approaches me, I snap.

I say, 'Derek. You're making it worse. Please.' I say this through clenched teeth and in a voice I usually reserve for nuisance callers.

Derek looks like a wounded child and I feel like a dick.

96

I run into Jerry in the corner shop again. I try to dash behind the cereal aisle, but he spots me.

'Haven't heard you clomping around for a while,' he greets me.

The hypocrisy of this comment makes it impossible for me to reply.

'And I haven't seen that woman lately, either.'

I can only assume he's talking about Tom's mum. I still don't speak, just gently caress the corner of the oven pizza I'm holding.

'Has there been a change of living arrangement?' he says, cheerfully.

I feel as though I'm being interrogated by the council.

'You could say that,' I say, both of my eyebrows rising against my will.

'Oh?'

I can see he's not going to leave it there, so I say, with as much poise as I can manage, 'Tom and I are having some time apart, unfortunately.'

To my surprise, I see a glint of pity in Jerry's eyes. He wasn't expecting me to say what I've just said.

'Ah, well,' he bumbles. 'These things happen. You're young. You'll find someone else.' He must see the look on my face, because he adds, 'Not like me.'

Looking at his standard half-pint of cow's milk, and his bag of white Hovis, I am suddenly struck with the realisation that of course this man has had romantic disappointments of his own. He didn't just end up alone by accident. Jerry will have been dumped, he will have broken someone's heart, he will have lost someone he loved. It has dawned on me in this tiny corner shop that Jerry is not only a living, breathing annoyance, but also a living, breathing human being, just like me. I have a feeling not unlike tenderness towards him. I find myself offering up a little smile. I feel generous.

I say, 'I don't suppose you fancy a coffee?'

'Now?' He takes a little step backwards. 'With you?'

I see that I have made a mistake. 'Only if you're not busy.' He's very obviously not busy.

'No, that would be . . .' he says. There's a brief pause as he hunts for the right word. 'Nice. Would you like to come to mine?'

Oh. I had imagined the café across the road, not our actual house. It's too late now. I've done it. 'Sure. Thank you.'

One after the other, we awkwardly pay for our items, and cross back over to our side of the street in near silence. Neither of us knows how to manoeuvre this. We don't have any house admin to discuss, no building work to agree on, no barbed complaints to make. So that leaves friendly chat, which isn't something we've ever properly attempted before.

At the house, we both reach for our keys at the same time, and laugh. He gets to the keyhole first and lets us in. I motion up the stairs with my pizza.

'I'll just pop this in the freezer and come back down,' I say. I want to give him a couple of minutes to hide things away, if he needs to, to make the space guest-appropriate.

In my flat, I am regretful. I could be pouring myself a glass of wine now, preheating the oven, drawing the curtains closed, hibernating. Instead, I have to go back downstairs and be charming and sociable with someone I spend a lot of my time resenting. And it was my own bloody suggestion. I take my time. I can't decide whether to take my shoes off or not.

When I go back downstairs, Jerry has left his door ajar for me.

I call, 'Hellooo,' as I go inside.

I've only ever glimpsed a triangle-slice of the entryway when I've come past on my way to my own flat; I've certainly never made it past his threshold. I've imagined that he might have a lot of stuff, because of the amount of parcels he receives and the overflow of junk into the hallway and garden. I hadn't quite gone as far as imagining what I see before me now. I swallow a gasp. I can't believe he would willingly allow another person to see this. There are stacks upon stacks of plastic containers of every description. Piles of books cover every available surface and topple precariously in tall, Jenga-esque formations on the floor. I have found someone who loves reading more than I do. I am unable to see what type of flooring he has underneath it all. It may be carpet, it may be lino, it could be the original floorboards. I have an overwhelming urge to take a photo to send to Tom.

'Is instant okay for you?' Jerry calls from around a corner.

I struggle to join him, stepping gingerly over a LaserJet printer and a tin of emulsion. He's in the kitchen, a huge space, similarly cluttered with what can only be described as shit. I wait for some sort of acknowledgement of the mess he has brought me into, but nothing comes.

He peers over his shoulder at me, and says, 'Instant?' again.

'Yeah,' I say. 'Instant is good.'

I look around, curious as to where we could possibly sit. I spot the washing machine that has kept me up at night, and in another corner, on top of a stack of atlases, the radio, which has tormented both me and Tom on so many occasions. It's weird to see the source of all the noise. It's a large, black, Nineties-looking thing, the type that builders use. I'm still expecting an apology, or an excuse for the state of the place; maybe Jerry will say he's in the process of having a clear out or something.

'Milk?' he says.

I say, 'Please.'

Jerry hands me a chipped mug. It's a Leicester City Football Club one, the blue badge with the fox's head. 'Are they your team?' I ask, thinking that we might bond over the Midlands.

'Who? Leicester? No, no,' he says. He doesn't expand.

Though the coffee he's made me is beige and anaemic-looking, the mug is hot in my hand. I'd like to put it down.

'So,' he says, and I realise that we will be drinking this coffee standing. 'What went wrong?'

Wow. Just like that.

'Tom's training to be a teacher,' I start. 'It's quite a lot of work, and I think he's finding it a bit hard.' I sip, even though the coffee's still boiling. I wince. 'Very hard, actually. And he's been homesick. I don't think he's made for London life.'

'It's not for everybody,' Jerry agrees. 'So he's given up?'

'I don't know about given up. But he's taking a breather. Recalibrating, you know.'

'And you've called it a day?'

186

'Well.' This is the real question, the one I'm genuinely unable to answer any time I'm asked it. 'I honestly don't know.'

'What do you want?'

He's direct, I'll give him that.

'I'm not sure.' I sigh. 'He's my best friend. Really he is. I know that's twee, and everybody thinks that about the person they're with, but with Tom, it's actually true. Nobody makes me laugh more. Nobody has ever looked after me like he does. And so now that the tables have turned and he needs looking after, I don't want to turn my back on him just because it's become hard.'

I've surprised myself by saying this thing out loud that I've maybe not yet admitted to myself, even in my head.

'You can't stay with someone out of a sense of duty, though,' he says. He looks as though he's speaking from experience, and I wonder which one of his exes he may be thinking about. 'I've been in a similar situation before.'

'Oh?'

'My ex. I was with her for ten years. She wanted me to move to Dublin with her. I'm talking about the year 1990 here, mind you. We'd been in this flat together a while at that point. I thought we were fine – happy, even – and then she sprang this proposal on me. She was Irish, you see. Her sister had had a baby, and she wanted to be closer to them, and I couldn't do it. I really wanted to be able to say, *Okay, why not*, but I couldn't. I'd been in this same house since I was born, and I just couldn't picture living anywhere else. She stayed with me for another year or so after that, but she grew more and more resentful, and she never got over the sacrifice that she felt I'd forced her to make.'

My chest constricts. This isn't what I want to hear. 'So what happened? Did she move back to Ireland?'

He shakes his head. 'She lives in Camden. In the end, she decided that Christmas and birthdays were ample family time, and then she fell pregnant herself, with the man she met after me.'

I watch him take a cautious drink from his cup, leaning against the sink. He is feigning nonchalance, but I can tell that this story still affects him.

'I'm sorry,' I say. 'That must've been hard. But you've had partners since?'

'Nope!' he says.

Jesus.

'So you never see her?'

'I saw her just once after we broke up,' he says. 'She was by the locks, holding her daughter's hand. The little girl must've been three or four by then. Her hair was the exact same shade of red as her mother's, and they were singing a song together. It was that Eurythmics one. About angels. It was like they were completely alone in the world. Neither of them saw me.'

97

I finally try a phone call. It's taken me this long to build up the courage. I don't know whether he'll answer, and I don't know what I'll say if he does. I sit up on the window seat in the kitchen, looking down into the street below, at the dog walkers and parents with pushchairs and shopping bags. I cradle a mug of mint tea in my free hand, more for comfort than for thirst.

I've timed it carefully. Since being signed off work, Tom's best and calmest moment of the day is very early evening, before dinner, when the whole night is still stretching ahead. It's just turned six o'clock. I press my thumb down on the three letters of his name.

It rings five, six, seven, eight, nine times. I wonder whether I have it in me to leave a voicemail. Saying what?

'Hello?' It's Tom's voice, slightly out of breath, but there, in my ear.

'Tom,' I say. That's all I can manage.

'Mara,' he says. He sounds so close and so distant, all at once.

Nothing more is said. I have the pressure and tightness in my throat which precedes tears. I don't want to cry. It's too obvious. We breathe.

'How are you?' he says. His tone is unexpected, slightly formal.

I can't answer right away. I do a long sigh and press my forehead against the cold glass of the window.

'It's you,' I say, when I'm ready.

'Mara,' he says. 'I don't know if this is okay for me to say, but I can't have a heavy conversation right now.'

This winds me. I've waited all this time to speak to him, and now he's going to tell me my emotions are inconvenient?

He continues, haltingly. 'I know we have a lot to talk about – and it's so nice to hear your voice, really it is. I just – all my energy is taken up at the minute, and I really, I'm not strong enough, or on top of this enough, to explain to anyone else what's going on with me. Not yet.'

'Right,' I say. I wonder whether his mum has briefed him to make this announcement. 'So where does that leave me?' I stop there, even though there's a lot more I want to say. This is already not going anything like how I hoped it would.

'I'm sorry. I know this must be hard for you too,' he says.

The tears have come. 'Tom. It's more than hard. I miss our life. I just want to see you.'

I hear him gulp.

'Could I see you?' I say.

'I don't think that would be a very good idea.'

'Why not? Just for a coffee or something?' My voice is breaking, getting desperate.

'You can't come to Birmingham just for a coffee,' he says. 'It doesn't make any sense. It wouldn't be fair on you.'

I feel suddenly furious. 'What's not fair is you leaving from one day to the next and not even telling me where I stand. That's what's not fucking fair.'

Tom is silent. Until he's not. He begins to whimper and moan, quietly at first, then growing gradually louder and louder.

Oh god.

'Tom.' I say his name as softly as I possibly can. 'I'm sorry. I'm just upset.'

'But you're right,' he says. 'I hate myself for what I've done to you. To us. I can't believe you even still want to talk to me.'

'Of course I want to talk to you. I love you. I haven't stopped loving you just because you're ill.' I want him to know this, and I also want to hear it back. I need a tiny shred of hope to cling to.

This is not what I get.

'I'm a horrible person,' he says. 'A piece of shit. You deserve to be with someone so much better than me.'

Once Tom starts down this road, there's no more reason to be had. I exhale. It hurts me to hear him talk about himself in this way.

'I'm not doing this,' I say.

Tom cries for a while, and I listen to him.

Once his breathing has steadied, I say, 'What are you doing to try to make yourself feel better?'

'I'm on the waiting list for some therapy. And I'm reading this book about coping mechanisms?' He says this tremulously, like I'm testing him, and might ask follow-up questions about it.

'That's good,' I say. 'That's really good. Are you sleeping? Eating properly?'

'Yes,' he says, a little boy. 'I am. I've been having some really bad dreams, though.'

'What sort of bad dreams?'

He clears his throat quietly, takes a beat before answering. 'Ones about all the people.'

'What people?' I try to keep the concern out of my voice, keep my tone neutral.

'All of us. There's too many of us. I dream about us all crowding into a tiny room, pushing and pushing.'

'Okay,' I say, sensing that he's working himself up. 'That's a normal thing to worry about, I think. We all stress about overpopulation sometimes.'

'But I stress about it constantly.'

'You do?'

'I find it hard to think about anything else.'

I see now that there's not going to be any form of love declaration. I'm nervous of saying the wrong thing.

'And the weather,' he says. 'It's wild to me that we can all carry on with our normal little lives while the weather tries to tell us in every possible way that we're destroying the planet.'

'I worry about those things too,' I say.

'But you don't let it take over your life,' he says. 'And that's the difference.'

98

Derek becomes ever more present, always looking over at me and grinning or giving me a thumbs up. Wherever I am, he's there. When he pops out to the shop, he brings me little presents back: a Twix, a can of Coke, a bag of easy peelers. I accept them begrudgingly, sure that there is some secret string attached.

99

Lewis sends me a text out of the blue.

Hey! Been ages. Glass of wine and a catch-up this weekend?

I feel as though he's contacting me from a different life. Can it even be called a *catch-up* if it's a full six months you have to fill the other person in on? I'm surprised he's taking this tack, really. I thought it was a given that we just weren't friends anymore. It suits me and I assumed it suited him too.

I wait an hour, then I reply, *This weekend is a bit hectic for me . . . Soon, though!*

Tomorrow, then? He pings back.

It seems he's determined.

I squint, and type, *Sure. I finish at 6, but I know you don't.*

No, it's fine! I can dip out early for my old friend ;)

Jesus. I could really live without this.

100

We meet at a wine bar in Soho. It's roughly halfway between Homerton and Notting Hill, where Lewis is now apparently living. I arrive first, as expected. I feel conspicuous in my work clothes. I'm wearing one of Tom's shirts, tucked into some very plain, loose black slacks. In my mind, this morning, the look I was going for was high fashion, off-duty. It didn't translate. I just look like someone wearing their dad's clothes. I get a pang in my chest at this thought. My dad never wore shirts. He favoured worn-out band t-shirts at all times of year, even in the dead of winter. Mum only kept one of them. The Clash, from their 1981 tour. It used to hang up next to her silk blouses in their wardrobe, but I haven't been home for a really long time, and I don't know whether it's still there. It's suddenly very pressing that I find this information out.

'Well hello there, stranger,' I hear.

I look up. There's Lewis, grinning wildly, also in his work clothes, but well tailored and expensive-looking and right for this bar.

'Alright, Lew,' I say.

'You remember Hattie?' he says, and I notice that he has brought someone else along.

I have a jolt of recognition. It's the girl he started seeing right before we moved out of our shared flat. She's survived.

'Hattie!' I say, flashing her a huge, insincere smile. 'How lovely!'

I'm even less sure now of what this is, or what I'm doing here. I didn't want to come in the first place, and this unannounced third person really takes the piss.

'You girls catch up. I'll go and get some drinks.' Lewis winks in our general direction, then swerves off towards the bar.

It's just me and Hattie. I nod at her. It's not her fault.

'Do you wanna sit down?' I say.

'Probably should do, yes,' she laughs. 'It's great that we could find a free evening. Lewis has been so excited to see you.'

194

I find this hard to believe. Hattie shrugs out of her denim jacket and lays it gently on the back of the chair closest to her. I see that the label reads Burberry. I didn't even realise Burberry did jeans.

'Aw,' I say.

Hattie is looking at me expectantly as she takes a seat.

'So,' I try. 'You're living in Notting Hill too, are you?'

Her brow furrows in what looks like genuine confusion. 'I live with Lewis. Did he not tell you that?'

'Ah. I'm sure he would have, but we've been out of touch for a little while.' I grit my teeth and shrug, to show her there's no hard feelings. 'I think we both found living together a bit testing.'

'I didn't realise,' she says. She takes a strand of professionally blow-dried hair and loops it around her finger. 'It was a tough year for him, last year. With work, you know. He felt he had a lot to prove. I'm sure it was nothing personal.'

I'm sure it was.

Lewis reappears, still grinning like mad, brandishing a bottle of champagne. This, even given the bizarre situation, seems inappropriate.

'I meant to say,' Lewis says, placing the bottle ceremoniously down on the table, 'Tom was very welcome to join us.'

And yet you didn't say. You're only saying it now that we're already here.

'I might as well lead with that, then,' I say, resigned. 'Tom's gone back to Birmingham for a while.'

Lewis does a short, sharp gasp, and Hattie looks at him to see how she should react. Seeing his shock, she widens her eyes and drops her bottom lip slightly.

'You're joking?' Lewis says.

'That would be a shit joke even for me.'

'So you've split up?' Hattie says.

'It's not quite as simple as that,' I say. 'Shall we get that open before we get into all this?'

Lewis comes towards me, arms outstretched. I flinch.

'I'm sorry, Mar,' he says. 'I wish you would've reached out.'

'It's not for you to be sorry,' I say.

The two of them fuss over me for a long time after my announcement. They ask enthusiastic questions about my job and the flat, and Lewis brings up childhood memories, and Hattie makes sure my glass is always full to the brim.

Soon enough, though, the real reason for this get-together becomes apparent.

Hattie sits up straight, and Lewis clears his throat. 'We've actually got something to tell you,' he says, glass already raised for his own toast.

The use of the word *we* can mean only two things: they're either getting married or having a baby. Both these options leave me cold. I imagine I'm meant to care.

'We're engaged!' Lewis cheers.

As I watch, a tear falls from Hattie's left eye.

I try really hard to give them the reaction they probably deserve. 'You guys,' I say, lifting my glass to cover as much of my face as I can. 'This is so great. How exciting. Such a whirlwind.' I can't quite bring myself to offer any more than that. I smile and I smile.

Lewis clinks me, and says, under his breath, 'The timing is terrible, I know. I don't want to make you feel any worse than you already do.' He must see the look on my face, because he adds, 'About Tom leaving you, you know.'

Hattie says, 'Lew, what about the other thing?'

Lewis looks fit to burst, as he says, 'Well, the other thing is, that obviously me and you have known each other forever, since we were kids, and it wouldn't be right not to include you in the wedding somehow. So me and Hattie wanted to ask you—'

Oh god, please no.

'—whether you'd do us the honour of—'

I beg you, please don't do it.

'—being our flower girl?'

Fucksake.

'Your what?' I say. 'Isn't that a job for kids, normally?'

Hattie does a proud little giggle. 'That's why we thought it'd be so fun. We don't want to do everything super traditionally. We want to put our own spin on things.'

At my expense? I wonder whether I'm allowed to turn the offer down. I don't even know when the wedding is, so can't invent a holiday or prior engagement.

All I can do is say, 'Thank you. Both of you. It's very sweet of you to think of me.'

101

My phone wakes me. I peel my eyes open and flail around for it in the covers.

It takes a few seconds for my eyes to adjust to the aggressive light of the screen, before I can decipher that it's Tom's name, and two little words: *You up?*

I am now, I reply. *Everything okay?*

It's 01:16.

Can't sleep. Been thinking about our conversation the other day.

Yeah?

I realised that in the whole time we talked, I didn't ask one single thing about you

No, he did not.

Did you not? I text.

No. I feel terrible about it. I wanted to ask how you're doing?

I'm doing okay, Tom

Really though. How are you doing? Don't try and placate me. I can handle it.

I'm being honest. I genuinely do feel okay. I obviously miss you, but I'm getting used to the feeling

He types, then stops, then starts up again. He types for a long time.

Ugh. I know I'm probably not meant to admit this but that was really hard for me to read. I'm definitely not meant to say this next thing either, and yet here I am, saying it: I don't want you to get used to being without me.

I read the message through twice, trying to hear his voice. I have the clichéd butterflies doing laps in my stomach.

Tom . . .

Trust me, I realise I'm being unfair.

What am I meant to do with that? I'm doing my best in an impossible situation.

And I appreciate that so, so much. You've put me first, like you always have, and have been getting hardly anything in return, and I can't imagine how discouraging that must be. But you've been on my mind every single day. I really need you to know that.

Every day? I think about this boy ten times an hour.

I understand that your priority needs to be yourself right now, I type, deliberating over each word. I'm fully awake now. *So I'm trying not to take this distance personally.* I pause, thinking about how best to frame this. *But I'm also not a robot. I can accept on an intellectual level that you're going through something really big and that I need to let you do that, and at the same time, on an emotional level, I can feel abandoned and sore and like I've been left completely in the dark. Do you get that?*

I see the two blue ticks. He's read it, and it's good that I've said what I wanted to say. Even so, I'm nervous that I've revealed too much. It's a very fragile balance that we have at the moment, one that can be thrown off with a single misjudged text. I fall back against my pillows, and wait.

Nothing comes for whole minutes.

Then, all at once: *You're the love of my life, Mara. I can't lose you.*

102

My mum has a sixth sense when it comes to knowing I need her. I guess a lot of mums do. She starts sending me nightly texts, which isn't the sort of thing she usually goes in for.

You had a good day, love? I get on Monday.

Look at this banana. Isn't it obscene?? She sends on Tuesday, with a photo attachment.

Wednesday's message: *What was that thriller you said was good on Channel 4, again?*

Mary Berry reckons the secret to the best ragu ever is a spoonful of redcurrant jelly. The mad bitch. Thursday.

I heard about Lewis! Ran into his mum in the Lidl. She was brimming over. Three eye-rolling emojis. Friday's offering.

On Saturday, she sends, *You got time for a visit soon? I need some help picking out a new washing machine.*

Sunday: *Has Vernon Kay been cancelled, or are we still allowed to like him??*

After that one, I call her.

'Finally,' she says. 'I thought you'd never take the bait.'

'Hi.'

'Gosh, it's worse than I thought.'

'What is?'

'Please,' she says. 'Remember who you're talking to. Your voice sounds terrible.'

I breathe out heavily. 'Things aren't going very well, to be honest.' I suddenly wish very strongly that I could be in my mum's kitchen, sitting opposite her over a cup of over-stewed camomile.

'Is it just the Tom thing, or something else?'

I feel as though I've been terribly naive in trying to hide the break from my mum. By shielding her from the news, I thought it'd make it simpler once me and Tom worked things out, but I see now that there's no guarantee that we will indeed get back on track, and in the meantime I've tricked myself out of receiving my mum's precious advice.

'The Tom thing is forcing me to confront other things,' I admit.

'Go on.'

I love her so much for not asking what went wrong between us.

'Well, like what I want to do with my life.'

My mum scoffs. 'I *still* don't know what I want to do with my life.'

'Just some of the bigger stuff. Like where to live.'

'Well, I know that one's sorted, at least? Or are you already bored of that flat we just bought?'

I weigh up how much to say next. 'My downstairs neighbour told me this really sad story about how he lost the great love of his life just because he refused to move to Ireland with her.'

'Right.'

'Surely home is the place where the person you love is.'

'I completely agree,' she says. 'So, in that same vein, shouldn't your neighbour's partner have been happy to stay in the flat where your neighbour already lived?'

Shit.

103

Late, I get dressed in a hurry, putting on a combination of things that have accumulated on my bedroom chair from the weekend. A warm start to September, the sun has been beating through the big windows of the library in the afternoons. Still, the morning air is sharp against my bare legs, and I wish I'd grabbed some tights.

It's 09:06 as I put my key in the lock. It's my day to open up, and everyone else will get here for ten, but there's a lot to do before then. There's a book delivery upstairs in the store room, so I get to work straightaway, organising it. I have my earphones in, listening to a playlist called *Up and At Em!* Gently lifting the books out of the cardboard box, I tick them off on the purchase order, and alphabetise them as I go. It's the sort of task I like best, where I can see the fruits of my labour, rather than when I have to sit behind the front desk, looking alert and approachable, and the time never seems to pass.

I'm nearly finished when I feel somebody behind me, and spin around to see who it is. Derek is standing in the open doorway, hands on hips, softly laughing, his mouth wide. I yank my earphones out, smooth my skirt down.

'How long have you been standing there?' I ask.

He shakes his head, sort of wistfully, without saying anything.

I feel the colour rising in my neck and cheeks, prickling.

'Derek,' I say.

'Ah,' he breathes. 'Our older clientele will get a shock when they see you today. What a look.' He peers pointedly at my thighs.

I am suddenly hyperaware of my whole body, in a way that I don't enjoy at all. I purposely don't look down. I know what I'm wearing. I have on a cream sweatshirt and a skirt. Derek clearly isn't referring to the sweatshirt. The skirt is white denim, and it definitely touches my knees, and the material is thick and not see-through in the slightest. I know this for certain, because I've checked multiple times in the mirror in the past, and even asked Noor to confirm it for me. Admittedly, it may well be slightly tighter than it has been before; the waistband is pressing into my stomach, and my knees now feel trapped in place, restricted.

We're still standing opposite each other, Derek's eyes fixed on my lower half. I'm starting to sweat. I need more than anything for him to go away. I grasp desperately for a retort to even the playing field. I could say, *Well you need a haircut*, or, *Didn't you wear that t-shirt three days in a row last week?* or, *I see you chose to accessorise with some pit stains this morning*. But I don't say anything like that.

I say, 'I've nearly finished here. Do you want to start taking these downstairs?'

On my lunch break, I rush home and change into jeans. Though Derek must notice this, he doesn't mention it.

Nothing has technically happened, yet I can't shake my discomfort for the rest of the day. That night, I sleep for a total of about ten minutes.

104

Tom asks to see me. Though I'm happy at the prospect, I'm also terrified. We agree that it shouldn't be at the flat, and that it's best if it's not in Birmingham either. For the sake of fairness, we choose a midway point: Milton Keynes. Far enough away to have the time to psych ourselves up, but not too far that either of us might have the chance to chicken out.

I find that I don't know what to wear. I feel as though it would be an unfair tactic to put on something that I know he likes, and that it would be a statement of having moved on if I choose an item that I've bought since he left London. Anything too formal could lend too much seriousness to the event; anything too casual might suggest I don't care. I want to call Noor and ask her what to do. In lieu of that, I open Instagram and type her name. There are no new posts, and this makes me miss her even more.

I end up in a navy blue silk shirt tucked into dark jeans, and my Converse. I look like me, and I think that might end up being the most important thing on a day like today.

At Euston station, I pace under the departure boards. I don't want to get a coffee – I already have palpitations. I know there's no point in trying to read or follow a podcast. I don't particularly want to communicate with Tom before seeing him. So I walk up and down and up and down. I'm twenty minutes early for my train, and I feel every single last second of them.

Eventually, over the loudspeaker, I hear, *Crewe, 10:46.* Usually, I sneer at anyone who runs through the station, thinking them unnecessarily hectic. Today, I am one of them.

On the train, I find a seat, alone, next to the loos. I wouldn't mind someone to sit opposite me, even a phone-chatter, so I can listen in to pass the time. Before the train doors close, my wish is granted. Two women take up residence a couple of rows in front, facing me. They each have a Selfridges bag, a rolly suitcase and a fresh blow-dry.

As we judder into movement, the woman with the bouncier curls begins to pluck out beauty products from her Selfridges haul. One after the other, she holds out slim packages for her friend to examine. She seems proud of her loot.

'So what sort of palette were you thinking?' The woman with softer waves asks, unscrewing the lid off a pink lipstick. 'Ooh, I love this. I picked up a similar – yeah, hand me that. Oh my god, what's my one called?'

'Jam Donut.'

'Is that what yours—?' Wavy looks up to see Curly nodding emphatically. 'No way. You're joking? We've got the same one?'

The two of them laugh about this for tens of seconds, in a performative way. When I realise that I'm the only other person in the carriage, and that it must therefore be for my benefit, I'm almost flattered. I look down at my blank phone screen, to avoid giving them the satisfaction.

'You won't do a bold lip on the day, though?' Wavy says, once they've managed to calm down somewhat.

'God no. I want to be a natural bride. That's what Danny wants too. It's going to be easy, carefree, you know?'

'Completely. And at the end of the day, you want to still look like you, don't you?'

'Hundred percent,' Curly says, painting a strip of coral onto her thumbnail and moving it away from her face to inspect the colour. 'I've got my mani pedi on Thursday, then I was thinking of getting a little spray tan? On the Friday morning?'

Wavy mulls this over for some time. 'I wouldn't risk it. Too many variables. You could be naughty, and do a sun bed. Just one. A twelve-minute blast?'

'Mmm, I did think that. And then I've got a base for honeymoon too.'

'We could both pop in when we get home?'

They bump shoulders together, pact made. I wonder where they're friends from. They look to be around my age, give or take a couple of years. I don't think it goes back to their school days. They're being too formally nice to each other. It's not a uni friendship either. I would guess that they're work colleagues. An unexpected bubble of laughter rises in my throat at the idea of me and Derek going to get a sun bed together before a big event in one of our lives. I realise with sudden, sharp certainty that I need to find a new job. It shouldn't be like this. I should be able to call Derek out, tell him that I want our relationship to be boundaried again, but I know myself and I know I won't do this, wouldn't have the nerve, and I also know that Derek – whether purposely or not – has never done anything bad enough that I could legitimately report it. What would I say? He buys me too many snacks? I don't like the way he looks at me?

Something about Tom's breakdown has been gnawing away at me ever since it happened. I see now, that in a perverse way, I've been jealous that he could care enough about his career that he would bring it home with him every day, fret over it, worry about not being there, bond with his colleagues over the workload and stress of it all. I've never taken worry about work home with me. It doesn't matter enough to me. It's just a job.

'Who's going to hand the drink tokens out?' Wavy is saying. 'Me?'

'Would you mind? Me and Danny could do it, but I just think it's a bit formal, isn't it? Hello, thank you for coming, here's your one free drink.'

'No way! It can't be you! Anyone but you. I'll do it, it's no bother.'

'You would?'

'What am I here for if not to help?'

I type Noor's name into Instagram again. There's something new now. A photo of a mural that I recognise as being on a wall outside a pub in Clapton. It says, *Talk to someone, anyone, about anything.* I get a cold shiver. There are thirty-six likes and someone has commented underneath it with a sad face emoji and a line of kisses. I click on the person's thumbnail. It's a tall guy with a shaved head and crooked bottom teeth. I scroll down and see a photo of him hugging Noor in Victoria Park. On his feet, big oxblood Doc Martens. I feel sick. I'm missing too many things.

I send a text. *Hope you're okay? Whatever's happening, I'm still here and want to be a part of your life.*

The tone is melodramatic, yet seems appropriate. Considering where I'm heading and how much is riding on this trip, my emotions are heightened and I'm ready to be open. I see the double ticks that signal that the message has been delivered, and then the ticks turning blue that show me that Noor has opened it and read my words. Why do I feel nervous? It's just Noor. I feel guilty too, that I've let it get to this point, that I could feel hesitant about contacting my own best friend, that I could be envious of the relationship between two strangers comparing lipstick swatches on a train.

105

The logistics of the thing are fuzzy. The original idea was that we'd meet in a café, but neither of us are particularly familiar with Milton Keynes, so it proves difficult to choose anywhere. The back and forth of suggestions starts to eat into the ceremony of the occasion.

Bogota?

How far is that from the station?

Erm, Google Maps says 14 mins

Okay, shall we try one a bit closer?

Well the Morrisons cafe is only 7 mins away . . .

Please no. Can you think of anything more bleak? Green Elephant looks cheerful?

Once in the station, the phone signal becomes patchy, so the WhatsApp conversation is killed dead. What actually ends up happening is that I spot Tom's back by the turnstiles and have to approach him from behind with a pounding chest and clammy hands.

'Hi,' I say.

He doesn't hear me at first.

'Tom,' I say, when I'm nearly on top of him.

He turns and, eyes wide, does two steps backwards and bashes into the barrier behind him. He looks small. Smaller than usual. Tender. He has on a black denim shirt done up to the top, and I'm touched. He moves in the right direction now, towards me, and we slam into each other in a sloppy hug. He smells sweet and musky, slightly different than I remember.

'It's really you,' he says.

'Who did you think it'd be, silly?' I whisper into his warm neck.

'Aww, look,' I hear. 'So sweet.' It's Curly and Wavy, smiling at mine and Tom's embrace. They edge past us, still grinning. Curly looks at me with an expression that says, *That's how me and my Danny reunite too.*

I want very badly to be completely alone with Tom. I don't know if I'm allowed to kiss him, or whether I should, or if he even wants me to. He pulls me in tighter. In Milton Keynes train station, with a ticket inspector self-consciously looking away from us, my handbag fallen at my feet, I am home.

106

Green Elephant isn't quite as cheery as we hoped it'd be. Apart from us, there are only two other patrons: an elderly woman reading the *Daily Mail*, and a flustered young mum with two under two. The smaller child is hysterical, and the shrill cries set the tone for the afternoon.

Tom orders us a flat white each, and brings over a large chocolate coin for me. I have the vague feeling that there's a historical personal joke in there somewhere, but I have too many thoughts and emotions crowding my brain to unearth it right now.

'So,' he says, sitting opposite me. 'Here we are.'

'Don't be stiff,' I say. 'Please.'

He laughs, a real laugh. 'I'm sorry. I'm really fucking nervous.'

'Of what? It's just me and you.'

He rubs at his eyes with his fists, like a little baby. 'Yeah.'

'Are you doing okay? Like, generally?' I think it best to start with the basics.

'Actually yes. Better than I have been in ages, honestly.'

This stings, and I feel like shit that I could be disappointed about Tom feeling better. The improvement part is great, it's just the fact that he's only able to feel better when he's away from me, once we've basically broken up.

'That's really great,' I say. 'And you're keeping busy?'

'I've been running a lot.' He looks sheepish. 'Real running. Not sitting-on-a-bench running. And I joined the gym.'

Another commitment in Birmingham, something else tying him there.

'You look well,' I say. And he does. He's grown his facial hair out a little, and he looks rugged, outdoorsy, healthy.

As Tom and I smile shyly at each other, the older of the two children at the table next to ours screams, 'But I *love* it! I want it!'

'Okay,' the mum says, quietly. 'You can have it in a minute. But don't shout at me. That's not how we talk to each other, is it?'

'Yes!' the little boy shouts. 'It *is*, Mummy! Please!'

I raise my eyebrows, like, *Oh, wow.* Tom does the same back. I always assumed that me and Tom would have children together one day. I thought he'd make such a good dad. I still think he would. He's so patient, and he used to be so good with me any time I was upset. Tears didn't used to scare him. Now I filter my feelings before I present them to him, try really hard to make them easily digestible.

'How's work?' Tom asks.

I'm surprised that that's the first real thing he can think to ask me. But then again, maybe work is something that's playing a lot on his mind.

'It's—' I think before continuing. 'It feels a lot like work at the moment. Derek is demanding too much of my energy. I'm not enjoying it that much.' I see Tom's face and try to inject some posi-tivity into my tone. 'But that's okay! Maybe this will push me to find something I really love. It could be a blessing, who knows.'

'I'm sorry about Derek,' Tom says. 'It sounds like he takes the piss sometimes.'

'Mmm,' I say.

Tom's phone starts to ring. He has his ringtone set to the same tune I have my alarm set to. It makes me jump. He takes it out of his jeans pocket, looks at it, and slips it back into his pocket again.

'You can take that, if you want,' I say.

'It's nothing important.'

There was a time, not so long ago, when I would have felt I had every right to ask him who it was.

'Nothing as important as this, anyway,' he adds, offering up a little smile.

I smile back.

'I like strawberries so much! Not this one! Mummy, no!'

'What have I just said to you, please? You need to stop raising your voice at me, or you don't get any strawberries or blueberries and we just go home. Right?'

'You are a *nasty* mummy and I hate you!'

Tom blinks fast and tilts his head towards the door. I nod in agreement, and drain my coffee.

Outside, it's grey and muggy, my worst kind of weather. I feel my hair expanding with every drop of moisture.

I speak without really thinking. I say, 'So we're friends now, are we? Is that what we're doing?' There's been no touching since the train station.

Tom inhales audibly. 'That's a big question to ask so casually, Mara.'

'Well, we can go all round the houses and have polite conversation and idle chit chat all day if it'll make you happy, but what's the point? We haven't come to Milton Keynes on a pleasure cruise.'

Tom places his right elbow into his left palm, and stretches his free arm across his body.

'That is why we're here, isn't it?' I say, facing resolutely ahead, away from his panicked gaze. 'To talk about next steps? If there are any.'

'Yes,' he says. 'That's why we're here.'

'And, not to use your own words against you, but you did say that you don't want to lose me.'

Tom starts to say something, then stops before a full word is out. He reaches a hand towards me and lets it graze my shoulder, before dropping it back down to his side. He tries again. 'And I can't. Lose you, I mean. You're my favourite person in the world.'

We're still walking, if very slowly. There's a big red-brick library on my right, and I say, stupidly, 'We could move here. A happy medium. I could work in there.'

I swear I hear Tom grimace. 'Mara,' he says.

'You're never moving back to London, are you?' I say.

Tom does the decent thing and answers fast. 'I can't see it happening in the near future, no.'

It's not a surprise to hear him say that. I already knew it in my bones. 'But I own a flat in London,' I say.

'Yes, you do.'

I chew the inside of my cheek. 'Why did you let me do that, if you knew you couldn't live there? You should've spoken up.'

I turn to look at him now. His arms are crossed protectively across his torso. He's rocking back and forth on the balls of his feet. He looks calm. He looks like he's relieved to be finally having this conversation.

'That wasn't my place to do. What would I have said? *Stop your plans while I work out what I want to do with my life?* That would've been mad.'

'Not as mad as what we're doing now.'

'You know it's not as straightforward as that.' Tom rubs his palms up and down his upper arms, as though he's cold. 'I wanted to give it a proper chance. I think I thought London might end up growing on me. It's a famously cruel city to move to as an outsider. But I had you. And I had a good job. And I couldn't work out why I couldn't appreciate those things.'

A wave of spite washes over me, and I say, 'In the end, you just love Birmingham more than you love me.'

'Fuckin'ell, Mara, don't do that.'

'It's true, though. You made a choice.'

'It didn't feel like a choice,' he says, sadly. 'It felt completely out of my hands.'

This is too annoying for me to swallow. 'Take some fucking agency, Tom. You *chose* to go back home.'

'Okay, yes. I made a choice.' He has unfolded his arms, and is now rubbing his palms together furiously, almost as though he's trying to start a fire. 'I couldn't cope in London, and I missed my home comforts, and I thought I might feel better back in Birmingham and, look, I do feel better now I'm back in Birmingham.'

'Great. So what is there left to say?' I know I'm being spiky, when I wanted to remain composed and level.

'That I love you.'

These words don't have the intended effect. They actually make me quite furious. What am I to do with them? Cling to them and hope that something will change, even though every single sign is pointing the opposite way? Put my life on hold and pray that Tom will one day realise that London isn't the devil? Sell my new flat and move in with Tom's parents?

'And I love you,' I say through gritted teeth. 'But that isn't always enough. We'll end up hating each other if we go down this road, and I don't ever want to hate you.'

'Oh, fuck,' Tom says, and I see that his eyes are filling up. 'Ah, Jesus.'

'Come on,' I say, suddenly resigned. 'Let's not dwell on this thing we can't fix. We're in bloody Milton Keynes, let's make the most of it.'

107

Three cocktails deep in the Wetherspoons, and nothing feels so heavy anymore. Tom keeps doing impressions of Jerry, and is making me howl.

'As per my correspondence dated the fifteenth of May,' he says, with real gusto, 'I hereby remind you that you must give me written warning if you are going to *pop* – in your words – outside to drop the bins out. As previously agreed, the front door must be immediately locked upon leaving the property and immediately locked after returning inside the above-mentioned property *sans bins*. As per legislation ninety-five point six in the waste management constitution, bin-dropping should legally take no more than thirty-six seconds. If, for any unforeseen circumstances – such as, but not limited to, extreme weather conditions, acts of god, or death – the dropping off of bins should take longer than thirty-six seconds, then all neighbours should receive formal warning of this at least seven working days in advance.'

Cheap mojito spurts out of my mouth. 'Nah,' I say. 'You spent way too long listening in to that man's life. It's uncanny.'

'Mate,' Tom says. 'I was fucking obsessed with him. I can't believe he's real.'

'Pfff,' I say. 'He's very real.'

'How are the other two? The top shaggers?'

'They're alright. We're all sort of friends now, you know.'

'I don't care about friends. I want to know about the sex.'

I laugh. 'It's steady. It's actually increased to three times a week since they started trying for a baby.'

'Whose height do you think it'll inherit?'

'Adele's, if it's lucky. And her manners.' In her voice, I sigh out a, *'Thank you.'*

Tom gratifies me with a hearty laugh.

Smug, I point to my empty glass. 'Another?'

'Please.'

I go up to the bar and signal for service.

'Same again?' the bartender asks. She looks underage.

'Yes. And shots.'

'That type of night, is it?' she says. 'What you having?'

I realise that I don't really know what a good shot is anymore. Me and Noor would always order sambucas, but that was her choice, and the thought of that lingering aniseed taste makes my stomach flip. 'Whatever your favourite is,' I say.

The bartender makes two mojitos from ready-made mix and pours two complicated-looking dark shots.

'Baby Guinness,' she clarifies, seeing my confused expression.

Tom groans as I carry the glasses over. I sit next to him, rather than opposite, so that we can slam our drinks back together.

'Wait, wait,' Tom says. 'Can I just say one thing first?' His voice is a little slurred. The last drink tipped him over the edge.

'Of course. Say your piece.'

'Woah,' he says. 'I wanted to say, *woah.*'

'About what?'

'You. I didn't say it before because I was shy, but you look *so good.*'

'Oh? You like my stuff?'

'Yeah. You're hot.'

'Tom,' I say. 'Are you flirting with me?'

'What if I am?'

'That would be fine,' I say. 'Now stop stalling and drink.' I tip the Baby Guinness straight down my throat. It slips down a dream.

Tom follows suit. We both shudder simultaneously, and in shuddering, our shoulders touch. I get a little frisson of pleasure from the connection. I lean into him slightly, wanting to stay close.

'My mum misses you a lot,' he says, softly. 'She talks about you all the time.'

This is not something I would have expected him to share.

'Oh?'

'What do you mean, oh?'

'Just. She's been quite closed off with me since that day she took you away.'

Tom lets his head flop back on his neck, closing his eyes. 'She didn't take me away, babe.'

'Sorry. It's just semantics. That day that you voluntarily left, then.'

His eyes are still scrunched up. 'She probably felt like that's what she had to do. She's said more than once that she hopes we'll fix things.'

'Really?'

My own mum has said nothing of the sort. If anything, she's said the opposite. She doesn't know that I've come here today, and I don't think I'll tell her.

'Of course. You're part of the family. You *are* my family.'

I drop my head onto Tom's shoulder. I'm tired. I don't want to pretend to be coy and detached anymore. I just want my boyfriend back. In one swift motion, he encases my hand with his and squeezes tight, as though he's trying to deflate it. We sit like this for whole minutes, breathing in synchrony, occasionally sighing. What is there to do? What can we try next?

108

We go to two more bars before realising that we should probably eat something.

'Could you fancy a chippy?' Tom says.

'More than anything,' I breathe.

There's one on the corner, called Moores, and Tom motions for me to wait for him outside. He knows my order, anyway.

After a few minutes, while I've been hopping from foot to foot, dying for a piss, he comes back out, laden down with paper packages.

'Bloody'ell,' I say. 'Who else have you invited?'

'I'm pissed, love. Need to carb up.'

'And I need to pee. Come and spot me.'

There's a little stretch of grassland, a square of sorts, up ahead, and I run to it, into the bushes, Tom not far behind me.

When I'm halfway through, I hear Tom saying, 'Lovely evening for it,' to someone. Then, 'Nothing to see here, folks. Just a small spring of natural freshwater.'

This strikes me as the funniest thing that's ever happened. We're like two kids on a school trip, being naughty.

Once the coast is clear, Tom calls out, 'Good spot for a picnic?' and this makes me laugh even more.

I'm not silly like this with anyone else. Nobody else makes me feel so much myself. In this precise moment, I am filled with love for Tom. True love can succeed. It has to.

We sit huddled on the kerb, mere metres away from my piss puddle, and Tom hands me my food. A saveloy – which in all the years of knowing me, he's never been able to get his head around me liking – chips, mushy peas and curry sauce. For himself, he's got his usual steak and kidney pie and chips. Inexplicably, he's also got us a couple of Spam fritters.

'On holiday, aren't we?' he says, by way of explanation.

We eat ravenously, stuffing handfuls of salty chips into our mouths at once. Tom feeds me a forkful of pie and I shove the saveloy into his face, as he backs away. The food's hot and tasty, and I get the impression that it's a meal I'll remember for a long time.

With the remnants of our feast scattered around us, Tom says, 'What do you want to do now?' He pulls his phone out and looks at the screen. 'Oh shit, it's nine forty.'

'Oh,' I say. 'Shit.'

'What time's your last train?'

'I don't actually know. I didn't really think about the end of the day. I was too focused on the start of it.'

Tom taps away at his phone for a few seconds. I assume he's looking at train times, but he looks up at me blankly when he's finished and says, 'So?'

'Have a look yourself. Your phone's literally in your hand.'

'Yeah, sorry. I'm in a bit of a daze.' He types something and waits. 'Okay, so. They're quite regular. Next one is nine fifty-one. But you wouldn't make that, obviously. And then they seem to be . . . every few minutes until about half past midnight.'

The thought of just going home now seems absurd.

My face must reflect this thought, because Tom scrolls down with his thumb, and says, brightly, 'But the first morning one is at three thirty, so.'

'I have nothing to rush back for.' I realise as I say this how very true it actually is. 'But maybe someone will be waiting for you back home?'

'I might just call my mum, if that's okay?'

'Of course.'

Tom wanders off to make the call in private, and I gather up all our rubbish, hunting for a bin. Talking about logistics has sobered me up. I feel wide awake and hyperaware that whatever happens next will end up being hugely significant. I have precisely zero desire to go home. I can't even begin to picture the journey back, the cold bus from the station, opening the front door and going into my dark flat, alone.

Tom is smiling when he comes back over to me. 'She said she won't wait up, and to have a good time.'

Now that he's been granted permission to stay out, he's keen to find an activity for us to do. I listen as he reels off our options.

'Here it says, *bar hopping at the Hub*,' he says. 'Or the casino? Cineworld? Hollywood Bowl? Creams for dessert?'

'Tom,' I say.

He looks up at me. Something shifts, ever so slightly.

He says, 'I'm just putting off the inevitable, aren't I?'

I nod.

'I should just be doing this, shouldn't I?' He reaches out and cradles my face with a cupped palm.

I nod, and close my eyes. It's so good to have his hands on my skin.

'And this?' He closes the gap between us by putting his other hand on my hip.

My head barely moves, but I think I make a little noise of assent.

'And this.' He leans his face towards mine and we stay like that for a few breaths, almost touching but not quite.

It's me that kisses him first. I can't fully remember our first ever kiss, but I imagine it wasn't as good as this one. This one is excitement and relief and an exhale of a held breath. It speaks of a shared history, a present moment held in amber, the desire for more future, for endless kissing. I feel faint with it. Tom is shaking a little.

When we eventually pull away, neither of us talks. We clutch hands and walk and walk, squeezing at one another's fingers every now and then. When we see a Jurys Inn, it doesn't require a conversation. We approach it together, and enter it as one.

'Do you have any rooms for tonight?' Tom asks the woman behind the desk.

'For the two of youse?'

'Yes,' I say.

'Let me just have a little look. I think that should be completely fine, though.' She hums and taps an upturned fist against the counter, as her computer loads.

I don't want it to take this long. I want to already be in the room. The lights in here are way too bright, and I don't want anything to break the spell.

'Had a good day out?' she says now, cheerily.

Oh for godsake.

'Really, really nice, yeah,' Tom says.

'Where's that accent from?' she says. 'Brummie, are you?'

Tom says, 'I am, yeah.'

'Aw, I love it over there. Great for shopping. Absolutely love the Bullring.'

Shut up, woman.

I wrap an arm around Tom's waist, pull him into me, reminding him.

'My fella's a Birmingham City supporter, if you'll believe it. So we get over there quite often.' She beams. 'Oh, here we go. We've got a nice double for youse. That'll be a hundred and four pounds today.'

I grimace, but Tom says, 'Great.'

He reaches for his wallet, and I wonder how he'll be affording this. To have a concrete price put on this particular evening feels too tacky to even contemplate.

'Babe, do you want me to——?' I say.

'You've gotta be joking,' he says.

'Aw, got yourself a real gent, there,' the woman says.

Everything that she's saying is grating on me. I just need this interaction to be over. But there's a form to fill in, and instructions about checkout and breakfast times to listen to. Tom handles it all. When he's finished with the paperwork, he nudges me with his elbow and points down at the page.

There are basic multiple choice questions asking whether we're there for work or pleasure, and a section about other guests. In his precious little handwriting, he's written my name, and date of birth, and then in the space where it says: *Relationship to main guest*, he's written: *She's my fave.*

Suddenly, it's all fine again. We're back on track. It's us. Me and my Tom.

We make it into the room. Room 108. And we undress each other urgently, getting tangled up in jeans legs and armholes and laughing the whole time. We collapse onto the bed, on top of the covers, and lie there naked, just looking.

'Yours is my best body,' I say.

'Yeah? Yours is mine.'

He traces shapes on my stomach and my groin and my shoulders. He flips me over, onto my front, and with his finger, he writes *M I N E* on my back.

109

It's novel to have a chilled Sunday morning together. Tom is in no rush to get up or go anywhere. We shower together, scrubbing each other in a jokey way, until Tom pushes me up against the shower wall and starts panting in my ear. I'm heartened by his aggression. We miss breakfast, so Tom calls down to reception and requests two fry-ups to be brought up to the room. We eat in bed, making the sheets sticky with bacon fat and butter.

When we eventually open the curtains, it's a bright, fresh-looking day outside.

'Walk?' Tom suggests, and I'm so happy that our time doesn't have to be over yet.

'Walk,' I say.

We check out of the Jurys Inn, and make our way to North Loughton Valley Park. I buy us takeaway coffees from a greasy spoon, and the sun is shining brightly enough to almost be warm, and Tom holds my hand as though it's the most natural thing in the world, which really it is. I want very badly for us to talk about what's going on and what we want. I also want very badly to keep that conversation at bay and to just enjoy the afternoon together.

By a clichéd babbling brook, Tom says, 'I can't believe I almost let this go.'

I wait for him to expand.

'A couple of weeks ago, I was thinking about how I'd feel and what I'd do if I found out you were seeing someone else.'

'Oh, babe,' I say. I don't want him to go down this path. I think about Derek's corner-shop gifts, his lingering looks.

'I felt sick to my fucking stomach. And then I just thought, *Well if that's how you feel, then you need to do something about it, because it won't take long for someone to snap that girl up.*'

'I'm not available for snapping,' I say. 'I'm already snapped.'

Tom raises my hand to his mouth and gives it a dry kiss. 'Is it true? You still want me?'

'I think I'll always want you.'

'Mara,' he says, kissing my mouth. 'Mara, Mara, Mara, my Mara,' in between kisses. 'It's going to be okay because we love each other.'

I'm careful. I say, with as neutral a tone as I can manage, 'You don't think we're doomed?'

He draws back to look into my eyes. 'Doomed? Not at all. I think I lost track of myself and then of us, and it was almost a disaster, but we're pulling it back now. And I'm incredibly lucky that you're willing to. It's a real relationship with real ups and downs.'

I nod as he talks. He's saying things that I want to hear. I need him to keep talking. I want him to say more.

'This is just a tiny blip. If we're going to spend our lives together – which I truly believe we are – then this will be this weird little thing we look back on and marvel at. We'll tell our kids for shock value, and they won't believe it ever happened.'

'Yeah?'

'Oh, one hundred percent. You're my One.'

It comes out almost of its own accord. 'But practically, though? How do we do this?'

'Well. I've been thinking about it. I didn't sleep much last night trying to work it out. I think, to start, we do fortnightly visits. Alternate cities. And then later on, down the line, we work out how to manage it more long-term.'

This isn't really enough of a plan to put my mind at ease. It's certainly something, but to go from living together – however briefly – to long-distance, feels cruel.

'I'll be thirty in a few years, Tom,' I say, and let this hang there. 'And so will I.'

'It's different for men. You know it is. I know nothing is promised, but what are the chances of this paying off?' I can't face another minute of uncertainty. 'Will I have to move to Birmingham to have a real life with you? Be honest.'

He chews at the corner of his bottom lip. 'I don't think so.'

'I need more than *don't think so*, Tom. Seriously.'

'No. No, you won't. I just needed to be at home in order to get better. It won't always be like this. I promise.'

He can't possibly know this. All he can do is speculate, same as me.

So I do the only thing that I want to do, and I follow my heart. I say, 'Okay, let's do it.'

110

On the train back to London, my phone pings. I'm giddy. Tom has been texting me cute little messages ever since we kissed goodbye.

I grin as I unlock my phone.

Thanks for the text. Actually not great at all. My mum's in the hospital. It's a whole big mess.

I do a double take, and realise that the WhatsApp is from Noor, and not Tom.

I text back with frantic thumbs. *Babe! Oh my god, what's happened??*

She's online. She replies quickly. *It might not be a texting conversation.*

My heart is hammering. I feel as bad as I could feel. Something scary has been happening to Noor while I've been luxuriating in the parks of Milton Keynes.

I'm so, so sorry, I text. *Are you with someone? Can I do anything? Sending all my solidarity.*

I'm with Luther. Don't worry.

Her tone is undeniably frosty. I guess Luther is the boyfriend. I feel a stab of jealousy that he knows what's going on before I do. And then I feel guilty about feeling jealous. I should feel glad that she has someone there to support her.

I do worry, I text. *I'll try and call you tomorrow? I'm really sorry about our bickering recently. I know I've not been great. I'd really love it if we could sort things out. Love you.*

As soon as I press send, I know I've said the wrong thing. Noor's having a personal crisis and I've made it about me and her. Probably the last thing she wants is to have to think about anything that's not her mum right now. I think about sending an amendment, but what's the point? I've said it now.

Thankfully, she replies, friendly enough. *Sure. Let's speak tomorrow.*

A few beats later, another text: *Love you too.*

111

I set up job alerts on my phone. I start off vague. I choose *Media, Editing*, and in a fuck-it frame of mind, *TV*. Though I'm quite sure that nobody ever finds their dream job via these channels, it's still worth a shot, and I know that the secret of it will make me feel strong when I'm having a bad day at the library.

Derek asks me three times what I got up to at the weekend, and in the end, I say, 'I met up with Tom in Milton Keynes, and now we're back together, okay?'

'You are *not*,' he says.

'We fucking are,' I say.

He does a kicked-puppy face, but I let it wash over me. My personal life shouldn't be his business, anyway. I carry on adding the plastic cover to the John Grisham in my hands.

'Are you sure about this?' Derek says.

'Derek, respectfully, you don't know the half of it.'

He backs away, palms raised in surrender. 'You shouldn't really speak to your boss like that,' he says, 'respectfully.'

Bye.

I look back down. I see that it's 12:25. In five minutes, I'll go for my lunch break. It's claustrophobic in this bloody library. *Fuck it.* I'm an adult, I can go for my lunch at 12:25 if I want. I take my jacket off the back of my chair and stand up.

'Derek,' I say, quietly. I signal towards the doorway with my chin.

'Bon app,' he says. He looks completely downcast. I hate him for that. How dare he be disappointed about my good news?

I go to Souvlakiland and get a big kebab with all the trimmings. Putting my earphones in, I call Noor.

She picks up on the second ring.

'Oh,' I say. 'That was quick.'

'I've got time to kill,' she says. She sounds flat and tired.

'How are you?' I say. A feeble question.

'Yeah,' she says. 'You know.'

I perch against the wall outside St Barnabas. Flanked by adults on all sides, a wriggly line of toddlers in high-vis make their way across the road. At least three of the children are crying. Funny to think that even tiny humans have their dramas and stressors.

'I'm so sorry your mum's not well,' I say, playing with a chip, pulling it up out of the wrap.

'Me too.'

'Can I ask what happened?'

'The worst thing.' I hear a gulp. 'She took some pills—' Noor's voice cuts out entirely, then. I hear a different voice murmuring in the background, then Noor saying, 'No, it's okay, I'll just step outside. It's my friend.' There's the sound of a door swinging shut. 'Sorry, Mara, let me go somewhere a bit more private.'

'Yeah, of course.'

An exhale. 'I was saying. She took some pills. Too many. She'd done it before when I was very little. It's all been extremely triggering.'

'I'm so fucking sorry. That's horrible.'

'Pretty shit, yeah.'

'Is she . . .' I try to think of an appropriate word. 'Stable?'

'Thankfully yes. Sort of comes in and out of focus. Sometimes she's just mum, and sometimes she's like a zombie.'

'Where actually are you?'

'Mile End Hospital.'

'How long has she been in?'

'Couple of days. They'll be sending her home soon, which is mad to me, but what can I do?'

'That doesn't seem right. Will she get any follow-up treatment once she's home?'

Noor makes a wet tut. 'Couple of visits, but then it's on me. Like always.' She's audibly crying now.

'I don't know if this is helpful at all, and say no if it's completely the wrong thing.' I pause. 'But I'm on my way.'

Noor sniffles a couple of times, and then says, 'See you soon.'

PART V

Autumn

112

What do you think we'll do this weekend? I text.

Don't you worry about that! It's all under control! Tom texts back.

I zip up my overnight bag, smiling to myself. It does feel as though it's all under control. Unlike the very transitory arrangements we had when we were both in London but not in the same house, we've organised things properly now. I have a designated drawer at Tom's mum and dad's. In it, I have five pairs of pants, five pairs of socks, a hairbrush, dry shampoo, a deodorant, a toothbrush, sanitary products, a travel hairdryer, a pair of jogging bottoms and face cream, items which live there all the time, waiting for me whenever I may need them. Here, in my Hackney flat, Tom has similar essentials.

There's an excitement attached to our time together. Each visit a little holiday. He has vowed to always meet me at the station, and I have promised to always have cold beers in the fridge. We almost lost each other and we want to celebrate the fact that we didn't. Today, it's my turn to go to him. I'm happy to be hosted, to let go, to not have to think, and to do whatever he wants us to do.

One hour and forty and I'm with him. Five chapters of a book. Two podcasts. Or one film watched on the tiny screen of my phone. I vibrate with nervous energy the whole way. And then the weekend begins.

113

He takes my bag from me, hoists it onto his shoulder, and scoops me into a hug, audibly inhaling as though to breathe me in.

'Hello, hello, hello,' he says, kissing the inside of my neck after each word.

I laugh. 'Hi, you. Chirpy.'

He pushes me away from his body by my arms, then yanks me back in. 'You're gorgeous today.'

'So are you. I like your attitude.'

'I like yours. Are you up for a drink, or did you want to go home first?'

'Happy to do anything. A drink sounds great, actually.'

'Perfect,' he says. 'There's this place I just found, that I'd never been to before somehow, even though it's been here ages, and it's alright, you know. I think you'll like it. Have you done something to your hair? It's so shiny. No. It's that shade of lipstick. I've not seen that before.'

'You have, babe.' I reach out for his hand, and let myself be led out of the station. 'It's my normal one.'

He squeezes his fingers in between mine, his grip tight. I have this flashing thought, *I would've been okay without you, but I'm so glad I don't have to think about that anymore.* I briefly consider saying it out loud.

Tom points out various cafés and bars that have opened up since my last visit. More than once, we stop so that he can say hi to someone he knows. Our chatting is punctuated by calls of, *Alright, mate.*

We make our way along the canal, until he motions for me to go into a large warehouse-type building called The Distillery.

'It's lovely by the water, isn't it?' he says.

I nod.

'Do you like this? Is this okay?'

I tilt my head to the side, observing him. 'Tom,' I say. 'It's more than okay.'

'You're sure?'

I lean against the door and go inside. 'Come on.'

At the bar, I order us a couple of pints and a bowl of chips.

'No gins for either of you?' the bartender asks. 'That's our speciality, you know.'

Tom has caught me up, and wraps a hand around my waist from behind.

'In that case,' I say, 'two of your favourite gin cocktails, then. Right?' I ask Tom.

'Please. My round, though.'

'Go and find us a nice table. You can get the next one.'

Tom wanders off. Waiting for our drinks, I look around the space. People are more dressed up than they would be at a similar location in London. The women have really made an effort, in cropped jumpers and high-waisted trousers or satin skirts with bodysuits. They're all in heels or platform boots. The men are in shirts, and sincere shoes. I wiggle my toes inside my Converse. Tom's a little dressed up himself. He has a cream mac on that must be new. I don't know how he's paying for stuff at the minute, whether he still has savings, or whether he's getting help from his parents. I know I won't ask.

'Date night?' the bartender asks, cocktail shaker in hand.

'Yep,' I say, scrunching up my nose. 'We're a weekend couple.'

'Oh?'

'I live in London, he lives here.'

The bartender stops what he's doing to look at me. 'With that accent? You're a Brummie originally, then?'

I laugh. 'Rugby.'

'Ah. But the capital pulled you in?'

'Something like that.'

'Don't you find the people a bit . . . cold?' he says, pouring the first drink into a tall, frosted glass.

My defences go up. 'You get cold people everywhere.'

'Much less so here, though. You have to admit. I've never got the appeal, myself. Birmingham is just as good, but twice as friendly. We've never got the credit we deserve. Do you not think?'

I hum in a way that he could take as assent if he wanted to.

231

'I just think, if you like city life, why would you not move here?'
I shrug. I'm done.

'We've got the water, we've got the shopping, the cathedral, we're close to everywhere else. Your boyfriend's here. What's not to love?'

'I like London,' I say. My tone has shifted now, I no longer have any desire to be polite. He's actually getting on my nerves. 'I don't really see why I have to justify my living arrangements on a Friday night when I'm trying to relax.' I force out a mirthless laugh. 'You have to live somewhere, and that's where I live.'

He widens his eyes at me, like, *Oh-kay.*

I scan my debit card on the reader and take the two drinks.

114

Tom suggests Turtle Bay for food, and when we get there, we order loads. We get sweetcorn fritters, and jerk chicken, and ribs, and mac and cheese, and plantain, and rice and peas, and sweet potato fries, and cocktail after cocktail.

Tom is giggly and keeps pointing out various couples on different tables, trying to guess how long they've been together.

'They met today,' he says, pointing discreetly at two women kissing passionately in a corner booth. 'Instant attraction. Probably been talking on a dating app for a week or so before tonight.'

'Could be an anniversary?'

'No way,' he says. 'It's got first date written all over it. Whereas that one,' he whispers, angling his head towards a middle-aged pair, sharing a bowl of curry goat, 'that's a second date. Third, tops.'

'Why?'

'Well. She's incredibly dolled up, and he's listening to everything she's saying as intently as if she were the *News at Ten*.'

'Do you not listen intently to everything I say?'

'Of course. But we're different.'

'How are we different?' I feed him a chip.

'We've had phases, haven't we? So even though we've been together a long time, it's still really fresh.'

I think about this. I smile at him. 'That's a really nice way to think about it,' I say. I nod in the direction of an elderly couple who are staring into space, their plates empty in front of them. 'What about them?'

'Four hundred and eightieth date,' he says.

115

He takes me to the Library of Birmingham on Saturday afternoon. I've never actually been inside before. Though I can tell he's had enough after twenty minutes or so, he trails after me for nearly two hours, smiling the whole time, as I stroke the spines of innumerable books.

I say, over and over, 'Imagine how long it'd take to read every book in here.'

He says, repeatedly, with pride in his voice, 'They spent nearly two hundred million on this, you know.'

116

On Sunday evening, I get one of the latest trains I can viably get. In the station, I cling to Tom.

117

I start spending a lot of time at Noor's mum's. Considering the circumstances, it's a surprisingly upbeat atmosphere there. I meet Luther, who I like a lot. I'd prepared myself for him to be tall, but he must be six foot six. Broad too. He's tender with Noor, laughs indulgently at her nasty jokes, scolds her gently if he thinks she's gone too far. And she's softer around him too. Sometimes I walk into a room where they were previously alone, and they spring away from each other as though they've been caught in flagrante, even when all they're doing is chatting. I'm jealous of the newness of their relationship. They have all the good stuff already, with even better stuff to follow.

One Saturday morning, when Luther's popped out to get breakfast for us all, Noor and I stand side by side at the kitchen sink, washing dishes.

'He's great,' I say.

Noor's unable to hide her grin. 'He is, isn't he?'

'I like the way he talks to your mum. He's very respectful, but not, like, formal, you know?'

'She's happy to have him around,' Noor says, passing me a plate to dry. 'She'd never admit it, but she misses having that male presence in the house.'

'She's never really dated since your dad?' Though I think I know the answer to this question, I don't want to take anything for granted. I'm still treading cautiously in matters of Noor's private life.

'Few casual things. Nothing that stuck. I had an Uncle Ian for a bit, who was harmless enough, but I guess the men could all sense that she was still pining for my dad. She's never got over him.'

I do an involuntary cluck, like, *Aww*, and Noor gives me a look.

'It's not cute. It's sad. She's not a widow. He left her on purpose.'

'Still,' I say. 'It must be hard trying to replace someone you thought was perfect.'

Noor is swiping at the inside of a Birmingham University mug with a sponge on a stick. 'You *will* find someone else.' She hands me the mug. 'Someone better.'

Oh. I've been putting this revelation off for a number of reasons, partly because I want to focus on my friend, but largely because I'm nervous of her reaction. That said, it's a much greater crime to openly deny mine and Tom's reunion than to just fail to mention it.

'Ah,' I say. 'So here's the thing.'

'Oh,' Noor says, raising a soapy hand to her forehead. 'No.'

'You know the end of the story?'

'I can make a pretty decent guess.'

'We just felt like we owed it to each other to give it a proper go. We missed each other.'

I can see Noor taking her time to answer. Eventually, she says, 'If you miss your ex, you look at old photos and cry, you don't get back with them.'

'What, ever?'

'You know my stance on this.'

'Well, I want to hear it.'

'I just don't think it works. Not in the long run. It's normal to miss someone you loved. Of course it is. But you have to push through that phase. All you're doing now is delaying the inevitable.'

'Why is it inevitable, though?'

'Name one solid couple that broke up and got back together. And *stayed* together.'

When me and Tom first started our break, in a fit of despondency, I Googled *Famous couples that have broken up and got back together*, so I have a handful ready to quote.

I run through my list, while Noor shakes her head. When I get to Katy Perry and Orlando Bloom, she says, 'Exception to the rule.'

'Me and Tom might be the exception to the rule, too.'

'If that's what you truly want, then I hope so. For your sake.'

'You don't sound very optimistic.'

'I'm not.'

I feel as though she's about to say something I really, really don't want to hear.

'Say what you want to say.'

Noor pulls the plug and her words are slightly muffled by the noise of the water draining out of the sink. 'Talking from experience, growing up, when my mum was at her lowest points, she would retreat. She could be irritable, she could push us away, hold us at arm's length, all those horrible things. But never, ever, did she even *threaten* to leave my dad. Never.'

I let this sink in.

'Maybe you guys broke up because Tom wasn't well. Maybe that's it. But did you ever think that you might have broken up for other reasons too?'

118

'I've been invited to Lewis and Hattie's cake tasting,' I say to my mum, over the phone. 'It's not a job you'd usually need your flower girl to be involved with, is it?'

'It's Lewis's way of trying to include you. He wants you and his wife to be best mates.' There's laughter in her voice.

'It's on a bloody Saturday morning. At nine.'

'Good excuse to get you up nice and early.' I hear her take a sip of something. 'Isn't Tom due to be there on that weekend?'

My mum took the news a lot better than Noor did. She gave me a couple of motherly warnings, but ended her speech by saying, 'I would do anything for a single extra day with your dad, so if it makes you happy to spend more time with Tom, then I support you.' I'd ended the FaceTime and promptly burst into tears.

'Yeah,' I say, now. 'I can't subject him to that, surely?'

'Why not? If he wants to be with you, then he has to do some of the things that interest you. Your hobbies. Your pastimes.' She bursts out laughing.

'Bye,' I say. 'Thanks for your support.'

119

Derek pulls me to the side on Thursday morning. I'm texting Noor under the desk, touch typing, so that it's not so obvious to anyone walking past.

'Hello,' Derek says. 'Sorry to interrupt you when you're so busy.'

I shove my phone into my trouser pocket, as though he hasn't already seen it.

'I'm not busy,' I say, and then wish I hadn't.

'Could you come back here a second,' he says. Though it's technically a question, it doesn't feel like one. He's using a new tone, one I've not heard from him before.

I follow in silence, as he leads me upstairs and into the tiny meeting room. There's nobody else in there.

'Take a seat,' he says. A loaded request.

I don't really want to. Still, I do as I'm told, placing as little of my bum on the edge of a perforated plastic chair as I can. He does not sit.

He starts talking, all in a flurry, with no preamble, as though he doesn't want to give himself the chance to back out. 'What I did for you,' he says, 'wasn't a small thing. I could get into a lot of trouble for it. I could lose my job. And I did it in good faith, because you were in a bind and until recently you'd always been a really good little worker, and I thought I could trust you.' He takes a breath, purposely not looking directly at me. 'However, your behaviour of late has been a real cause for concern. It's made me start to wonder whether I may have made a big mistake in amending your paperwork. I will keep this brief, but I think it goes without saying that I want to see a lot more real commitment from you. Smiles for our patrons, a can-do attitude, friendliness with your colleagues. And much, much shorter lunch breaks.'

A wave of icy coldness is washing over my neck and spine.

'I hope I've made myself clear,' he concludes.

There's nothing I can say to this. Derek is glowing with his own self-righteousness, his power on display. I dared to think I could have a personal life, I dared to spurn his proffered friendship, and now look. How silly I was, how naive. How fucking stupid.

I stay sitting in that plastic chair for whole minutes after he's gone back into the main library. I stay there until I realise that my can-do attitude should probably start right this instant.

120

That evening, Adele knocks on my door. I'm still in a mild state of shock. I think some part of me assumes that anyone who wants to speak to me today wants something concrete from me, some sort of commitment, some kind of promise.

'Come in,' I say.

Adele is dressed head-to-toe in Ganni. She looks like London Fields personified.

'Is it a good time?' she says, one foot already over the threshold.

'Course, I'll pop the kettle on.'

Adele takes herself through to the living room and sits down. She shouts through the kitchen hatch at me, 'I'm just here for a gossip, really!'

I peer through the little hole in the wall at her. She looks flushed, excited.

'Oh?'

'You would've been at work first thing this morning?' she calls. 'Opening up?'

'Mmhmm!'

'So you don't know anything about the police?'

'What police?' I say, popping two teabags into two mugs.

'Someone called the police on Jerry.'

I poke my head right through the hatch. 'Excuse me?'

She laughs, savouring my disbelief. 'Yep. One of the guys a couple of houses down said Jerry's been harassing him.'

'Oh my god,' I breathe. 'That's amazing. Let me finish making these, and then tell me everything.'

I add the hot water and milk, and carry the teas through, placing them down on my teak coffee table.

Adele has kicked her ankle boots off and has curled one of her legs up under her bum. She grins, as she says, 'I heard the whole thing. I was tempted to video it, but I couldn't tear myself away to go and grab my phone. So you know how funny Jerry is about the parking spots?'

Jerry is notorious for being funny about parking. The rules are foggy for the normal resident, but he seems to know exactly who's allowed a spot, and who's not, and how many each house has, and which one belongs to who. I nod.

'So the guy – Rob, I think he's called – has this little green Ka, which takes up half a spot at best. And Jerry's decided that Rob keeps parking in his – Jerry's – spot. Please don't ask me how Jerry has decided that's his spot, but apparently he's been parking there since—'

'Before we were born,' I say.

Adele laughs. 'Exactly. So Jerry keeps leaving these notes on Rob's car. *Please remove your vehicle. This is Jerry Bates's parking space*, et cetera. And Rob mostly ignores them. But then this morning, I look out and there's bloody spray paint all over the side of Rob's Ka.'

'No!'

'Yes! And it spells out: *Last warning. Please remove this car.*'

I put my head in my hands. I've had a really shit day, but Rob's has been just as bad.

'I'm hooked at this point, so I keep going back to check. It's still early enough that Rob won't have gone outside yet, and then, at around ten, I'm in the bathroom and I hear screaming. So I run back through to the kitchen, and Rob is going absolutely mental, rubbing at the paint on his car, and it's not coming off. I watch him spin around on the spot, and I see how angry he is, and then he's heading towards our house. Oh my god, it's so good. I'm sure Jerry will be too scared to go out, but after a couple of minutes he does. And Rob is calling him every name under the sun, saying he's crazy, he needs to be institutionalised, he's the most selfish, unneighbourly person he's ever met. And the whole time, I can't hear a word that Jerry's saying. He must be really keeping his cool. After a while, Jerry walks over to the car, and he goes to touch it, to make a point about the paint or whatever, and Rob slaps his hand away. That's when it gets really good. Jerry starts shouting, *Assault! Assault!* and gets his phone out of his pocket and dials. Then Rob gets *his* phone out of *his* pocket, and dials too. And they just stand there in silence, with their hands on their hips, and wait for the police to arrive.'

'Jesus,' I say. 'So what happened when the police came?'

'Well that's the thing. I had to go to an appointment then, so I didn't see how it ended. I left the house just as the police cars arrived. Two! Can you believe it? I went past and was like, *Morning, officer.* And Rob shouts out, *Tell them how he's been harassing me!* And I'm like, *Sorry guys, I'm in a bit of a rush.*' Adele takes a sip of her drink. 'They could both be in jail right now.'

'Well, Jerry's not,' I say, pointing at the floor. There's the dim sound of his radio coming up through my carpet.

'Jerry always lands on his feet,' Adele says.

'I'm happy you came to tell me that. It's cheered me right up.'

'Did you need cheering?'

'A bit. I think my boss threatened me today?'

'Sorry, what?'

I tell Adele the story, and she gasps in all the right places.

When I'm finished, she says, 'You know he'll never take it further. It's not in his best interest.'

'It seems like quite a risky strategy to assume that, though,' I say, flattening my back against the sofa cushions, and stifling a yawn.

'I bet he's all talk. Still, it sounds like it might be an idea to get out of there.'

'Why should I be the one to leave my job though, just because he's sulking?'

She sighs. 'I left my last job because my boss touched my bum at the Christmas party. It shouldn't go like that, but it does. I could've stayed, or I could've confronted him, or reported him, but what's the point?'

'Oh, Adele,' I say. 'That's horrible.'

'Yes,' she says. 'It is.'

121

About ten minutes after she's gone back upstairs, I get a text from Adele.

With all the excitement of parking-gate, I completely forgot to tell you the real reason I came down . . . Me and Baz are pregnant!

I bang my mop against the ceiling and call, 'Wahooo!'

Adele bangs back and I hear her laughing.

122

Through my kitchen window, the next morning, I see Jerry cheerfully loading up the boot of his car with all sorts of trash. His car is in its rightful place. He's taking his time, whistling. He pops in a bundle of newspapers, an ancient-looking tin of Dulux, a sports bag. I try to make out the tune. It's familiar. I wonder if he slept okay after his dramatic day. He seems genuinely fine. He's in no rush to get off the forecourt. I look for the green Ka, and see that it's at the far left-hand side of the parking area. Rob lives on the far right-hand side of the row of flats. Jerry has won. With a jolt, I realise what the song Jerry's humming is. 'Eye of the Tiger'.

123

I meet Tom at Euston on Friday, after work. He's jittery with excitement when he gets off the train, in a weird mix of work clothes and weekend clothes. He has a light blue shirt on – one he used to regularly wear to school, tucked into his black jeans, and his Vans on his feet. I see that he has cufflinks on, and tease him about this.

'I was in a rush!' he says. 'I couldn't wait to be with you. Anyway, shhh, and give me a kiss.'

I oblige, before saying, 'Explain the get-up, then.'

'I had an interview this afternoon.' He's proud.

My stomach lurches. We've never actually talked about him quitting his London job, so I don't know exactly when he did it. I just know he doesn't work there anymore.

He sees my face, and says, quickly, 'For an online tutoring gig.'

I try to fix my expression. 'That's great, Tom. You didn't say.'

'I didn't want to jinx it. I didn't feel qualified.'

I take his hand and we walk together towards the tube. 'You're literally qualified, babe,' I say. 'So how did it go?'

'The girl doing it was really friendly, about our age, and that helped, I think. She said they'd let me know after the weekend, so.' He shrugs, but he's smiling.

I nudge him with my hip. 'Well done, you,' I say. I swallow something nasty down. Something that feels a bit like jealousy. Did he not need my encouragement before doing something as big as a job interview? Did he not want my advice?

'Thank you,' he says. 'It's not a done deal, though.'

'They'd be lucky to have you,' I say, pointing towards the ticket machines.

'Oh, it's fine. I lost my Oyster card ages ago. I can just pay with my contactless,' he says. 'Unless you need to top up?'

'No, no,' I say.

We head through the turnstiles one after the other, and I follow

Tom towards the Victoria line. There's something new in Tom's walk, a little swagger, some confidence that hasn't been there for a while. It feels like I'm on an early date with someone I want to impress. I talk quickly, trying to cram all my week's news into a few minutes. I stick to the positive highlights, deciding to save the heavier stuff for home, or even to avoid sharing it altogether.

'Adele's expecting,' I say. 'She's only eight weeks, but she was desperate to tell me. We've got closer lately, you know. I have a cup of tea with her a couple of times a week now. It's actually nice.'

'That's great, babe. They really wanted that, didn't they?' He smiles as he steps off the end of the escalator.

'I was thinking we could get them some flowers? Go to Columbia Road on Sunday?'

'Sounds like a lovely idea.' He purses his lips into a little air kiss. I blow him one back. 'Noor's mum's doing loads better,' I say.

'Yeah?'

'And Noor's boyfriend's super nice. I think he's the best thing that could have happened to her right now. He's just this really calm, straightforward person. And she's chilled *right* out. She just seems much more at peace. Picking her battles, and stuff. She's like the old Noor again. He's a blessing.'

'Fit, too,' Tom says. 'I've seen him on her Instagram. Good for her.'

'Good for them both, you mean,' I say.

'Of course.'

124

Tom is surprisingly on board with the cake outing. It's at a bakery in Holborn. We leave the flat just after eight. It's a bright morning, with a fresh crispness in the air.

'Want to go for breakfast?' I say, once we're at Liverpool Street. 'A quick one?'

Tom looks at me like I'm mad. 'We're on our way to try a hundred different cakes, babe,' he says.

'Oh yeah.'

I've dressed up a bit, unsure as to what's actually required from a guest at something like this. I'm in a floral dress with tights, and feel stiff in these unfamiliar clothes. Tom is wearing the shirt from yesterday with some smart trousers I've never seen before. Reassuringly, he's chosen his Vans again. That's something. The whole thing is very foreign. The last time I saw Lewis or Hattie was on the champagne announcement night, and I have a nervous belly. I hope it'll only take an hour or so. I don't want to spend a whole Saturday celebrating someone else's love, when I finally have my own back on track.

We take the Central line to Chancery Lane, and Tom holds one of my hands with both of his, clutching it in his lap. Opposite us, there's a young couple with a baby in a pushchair and a five or six-year-old boy. The older child keeps peering into the buggy.

'Shhh, shhh,' he whispers, even though the baby isn't making any noise. 'It's okay. It's not far now.' He turns and sees me smiling to myself. 'We're going to my granny's,' he says, proudly.

'Oh?' Tom says. 'Lucky you. Will you be having some lunch with her?'

The little boy steps closer to us. He drops his head to one side, considering Tom. 'It's morning time . . .'

Tom slaps his forehead, clowning around. 'Silly me! I forgot about a whole meal! Are you having breakfast with her, then?'

I look over at the parents. They're grinning indulgently. A few other people in the carriage are looking up from their phone screens and *Metro*s, corners of mouths lifted.

'I had an egg at my house, but my granny has doughnuts and I'm going to ask her for a doughnut, and I think she'll give me one to eat, but not for Molly because she's too little and she just has mummy's milk.'

'Wow,' I say. 'Yum.'

The little boy cranes his neck to examine this new interlocutor.

'Hello,' I say.

'What's your name? Mine's Frank.'

'I'm Mara,' I say. 'And this is Tom.'

'My best friend is called Tom,' Frank says.

'He sounds like he might be cool,' Tom says. 'Is he?'

Frank nods. 'But I like Molly best, even though she's only a little baby.'

His parents have stood up. 'Come on, Frank. This is our stop,' his mum says. 'Say bye-bye to your new friends.'

Me and Tom wave.

'Bye Mah-ra. Bye Tommy,' Frank says.

Tom grabs hold of my hand again, and squeezes. I am warmed through.

'Mummy,' Frank says, as he steps off the train. 'They were boyfriend and girlfriend. Did you see?'

125

Hattie greets us enthusiastically outside the cake shop. She's wearing a cream suit with no top underneath. She has one of those chic, unselfconscious flat chests. There's a thin gold chain around her neck, with a tiny H charm dangling right in the middle of her clavicle.

'Lewis is already inside,' she says, beaming.

'Are we late?' I say, giving her a half-hug.

It turns out it's just the four of us at the tasting. Following behind Hattie, me and Tom exchange perplexed glances. At least we're in it together.

'Mara!' Lewis calls. 'And Tom! Amazing!'

He's in a crisp white shirt, and actually looks well. If I'm being generous, he looks handsome. Happy. That's what it is. He looks really fucking happy.

Tom falters, does something wince-adjacent, then says, 'We've come hungry!'

Lewis does some loud laughing, and even bends at the waist to slap his knee. Hattie is audibly smiling, doing a sort of *hmm* sound through a grin.

'Well good news, pal, because there is bloody *loads* of cake to taste through here,' Lewis says.

We sit in a neat little dove-grey banquette, and ceramic plates are brought out to us one by one. Hattie and Lewis hand us a voting card to keep a log of each offering. The categories are: *appearance, texture, taste, moistness, crowd-pleasing-potential.* To start, there is the classic fruitcake. This is followed by double chocolate fudge. Vanilla cream. Peanut butter and raspberry jam. Lime and ginger. Apple, cinnamon and raisin. Burnt butter. One made up of lots of tiny profiteroles. Pineapple upside-down cake. Banana and coconut. Red velvet. Carrot and pumpkin. Lavender and Earl Grey. Coffee and walnut. Matcha with green tea buttercream.

I start to feel sugar-drunk and quite mad. I look around at the others, who are all out of it too, moving slightly more slowly than usual. I catch Hattie's eye and we share a brief moment of camaraderie, scrunching our faces up at each other. I see that she's genuinely open to me, wants us to enjoy this activity together. There's nothing sinister behind any of it. It's exactly what it promised to be: a cake tasting among friends. I can completely see the appeal of a nice, straightforward girl like her. She's content here in this backroom of a bakery. She has no visible desire to be anywhere else, nothing is making her feel out of place, she has the right person by her side. She's good. I look to Lewis. He's licking his front teeth, gathering up some lost crumb, his upper lip bulging out. His left thumb is idly stroking the inside of his ring finger, where quite soon there will be a gold band. I realise that this is a nervous tic that he's had for some time, maybe even since our school days. I glance towards Tom. He has one fist in his trouser pocket and the other is rubbing at his eye socket. So far, he's given almost all the cakes a seven out of ten in all the categories.

I break our sleepy silence. 'Any clear frontrunners?'

'What do you think?' Hattie says.

Tom starts to speak, and I nudge him. 'Wait. We don't want to influence them yet,' I say.

Lewis looks at Hattie and says, 'I know which ones you're going to say.'

'I might surprise you!' she says.

He smirks, proud of his insider knowledge.

'Go on, then,' she says, tilting her head to one side. 'Let's hear it.'

'Okay,' Lewis says. 'Write your top three down, so everyone knows I haven't cheated.'

Hattie obliges, scribbling away on the back of a paper napkin, shielding it with her spare hand.

'Ready?' Lewis asks. 'So, in third place, you're going to have the lavender.'

Hattie giggles.

'Second place is lime and ginger.'

Hattie does a little squeak.

'And in first place, you'll admit your real favourite, even though you know it's a bit predictable, and you'll have written – drum roll, please – red velvet!'

Hattie hides her face in the crook of her arm. 'Aah,' she says. 'I'm so basic.'

'Hey,' I say. 'We like what we like. Lewis, what are your top three?'

'It doesn't matter,' he says. 'We already have our winner.'

The couple hold onto each other and rock a little.

I think Tom's top three would be the carrot, the vanilla sponge, and the coffee and walnut, but I don't ask him to confirm this.

126

There is a tiny hole in the sleeve of my wool winter coat. I run my hand over the rest of the fabric and find a cluster of five or six other jagged holes near the hem. I hang it back up and close the wardrobe door.

127

On weekdays, Tom and I establish a routine. It happens naturally. We don't explicitly lay down any rules, but the consistency of it is of great comfort to me. We have a short texting conversation first thing in the morning, while we're still in bed, him on his Birmingham mattress, me on my Hackney one. We exchange a few texts at lunch, a few when we finish work, and then, the best bit of my day, our nightly phone call. Unofficially, the phone will ring at nine thirty, but it can be at nine or ten too. Every couple of days we do a FaceTime. And every other Friday one of us gets on a train headed towards the other.

128

At Noor's mum's, one Monday, Luther runs out to get a chippy for the four of us. Noor's mum is in a really level, cheerful mood, and sets the table with her wedding crockery, humming along to Stevie Wonder. Noor combs her fingers through the front of my hair, raking it into a slicked-back, wet-look sort of arrangement.

'Get off,' I say.

'You should cut your hair short,' Noor says.

'What short?' I say, yanking my head away from her hands. 'Worry about your own hair.'

'Yes,' Noor's mum says. 'Busybody.' She brings over a pack of cheese straws for us, and winks.

'How's it going at work?' Noor asks me, letting a strand of my hair slip in between her fingers.

I sigh. 'Just avoiding him really. Biding my time.'

'Still keeping your eye open for something else?'

'God yeah. The thing is, if it wasn't for him, I'd probably be pretty happy there.'

'There's a position going in the electricals department at work?'

I raise an eyebrow.

'What? It's all product, isn't it? Books, washing machines, it's interchangeable.'

'Are you taking the piss?'

Noor laughs. 'I'm actually not. The pay's alright, you know.'

'You've changed your tune.'

'She got her fifteen percent!' Noor's mum calls.

'Wait, what? Why am I only just hearing about this?'

Noor shrugs. 'I was being diplomatic. It's not nice to brag about your job when someone else is having a shit time at theirs.'

'Well aren't you thoughtful?' I flare my nostrils. 'Seriously, though, that's great. Well done.'

The front door bangs shut.

'They had no saveloys, Mara,' Luther says as he pushes his way into the kitchen, arms laden down with paper packages. He looks genuinely worried about passing on this news. 'So I got you a jumbo sausage instead. Is that okay? Noor's told me how important it is for you that it be an actual saveloy.'

I laugh as I get up to help him with the food. 'Jumbo is fine,' I say. 'Everything tastes the same if you put enough salt on it.'

Noor's mum shakes her head as she unfolds one of the large parcels. 'Such big portions,' she says. 'Terrible.'

Now that Noor's abandoned my hair, she fusses around Luther, wrapping her arms around his waist, pushing her hands into his pockets. 'She says that,' she whispers into Luther's back, 'but just watch her finish her portion and everyone else's too.'

I catch Noor's mum smiling to herself.

Something shifts very slightly in my stomach. Mixed in with my hunger, there's a longing.

129

I've recently discovered *People Just Do Nothing* and can't get enough of it. Back in my flat, I settle down on the sofa, huge mug of mint tea on the coffee table in front of me, and happily rub my bloated stomach as I watch episode after episode. I've just started series two when I hear a shout. I look around me. Everything is in its place.

'Always the fucking same!'

I pause my show, and crane my neck, trying to make out the words. It sounds like Adele. I don't think I've ever heard her raise her voice before.

'No. Shut – just shut—!'

I grimace into my flat, then tiptoe out to my hallway in order to hear better.

'How do you think I feel!'

I can't hear Baz. It's as though Adele's arguing with herself. I assume he's answering her more quietly, and I'm relieved about that, at least. She shouldn't be getting stressed like this with a little life in her belly.

'And what if – the other way round?'

This is just as loud, but more shrill somehow.

'What then? Tell me. Put the shoe on the other fucking—!'

I hear a door slam above my head. My own bedroom door rocks in its cradle with the force from upstairs.

I feel as though I should act in some way. But how? I start to draft a text.

All okay? Delete that.

I wasn't eavesdropping but . . . But of course I was eavesdropping. *Heard a bit of shouting. Can I do anything?* That's not right either. *Do you want to pop down here for a bit?* Nope.

I click off the messaging app and go back into the front room. I'll wait ten more minutes, and if I hear anything else, I'll send a message. I press play on my show, but the end credits roll before I realise that I'm still staring at the ceiling.

PART VI

Spring

130

Derek sends out an all-staff email with the subject heading: *Getting to know each other!*

I feel as though Derek already knows me too well, so I avoid opening the email all morning, until my curiosity gets too much, and I click on it just before lunch. A pop-up appears on my screen.

The sender requested a read receipt be sent when this message is read. Do you want to send a receipt?

I click on the *Don't ask me about sending receipts again*. And then I click on *No*. This idiot thinks he owns us. He doesn't own me.

Hi guys!
Just a quick one. Of late, I've noticed some glum faces around our beloved library – patrons and staff alike! The world can be a dark place, and Homerton is no exception. That's why I thought we should make a real effort to remember why we choose to be librarians and what it's really all about. Friday evening at 6pm, we have a very special guest coming in to get us all talking and hopefully free up our chakras a bit. If it's not your usual working day, please do make an effort to be here regardless. Though it's bound to be a brill event, we'll have to class it as compulsory training ;)
Your boss and friend,
Derek

131

Now that the weather has turned for the better, I take meandering, convoluted routes home from work most days. There's less rush to get inside. I walk along the canal, wander into Hackney Marshes. On nights when I have no plans to see Noor, I eat little picky dinners in the park: pre-packaged sushi, a baguette stuffed with cured meats, little pots of fresh fruit.

On this particular evening, I feel really hungry. I walk to the Chesham Arms. It's usually packed, but I get there early enough to grab a wooden table in the beer garden, and I order a Yard Sale pizza from my phone. I have a book in my bag, which I take out and place in front of me – the second in Ferrante's Neapolitan Quartet – but I don't feel like reading. I watch as people arrive with their friends and their partners and their dogs. I can't remember if I've brought Tom here before. It's not really his type of pub. On the table next to mine, a man five to ten years older than me – I can never accurately tell a man's age; they all look roughly the same to me once they're no longer young and not yet elderly – is unhurriedly filling in a crossword. He has interesting trainers on, fuchsia suede Adidas of some description. In front of him is a glass of white wine. Every now and then, he lifts his face to the sky, with his eyes closed, letting the sun stroke his eyelids. I have a glass of white wine too, which I'm sipping slowly.

Though he's not obviously attractive, I picture an alternative evening where we get chatting. After a few awkward, timid glances, he'd ask me about my novel. He'd assure me that he wasn't trying to chat me up, it was just that he'd seen this author's name everywhere lately and would love to hear what all the fuss was about. Brave, now that the ice was broken, I'd tell him that I liked his trainers. He'd invite me to help him with his crossword clues, and I'd lean over to point at the empty squares, until we'd laugh and suggest sharing a table, freeing up the spare one for anyone else who may need it. Once our glasses were empty, we'd order a bottle, deciding together that it made more financial sense. My pizza would arrive and we'd share that too. He might mention that he worked in publishing – although maybe it would have to be a different industry, considering that he'd never read any Elena Ferrante. He might coax out from me the fact that I'm ready to move on in my career, and suggest a few roles going at his firm. He'd scribble his phone number on the back of a grease-soaked napkin, then scrunch it up, laughing, and ask me to hand him my phone instead – after all, I'd only lose the napkin, and it's not a Nora Ephron film!

I watch, in real time, as he misses his mouth with his glass and dribbles wine down his chin. I listen, in real time, as he says, 'Oh, crumbs.' And, I see, in real time, when he stands to go and search for a napkin, that on the boxers which poke out of the waist-band of his jeans there are cartoon hot dogs dancing all over the fabric.

I tip my own head back and smile into the sun.

On my other side, an adult woman with pigtails is chattering excitedly to another adult woman with braces. I tune into their conversation.

'So maybe we get really rich in a short span of time, and we make clones of ourselves. Baby clones. And we raise them and teach them the ways of the world, and then when we're close to death we upload our consciousness into the clones, and we go on living forever like that? What do you think? Pretty good idea, no?'

'And do we have real children too, or just take care of our clones?'

'I think the clones will be plenty. You'd never lose your patience with them or find them annoying, because it's basically just you.'

'What, and you never find yourself annoying?'

'Well. It'd be a kid version of me, so I'd be able to make more allowances.'

A voice shouts, 'Mara! Mara!'

I jump up, looking this way and that.

'Pizza for Mara!'

I cross the garden, and make my way to the bottom of the wooden steps to collect the outstretched pizza box from the waitress's hand.

'Marg for Mara,' the waitress says, pleased with her little joke.

'Yes, but it's got nduja on it,' I say. 'Right?'

Her face falls.

'Marg for Mara!' I say, but the waitress has already turned away.

132

Back at the flat, I lie face up on my bed. The sun is still shining resolutely, warming the sheets. The light at this time of day is my favourite. I text Tom.

Do you ever get the impression that everyone around you finds being alive so much easier than you do?

I've pressed send before I realise that the tone is all wrong. It's meant to be playful. I call him.

'Hey,' he says. He sounds breathless.

'I just sent you a weird text,' I say. 'I thought I'd try to get in there before you read it to reassure you that I'm not suicidal.'

Tom does me the courtesy of laughing. 'What's up, babe?' he says.

'Just had a little solo al fresco pizza party. Did some good people watching. It's really nice now the nights are longer that we suddenly have all this free time after work again.' A very basic observation for me to make, but I'm sure Tom'll allow it. 'Isn't it? What about you? Why are you huffing and puffing?'

'In the gym,' he says. 'Treadmill.'

'Want me to call you back later? Usual time?'

'No, no, it's fine,' he pants.

'Sure?'

'Yeah, yeah,' he says. 'Going the pub with the lads later, so.'

'Bet you look cute in your little gym outfit,' I say, curling up to better fit in the sun patch.

Tom does another wheezy laugh.

'Are your knees out?' I ask.

'Big time.'

'Stop, you're making me all hot and bothered.'

'Won't stop. Like it.'

'Want me to tell you the status of my knees?' I ask.

'Yes.'

'Very much out,' I say. 'It's no-tights weather, and this is me until September now.'

'Hot,' Tom says.

I can hear the sound of his feet banging against the treadmill. It seems to be getting faster.

'So you've got a big night planned, then?'

'Medium.'

'Is it just the lads, or?'

'Some of the,' slap, slap, slap, 'girlfriends too.'

'Oh, nice.' I stand and pad across to the window. I look down into Jerry's garden. 'Jerry never seems to set foot in that huge garden, you know. It's such a waste.'

'Ask,' bang, bang, bang, 'whether you can,' bang, bang, bang, 'use it this summer.'

'Fuck off,' I say. 'As if.'

'Why not?'

'You can only access it via Jerry's back door. What am I going to do, go down there in my bikini and say, *Hiya Jerry, just popping out back, would you mind letting me through?*'

'Mmm,' Tom says, through laboured breaths. 'Bikini.'

'Alright, this is silly. Get back to what you're doing and I'll chat to you properly tomorrow.'

'Yes,' he says. 'Love you.'

'Love you. Have fun with your friends.'

133

I'm happy when I hear the bedsprings going above my head. Though I'd quite like to be having sex myself, I'm glad that Adele and Baz are back at it. There's not been much in the way of creaking headboards over the last few months.

It goes on for a long time. Just when I think it's over, the noises start back up again. It's frantic and fast, and I wonder how it feels to be energetically penetrated when you're heavily pregnant. I think that if it were me, I'd want it to be gentler, more deliberate. But maybe that's old-fashioned. Maybe Adele needs exactly this. Fully awake, I reach for my bedside water and down it. I push my legs up and out of the covers, and over the side of the bed. Taking my phone out from its hiding spot under my Ferrante, I see that it's 02:06.

There's a text from Tom: *You are the very best!* Sent at 01:15.

It seems that everyone but me still knows how to make the most of their nights. In the dark, I make my way to the bathroom, sit down on the loo, and pee. A decidedly steady stream. I'm surprised that my bladder didn't wake me up before now. I don't flush and I don't wash my hands. I'm reminded of Derek, and a punch of dread hits me in the chest at the thought of the team building that awaits me later today. I'm due to go to Birmingham after work, and all this chakra nonsense is bound to hold up my departure by hours.

On my way back to bed, something tiny flutters in front of my face, almost touching my nose. I flick the hallway light switch and see the jittery beige body of a moth in flight. I watch as she hops from the corner of a picture frame to the empty white wall. Biding my time, I allow her a few more wing flutters, my palm already spread. She becomes still. I smash my open hand against her body, flattening her against the wall. It's satisfying to see the papery dust of her, the confirmation that she's gone. I flick her onto the floor with the index finger of my other hand, and blow the remnants into the air. Back in my bedroom, the window panes are still rattling with the sounds of other people's pleasure. I get into bed and smoosh my pillow over my ears.

134

Derek is overexcited all day. He's wearing a 'fun' shirt with a little surfboard on the chest pocket, and he hums as he replaces books on the shelves. I've also made the effort to look nice today, but I make a point of looking out the window a lot and smiling, so that it's very clear to everyone that it's not for Derek or the library's benefit, but for my real life, my life outside this building. I'm in a lilac silk shirt dress that I know Tom likes, and have on some gold sandals that I unearthed from a box stored inside my window seat storage. My shift drags. After lunch, a familiar face returns.

'Well hello, trouble!' I hear Derek say, and I know immediately who he's speaking to.

I look at the calendar on my desk. It's been so long since I banned Starey Man from the library that I assumed he'd found another spot in which to spend his time, another woman to bother. I sense him looking for me, feel his eyes roaming around the space.

'The library missed you!' Derek says, throwing his arms wide for his prodigal son.

'Did all of you miss me?' Starey Man says. 'Even her?'

'I can't speak for her,' Derek says. 'Wouldn't dare. You'll have to ask her yourself.'

Both men laugh and laugh. I suddenly wish I wasn't wearing my nice silk dress and flashy shoes after all, wish instead that I was tucked up safely in my roll-neck and wool trousers.

Do not come over here, I will him. *Not today. Please just stay there with your little mate.*

I look up and he's right in front of me, grinning.

I speak before he's able to. 'I assume we'll be having no trouble from you from now on?'

Starey Man sniggers. 'That depends.'

'No,' I say, before he can say anything about me being a naughty girl, or a good girl, or deserving anything, or having to be punished.

'It does not. There is an established contract between this library and its patrons. An unspoken agreement, if you will. When you use this space, you have to respect the rules. And that includes not smearing sandwich fillings on our books, and it certainly includes not harassing the staff.'

Starey Man is still smiling his horrible smile, flashing every tooth in his head at me. 'Strict,' he says. 'Lovely.'

'Have you seen our new Ian Rankins?' Derek calls in a loud whisper.

I know that this time he's not doing it to help me out of a bind. He's doing it simply because he wants to show Starey Man the new Ian Rankins.

Later, when I'm forced to circle around the two of them to replace some books on the crime shelves, I hear Derek say, 'You should come tonight, mate. Seriously. I've already asked a few of our regulars, but I didn't know if you'd be back. You know, after the misunderstanding.'

This is above and beyond, and I snap my head round to glare at Derek. He does his utmost to not make eye contact.

135

Our team building activity is a sound bath. After closing, Derek makes us move all the furniture to the sides of the library, and then closes the blinds, even before the woman arrives with her collection of bowls. There are eye masks, and Derek takes great pride in handing them out, a knowing expression on his face.

'So guys. Guys! Some quiet, please!' Derek calls. 'We're a library, we should know how!'

A hush falls over the space. There are around twelve of us, a mixture of staff and patrons coerced to stay after hours.

'Ximena will be here any second,' he says, pronouncing the X.

I can hear Starey Man murmuring his approval from the far corner.

'I want you to engage with this properly. Be present, be open, be vulnerable. You'll get out of this what you put into it. Yeah?'

There are some mild sounds of engagement.

'I *said* . . .' Derek says, louder now. 'Yeah?'

'Yeah,' we all say.

I'm next to an elderly woman who often comes into the library to use our loo and freshen up. I think she's called Deidre or Deidra. She looks a little confused. She has a Philippa Gregory under her arm and is clutching onto it as though for support.

I nudge her gently with the crook of my arm, and say, 'Bit nervous for all this, myself.'

'What is it?' she says. 'What's this for?' She's holding up an eye mask with her free hand. 'I don't like putting things on my face.'

'Don't worry,' I say. 'You don't have to do anything you don't want to do.' I'm not sure this is strictly true.

Ximena arrives, and she looks neutral. She's just a woman. In her early forties, I'd guess, in a white t-shirt, light jeans and some Reebok Classics. She has salt and pepper hair in a messy bun on top of her head. I try to nod at her, wanting to get her on side. Women together. She doesn't see me.

She nods at Derek instead, then nods at a lone chair left in the centre of the room. 'Can we move this, please? I need a completely free area.'

Derek says, 'Mara. Please.'

I oblige, dragging the chair clumsily across the carpet, then bashing it into place by the wall. 'There you go,' I say.

'Shoes off, everyone,' Ximena says, curtly. 'And take a seat on the floor.' She kicks her Reeboks off and sinks onto the ground.

I make my way back over to Deidre/Deidra. She has begun to sit but seems to be stuck halfway down.

'Can people use chairs if they need them?' I ask.

'It's best if you're closer to the earth,' Derek says. 'It's more grounding.'

'Derek,' I say.

'Well,' he says. 'Ximena? Could this lady potentially be excused from full floorwork?'

'Yes,' Ximena says. 'She absolutely can. We don't want any injuries. It's a gentle practice.'

I return the original chair back to its original spot in the middle of the room and lead Deidre/Deidra to it, helping her to take a seat. I take the Philippa Gregory from her, gently prising it from her hands.

'I'll keep this safe for you,' I say.

She looks unconvinced.

Derek is milling around the group, seemingly with the express intention of saying, 'Yes, well done, lovely,' to everyone who's managed to follow the first instruction and sit down on the floor. I see him pause next to Starey Man.

'Great posture, mate,' he says.

Ximena says, 'Derek, if you could take your own seat now, please.' She rolls her shoulders back, and says, 'I need to light a couple of candles. Is that allowed?'

A cowed Derek says, 'Mmm, not too sure about that, X. Quite a flammable environment as you might imagine. I can turn on the light in the hallway and pop the door ajar? That would mean standing back up, though, of course.'

'It's okay,' Ximena says. 'We'll make do.'

I wonder how much we're paying her to be here. Not much, I imagine.

'So, if you'll allow it, Derek, I'm going to do a sonic smudging of the library, in preparation.'

Derek, from his cross-legged spot on the floor, widens his eyes. 'You do you.'

With that, Ximena drifts around the space, sporadically hitting one of the medium-sized bowls with a little mallet. It's a relaxing sound, which fills my chest with a sort of gushy, liquid sensation. I stop looking at Derek, and focus on Ximena's gentle progress. I lose track of time as I watch.

Eventually, she stops.

'Now,' she says. 'This is the most important part of the practice. I want you all to *set your intentions*. Unfortunately, I don't have quite enough bowls for you to have one each, or usually I'd have you set your intention directly to a bowl, in order to connect. Instead, you'll have to do your very best to connect with yourself. Your intention could be a big one: love or peace or wellness. Or you could opt for something very specific, like, *Give me the strength to leave my cheating partner.*'

I'm jolted from my reverie. People around me are softly nodding, lapping it up.

'Maybe close your eyes for this. I'll give you a minute or two. There's no need to use the eye masks if you don't want to. They're entirely optional.'

I am very aware of the rough carpet on my bare legs. It's not the cleanest. I can hear Deidre/Deidra's deep breathing, her inhale catching and turning into a sniff, every other breath.

What should my intention be? It could be plenty of things. *Let me be braver than I am. Let me take control of my own life. Give me the clarity to work out what should come next.* And more specific than that? *Give me the energy to stand up to Derek. Let me talk more openly with Tom so that we can start making real plans together. Unblock me from this difficulty I have with speaking to my mum about my dad.* Jesus, where did that come from?

'Okay, that's wonderful. We can begin in earnest,' Ximena says.

Nothing about Ximena seems neutral anymore. The feeling in my chest is down to the tone of this woman's voice, her way of moving, and the manner in which nothing seems like a rush to her. I am unmoored. I wait for the next part.

'Hold your intention in your heart and in your mind. Stay concentrated and present. Breathe deeply at all times throughout the next hour. That's crucial. I will approach some of you if I feel as though you could benefit from it, but I will never touch you. I will start off with just the bowls, and as we move through the practice, you will notice that I'll add my voice to the sounds. If the feeling takes you, you are more than welcome to join in and make some noise yourselves. So, I will begin now.'

I let the sounds wash over me, like music. The closest experience I've had to this is listening to the rainforest white noise video on YouTube, but now that's lost any positive power it ever had, through its close association with blocking Jerry's radio out. Rather than repeating my intention, I let images and memories of my dad flit in and out of my head. A seaside scene, him picking pieces of swede out of a Cornish pasty for me. Watching *Top of the Pops* together, singing along to Shania Twain. He and my mum kissing on the mouth, always on the mouth, and me always saying *Urgh* but being happy that they were such good friends. Him shouting at a boy who'd kicked my sandcastle down and me being so proud, feeling so untouchable. Practising for a magic show we were going to put on for my twelfth birthday, my last one with him, doing the same trick over and over until we'd got it just right for my friends. Him in bed, sick. No, not that. Not that. The scent of his t-shirts when he hugged me. The hours and hours spent playing *The Sims* together on the PC. The hundreds of houses we built together. Each room carefully decked out. Every piece of furniture just right. He never let me cheat, never let me use the codes that got you free Simoleons, the Sims currency.

I don't notice that I'm humming, louder and louder, until I feel Deidre/Deidra's foot in my back.

'Shhh,' she mutters. 'I can't hear myself think.'

I open my eyes, shake my head. My cheeks are wet. Starey Man's eyes are on me, and I have no idea how long he's been watching. He nods his head and puckers his lips, blowing me a kiss.

136

Afterwards, I call my mum, and we cry and cry and cry.

137

It's difficult to try to explain to Tom what happened to me in the library, when I'm not even sure I know myself.

On the phone, I say, 'It wasn't faddy. I know it sounds it, but trust me. It was profound. It was . . . elemental or something.'

He's huffing and puffing.

'Are you in the gym again?' I ask. I feel as though I want to protect the experience that I've had, don't want to sully it with any scepticism. I want Tom's full attention.

'No, no,' he says. 'Was on a run, but I've stopped now. That might be my lot. I'm just going to pop into the Asda.'

Not the bloody Asda. I want him focused.

'Shall I just call you later, from the train?' I say. 'After your shower and that?'

'No,' he says, quickly. 'I'm here. I'm all ears. Please. Tell me all about these gongs.'

'Babe. They weren't gongs.'

'Well, did Derek take part? Was he alright?'

'No worse than usual. I think when he saw me crying, he felt like he was personally responsible. He kept insisting that we all go to the pub to *keep exploring.*'

'Prick.' Tom coughs. 'You didn't want to go . . .?'

'Of course not. I'm coming to you. I think he managed to convince Ximena, though. I maybe should have gone just to speak to her a bit more. She was so great.'

'She sounds like an interesting woman.'

'Would you be up for doing something like that?' I say, expecting an easy yes.

'Mmm,' he says. 'Don't know. Maybe not.'

'What, why?' I'm personally affronted somehow. After everything I've just shared, why would he not want to do it too? I'm the perfect advertisement for the practice.

'I've got nothing against anything that makes someone feel good, but essentially it is just bullshit, isn't it?'

I don't say anything.

'Mara? I don't mean that what came up for you was bullshit. Obviously. That's beautiful and special. But you did that. It wasn't this shaman or the group or the dark room or the gongs.'

I'm angry that he keeps saying the word *gongs*.

'It was all you,' he continues. 'You could have had that same experience by just looking out the window at a pretty sunset, or by reading a book that reminds you of your own situation, or by going to your dad's grave. You know? That's all I'm saying.'

I'm really bristling now. He knows how I feel about cemeteries and he knows how little I get from going to my dad's grave. I get less than nothing. He's so fucking full of it. A few months of exercise and clean living and he thinks he knows it all.

'Tom,' I say. 'You're actually doing my head in. You're being very rude.'

'What—?' he starts to say.

'You go and do your little shop, and I'll speak to you another time. It probably doesn't make sense for me to come tonight now, either. It's late.'

'Mara.'

'No. You've pissed me off. I don't want you to take the magic out of this for me.'

I hang up. Angry as I am, I'm relieved that I finally feel free to speak to him without the filter of a mollycoddle. We can argue and it's fine. Nothing will implode, nothing has to change, and everyone will be fine in the morning.

138

'Mara?' my mum says, over the phone. 'Do you think you might pop home soon?'

Though it's my rescheduled designated weekend with Tom, I say, 'What about Friday?'

'Oh.' She tries to keep something out of her voice. Is it relief? Excitement? I can't tell. 'If you can make that work, then yeah, that'd be really, really nice.'

'Course I can make it work.'

I feel bad after our call. I don't like the idea that she would sound *grateful* – and yes, now that I've dwelled on it a little bit, I can see that that's what the hidden emotion was, *gratefulness* – about me going home for a visit. I've lost track of the important things, I realise. I've been so focused on my new little family of me and Tom, that I've neglected my original family of me and my mum.

Tom's been sucking up since our tiff. He keeps sending me saccharine texts that say things like, *You're my world*, or, *I'm so lucky to have you*. That he's giving me these platitudes rather than actually apologising for his tactlessness makes me loath to reply. I text back, *xxx*, and, *You too*.

I only call to tell him I'm not coming to Birmingham on the Friday morning. I'm on my way to work, harried, and the conversation starts off on the wrong foot.

I say, 'So, about this weekend.'

'I can't wait,' Tom says, his tone overly keen, strained.

'I'm not actually coming.'

Tom doesn't say anything to that.

'Tom?'

He exhales. 'I said I was sorry?'

'Well, actually you didn't, but it's not because of that.' I dart between a Honda and a Volvo, crossing the road with at least two blind spots. 'Fuck,' I say, having to sprint the last metre.

He doesn't wait to hear what the actual reason is. 'But I booked in for that new Indian for us,' he says.

'I need to spend some time with my mum.'

There's nothing he can say to that – my trump card – so he doesn't.

'Okay?' I say. 'I'll come next weekend instead?'

'It's not obligatory.'

'So if you can't see me this weekend, then you don't want to see me at all?'

'Did I say that?'

'Tom. Seeing each other can be flexible. Something's come up. I can't come when I thought I could, so we have to reschedule. That's all that's happening here.'

I'm not sure if I believe what's coming out of my own mouth. It feels very much as though something else is happening.

He starts to speak. He says, 'Mara.' Stops. Starts again. 'You've cancelled twice now. We have a contract.'

'Excuse me?'

'I don't mean that – I mean, we have an unspoken agreement.'

'Right?'

'Doing long-distance, we have to stick to our weekends together, otherwise what *is* there?'

I'm right by the entrance to the library now, and am already a few minutes late for work. I don't have time for this argument, but I also really want to have it. I want to lash out.

'That's rich,' I say, spitting the two words out.

'Why? I've never missed a weekend.'

'What about the rest of the time, though? Our phone calls? You think you've always been fully engaged when we speak on the phone? You think you never rush me off? Never treat me as another task to tick off your to-do list?'

I hear him sigh.

'I actually want an answer to those questions,' I say.

'There's not always a lot to say, Mara.'

'I'm happy to hear any—'

'And sometimes it's like you're trying to trip me up.'

'What?'

'Like reading between the lines to see if I'm actually doing as well as I say I am.' He sounds shaky now.

'And why do you think I have to do that? It's because you don't fucking disclose anything to me.'

'Can you understand that I may not constantly want to dwell on my mental state? That I might not want to be reminded all the time that I'm only one bad night away from feeling suicidal again?'

My heart skips a beat. I wish he hadn't said that. I double back on myself, turn a sharp left, away from the squat shape of the library. He's never said that word to me before. I can hear him softly sobbing now, and I realise with horror that he may just be articulating it to himself for the first time. Now, at five past nine on a Friday morning.

He doesn't expand on what he's just said, just cries, wet and loud, into the phone. I don't know what it says about me that I have no energy to comfort him. The thought that keeps spinning round and round in my mind is, *How can I build a life with someone if I'm too scared to ever have a disagreement with him, in case it pushes him over the edge?* I feel as despondent as I ever have about our relationship. My phone signals that I have another call coming through. I pull it from my ear so that I can look at the screen. Derek. I remember Derek's threat. I remember that I'm meant to be on my best behaviour, be the perfect employee.

'I have to go, Tom,' I say. 'I'm late for work and Derek is calling me.'

Tom's still crying.

Maybe I should say that I'll come to see him after all. My mum would get it. But it's her turn. And I want to go home.

280

139

My mum picks me up from Rugby train station. She's waiting for me on the platform, and waves the whole time that the train is slowing to a halt. Maybe for a full thirty seconds. I'm sure she can't know which carriage I'm in. I'm so happy to see her, in her familiar dark jeans and a beige hoodie I've never seen before. She looks younger and older at the same time. I hop off the train and join her.

'Oh dear,' she says, taking my backpack off my shoulders and putting it onto her own. 'Are we going to talk about it, or would you rather not?'

I thought I was doing my best to appear cheerful, but my mother can't be fooled.

I shake my head, aggressively left to right. 'No, thank you. I actually really don't want to think about it at all for a couple of days.'

She gives me a light tap on the back of my neck in lieu of a hug. She probably knows that a hug would release something I don't want to release.

'Come on, then, little donkey.' She walks with purpose out of the station and into the car park.

I follow, meek. I swallow, trying to force the tension out of my throat. This weekend is not about Tom. I need a break and I need my mum. I try not to dwell on the fact that she clearly needs me too.

The car smells like Polo mints and Body Shop white musk. As my mum puts the car into gear, the radio comes on. It's that HAIM song that I'd decided would be the anthem for my new flat. 'Days Are Gone'. I don't think I've ever heard it on the radio before. My mum hums along, sort of in tune.

She drives fast and jerkily, as she always has, cheerfully calling out colourful insults to anyone she deems to be driving too slowly or carefully.

'Where'd you fucking learn to drive? The Go Kart range?'

'Wanker.' A classic. This to an elderly woman in a Fiat.

'That's it, you trollop,' she shouts at another car, a couple of minutes later. 'The indicator's just there for aesthetic reasons!'

At this one, I manage a laugh. 'Trollop? That's a throwback, even for you.'

My mum grins, turning the radio down with one hand and using the other to swerve into our drive. 'Sometimes only *trollop* will do the trick.'

I unbuckle my seatbelt.

'Hey,' she says, switching off the ignition. 'Can I just say one thing? I'll say it now, and then it can stay here in the car. We don't have to bring it into the house or into the weekend with us.'

I nod.

'It's not supposed to be this difficult.' She places her hand on top of mine, which is still hovering over the seatbelt buckle. 'I really want you to remember that. It isn't meant to be a battle or an uphill struggle or something that just hangs on by a thread. I say this with absolutely no judgement, and you know I love Tom, and only want good things for him. Of course, he's already got the best thing, having you by his side. But you could still be there for him in a different capacity, without jeopardising your own happiness. I hope you know that? You wouldn't be abandoning him or letting him down or anything like that.' She's not looking at me, instead looking directly through the windscreen at the house. My childhood home. Red-brick and very square, just like the kind of house children draw. There's even a little shrub in a pot right by the front door that could be depicted with a brown crayon and a green crayon.

'I—'

'No, I don't want you to speak. I just want you to think. I can say this next thing to you, because I am your mother. Tom is your first love. And you know what? I think that you simply don't have the imagination to picture anyone but him at this stage in your life.'

The pressure in my throat feels ready to pop.

'Do you know something else?'

I chew on the inside of my cheek, look out the passenger seat window. I say, 'What?'

'There's no such thing as *the love of your life.*'

'What about dad?' I say, in a small voice.

My mum makes a sort of clucking noise in the back of her throat. She takes a few beats before responding. 'Your dad was my favourite person I ever met – I'm not including you because I made you from scratch.' She cocks her head. 'I always felt so lucky to have met him, and so unlucky to have not had him for longer.'

I've only heard the story of how my parents met a handful of times, but it's a modern legend I've treasured and held close my whole life. Like me and Tom, they studied together at Birmingham University. They were friends for three years, went out with different people, never saw each other in a romantic light. A few months before final exams, my mum's mum – my grandma – got ill. My mum had to take the final term off to be at home with her. In solidarity, my dad applied to postpone his final term too, and was at my mum's beck and call whenever she needed to unwind. When my grandma died, my dad convinced my mum to go travelling with him, and in the South of France, they fell in love.

'Life isn't just one thing, Mara,' my mum says. 'There isn't just one possible outcome. Yes, in my life I have only ever loved one man. But if it hadn't been him, it might've been someone else. I could've had a beautiful life with a different man. I could've even had a different child. I'm so thankful that I had the husband and daughter that I did have, *but* if I'd gone down a different path, I wouldn't have known any different, and might still have been perfectly happy.'

I've been instructed not to speak, so I don't.

My mum says, 'We're going to go into the house now, and I'm going to uncork a nice bottle of red, and we're going to watch some trash. Okay, my heart?'

140

Me and my mum run into Lewis's mum in the big Tesco on Saturday afternoon. We have a basket filled with oven pizzas, cheap garlic bread, and a six-pack of Moretti.

'Girls!' Lewis's mum calls by the canned veg.

'Well, hello,' my mum says. 'If it isn't the mother of the groom!'

Lewis's mum beams, holding tightly onto a can of cannellini beans. 'Rach,' she says, conspiratorially. 'I didn't dare say this last time I ran into you, because I always put my foot in it, but Lewis has said he'd absolutely *love* it if you came along to the wedding. He did forget to ask you, I'm ashamed to admit, and he was just *mortified* when he realised. And then he felt too shy to send an invitation out after Mara had already had hers.'

I elbow my mum. 'Go on. You've got to come.'

'I'm worried it might make me feel ancient.'

'And how do you think it makes me feel?' Lewis's mum says. 'This is the third one of mine I'll see walking down the aisle.' She drops the can into her trolley, and I watch as it lands right on top of a loaf of sliced wholemeal bread.

'You'll already have an outfit ready, at least,' my mum says.

'Gosh, no. I'd never repeat a look. I'm going to go into Birmingham next weekend and get a new skirt suit. I'm thinking a nice, tasteful light blue. But it's not the done thing to wear a hat anymore. Don't know why. I always thought it was such a lovely touch. Might still do a fascinator. We'll see. Don't want to give it all away now. I'll be telling you about Hattie's dress in a minute, if I'm not careful.' She winks at me. 'No sleeves, but I won't say any more than that. And she's gone for cream rather than stark white.' She mimes zipping her lips closed. 'Fishtail. Oh gosh, what am I like? I'm just so excited.'

'She's a nice girl,' I say.

'Isn't she just gorgeous!' The colour has gone up in Lewis's mum's face.

'She's a nice girl,' I repeat.

'I'm just so, so happy they found each other. It's as though they're two parts of the same puzzle, and now they can slot together, just so.'

I nod, and my mum nods.

Lewis's mum throws her head back, eyes closed, apparently in the throes of pure ecstasy. 'My Lewis and his Hattie.'

Me and my mum exchange panicked looks.

'Are you okay?' my mum asks her.

Lewis's mum comes to. 'Gosh.' There's a tear in one of her eyes. 'And you, Mara?'

My heart takes a nosedive.

'Must be your turn soon?'

'Not quite.' I wave my left hand in the air, showing off the lack of rings.

'Won't be long.' She does another one of those winks.

'It's not the only thing in life though, is it?' my mum says, reaching nonchalantly for a can of baked beans and mini sausages.

'Ooh goodness, but it helps, doesn't it? To know they're settled.'

'They can be settled and be on their own.'

I want us to leave this exchange now.

'Thanks for asking mum along, anyway,' I say. 'It'll be nice to have her there.' I realise as I'm saying this, just how true it is.

141

I'm sent back to London with a multipack of dishcloths and a bottle of Glen's vodka. I am restless on the train, shifting around in my seat, unable to concentrate on my book or my Zodiac Killer podcast. I unlock and lock my phone. I go to the bathroom twice, once just to clutch onto the edges of the sink and stare in the mirror. Me and Tom haven't exchanged a single message all weekend. I have endless things I want to say to him, and at the same time, nothing.

Back in my seat, I watch as the couple sitting opposite me hold hands in various ways. They interlock fingers, first in one direction, then the other. The woman makes a fist around the man's thumb, twisting her fingers round and round it. They admire the way the two hands look together, hold them up to the light to better see them. They briefly let go, before touching the pads of their fingers together, one by one. I wish they were both dead.

142

I hear moaning as soon as I close the door to the flat behind me. This seems a cruelty too big to stomach. I open the door to the flat again, and slam it shut.

I'm here! I'm in! You're no longer alone in the world!

There is the repetitive creak of the floorboards where the bed is being pushed back and forwards with their exertion. I drop my bag onto the floor and go into the kitchen to make a cup of tea. I can still hear the creaking, even over the whistle of the kettle.

Tom calls. I send him to voicemail with one tap of my thumb.

I make a nettle tea and try to find a corner of the flat where I don't have to experience Baz and Adele's love for each other in quite such an involved fashion. The quietest spot is right by the living-room window, so I stand there, cradling my mug and squinting through the murky window at the passersby below. I'm yet to get around to finding a window cleaner. It's one of the house tasks I've put off for longest, as I know it'll involve asking Jerry for access to his back garden, and I'd really rather not have to ask any more men for any more favours.

Out in the world, there's a woman walking on the other side of the road. She appears to be in no rush at all. She has her phone by her ear and I can see that she's laughing. She has on a double denim outfit and some very shiny loafers – all items that I own versions of, but would never think to wear at the same time. She has shiny brown hair – I can see that even from here – and it's pulled back into a sleek ponytail. I wonder who she's talking to, if she's ever declined a call from the person she thought was her Big Love, whether she's ever had a weight on her chest which feels like choking.

The window in front of me rattles and rattles in its frame, blurring my view of the shiny-haired woman, and I ask myself whether Baz and Adele may have moved from the bed to the sofa.

I can hear one of them whining, an animal noise which shocks me with its vulnerability. The action is reaching its crescendo. A wail, and it's over.

There's no *thank you* this time.

143

I get a text from Sarah, Tom's sister. Her name on my screen startles me. I'm at work, counting down the minutes until my lunch break, and trying not to look at Starey Man, who is doing something weird with one of his socks. Though I have no desire to read it, I click the message open quickly, wanting the experience to be over.

I wouldn't usually get involved, but is everything okay?? her text says. *Tom's gone all introverted again and won't talk to any of us. Give me a call when you finish work?? (Sorry if this is overstepping!!)*

That he's acting weird at home as well as with me is a salve of sorts. I'm grateful when other people receive the brunt of Tom's depression. It makes me feel less alone, as though I can hand the baton over to someone else for a while. He's not badly behaved, I remind myself, he's depressed. But which parts are his personality, and which parts are the depression?

In a rush of adrenaline, I draft a message to Tom: *Can you talk to your sister, please? She's asking me questions I don't know the answers to.*

My stomach does a little flip when I see that the most recent text above mine in our exchange is one from him which says: *You are my ray of sunshine!*

Lately, he's been simultaneously doing a lot and not enough. I haven't felt relaxed in my relationship for, how long? Weeks? Months? Longer? I can't always breathe freely around him.

I send the text. The ticks double, then turn blue, almost imme-diately. He's online. I watch him type. Five words come through.

I'll speak to her tonight x

I wait for the rest, for more. Nothing comes. Next to his name, it says *online, online, online.*

Then it says, *last seen today at 11:18.*

For the rest of the day, whenever I check, it continues to say: *last seen today at 11:18.*

144

Instead of calling Tom or Sarah after work, I call Noor.

'How's your mum?' she says.

'Fine. How's yours?'

'She's good. And Tom?'

'Eh. How's Luther?'

'Do you want to just talk about ourselves for once?' Noor says.

'So much,' I say.

'So, look. I ordered this really well-reviewed at-home bleach kit. And I think we should both go blonde.'

'Noor.'

'I'm serious. Why not? It'll be a laugh. Now's the time. We'll never be this young again.'

I breathe out, releasing some of the tension that's been gathering all day. 'Okay,' I say. 'When?'

'Want to come over now? My mum's popped out with a friend for a bit of dinner.'

'Has she! That's so great. Which friend is it?'

'Mara, we literally just said ten seconds ago that we're not talking about mums or boyfriends.'

'Right. So I'll come now, then?'

'Yep.'

145

The bleaching kit doesn't look particularly fancy or professional. On the front of the box, there's a picture of a woman with a pure-white bob, head thrown back in glee.

'Where'd you get this?' I ask, my head over the side of Noor's bathtub. 'And why am I the one who has to go first?'

The whole way over, all I could think about was the woman with the shiny brown ponytail who I watched through my window. I've never dyed my hair before, never really seen it as an option available to me. Strange the things we willingly exclude ourselves from in life. There's nothing actually stopping me from having peroxide blonde hair, or wearing double denim, or working somewhere that isn't Homerton Library, or choosing not to indulge my boyfriend's every need and whim. Now, with my head jammed against the porcelain of the bath, I think about who might dye Jerry's hair for him. I can only assume, based on the amateurish finish, that he does it himself. To think that he might periodically rinse raven-black Just For Men through his hair in exactly the same way as Noor is applying the bleach to my hair now, makes me laugh. I start laughing and can't stop.

'What is it?' Noor says. 'Stop moving.'

'It's just that Jerry . . .' I manage, before erupting into fresh peals of laughter. 'Jerry has . . .' More laughing still. I slip and bang my nose against the hot tap. I wonder if this is bonafide hysteria.

'You're bleeding.' Noor pulls me up by the shoulders. 'For fucksake.'

I stem the flow of blood from my nose with the back of my wrist, and am still laughing.

Noor's eyes are wide open and she's shaking her head, but there's a smile on her face.

'Honestly,' she says. 'You didn't used to be this unhinged.'

She stands up and starts opening cupboards, looking for something to stop the bleeding. Brandishing a packet of cotton wool, she tears a strip from it, hands it to me.

I ball it up and stick it up my nose, leaning back against the bath, steadying my breathing now that I only have one free nostril.

'You actually okay?' Noor says.

I lift my shoulders up and down, suddenly quite calm.

'That job's still going at my department store?' Noor says, joining me on the floor.

'Do you think I have a lack of imagination?'

Noor does me the courtesy of visibly considering this. Still, a bit too quickly, she says, 'Maybe.'

'I like routine, though. I like knowing what's what. I like knowing where I am. That's okay, isn't it?'

'Of course it is. But you do need to leave room for the variables to come in too. That's where the really fun stuff happens.'

'I find it scary.'

'I know you do.' Noor places her hand on top of mine, lightly. She doesn't squeeze, doesn't hold. 'We're only twenty-six, babe.'

She lets this statement sit there. We sit there. It's nice. I feel like everything is probably going to be fine. I have a feeling that I'll look back at this moment in the future, that I'll remember it fondly. The evening me and Noor turned blonde and turned a corner.

'Shit,' Noor says.

'What?'

'I forgot to put a timer on. How long has that shit been on your head?' She's scrambling up, grabbing for the bleach box, scanning the tiny writing on the back. 'Oh, fuck. It says fifteen minutes for fine hair. We've been bleeding and having heart-to-hearts for ages. Quick. Put your head in there. Hurry up.'

I follow her instructions. I know I should feel some degree of panic, but I don't. It's only hair.

146

I can't stop crying about my hair. Once dry, there is not one single angle from which it looks okay. We flip it this way and that, change the parting, scrape it up, plait it, curl it. I look like a giraffe. There are orange spots and yellow patches all over my scalp. Even with eyes half-closed and a generous spirit, nobody could describe any section of my hair as blonde. Noor won't stop laughing.

'Please,' I say, the cotton ball still up my nose, tears streaming. 'Do something.'

'I'm not a professional,' Noor says. 'For this, we need professionals.'

'You're meant to be my friend!'

The door slams shut downstairs.

'Hellooo,' Noor's mum calls.

'Oh god,' I say. 'More witnesses.'

I dread to think what it looks like to Noor's mum when she first enters the bathroom. I'm on the floor with leopard print hair, Noor's on the closed toilet lid, clutching her sides, there's blood all over the towels and the bathmat, and the smell of ammonia is entirely overpowering. The smile Noor's mum had when she first rounded the corner drops from her face.

'Are you doing a ritual?' she says. She is hesitant, waiting for us to explain.

'We were just trying to be young,' I say, through a hiccuping sob.

147

It ends up costing me £245 to sort my hair out. Francesco, the hairdresser who has been assigned to 'colour correct' me, won't stop saying, 'Who *did* this to you?'

'My friend, Noor. She said she knew what she was doing.'

'And this person,' he says, picking up a section of hair and sniffing it, 'you are sure she does not wish you any harm?'

I shake my head in between his two hands.

'There is a real reason we train for months and months, just making the cups of tea and doing the washing of the hair, before we are allowed anywhere near the dye,' he says. 'We are going to get rid of quite a lot of length. That's okay?'

'Do whatever you want,' I say. 'I really don't care.'

I've never spent a whole afternoon in a salon. I give myself over to the experience, chatting to Francesco about my weekend plans and my holiday plans and the weather and my split ends, as the dye develops on my head.

As the hours tick by, talk turns more serious.

'You're obviously not a London native?' I say, referring to his Italian accent.

'*Ohi madonna mia*,' he says. 'And I thought I was so convincing.' There's laughter in his voice, he has a friendly face. 'No. I'm from Calabria. This tiny little town in the mountains.'

'A big culture shock when you first came here, then?'

'I tell you something. The real culture shock is whenever I go back.'

'Yeah?'

'My nonna, she is always saying, *Francé, quando te ne torni?* When you are coming back? And I say to her, when you find me a nice job there and a nice man.'

'She misses you.'

'And I miss her. Of course. I miss plenty things. The weather, to start.' He nudges his chin towards the glass front of the salon, indicating the downpour outside. 'This shit is enough to make anyone feel depressed. Honestly. But all together, I have a better life here. My family, they have come to terms with me being gay, but it's still a little bit a secret in the town. Me? I don't care. Of course. My parents, too, eventually, they accept. But they get worried about what people will think. The neighbours. The older generation. Here? I am just another gay man. No big deal.' He lifts a piece of foil from my roots, examines the hair underneath. 'And there is always, always something to do here. In my town back home, we have the big saints' day every summer, and this is it. That's the end.'

I notice that he still describes it as *home*, though.

'How often do you manage to get back there?' I ask, taking a sip of the now tepid cup of jasmine tea he gave me when I first sat down.

In the mirror, I watch him thinking.

'At Christmas, I never miss a trip. Nowhere else is the same. And I like to spend a week with some actual sun in the summer, but this year, maybe not.'

I notice the glint in his eye. 'Someone keeping you here?' I ask.

'There's a man,' he says. 'It's very casual, but maybe we will go to Croatia in August. I haven't told my nonna yet. She will cry and make me feel bad, and it's not sure anyway.' He is applying bleach at the roots now, where it takes the least amount of time to develop. 'And you? You have someone?'

I run my tongue back and forth over my front teeth. 'I do.'

'And?'

'We're not in a great place right now,' I say.

Francesco tuts.

'He suffers with his mental health.'

Francesco's eyes widen, and he lifts both his eyebrows, in solidarity.

'We're doing long-distance.'

'*Ohimè*, what a combination.'

'A lot of stuff seems to be getting lost in translation at the moment.'

'That is when you need to just go to bed together. It's the universal language.'

'I think we do that too much, rather than tackling the root of the problem.' I chew the inside of my cheek. 'He doesn't talk to me anymore.' As this comes out of my mouth, it dawns on me that this is the most painful part of the whole ordeal for me. We used to talk for hours. We would untangle things together, approach issues from every possible angle. We were open with each other, nothing was off limits. I'm having more of an open conversation with Francesco than I've had with Tom in months.

148

I decide to have a clear out. I start with my underwear drawer. It's overflowing with mismatched socks and too-tight thongs and fussy bras that I'll never get around to wearing again. I scoop up the contents in my arms and throw everything onto the bed. In the mix, there are a few pairs of Tom's boxers. Not his nicest pairs, more like emergency spares. There's a novelty maroon pair from Freshers Week that have the name of his student halls printed on the waistband in block capitals. They're well-loved and fraying, and are so synonymous with Tom that I no longer even think of them as a joke. They're just his pants. I fold them up tenderly and place them straight back into the drawer. I do the same with all his other pairs. I count six. So if he came to stay and forgot to bring any underwear, he'd only have enough to last him just under a week. The thought makes me sad. There was a time that every item of clothing Tom owned lived right here, nestled in among my own clothes.

I pair together the larger socks, also Tom's. There are only five pairs of these. I push them into the drawer, next to the boxers. Next, I identify the g-strings, the t-strings and all the laciest briefs, some in fluorescent colours, shades of neon pink and orange and purple. I transfer them directly to the bin in the kitchen. I barely remember buying these items, and I can't imagine a time where I'd willingly choose any of them over a pair of cotton briefs. Back in the bedroom, I discard a green satin teddy and a huge pair of beige high-waisted pants, bought years ago to be worn under a bodycon dress. I pluck from the pile a black thong with a sequin heart on the front. The sequins have all lost their original shine. I wrinkle my nose and drop it to the floor. I feel more myself in simple shapes, in soft materials in blacks and whites and creams. I've always got the impression that Tom doesn't notice these types of things anyway. When we're having sex, he's so quick to remove anything I'm wearing, that I don't think he even registers what underwear I have on. As I throw a peach-coloured triangle bra over my shoulder, I'm reminded of my second viewing of the flat, when I came here with my mum, and there were tens of silly little bras just like this one, drying over the bath. I find that I'm smiling as I think of the previous owner, wondering where she is right this minute, what she's doing, who she's with.

Once I've finished with the drawer, I move onto the wardrobe. There's plenty of space in here, now that Tom's clothes are all back in Birmingham, bar a couple of sweatshirts that I held onto. Still, I lift out a pile of jumpers from the middle shelf, and get to work on separating them into three piles: *love, don't care, hate*. Near the bottom of the pile, there's a roll-neck I've forgotten about. A dark navy, cashmere-mix. Though it's out of season, I'm happy to be reunited with it, and hold it up, press it against my body. I pull it over my head, to make sure it still fits. It's a lovely jumper, the neck looser than most roll-necks, making it chicer somehow. I look in the mirror, and am pleased with how it looks.

I turn back towards the bed, but stop in my tracks as something catches my eye. I rotate back round to the mirror, slowly. There are little white dots near the neck and the armpits and, now that I really look harder, all over. I rub at one of them, thinking it must be dust or congealed laundry detergent. It doesn't move. My finger gets caught, and I see that it's a teeny, tiny hole. I pull the hem down, stretching the expensive material taut, and can tell now that it's riddled with minuscule holes. I shudder, anxiously pulling the jumper up and over my head. My skin starts to itch. I rifle through the rest of the pile, holding each item up to the light. There are at least five jumpers that are completely unsalvageable. One of them is Tom's Nike hoodie that I love. Without thinking, my fingernails still scratching compulsively at my skin, I throw each of the offending items into the bin, tie the top closed, and take it downstairs and outside to the wheelie bin.

Once the lid has slammed shut and I'm empty-handed, I stand there, shivering for a while. I don't notice Jerry at first.

'Doing a bit of cleaning?' he says, and I jump.

He's standing by the door to the basement portion of his flat, fiddling with a paintbrush.

'Didn't see you there,' I say.

I can't work out what he's doing. There doesn't seem to be any paint anywhere near him. I'm reminded of how, when I was little, my parents used to get me to 'paint' the fence with water to keep me busy for an hour or two.

Before Jerry can say anything else, I blurt out, 'Have you noticed any moths? I mean, have you had any problems with them this year?'

He looks up at me. 'Moths?'

'Yes, moths. I've just had to throw away a load of jumpers.'

He transfers air from one cheek to the other, thinking. 'Don't think so, no. Might be worth getting some dried lavender up there. They don't like that.'

Back upstairs, I spend the rest of my day Googling ways to rid the home of moths. I order cedar blocks online. I empty my wardrobe and drawers and deep clean them with bowls of soapy water. Dissatisfied and still itching, I go back over the surfaces with vinegar and any sprays I can get my hands on. I spritz and spritz and spritz until I am wheezing from the fumes. I do load after load of laundry, dialling the temperature up to fifty and sixty degrees. Exhausted, and unsure what to do with my riddled winter coat, I bundle it up in a plastic bag and hide it inside the window seat.

149

On high alert, I toss and turn through an anxious, light sleep. Upstairs, Baz and Adele have noisy, rampant sex until the early hours, and their moans mingle with images of crawling insects to create vivid, unsettling dreams.

Before work, I start my disinfection project again in earnest. I rearrange packets of breaded cod and oven pizzas to make room in the freezer. I fill the drawers with bags of my more delicate clothes: camisoles, a silk dress, my cashmere, a couple of pairs of wool trousers. I have read online that the larvae die in extreme temperatures, either very hot or very cold.

Whenever I think of the infestation, I picture hundreds, if not thousands, of moths. The image makes my stomach clench. I can't stop yawning.

Scrubbing away, I mutter to myself, 'This is a one-woman flat. You can't live here with me.'

I struggle to get dressed, holding various items of clothing up to the light to check for holes. None of them feel particularly appealing. The sturdier, man-made materials seem safer somehow, so I put on some stiff denim and a polyester blouse.

Just as I am about to leave for the library, I remember my bagged coat. I lift it out of the window seat box and remove it from its carrier. It has a strange feel to it, and, as I realise what's off about it, I drop the garment in horror. The material is teeming with tiny white, wriggling bodies. I kick it away from me.

'Urgh, urgh, urgh, urgh,' I say, backing out of the room. 'No, no, no.'

I am getting very hot and my skin is prickling and I know I can't leave the coat on the kitchen floor and I also know that I cannot step back into that room without some support. I want Adele.

I knock for her. It's too early to be knocking on her door, but I can see my fist and it's pounding on the wood and I can also hear my voice, saying, really quite loudly, 'Adele! Adele, can you come, please?'

There will be plenty of time to be embarrassed about this later. Now, the only thing that matters is removing that horrible thing from my home.

There's the sound of padding footsteps, and a long pause.

'Adele!' I call again. 'I'm sorry, it's only me, I just need some help.'

The door opens. It's Baz.

'Everything okay?' he says, through a small gap. His eyes are bleary, his stubble overgrown.

He's not opening the door fully, and I realise that maybe he's not dressed yet. I feel very strongly that I don't want a man to help me with this particular issue. I don't want to be made to feel silly or like I'm overreacting. As nice as Baz is, he's not the right person for the job.

'Could you get Adele, please?' I say.

'She's not here,' he says. 'Is it something I could help with?'

I am taken aback. What does he mean, she's not here? It's only eight o'clock.

'Where is she?' I say, though this is not technically my business.

I see Baz shift from one foot to the other. 'She's away, visiting her sister.'

I recalibrate quickly, glance up at the ceiling, swallow down a further question. I look at Baz. He gives me a half-smile, and I can't tell what it means. All thoughts of moths have left my head.

I say, 'Don't worry. It's more of a girl thing. I'll handle it on my own. Sorry for disturbing you.'

'It's no trouble?' he says. 'If you do need something?'

My mouth is full of saliva. I can only shake my head and step back into my own flat. I do a little wave and close my door. I rub my palms over my face. I hear faint voices.

150

'A lot of things have happened to me and you don't know about any of them!' I say, quickly and loudly, when Tom picks up the phone.

I'm happy to hear him laugh into the receiver.

'I have blonde hair and a moth infestation and Baz is having an affair,' I say, all in one breath.

'Woah, woah, woah,' Tom says. 'Blonde hair? Since when?'

'That's not the part you should be focusing on, Tom.' I allow myself to exhale.

There's a smile in his voice when he says, 'God, I've missed you.'

It's both painful and beautiful to hear him say that. I sink onto the window seat, facing into the kitchen, my back against the glass. I am quiet.

'I let things slip with you,' he says. 'Again. You're the one thing in my life that was working, and I should never have taken that for granted.'

'You were right about the contract thing,' I say. 'I shouldn't have cancelled those weekends at such short notice. It wasn't fair.'

'Listen,' Tom says.

'To what?'

'That absence of noise. No treadmill, no Asda, no other activities going on in the background.'

I rub at the hard cartilage of my ear. He's right. Silence. 'That's nice.'

'I'm at the gym, but as soon as I saw your name on my screen, I stepped outside to take the call properly.' He breathes in through his nose. 'You're my priority and I'm going to start treating you as though you are. Okay?'

Yes. I don't say it out loud. We just let his statement hang there. We're alright.

'What am I meant to do about the Baz thing, though?' I say. 'I literally heard him shagging someone else. Do I have to tell Adele?'

'I mean, yes, probably,' Tom says. 'Unless they have an arrangement?'

'What arrangement? She's heavily pregnant. There's no arrangement.'

'You'd want to know,' he says.

This rankles, before I have chance to catch myself. 'But you wouldn't do anything that I'd need to be told about anyway,' I say.

'Mara. I'm talking in hypotheticals. It's your friend's problem, not yours.'

Though this is technically true, I can't help but feel directly involved. Not for the first time, I wish my home was soundproofed with heavy insulation between each floor. I wish I'd never heard a thing.

'It's just so sordid,' I sigh.

'Well, what did you actually hear? Could it have been something else? Housework? An exercise video? Porn?'

'Mate. I know what Baz sounds like when he climaxes. Trust me. Nobody knows better than me.'

'I think I would go to him first,' Tom says, unexpectedly.

'Oh?'

'I'd rather confront the perpetrator than the victim. And the relationship you care about is the one you have with her, right?'

I hum my approval.

'So you don't care if he ends up hating you, but you probably do care if she can never look you in the eye again because you're the person who told her the father of her child was cheating on her.'

'Fuck,' I say. 'You're right. So I have to do that pretty soon, probably.'

'Hey, Mara,' Tom says, his tone gentle. 'You're a good neighbour.'

151

Whether fortunately or unfortunately, the decision of how to proceed with the Baz and Adele dilemma is taken out of my hands. Adele gets back from her sister's the very next day. I'm sitting on the sofa, Googling pest control quotes, when I hear a car door slam. I wince, edging towards the window, and peering around the curtain.

I watch as Adele leans against the Uber door to steady herself, slowly hoisting a leather holdall onto her shoulder. It takes her a long time to move. I wonder why the driver isn't offering to help. Maybe it's an insurance thing. Perhaps he's not allowed to. I realise that it will be much harder to corner Baz alone, now that Adele's home. I might have to tell her directly, after all. My stomach sloshes at the thought.

Adele finally begins to tackle the short walk to the front steps. To my horror, I hear the front door open and, moments later, Jerry's booming voice.

'Can I help you with that bag?'

I see Adele smiling and nodding gratefully at the hidden figure of Jerry.

'Give that – That's it. Coming from anywhere nice?'

'Just my sister's. Kent.'

'Don't know what's going on with our post. You'll tell me if you're missing anything? I've not had a bill for weeks.'

The door slams and I hear it being double locked. Their voices are clearer now that they're in the hallway, and I make my way closer to my own front door to hear them better.

'I was thinking – would be good to give these walls a fresh lick of paint, wouldn't it?'

'Before the baby comes?' Adele's voice.

'See if you can convince Mara,' Jerry's voice in a faux whisper. *'She never seems all that keen on home improvements.'*

I pull a face. Me? He's never bloody asked. I press my ear to my door. Now that I've heard my name, I'm even more loath to miss any of the conversation.

'*It's not too bad. I've always liked this shade.*' The sound of something heavy being dropped. '*Oh, don't worry, it's only clothes in there. My sister gave me loads of my niece's old bits for when mine comes.*' A little tinkly laugh. '*But yeah, I'm quite fond of this beige.*'

'*No need for a colour change. I should still have some tins of this somewhere. I'd just like to paint over these tyre marks here. And here. And well, they're all over the place really.*'

Neither Adele nor Jerry talks for a few moments, and I assume that Jerry is pointing out the various marks.

'*Oh yeah. How odd. I wonder where they've come from.*'

'*It's that girl.*'

My heart flutters.

'*What girl?*'

'*Your friend that's always coming round on her bike. You know, the brunette.*'

'*Our cleaner? I thought she drove.*'

Jerry does a bellowing laugh. '*Not the cleaner! I know the cleaner. It's not her. I'm talking about the woman who always comes to yours at one-ish on weekdays. Stays an hour or so.*'

I don't hear Adele say anything to that.

'*Oh come on. You must know who I mean. She's been staying overnight these last few days? Housesitting?*'

I think I've stopped breathing. Just at that moment, I hear the pounding of footsteps from above, and then the sound of Adele and Baz's door swinging open.

'*Adele? I thought that was you!*'

The bang-bang-bang of Baz's bare feet going down the stairs.

'*Ah, thanks, mate, I'll take that. Come on, Ad, you look knackered. See you in a bit, Jerry. Let me get my girls upstairs.*'

It seems to take a long time for the two sets of feet to make it up to my level. Baz is chattering away, asking how Adele's feeling and if there have been any developments with the bump and have there been any kicks and does she want to have a bath when they get inside. Adele doesn't say a word.

Right outside my door, Baz says, '*Honey?*'

In a voice that defies belief in its coldness and control, Adele says,

'Honey? I'd love for you to tell me who has been sleeping in my fucking flat while me and your unborn child have been away.'

Their door closes and I don't hear a sound for the rest of the day. There is no shouting, no screaming, no noise whatsoever. Nobody leaves and nobody arrives. It is absolutely terrifying.

152

In the lead-up to the big day, more than once, I've Googled: *What do flower girls even do??*

The long and short of it seems to be as follows: *Scatter petals, accompany the ring bearer to the altar, and generally keep things CUTE. Responsibilities end once you've walked down the aisle, when you take a seat next to your parents.*

When I've specified my age, I've also found: *Older flower girls can get ready with the bride on the morning of the wedding. Younger flower girls tend to get ready with their parents. This is usually down to the discretion of the bride, and depends on the flower girl's relationship with the bride and groom.*

Thankfully, Hattie has allowed me to get ready wherever I want, and where I wanted was my own flat with my own partner. I have been given dress. It's salmon pink, and silky, and I didn't have to pay for it myself, which is a distinct plus. It has an awkward, fussy neckline, which has made pairing a bra with it tricky, but it looks pretty nice, and I feel comfortable in it. That said, I'm holding off from putting it on until the very last minute.

I've finally mastered how to style my hair, now that it's so short. Over the course of a few sessions, an unusually patient Noor taught me how to use a curling wand, and I've only burnt myself twice creating some *casual* waves this morning. It's skew-whiff at the back, but if I tousle it enough throughout the day, I'm sure nobody will notice.

Tom is excitable and keeps telling me I look fit, even though I'm still in my pyjamas. He irons his shirt for about half an hour, until I tell him to stop. We listen to a wedding playlist, and sing along to 'Oops Upside Your Head' and 'Candy'.

'How much is appropriate to put in the card?' I say, looking up from my desk.

'A hundred?' Tom says.

'Are you alright? We can't put a hundred pounds in.'

'One fifty, then.'

'No, I meant that's way too much.'

'Oh,' Tom says. He has a tie in each hand. One is navy blue and shiny and the other is pink with orange stripes, an item I can't imagine him ever buying for himself. 'But if you think of it like a day out, we're basically paying fifty quid each to have a full meal and drinks and entry to the club.'

'The club?' I say. 'Where did you get that tie, please?'

'Online,' he says. 'I found this great seller on Etsy. Should I do the fun one, then?'

'What do you know about Etsy?'

'I'm allowed to know about Etsy, babe,' he says, holding each tie up to his neck in front of the fireplace mirror he bought for me when I first moved into the flat. 'I dunno. I like to wear cheerful shirts and ties for my online tutoring. It makes me feel good when I'm just sitting there in my joggers.'

I lean back on my chair, tipping my head towards him for a kiss. He comes over, lowers his head down and presses his lips to my forehead.

'Your dress is pink, right? It'll be nice to match.'

'Yes,' I say. 'Like little twins.'

Back at the start, I'd often meet Tom out somewhere and we'd find that we were wearing almost identical outfits: blue jeans and a navy jumper, or lumberjack shirts in the same shade of red. Even now, a lot of his wardrobe has bled into mine. My favourite sweatshirt is his old grey Nike one, now rotting in landfill somewhere. We've always been a similar size.

'How do you feel about today?' he asks.

I think before answering. 'I'm relieved that we made up in time for you to come with me.'

'Come on, babe. I was never not going to come to this.'

'I feel a bit apprehensive, maybe. Even though me and Lewis aren't really close anymore, it's weird to think that he's taking this huge step. It feels too soon. Like Hattie's a teen bride or something.'

'It's quite a normal age for two people to get married.'

'I know that. Just not *Lewis*.'

'No? He's always been very serious. Older than his years, and that.

Of all your friends, I would've definitely had him down as being the first to commit.'

The word *commit* seems like an odd choice. I would've said that me and Tom were *committed*. Maybe it's just semantics.

'Hmm,' I say. 'Shall I put on another quick pot of coffee?'

'Go on.'

In the kitchen, I call my mum.

'How you getting on?' I ask.

She's already at a hotel around the corner from the venue, where me and Tom will stay too, after the wedding party. I offered her the flat two or three times, told her she should stay here with us the night before, but she said no. She said she wanted room service and to turn the whole thing into a little holiday. It's weird that she's in London but not with me.

'Just blow-drying my hair,' she says. She sounds chirpy. 'Don't you just hate the weak little hotel hairdryers? My thumb is spasming from holding the button down, and the hot air comes out like baby's breath.'

'I've got a great hairdryer here. You're still in time to Uber over.'

'You must be joking. I can basically see the wedding from my balcony.'

'So we'll meet you there in about an hour and a half?'

'I'll just head over when I'm ready. Lewis's mum might need some moral support.'

'God yeah, I forgot about her.'

'We'll get her on the mimosas, she'll be fine.' I hear a faint sound, like a gust of wind. 'Hear that? It's going to take me an hour just to get my fringe dry. I'll have to go, love. Tom okay?'

'Yeah, yeah, he's good. Nearly ready. Got himself a tie from Etsy.'

'What does he know about Etsy?' she says.

153

The wedding is in Holland Park. At an art gallery called The Orangery. I suspect the location may have been more down to Hattie, than to Lewis. I dread to think what they've paid for this day. I think of all the times that Lewis sent me detailed breakdowns of household bills I owed him money for. Once, he invoiced me £1.45 for a breaded basa I'd mistakenly cooked for myself, thinking it was mine. People change, I guess. For the right person.

I leave Tom with my mum, and go to find a teary Hattie in her private rooms. She's sitting with an older woman who looks just like her, and both of them are dabbing delicately at the corners of their eyes with old-fashioned hankies.

'I'm interrupting,' I say, as I approach them.

The older woman looks up, surprised, and says, 'Who are you?'

A fair question.

'Mummy, this is my flower girl, Mara.' Hattie throws me a watery smile.

Hattie's mum still looks confused.

'Lewis's childhood friend,' Hattie clarifies.

It's surprising to hear myself described in this way, yet I suppose that's what I am.

At that, Hattie's mum stands up, her hankie falling to the floor. 'How wonderful. Come, come,' she says, welcoming me into her bosom.

Unable to deny her, I let myself be encased in her Parma-violet-scented embrace.

'I can't believe I'm only just meeting you,' she says. 'Don't you look gorgeous?' She pushes me away from her body, so as to take me in, head to toe. 'Lovely. So pretty. Hattie, I told you this pink would suit every skin tone.'

Hattie is still smiling, her gaze focused on the middle distance.

'How are you feeling?' I ask Hattie, over her mum's shoulder.

'You know. Mixed emotions.'

With her hands still firmly on my forearms, Hattie's mum says, 'Her father isn't here yet.' Her tone is sharp. 'He missed the rehearsal dinner, and we don't know – even at this incredibly late stage – whether he's bringing his new piece. Hattie's been tearing her hair out reorganising her table plans at his every whim.'

I grimace. 'I'm sorry, Hattie, that's really rough.'

I quickly recalibrate. Hattie doesn't strike me as someone who'd have a shit dad. Perversely, it makes me warm to her. She doesn't have a perfect life, after all.

'Whatever happens,' I say, suddenly full of solidarity, 'you've got us.'

'Thanks, Mara,' Hattie says, standing now.

Her dress is incredibly simple. Sleeveless, floor-length, ivory silk, with a boat neck. No bows, no frills, nothing sparkly. Her hair is gathered in a loose chignon at the nape of her neck and she has a tiny diamond stud in each ear. That's it. She looks exquisite, the perfect bride. I can't quite muster the words to tell her this, so I just tilt my head to the side and do a knowing half-smile.

'Look, we can't wait any longer,' Hattie's mum says. 'You can't be late to your own wedding. If he comes, he comes, but in the meantime, I'll be the one to give you away.'

This prompts a fresh round of tears from each of them, and I find that I have a small lump in my throat myself.

'I think that'd be apt,' Hattie manages to say. 'I think I'd prefer it, actually.'

'Well then, that's that sorted. Stay here a sec, while I go and let them know the change of plan.'

Me and Hattie are left temporarily alone. We look at each other.

'I know I don't look it, but I'm so happy,' she says, sniffing. 'I feel like I've hit the jackpot with Lewis. I can't believe my luck.'

It's strange to me that she could be so choked up about committing her life to someone who has probably given himself mercury poisoning with all the fish he consumes.

'I'm sure he feels the same,' I say.

'He treats me like a queen,' she says. 'The way he looks after me, and all the little things he does for me every day, it's just—' She's unable to finish her sentence.

I lean down to pick up her mother's abandoned hankie, and I pass it to Hattie. 'Don't cry. You look too beautiful to go out there with a red face.'

She widens her eyes, willing the tears to stay inside. She fans the air in front of her face.

Her mother returns.

'That's our cue, baby girl,' she says, as Mendelssohn's 'Wedding March' commences.

The three of us step outside together, where two of Hattie's actual friends are waiting, dressed in the same shade of pink as me. They look me up and down, eyes narrowed.

'Ready, ladies?' Hattie says.

'Are you!' her bridesmaids say, in tandem.

'As I'll ever be,' Hattie says. She smooths down the sides of her dress, and I notice, for the first time, that it has pockets. Again, I'm filled with something like respect for her.

One of the bridesmaids winks at Hattie and, taking the other bridesmaid's hand, starts the procession down the aisle.

I pick up the wicker basket of pink rose petals that has conveniently been left by the door for me. A guy in a grey suit with a crew cut offers me the crook of his elbow. He must be the ring bearer. I'm happy to see that, like me, he is also an adult. We follow closely behind the bridesmaids. I only remember to start scattering the petals when I'm halfway down the aisle. I have to dislodge myself from the ring bearer's arm to access the basket. I will myself not to look at either Tom or my mum. I keep my eyes focused towards the front of the space, where I can see the back of Lewis's head, tender with a fresh haircut, a bit shorter than he'd usually have it, a little too neat.

Somehow, I arrive at the makeshift altar. There's no space for me in the first row of chairs, reserved for immediate family, and I don't remember the formal rules of where I'm meant to go next. Just in time, I recall, *Responsibilities end once you've walked down the aisle, when you take a seat next to your parents*, from my extensive Google search, and I look this way and that to find my two familiar faces.

Tom does a little wave. They're in the third row from the front, and I nearly crash into Hattie and her mum, as I double back on myself to slide in between Tom and my mum.

'Smashed it, babe,' Tom whispers in my ear, a smile in his voice. I elbow him.

They've written their own vows. I didn't think people did that in real life. As Lewis starts talking, I squirm. It's too exposing.

'Henriette,' Lewis says, reaching for her hand. 'I promise to always be your biggest supporter, no matter what. I promise to bring you an almond latte every morning. I promise to always wait without complaint outside the changing rooms in Whistles. I promise we can spend every Christmas at your parents'.'

Next to me, I feel my mum stiffen. 'What's all that about?' she whispers, loudly. 'That's not right.'

Lewis continues, his voice catching, 'I promise – sorry. I promise – ugh, why is this so hard?'

There is a communal *Aww* from the spectators. I am silent.

'I promise I'll learn to love Lana Del Rey.'

Hattie snorts out a laugh and reaches out her other hand to hold onto Lewis's forearm.

'I promise to let you have seventy-five percent of our wardrobe space.' He pauses to accept the laugh from the crowd. 'I promise to bring fresh flowers home every week, to never stop telling you how beautiful you are, to treat every night like date night, to unscrew every jar for you, uncork every bottle for you, change every lightbulb.'

'Is she incapacitated?' my mum whispers.

'Shhh,' I hiss. 'It's sweet.'

She looks at me with a face that tells me she knows I don't think anything about this is sweet. It's like a Meg Ryan film. Not sweet, but saccharine.

'I promise to rub your feet when you've had a long day. I promise to proofread your work emails, and any difficult texts to your friends, and deal with all the awkward admin of daily life.'

'Is he promising to be a good husband, or a good PA?' my mum says, in a voice which is definitely too loud.

Tom giggles. 'Bit much, isn't it?' he says, into my ear.

Even though it definitely is too much, I feel suddenly protective of Lewis and Hattie. They're making themselves completely vulnerable to each other, shouting about their love in front of all these people. Surely there's something admirable in that?

I don't respond.

Hattie has started her vows now. She reels off a list of gender-normative things she'll do for Lewis throughout their married life, until she has to stop halfway through to do a little cry.

Lewis looks out at the rows of all their family and friends, and lifts his arms up. 'Let's give her some encouragement, guys!' he calls.

Everyone starts whooping and cheering.

'Come on, Hattie!' Tom shouts. 'You've got this!'

I thaw and lean into him. He kisses my bare shoulder. I see my mum watching us and smiling. I smile back.

'Help,' Hattie says. 'Right. Here we go. Let me try again. I promise to master at least five failsafe recipes that our children will be able to think back on fondly when they're grown up. I promise to learn how to iron and thread a needle and – wait for it – drive.'

'Wheeey!' Tom shouts.

I elbow him. 'I don't think this is an interactive part, babe.'

Eventually, rings are swapped and a kiss is given, and an announcement of man and wife is made. That's it. My oldest friend married off. Tom takes my hand and squeezes it. My mum takes my other hand and squeezes it.

'Weird, ey?' she says. 'They look happy, though. And his mum looks ready to spontaneously combust.'

The three of us manage to slope off during the photo segment of the proceedings.

'Can one of you find me a fag from somewhere?' my mum says.

'Mum!'

'What? It's a special occasion.'

Tom beams at my mum's naughtiness. 'I'll go and ask one of the staff,' he says.

Me and my mum are left alone for a couple of minutes.

'Okay, love?' she says.

'I'm good,' I say. I do feel good. The sky above us is crystal clear and shockingly blue, opening my chest up. I'm with my two favourite people in the world, and before long there'll be canapés and champagne.

'Tom seems well,' she says.

I nod, slowly.

'You two going to be the exception to the rule of long-distance never working?'

'Ha,' I say. 'Maybe.'

'You know it's not my style to interfere, but the advice I would give – if I was that way inclined – is that the secret to long-distance is to have an end date in mind.'

I murmur my assent.

'And you have that, yeah?'

Tom appears, grinning, proudly brandishing a cigarette.

'Thanks, love,' my mum says, accepting it. 'Got no light, though, either. Forgot to say.'

'One sec.' Tom pops off again.

'So?' my mum says. 'The end date?'

'Mum, don't ask questions I can't answer. We're playing it by ear. Taking it day by day.' I raise my eyebrows at her. My heart rate has increased dramatically. 'And today is a really good day.'

Tom's back, with a fluorescent green lighter. He cups a hand around the cigarette that's in the corner of my mum's mouth, and lights it for her. I don't like seeing my mum smoking, but don't say anything more about it. Tom heads off to return the lighter to its owner.

'Let's enjoy today, then,' my mum says, inhaling deeply. 'Being as it's a really good day.'

154

There are salmon blinis and scallops wrapped in bacon and lobster mango salad and fillets of sea bass with beurre blanc. My mum drinks two glasses of pinot during the meal, and a shot of sambuca with dessert, and becomes soft and wonky. She takes Tom to the side at one point, and I see them deep in conversation, my mum nodding sincerely, Tom gesticulating wildly.

I see Lewis alone by the brass band, tapping his foot in time to the music. They're doing a rendition of Beyoncé's 'Crazy in Love'. I approach him.

'Lew,' I say.

He turns towards me, giving me a generous smile. 'Mara. It's so good to have you here. Thanks for doing your duties so nicely.'

'Of course,' I say. 'It's been a beautiful day so far. Hattie looks amazing.'

'Doesn't she?' he says, scrunching up his nose, like a proud parent.

'Have you managed to be present? In the moment?' I ask. 'Not worrying about whether everyone has enough to drink and eat and stuff?'

'It's been a blur, really. I'm just starting to take stock now.' He shakes his head. 'I've just married my best friend. I can't believe it.'

I say, for absolutely no good reason at all, 'Remember when I used to be your best friend?'

Lewis looks unsurprisingly surprised by this comment.

'We've just.' He twirls his wedding band around his ring finger. 'Grown up, Mara. That's all.'

'I know. I was just saying. Funny how things change.'

The opening bars of Whitney's 'I Wanna Dance with Somebody' start up.

'Be rude not to?' Lewis says, holding out his hand for me to take. I nod, smile. 'Be rude not to.'

Lewis spins me around the dance floor. Initially, I'm stiff, self-conscious. I feel as though everyone must be looking at us, wondering who I am. I soon see that nobody is paying us any attention whatsoever. They're all too busy at the bar or in little chatty groups or in the photo booth, taking pictures in feather boas and pink cowboy hats. I shrug my shoulders back, twirl, pout. I do a little jog on the spot, and Lewis copies me. I shimmy forward, as he shimmies back. We're laughing together, being silly. We get almost to the end of the song, before Tom arrives.

'Do you mind, mate?' he says to Lewis. 'Could I steal her?'

'Go ahead, pal,' Lewis says. 'I'm going to find my bride.' He winks at me. 'Later.'

Tom looks relaxed. He says to me, 'Nice chat?'

'Actually yes,' I say, allowing myself to be encased in Tom's arms.

'You look so great,' he says. 'I feel very proud to have you on my arm today.'

'Yeah?' I say. 'Proud to be on your arm. Stud.'

We sway softly back and forth, waiting for the song to change. I don't recognise it at first. Tom works it out before me.

'Outkast,' he says.

'Ohhh,' I breathe.

It's 'The Way You Move', and we both know all the words, so take it in turns to do Big Boi's verses to each other. In one hand, I hitch my dress up over my knee, so I have more freedom to move. As Tom raps, he circles his head around, stretching his neck out. He pulses his shoulders back, snarls. His little pink tie swings this way and that with his movements.

155

Tom pushes me through the door to our hotel room. He's clumsy, kissing my neck, his tongue darting into my hair, his hand fumbling around under the hem of my dress, pulling it up, propelling me forward with his weight.

'You looked better than the bride tonight,' he whispers, in a husky tone not quite his own.

'Yeah?' I say. I reach around him, trying to close the door behind us.

He grabs at my hand before I've made contact with the door, pinning my arm to the wall by the doorframe.

'Tom,' I say. 'The door.'

He spins around with me in his arms, using his side to push the door closed. He's athletic. He's also drunk.

I find it so exciting when he's this decided. We've had a really fucking great night. It's Tom. My Tom. The Tom I've loved for the last six years.

'I love you,' I whisper, helping him loosen his tie.

'I love *you*.' He uses one of his feet to step out of the other shoe, kicks it across the room.

'Watch out,' I laugh.

'Want to do it on the balcony?' he says.

I bite down gently on his lower lip, say into his mouth, 'What're you talking about, balcony?'

'Come on. It'll be fun.'

I see now that he's dead serious. I let myself be pulled along behind him, allowing him to be in control.

'When did you turn into an exhibitionist?' I say, unhooking my bra, threading it through the armholes of my dress, and throwing it into the corner of the room.

'What do you mean? I've always liked it,' he says. 'Go through there.'

I pull my shoes off, rubbing at the sore places where I know blisters will soon appear. I go out onto the balcony, look around to see where we might be overlooked. It's a balmy night, there's a warm breeze which feels good on my skin.

'Maybe get the light?' I call through to Tom.

He joins me outside. 'I want to see,' he says. He's taken his suit jacket off, and his pink tie. He looks handsome in his blue shirt. I like him in blue. 'Lean over the railing,' he says.

I do as he says.

His hands grasp at me from behind, lift up my dress, bunching it up around my hips. I hear the sound of his zipper, feel the thrust of him. It's fast, urgent. I stop worrying about possible onlookers. We're alone in the world. Every time Tom touches me, my stomach fizzes.

'I won't take long,' I mutter.

'Good. I want you to feel good.'

He's close too. I can feel it.

This part has never been a problem. This is where we fit best together. It's natural, instinctive.

I shudder and let the pleasure wash over me. He's right behind me, juddering once, twice. We stay like this, attached, out on this balcony, for whole minutes.

'We'd better get inside,' I say, with Tom's head still on my shoulder.

That night, in the quiet hotel room, we both sleep like babies.

156

In the morning, Tom says, 'That was the last time, wasn't it?'
In the morning, I say, 'That was the last time.'

157

Now that the decision has been made, there is laughter, lightness, flirting, even. We sit in the hotel lobby, waiting for my mum to pack up and join us, or maybe waiting for permission to leave, I'm not sure. There are a few other wedding guests lazing in the lobby, in various states of disarray, some who I remember, some who ring no bells at all.

'Do you remember the first time we had sex?' Tom says.

'Course I do. What sort of question is that?'

Tom is only the second person I've ever slept with, and I barely count the first, which was sloppy and underwhelming and with someone whose face I can't conjure up now, no matter how hard I squint.

We'd gone back to Tom's student halls after the night out in Reflex. His space was personality-less, apart from the family photos Blu-Tacked to his wardrobe door. I can picture them now. There was one of him and Sarah as kids, dressed in matching snowsuits, and there was one of his mum with huge bouffant hair, pregnant with him.

We'd kissed for maybe three hours solid. With that out of the way, we'd talked about what it all might mean for another three hours or so. Exhausted, we'd fallen asleep, wrapped up in each other's limbs, at about ten or eleven in the morning.

The sex came once we'd decided it wasn't going to happen. Tom had ordered us pizzas, and we were eating them under the covers.

He'd said, 'You're actually sound as fuck.' I remember that that's what he said, because it was the unsexiest compliment he could have given me.

I pushed the pizza boxes onto the floor, and climbed on top of him. If I squint, I can still see the look on his face that day. Like he couldn't believe his luck. Nobody had ever looked at me like that before and nobody has ever looked at me like that since. I can't recall much about the actual shag. I'm sure it was fine. We were certainly keen to do it again straight after, so it must have been alright. But I'll never forget that look on Tom's face.

'Do you remember how the condom came off inside you?' he says, now.

'What?' I look at him blankly. 'Was that then?'

'Yep.'

'I thought that happened a few months in?'

'Nope. It was that very first time. Well, maybe the second time. But it was on that first day together.'

'Yeah?' It's weird to think that I could block out such a specific detail.

'And I had to fumble around inside you to try to get it out.'

I clench my legs together at the memory. He's right, it was then. I'd cried and he'd been so calm, clinical even. He'd made me lie back with my legs spread open, then when that hadn't worked, he'd told me to go on all fours to see if he could find it that way. There was no embarrassment, only panic. He was gentle with his fingers, kissing me softly on the insides of my thighs so that it wouldn't feel too much like a medical examination. Eventually, he'd said the best thing to do was to relax. He'd put on a film, and we'd finished the pizzas, and he'd made me laugh so much at one point that when I went to the bathroom to pee, I'd wiped and there the condom was on the toilet paper. I'd run out to show him, and we'd both been so happy. How did I forget that? Tom showed me his very essence in those few hours. He's a nurturer, a caregiver, patient, funny, kind. I knew that from the very beginning. I think I knew it even when he pushed his copy of *Sons and Lovers* across the desk to me, with the first little note written in the margins.

'Did we go and get the morning after pill?' I say.

Tom shakes his head. 'You said you fancied your odds.'

'Me?' That doesn't sound right either. 'When was I ever that relaxed? Did you not insist?'

'How could I insist? It's your body. But I was stressed as fuck for the next three weeks, I'll tell you that for free.'

I reach across the arm of the chair to take his hand. He laces his fingers through mine.

'Morning!' Lewis pushes through the lobby doors, looking red and happy and hungover.

Hattie follows closely behind, wearing a little white jumpsuit with *Just Married!* written in gemstones across the front. On anyone else it would be tacky, but on her it looks quite chic. I look down at my black hoodie and wonder whether it would look quite chic with *Just Broken Up!* written on it in gemstones.

'How's everyone's heads this morning?' Lewis says, lolling his tongue out of his mouth to demonstrate what feeling rough might look like.

We alternately shrug and nod.

'We're ready to do it all again!' Lewis says. He puts his arm around Hattie, looks at her, his eyes gooey. 'Ey, my girl?'

Hattie giggles. 'Absolutely. But seriously, thanks so much to all of you. We had the best day.'

From behind the couple, my mum pushes through the clear double doors with force, one eye scrunched closed, her holdall hanging loosely from one shoulder.

'Fuck me,' she says. 'Oh. Alright, Lewis, Hattie.' She catches my eye. 'Mara, Tom.'

I throw her a weak smile.

'Morning, mum,' I say.

'Morning, Rachel,' Tom and Lewis and Hattie say, in unison.

Lewis and Hattie have each taken three weeks of annual leave and will be going straight to the airport to fly out to Bali. There's a white Audi out the front of the hotel, waiting for them. There are no tin cans attached to the bumper, but we all follow them outside and make as much noise as we can with our hands and our mouths as they pull away. Tom holds my hand, tightly. My mum is at my other shoulder, catcalling.

They're gone in a matter of minutes.

Tom says, 'I might just pop back in quickly and use the loo before we get going.'

When he's out of earshot, my mum says, 'Everything okay?'

'Mmm,' I say.

'Anything you want to tell me?'

I purse my lips. 'I think you already know.'

'Oh, love,' she says. 'Can I give you a hug, or not right now?'

I feel for the first time as though I need to cry. I shake my head. 'Not right now. I can't.'

323

'Alright, let's get you home.'

'Are you going to come to the flat for a bit?'

'No, you donkey, I mean home-home. You're coming with me.'

Tom reappears. He looks tired.

'Come on, you two,' my mum says, with all the authority I don't feel. She puts an arm around Tom, kisses the air next to his cheek.

'Mara told you?' he says.

'Mother's instinct.'

The three of us head towards the tube, dragging our feet a little, my mum leading the way. I realise for the first time that Tom has quite a lot of stuff with him. He's brought his whole bag, not just the stuff he needed for the wedding, but everything he'd brought to London, almost as if he'd known he wouldn't be going back to the flat.

158

Baz moves out. I hear shouting, and then I hear silence, and then I hear weeping, and then I hear Adele saying over and over, *'Just go, please just go.'*

About an hour later, a long gold Honda pulls up, and a man who looks a bit like Baz gets out of it. The doorbell above my head sounds. There's the scurrying of feet, the sound of one of the sash windows being pulled up, Baz's voice.

'Give me ten minutes, mate!'

'Take your time!' the other man calls. I watch him light a fag, pace around the forecourt, get back into the Honda.

My chest pangs for Adele. I can't imagine going through what I'm going through and also being pregnant. It doesn't bear thinking about. Her hormones must be out of control. I want to text her, but don't.

After another five or so minutes, there's murmured chat. No more raised voices. The dragging of a wheelie suitcase. Trainered feet slapping down the stairs, making their way down to my level. The door closing. An audible sigh.

'Fuck,' I hear.

He doesn't move for a while, and I make my way into my hallway to see if I can hear anything more. I press my ear against my own door.

He's definitely still there. I can hear his heavy breathing.

Maybe he'll go back inside.

But no. There's the thump-thump-thump of the suitcase being dragged down the stairs, the rolling of the wheels along the little communal hallway downstairs. I pray for everyone's sake that Jerry stays safely inside his flat. His timing is never great, but this really does need to be a private moment. I step away from my door, and go into the kitchen, so I can peer out at the brothers.

The front door slams.

I see Baz hug the man. I'm surprised to see that there's only the one case. Baz's whole life condensed down to one bag. I wonder whether he's packed light on purpose, so that he can find excuses to come back. I wonder if Adele is looking down on this scene herself, up there. I wonder how she's going to afford the rent on her own. Her maternity is due to start. It's going to be really hard.

Baz's brother opens the boot of the car, and Baz throws the case into it. They both get in. The gold Honda does an awkward three-point turn, and then exits the forecourt. I hear a blood-curdling scream from above my head.

I want to help, do something proactive for her. I put on my slippers, open my door, and knock on hers.

'Adele,' I call. 'It's just me.'

Though I don't think she'll want company, after a few seconds, she comes to the door. Her eyes are wide, manic. Her curls are dishevelled and she's wearing a mad combination of clothes. A pair of basketball shorts and an enormous hoodie with *University of Life* written on it, which hides her bump.

'He's gone,' she says.

'I know, I'm so sorry.'

She stumbles back in the doorway and I instinctively grab for her, catching her by the waist.

'It's okay, you're okay,' I say.

Her breathing is noisy, she's hyperventilating. She feels very cold and clammy in my arms.

'Can you lean against me?' I say.

She's gone floppy. I'm scared we're both going to fall to the floor.

'Adele,' I say.

Her eyes flutter, close.

Oh god.

She slumps, sliding through my grip. I tighten my hands, and try to steady her descent, going slowly down with her.

'Can you hear me?' I say. 'Adele? Can you say something?'

She's passed out, her legs crumpled beneath her. My phone is in the flat.

'Shit,' I say, quietly.

I ease my legs out from under her. I try to think what you're meant to do when someone has fainted. Raise their legs? Or is that the wrong thing? Sherry's story about the woman with the Dalmatian comes to mind. I try to gently move Adele from her awkward position, make her level, turning her into the flat surface of the landing, away from the stairs. I lift her legs, one after the other, hold them up above her chest. I hope I'm not hurting her or the baby. Seconds tick by. My heart pounds. I wonder whether I should knock for Jerry, the real adult.

Adele's eyelids roll back and she appears to come to.

'Adele?' I say.

'Mmm,' she says. 'Baz.'

'It's Mara. You're with me. You just fainted, but I'm here. We're going to get you sorted.'

She starts to cry.

I tut. I say, 'It's okay. I'm going to call an ambulance, make sure you and baby are fine.'

'No,' she says. 'I don't want that. I want Baz.'

'I know. I know you do. Can I call a family member? Your mum?'

'Call Baz, I just want Baz.' She's shaking her head this way and that on the floorboards, getting herself worked up.

'Okay, okay,' I say. 'I'm calling Baz. Wait here one minute.'

I don't even know if I have Baz's number. I go into my living room and get my phone. I go back out to Adele.

'I'm just going to check on the online 111 thing what we're supposed to do,' I say.

I type into Google, *fainting after a shock*. The search results load. *Vasovagal syncope* is the first thing that shows up. I delete *fainting after a shock*, and write *fainting when pregnant*. The advice is as follows:

– *sit down and/or place your head between your legs*
– *lie on your side, if possible*
– *remove tight clothing*
– *ask someone to open a window*
– *drink some water*
– *eat something sugary*

'Okay,' I say. 'I don't think you're supposed to move at this stage.'

I look at her baggy clothes. That's that one sorted.

There are no windows in this space we find ourselves in, so I can't do anything on that front.

'I'm going to get you some water,' I say.

I step back into my flat, fill a pint glass with water and look for something sweet. In the cupboard, there's a small pot of Ambrosia. At a loss, I take that and a spoon too.

I help her to sit up and lean against the wall. I have to hold the glass for her to sip the water. She's helpless, like a child. Softly sobbing. I don't remember ever pitying anyone more. Maybe Tom that day on my bathroom floor. I shake the thought from my head.

'Can you try to eat a few spoons of this?' I say, showing her the custard.

'Yes,' she says.

I peel back the foil lid and dip the spoon in.

'Good girl,' I say, as she opens her mouth and receives the food. 'Well done. You're being so brave.'

And, even though she's sitting on the floor, despondent, arms cradled around her stomach, I do think she's being so brave.

'Does it get better?' she says, so quietly I almost don't hear her.

'A bit,' I say. I offer her another spoonful of custard. 'I'm probably not the best person to ask.'

'You seem to be doing so well,' she says.

'Do I? I feel like I'm making a big mess of it.'

She closes her eyes. 'What am I actually going to do?'

I put the Ambrosia down on the floor next to me. 'You're going to get through this first hour, then you're going to get through today, and after that you'll get through tomorrow, and you'll just take it day by day.'

She pushes her head back into the wall, groans.

'I'm sorry,' I say. 'That was a horribly clichéd thing to say.'

She nods, softly.

'But you will be okay.'

'Will I?'

'Absolutely,' I say. 'Look at what he's lost. You're one of the most beautiful women I've ever seen in real life.'

Adele snorts.

'What? You are. And you're one of those people who are genuinely just nice with no ulterior motives. It's baffling, really. And what have you lost?' I don't wait for her to answer. 'A cheat.'

Adele sighs and says, 'A cheat who I love more than anything in the world.'

'Not more than anything,' I say, placing my hand very lightly on her stomach.

She sniffs and says, 'No, not more than anything, you're right.'

'Are you ready to stand up?' I say.

'I think so.' Adele braces herself and accepts my proffered hand. 'You didn't call Baz, did you?'

'Nope,' I say. 'I did not.'

PART

W

PART VII

Winter

159

Happy birthday Tom! Hope you have a really lovely evening, whatever you're doing. I'd call you but I'm not sure it's wise/I can quite manage it. You're on my mind anyway, and sending you a virtual pair of novelty PJs! X

160

I go out with Noor. We share a pill that she's picked up from someone in the bathroom and we dance a bit and talk a lot. Luther's doing a DJ set and plays music that's hard to get into. Ambient music.

'I've been doing well, haven't I?' I say to Noor.

'Really well.'

'I feel like I've really got my shit together,' I say.

'You have.'

'I don't love him any less. I just think about loving him less.'

'That's not nothing.'

'Are you proud of me for how I've handled the breakup?' I say. 'I'm proud of myself.'

'Very proud.'

I say, 'I know I've been saying it for a long time, but now I really do mean it: I am *okay*.'

'You're doing great, babe.'

'I think it boils down to this. My heartbreak was the main thing in my life and everything else was secondary. Now the rest of my life is the main thing and my heartbreak is secondary.'

'Absolutely.'

She's humouring me. She's all consumed with watching Luther on the decks. When you're really okay, you don't have to keep saying you're okay.

We drink vodka Red Bulls, and I feel very aware of my heart in my chest, the pumping of blood around my body. I'm either having a really amazing night, or a bit of a shit night, I can't work it out. People are laughing loudly all around me, and there's a lot of sweat.

At one point, Noor whispers in my ear, 'If you were properly back on the market, you would be sold out within a week.'

I haven't said anything about wanting to be back on the market, but, after that, she diligently introduces me to all of Luther's friends, even the ones with girlfriends, and more than once she points at one of them, and says, 'What about him?'

'What about him, what?' I say.

'Just a thought,' she says, dancing away.

I get a taxi home much earlier than anyone else does, and am already dialling before I've closed my front door. I call a few times.

Eventually, he answers. I'm sitting on the toilet by this point, trying to pee, waiting, while nothing comes. For the duration of the call, I don't stand back up again.

When I hear his voice, I cry almost immediately and he does too. I've held off from talking to him for months, and it's unnatural. I always want to talk to him after a night with couples.

I don't know precisely what we say to each other, but I do know that I keep asking to see him.

I do know that he becomes agitated and says, *I'm not seeing you. I can't do this again.* It's easier to be at peace with your decision from afar. If he were to be presented with a walking, talking, breathing reminder of what he's lost, it might not be quite so straightforward.

I know that he says he's a long way from being over me. That he makes a promise to call me on Christmas Day. That I say some shit about wanting us to be in a good place, even though in that moment I think I'm referring to being back together, rather than being in regular contact and feeling happy about it. A good place isn't sporadic texts. A good place isn't checking his Instagram to find out whether he's okay.

I know that I torture myself and ask him if he thinks we'll ever have sex again. I already know the answer so I don't know why I make him say it out loud.

I know that I take every chance I can to keep repeating, *I love you*, so I can hear it back.

And I know that he ends the conversation because he needs to get up early or go to sleep or stop hearing me say, *I love you.*

161

When I tell Noor about the phone call, she downloads a dating app on my phone, and swipes away on my behalf, an echo of her own single days, when I found it so fun to get involved in her love life.

She sets up a date for me with a carpenter from Northampton. She does all the texting.

Looking up from my screen, she says, 'All you need to know is that he's witty and charming. Fast, too.'

'Oh god,' I say.

'But more important than any of that,' she reminds me, 'is that he's asked you out at a point when you really needed to be asked out.'

Once I've been entrusted to do my own correspondence again, I draft a nervous message. *To avoid anything too formal, I was thinking . . . I have some errands to run in central tomorrow, so could meet for coffee around Bond Street after?*

He replies, *I'd like that very much!*

My phone starts to ring. He's calling me. Noor is nodding, excitedly. The idea doesn't horrify me, so I pick up.

'Well, hi,' he says.

'Hi,' I say.

'You think you're cute enough to suggest a weekend date, then?' he says.

Oh.

'Sunday's basically a weekday, if you ask me,' I say.

He snorts. 'Nice. I like that. Yeah, arguably Sunday afternoon is actually the worst bit of the week, I'll grant you that.'

I'm having a conversation with a man, planning a date. I wonder if I sound convincing to him.

'I'm interested in the carpentry.' I know that this is a pathetic thing to say. Noor confirms this by grimacing.

'You are?'

'I am. I'm always impressed when people are good with their hands.'

He does the snort again. 'I'm certainly that.'

Okay, buddy.

We speak for a couple more minutes, and he seems normal enough. Bit of a performer, maybe, but I like that he's phoned. It makes the date seem safer somehow.

Shall we say 5ish? I text, after we hang up.

There is no reply, even after an hour.

'He'll text,' Noor says. 'Don't worry.'

Noor stays until late, and there's still nothing. I try not to think that he must have something against my voice.

Before she leaves, Noor kisses me on the cheek, and says, 'Maybe he just thinks five-ish is the firm plan, and there's nothing more to say?'

'Thanks for saying that.'

162

As planned, the next day, I go to Bond Street, because I really did need to. I'm on the hunt for curtain ties. In John Lewis, and Debenhams, and House of Fraser, I avoid looking at my phone.

The text never comes.

163

I write the non-encounter off as a bad judgement on my behalf – and Noor's – and jump straight back onto the app that same evening.

I start speaking to a guy originally from Leicester, who works in branding, and has a kind face and nice glasses, and we talk about books for a couple of hours.

This app is a little clunky, I send, at around ten o'clock, as I'm getting into my pyjamas. *Would you maybe like to switch to a different platform?*

I'm quite shy. Let's just talk later, he sends.

When I next check the app, he appears to have unmatched me.

I wonder if – like what happened with Noor's mum – these random men can sense that I still love my ex.

164

I match with an artist from Coventry. He has a big beard which makes it hard to tell how attractive he really is. He 'super' likes me, though, which is the boost I need, so I decide to give him a chance. Though it is him who's essentially chosen me, I send the first message.

Hey. It's a classic for a reason.

He replies, *Ey up pet,* then sends an unintelligible stream of foreign words.

I send a, *??*

German. I was living in Berlin for 3 years. And still I probably got that wrong just then.

Ha, I send. *You needn't have told me it was wrong. I wouldn't have known any better.*

But I knew :(

Berlin, though, I type, really trying. *That sounds like a fun time. For work or play?*

Work. I got a studio there. My fave place.

Tell me something else interesting about you?

You're pretty, he replies.

Thank you. I'm glad I chose my 5 little pictures well!

Lol

Are you a man of so few words in the real world?

When we are married with 3 kids . . . we can say we met on tinder

How depressing. Although, it's a bit like having a pen pal?

Er . . . what music do you like?

You have competition. Someone else just super liked me. Although his bio says 'would you rather drink lilt every day forever or never drink lilt again?' So you're probably safe. (And I'm ignoring your music question on purpose.)

Haha I think we will get on

What would you even answer to that shit? Never drink lilt again, right?

You seem nice
It's not even a memorable soft drink
I like u
Why do you not react directly to anything that's been said? You just say unrelated stuff
Yes. I dunno. Send me a pic of you perhaps?

I find a recent one of me and Noor and crop her out, then forward it to him. I write, *This was from yesterday so probably quite indicative of what I actually look like . . .*

I like your hair. The little centre parting. Cutie. One more pic??
I think that's your lot for tonight!
What shall we do then . . . when we meet
What do you suggest? I have no idea why I'm indulging this line of enquiry at this point.
Film. Food. Walk. And other stuff.
Sounds good. What are you up to tonight?
Thinking of uuuuuuuuu
Haha get it together! I'm going to bed x

For the first time I can remember, I switch my phone off. I sleep as soundly as I have in months.

165

When I switch my phone back on in the morning, there are multiple messages from the artist.

How's the tinder life then? First message.

Left swiping? Second message.

The tinder flick. Third message.

Eyes still half-closed, I write, *I've actually removed myself from the stack. Not because I'm in love with you, BUT because I don't think it's really for me.*

He replies instantly, *Hahahahahaha me either. It's just a thing for confidence really. I'm lacking all that big time. Some ego stuff.*

Great, I love a project . . . I type.

Send me a 'live' selfie?

Oh god, really?

Really!

I wonder whether all these photo requests are normal, or whether this person might be a bit intense. I sit up in bed, tilt my head to one side, and take a photo. I'm in my pyjamas and my hair is piled on top of my head. Absolutely nothing rides on this interaction with this man, so I send the photo to him.

He replies with a string of heart-eye emojis.

You like the pineapple head? I write.

Swear on me nan's grave! I fancy you. Natural!

Thanks, I guess!

You're such a super cutie. I keep looking at that photo. Your ears! Another heart-eyes emoji.

This is definitely too much. Just to confirm, I screenshot the last few messages and send them to Noor.

She replies with one word, all in caps: *BLOCK!*

166

I make a list of long overdue house tasks.

- *Lampshades in hallway*
- *Boiler service*
- *Coat hooks*
- *Modesty protector for bathroom window*
- *Repaint inside of fireplace*
- *Tiling in kitchen*
- *Extra plug point in living room*

Though Tom was never exactly handy, he was always on the other end of the phone to talk my plans over with. Now, I'm daunted by the idea of dealing with practical things like this alone.

I mention to Noor what I'm planning.

'My mum knows a guy,' she says.

'Does she? That would be amazing. I don't know where to start.'

'I'll text you his number.'

The guy in question is called Manuel and is extremely warm and friendly over the phone. He gives me an affordable quote and says he can do everything except the boiler service over the course of a couple of days. When I ask him when he's free, he says that he can come any time. Surprised by how easy the transaction has been so far, I arrange for Manuel to come on Saturday afternoon, and hang up feeling smug.

167

Saturday afternoon comes around, and my doorbell rings, once, twice, three times in jaunty succession.

'The parking here is not good,' a small-framed man says at the front door. He's dressed in ripped jeans and a smart pink shirt.

'Manuel?' I say.

'It's me.'

Upstairs, I show him the various things that I'd like him to do.

'No problem, no problem,' he says, in every room.

I hand him the ceramic lampshades that I want him to install, and leave him in the hallway while I go to sit on my bed. I am awkward in my own home.

I text Noor, *He is ladderless, and also seemingly toolless?*

Can't he just stand on your bed? she replies. *On a towel, no shoes.*

Well not really because the lampshades are going up in the hallway . . .

A few minutes later, I text her, *Update: he says not to worry he'll sort it and has now left the house.*

Manuel is gone nearly half an hour.

Oh good, he's come back with a three-legged chair that he found in someone's skip. I send Noor a photograph of said chair.

Seems secure! Noor replies.

I'm holding the chair up while he stands on it, I text.

He's quite a small man . . . I text.

Now he has put a stool on top of the three-legged chair, I text.

Noor stops replying after that. I can only assume that she's ashamed of her recommendation.

Somehow, Manuel successfully manages to install the three lampshades.

He comes through to the kitchen, a little later, shiny and pleased with himself, to tell me that he's done the coat hooks and the modesty protector, and is going to tackle the plug point next.

I am pouring myself a large glass of pinot, so instinctively say, 'Would you like one?'

'Thank you,' he says, without reflecting even for a second.

I pour him a small glass, but he widens his eyes and nods for more, so I fill the glass almost to the brim. He leans against the kitchen counter and closes his eyes.

Though he came approved by Noor's mum, I still took the precaution of putting a pair of Tom's forgotten trainers by the door. I look at them meaningfully when Manuel asks me, in a friendly tone, 'Where is your partner? Why he cannot do these jobs for you?'

I do a performative laugh and say, 'He's useless.'

'It's funny,' Manuel says. 'Boys these days are very weak. I taught my boys how to do everything around the house. I do not want their wives to ever have to call for help from outside.'

I realise that Manuel must be quite a bit older than I thought he was.

'If nobody ever had to call for help from outside,' I say, 'wouldn't you be out of a job?'

He shrugs. 'I'd just do something else.'

Just do something else, just do something else. These four words play incessantly in my head.

After the wine, Manuel doesn't complete any of the other jobs, mostly just hums and touches things instead.

'I work on Sundays,' he says. 'Don't worry. It's just another day, isn't it?'

'Yes, I suppose it is,' I say. Since the final breakup with Tom, I have come to loathe Sundays.

'I will be back in the morning,' Manuel says.

He goes, leaving the three-legged chair in his wake. I don't particularly want to have it in the flat. I've only just got on top of the moth situation, and the found chair has a very worn fabric seat that could contain any multitude of eggs or larvae. I place it downstairs in the communal hallway, in case he needs it again tomorrow. Once I close my own door behind me again, I feel a sharp stab of loneliness. Manuel is cheerful, optimistic, a family man. I liked having him here. I look down at Tom's shoes. They might be the last thing of his that I have. I decide that Manuel poses no threat to me. I pick up the old Vans and drop them into my pedal bin.

168

I start watching a sitcom about a stand-up comedian. Whenever he's not on stage, he seems utterly miserable. Sometimes, he seems quite dreary while he's performing too.

I have a romantic notion about stand-up. Even though I've only ever been to a handful of nights, I've always got the impression that the types of people in attendance were *my* people. I love the communal laughter, the generosity in giggling even when the comedy is bad. It seems so pure to me. I realise, midweek, that all I really want to do is sit in a crowded pub and howl and knee-slap with a load of strangers. I do a Google search for local events and find a fun-looking one in Angel.

I text Noor the link and write, *Comedy night tonight? Could you fancy it? Luther welcome too, obviously!*

She texts back, within less than a minute, *We bought a chicken in the reduced aisle at M&S and it goes off tomorrow! Was literally just going to text to see if you wanted to come to dinner!*

I think about it only for a few moments, before texting, *Maybe I'll go by myself, then . . .?*

Noor texts back, *!!!*, and I know they're exclamation marks of approval.

169

I get to the pub twenty minutes before the first comedian is due to perform.

The redhead on the door draws a smiley face on the back of my hand with a green felt-tip pen, and says, 'Alright, love. We've got a few extra performers who'll be popping out at the end, tonight. Be great if you could hang about for them. Only if you've got nowt better to do, of course!' She has a contrived Yorkshire accent, which I can't be sure really belongs to her.

'Sure,' I say. 'Why not.'

At the bar, I order a pint of Pilsner. I take it into the main room and sit in a middle seat in one of the middle rows. As proud as I am of myself for my solo outing, I still have my limits. The last thing I need is to be picked on. The space fills gradually, with little groups of twos and threes, already smiling or softly chuckling. I move my knees to one side more than once to let people past. A couple in their fifties settle in on my right. Two women. They're wearing athleisure wear and expensive New Balance trainers in tasteful shades of grey and navy, and are having a whispered argument.

'You're not objective, because everything she does is so charming to you,' the one closest to me hisses.

'It's not like I can't see through her,' the other says. 'I just genuinely find her funny.'

'Funny! Nothing that comes out of her mouth is her own. I've never heard her utter one original thought. And I don't know why she puts on that accent. She's from bastard Kent.'

An audible scoff. 'Let's leave it there, shall we? Before we get really nasty.'

'If we want to talk about nasty, all of your girl's jokes are her just insulting audience members. Thinks she's fucking Frankie Boyle.'

'Alright, lads and ladettes!' The redhead from earlier, now sporting a fluorescent shell suit, has made her way onto the makeshift stage. 'Let's 'ave it!'

Though the couple next to me have stopped bickering, I can still feel silent tension emanating from them both.

'Do we have anyone on the sesh tonight?' the redhead calls. She sloshes a pint glass this way and that, brings it to her mouth, mimes guzzling it.

A few cautious whoops from the audience.

'I *said*, any alkies in tonight?'

The woman closest to me sighs.

'Can see you lot are gonna be a barrel of bloody laughs!' the redhead says, taking a real gulp of beer this time. 'I should say, my name's Ginger, and I'll be your compère tonight. That's right!'

Some scattered clapping.

'Lads, come *on*. Let's hear it for this ginger nut!' Ginger says, pointing at her own chest with her own thumb.

One audience member does a faint wolf whistle.

'Oh yeah?' Ginger says, sashaying about. 'You like my shit? You're into *all this*?' She rubs a palm up and down her tracksuit top, then uses the same hand to push her fringe out of her eyes. It stands up on end with the static. She widens her eyes and says, 'This little number? Couture. A gentleman by the name of Monsieur Umbro. You've heard of him? Surely not! He only does made-to-measure.'

I glance to my right and see that my immediate neighbour is rolling her eyes.

'So, look, I have to say, I'd love a fag right now. Whenever I have a drink, I absolutely gag for a smoke. I'd even take a rollie at this point. Honestly. But health and safety, you know.' Ginger forms a gun with thumb and forefinger and aims for her open mouth. 'Plus, my vintage Umbro is highly flammable.' She throws her head back and does an artificial, squawking laugh. 'Alright, who put ten pence in me, ey? Let's have some real acts, shall we?'

'Please, yes,' the woman next to me mutters.

'Sorry!' Ginger calls. 'Was that some audience participation I heard?' She makes a visor out of her hand and looks out into the crowd. 'No! Don't tell me it's the big boss! It is! It's only bloody Vanya!'

The woman who must be Vanya goes rigid next to me. 'Nope,' she says, under her breath. 'Not tonight.'

'Do you wanna come up here and say hello, boss? This is the woman who came up with the whole concept of Wet-Yourself Wednesdays. Okay, no, that's me using some artistic licence, admittedly. We are, of course, Side-Splitter Sundays. Now expanded to other nights of the week. And it's all down to this comedy genius,' Ginger points at Vanya. 'Sorry, can we get the house lights up for a sec so everyone can see Vanya?'

Vanya shakes her head. 'No house lights, thank you. I'm just here to enjoy the show, like everyone else,' she says, through tight lips.

'Boo!' Ginger calls. 'Boo, hiss. Alright, well, I'm sure you'll all buy her – and me – a drink in the interval, but I'd better get on with it. Our first entertainer tonight is five-foot-nothing of pure muscle and lean, mean gags. You won't believe he's single, and you won't believe we've allowed him up here tonight. It's Jack Joseph Jones!'

170

The queue for the loos is long and there seems to be no real system in place. I hop from foot to foot. Vanya and her partner have popped behind the bar and are pouring themselves large measures of whisky. Vanya catches my eye, winks, and motions for me to join her. I look around, to make sure it's me that's being addressed.

She laughs. 'Yes, you! Come.'

'I can't lose my place in this line!' I call over.

'I'll make it worth your while.' She lifts the hatch on the bar and ushers me in.

I obey.

'Go through there,' she says, nodding towards a little back room. 'Staff loo.'

'Oh my god, thank you, thank you.'

She grabs my arm as I try to make my way past her.

'Hold on,' she says. 'You need to do something for me first.'

'Oh?' I say.

'For a piss and a whisky, I'd like your no-holds-barred thoughts on the night so far.'

Vanya's partner tuts, and says, 'Maybe let her go for the piss first?'

'Go on then.' Vanya lets go of my arm. 'Five-word review when you're back.'

I go through to the small bathroom behind the bar. The latch has been yanked off, so I hold the door handle as I squat over the toilet. As I pee, I try to formulate my review. I've certainly been having a nice time. The first act was a character comedian, whose bit was that he was a misogynist who had never heard of the 'U2' movement. In between jokes and verses of 'With Or Without You', he dropped to the floor to do push-ups. The second guy who came out didn't actually speak at all. He stood there, looking around at the audience, for the whole duration of his slot. The absurdity of it, and something about his facial expressions, made it so that the audience's nervous laughter gradually became real, and by the end, everyone was in bits. The third guy was a bisexual Japanese man, who did impressions of his mother trying to come to terms with his sexuality. I wipe, flush, and wash my hands.

Back behind the bar, facing Vanya, I say, counting the words off on my fingers, 'But where are the girls?'

'Thank you!' Vanya says, throwing her hands up. 'Exactly my point.'

The other woman is pouring me a whisky. 'Leanne,' she introduces herself, as she hands the glass to me. 'And this wallflower is Vanya.'

'I gathered that from the show,' I say. 'I'm Mara, and I'd like to say that I am genuinely enjoying myself, despite the lack of female representation.'

'There's Ginger?' Leanne says.

'Please,' Vanya says. 'We do not count Ginger.'

'What's with the voice?' I say.

'No, even I can admit that the voice isn't right,' Leanne says. 'I don't know why she does that.'

'Are there female comics in the second half?' I ask.

'There's one!' Leanne says.

'Whose onstage persona is a maniacal jilted bride,' Vanya says. 'Honestly. I'm ashamed to have my name attached to this thing sometimes.'

'Sorry about her,' Leanne says. 'She's on one today. Cheers.' She offers her glass for me to clink with. 'What's your story, then? What do you do when you're not at comedy nights?'

'I'm actually a librarian,' I say.

'How quaint!' Vanya says. 'Love that. Where?'

'Homerton.'

'A happy job?' Leanne asks.

'Ah.' I make a thinking noise. 'I don't know at the minute. Feeling a bit unstimulated and trapped.'

'Let me guess. Is your boss a,' Vanya whispers the next word, 'man?'

I take a sip of my whisky and wince. 'Yes, he is.'

Ginger pokes her head around the main room door and shouts, 'Bums back on seats, please, my loves! All of you! Chop, chop.'

171

The rest of the night is hazy. There's frenzied whispering and sour whisky breath and cackling and a few bars I've never been in before and a fake chicken sandwich made from salty seitan that makes me thirstier than I've ever been in my life. There's a cab. There's a huge apartment, some karaoke? More whisky. Other people. Lots of them. A nap on a sofa. A feeling of being safe and happy. Some plans. Deals made. Another cab. Some vomit in a bush. My own bed. A fitful sleep. Then oblivion.

172

I wake to tens of texts.
Are you home?
??
You promised you'd text when you were home!
Ok, leanne's saying you're probably asleep
Are you asleep?
Oh bloody hell, I can't settle until I know everyone's got home fine
It says you were last online four hours ago
Mara?
Just text one word and I'll be able to relax
Oh god
I'm going to call the cab company
We always use them, they're usually very trustworthy
It's fine. I'm sure it's fine.
Was so lovely meeting you, by the way!
And now you've probably been murdered
Text back, please!
Hi sweetheart, this is Leanne. Ignore Vanya's stressing – she can't help herself. Have a good sleep and we'll chat in the morning (or afternoon!) x
I'm not stressing. I just know the type of world we live in.
But alright yes. Speak tomorrow!!
Goodnight x

173

Once I've stopped throwing up, I call Vanya. It turns out we've made a pact that I'll be holding a stand-up night at the library next month. Just female performers. Only female audience members. I have absolutely no clue how I'm going to pull it off. I don't even know that many women. So far my guest list is:

Noor
Noor's mum
My mum
Adele
Hattie?
Vanya
Leanne
Deidre/Deidra

I also can't imagine sitting down with Derek to ask him whether I can put on an event that he expressly can't be a part of.

When I tentatively express this concern to Vanya, she says, 'You're not asking him. You're fucking telling him.'

Okay. So I also can't imagine sitting down with Derek to *tell* him that I will be putting on an event that he expressly can't be a part of.

174

Jerry's been undeniably quiet. No radio, no washing machine, no coughing. The only reason I even know he's around is because he picks up his post. The couple of times I catch a brief glimpse of him – one time getting into his car and the other picking up an empty Coke can from the street – he has a strong, proud posture. I am shocked to find that, in some perverse kind of way, I'm actually missing him.

175

In December, Derek gets a promotion. I am so angry about this, I can't speak. For a whole week, I walk around the library, mute, on the verge of frustrated tears, until I overhear him explaining to Starey Man that his new job opportunity means he'll be transferring to Swiss Cottage.

That same Friday afternoon, Derek calls an all-staff meeting, and says that there's now a vacancy for library manager here at Homerton.

176

I spend Christmas in Rugby with my mum. Knowing I don't have to rush off to spend New Year's Eve with Tom means it'll be the longest time I've spent at home in ages.

I drink a tiny bottle of Prosecco on the train, listen to the general cheer and chatter of the Christmas-Eve-Eve travellers. I keep my book stowed away in my bag. There's plenty of other ways to pass the time today. Someone at the far end of the carriage starts up with the first verse of 'Fairytale of New York', and as he progresses deeper into the song, others start to join in, until for the third verse, most of the passengers are at least humming the tune. I clap and sing the parts that I know.

When it gets to the F word, the first man sings it at the top of his lungs, rather than replacing it with something less offensive, and after that lots of people trail off and go quiet.

'Oh come *on*,' he says. 'It's the PC police gone fucking mental on this train. That's the actual fucking lyrics. I didn't write them, did I?'

Someone boos him, and another person says, 'Do you mind with the fucking swearing? I've got my kid with me.'

My mum picks me up from the station, wearing a Santa hat, and the image of her grinning in red behind the steering wheel is so tender that I want to cry.

'Oh, come here, my little donkey,' she says, squeezing me with one arm. 'Is it really so sad to be back here with me?'

I shake my head, no. That's not what's choking me up. I've been away for too long. Again.

She's put up fairy lights all around the front door – multicoloured, Nineties-looking ones – which she doesn't usually bother to do, and that makes me teary too.

'Go on upstairs and get yourself sorted, you softie,' she says, slapping my thigh, affectionately.

My bedroom is warm, pink, narrow. A womb. It looks exactly as it has always looked. I'm uneasy as I step inside, feeling as though I belong here but also have no business going in. The places I stayed while I was studying in Birmingham weren't home – even my final-year house with Noor – they were always too temporary. The flat I shared with Lewis was never home. Not even close. Now, when I get back to my Homerton flat after being away, it's a relief. I get, if not the same, then a similar feeling as the one I have right now, in my childhood home. The only difference is the lack of nostalgia. But what makes the flat feel like home? And when did that feeling start? On my first night there? Once I had all my clothes in the wardrobe and my pictures on the walls? Once I got to know my neighbours? Is the flat any less home now that I'm single and have no overnight guests? Was it more home when Tom was there too? Less? What about when his mum was there? Definitely less home then.

From the corner of my eye, I see the photo of my dad holding me as a toddler. I don't allow myself to look at it properly. I don't need to, I know it by heart. In it, I'm wearing a brown dress and could easily be mistaken for a sack of potatoes, the way he has me clutched under his arm.

Downstairs, I can hear my mum in the kitchen, ordering a curry for us, the same order as always: butter chicken, prawn balti, pilau rice and two peshwari naans. I can hear her cracking jokes, asking whether the owner will be delivering it himself or if he's still too lazy and will be sending his son, not that she minds, being as he's much more likely than his stingy old dad to whack in a couple of complimentary poppadoms.

I sink onto the single bed. Here I am cocooned, safe, can let go of all the demands on my time and attention. I could climb right inside this bed, under the covers, even now when dinner's on the way, and my mum would ask nothing of me, would require no more of my energy than I'm willing to give.

But then, she's my mother. She made me. Her love is as unconditional as it comes. I wonder whether that sort of love can only flow from a parent to their child. Siblings, too, maybe, but I wouldn't be able to confirm that. Can couples ever give each other unconditional love? And should they? I thought my love for Tom was unconditional, but it does in fact have conditions. I don't have to love him through everything. I'm not his mum.

'Love!' I hear from downstairs.

'Yeah?' I call back.

'Do you want to watch *Eight Out of Ten Cats Does Christmas*?'

I smile into the pink room. I sit up. My mum does need me, and I do have responsibilities. I can't hide away like a little girl anymore.

'Yeah!' I shout down. 'Coming!'

177

On Christmas Eve, me and my mum do our yearly tradition. We watch *Miracle on 34th Street* and eat huge bowls of mixed festive-flavoured crisps. This year we have Prosecco and brie Kettle Chips, pigs in blankets crinkle-cuts and turkey and stuffing puffs. We snuggle up next to each other on the two-seater in fleece pyjamas, my mum's legs draped over mine. We talk the whole way through the film.

'Do you remember that year I bought our turkey joint from that dodgy butcher and it turned out to be pheasant?' she says.

'It was actually nice,' I say. 'What about when we decided it'd be cute to only do stocking fillers instead of main gifts and, even though we'd agreed on it—'

'We both cried on Christmas Day because we felt short-changed?' My mum stuffs a handful of crisps into her mouth and nods, sagely. 'The real meaning of Christmas.'

'I've got you a big gift this year, don't worry,' I say.

'I have too.'

We stop reminiscing for a few minutes, and I wonder whether we might both be thinking about the Christmas morning a few years ago when I was in Birmingham with Tom and his family. Me and Tom had been together for long enough by then that it felt natural to spend Christmas together. Well, maybe not natural, but appropriate. I'd assumed that we'd do our first one in Rugby, so my mum wouldn't be alone, being as Tom's family is bigger than mine. But Tom insisted we do it fairly, and flip a coin. He picked heads and won. My mum was a good sport about it, and, even though I asked her over and over, she said she wouldn't feel comfortable intruding on Tom's family herself. The whole month of December I had a heavy heart, while Tom excitedly made plans and told me about all the elaborate things I could expect from an Atwood family Christmas. On the twenty-fifth, over salmon bagels and bellinis, I picked a huge fight with Tom, then locked myself in the bathroom and called my mum. I cried and said I was sorry and that it wasn't a real Christmas without her and could she please, please pick me up? She told me to get myself together and that it would be very rude of me to leave now, that I had to make it to at least the *Call the Midwife Christmas Special*, and then she would come and get me. And that's what I did. There was a lesson in there somewhere.

Our doorbell rings just as, on screen, Susan Walker is showing Kris Kringle a photo of her dream house, telling him she wants it for Christmas. Me and my mum look at each other.

'Who's that?' I say.

'Go and see.'

I point down at my tatty pyjamas. My mum raises her eyebrows and points at her own.

'Fine,' I say.

I get up and go to the door, wrapped up further in a fleecy blanket, covered in crisp crumbs. Through the mottled glass I can see a woman with something in her hand. I open the door, cautious.

It's Lewis's mum.

'Oh,' I say. 'Merry Christmas.'

'You're here!' she says. 'How lovely for your mum. I wasn't sure whether you would be.'

This really rubs me up the wrong way. I bristle.

'Yes,' I say, through thin lips, 'here I am.'

Lewis's mum hands me the tin that she's been clutching to her chest. 'Christmas cake,' she clarifies. 'Been working on it since August.'

'Mum!' I call. 'It's Lewis's mum!'

My mum joins me in the porch.

'Bloody 'ell, that's gorgeous,' she says, lifting the lid off the proffered tin and inhaling the scent of brandy and dried fruit. 'Hiya, love.'

'Are you both well?' Lewis's mum says.

'We're alright,' my mum says. 'We're always alright, us. And how are the newlyweds?'

Lewis's mum does a wide, toothy smile. 'Oh, they're gorgeous. So happy.'

'So you've got everyone round at yours tomorrow? Full fridge?'

The smile sags a little on Lewis's mum's face. 'Well, we're a little short on numbers this year, actually.'

'Oh?'

361

'Lewis was invited to his in-laws, so he's in London. Rebecca's taken the kids to Disneyland Paris, and Jamie said he'd work. So, actually, it's just me and Grant tomorrow.'

I know she's going to ask before the words come out of her mouth.

'Did you want to come over here, then? We've got plenty of food,' my mum says. 'Before you even say it, it'd be no bother.'

Lewis's mum taps a patent toe against the front step, widens her eyes. 'We couldn't.'

'I'm not arguing about whether or not you can.' My mum tilts her head to one side. 'I'm just asking whether you'd like to.'

'Well,' Lewis's mum says, flustered, 'in that case, yes. Yes please. I'll check with Grant, but he's happy wherever there's a sofa and a telly.'

'Lovely,' my mum says, kissing the air next to Lewis's mum's head. 'Lunch will be around two. Or three. Come just before that.'

Once the front door is closed and I'm following her back into the living room, I hiss, '*Mum.*'

She turns around and hisses back, 'Christmas. Spirit.'

178

My mum drives me back to London on the thirtieth. She says it's so that I can avoid the trains and the mad rush of people heading to the capital for New Year's Eve, but it's a flimsy lie. We both need to spend a few more days together.

Since I was little, as a stocking filler, she's always made me a CD. One year, I was obsessed with Michael Flatley, so I received his *Lord of the Dance*. As I got older, it was Steps albums, then Mis-Teeq, a long fixation with Nelly, Motown compilations, Beyoncé one year when I hadn't spoken to my mum as much and she'd just had to hazard a guess. In the car, she slots this year's offering into the CD player.

'It's that band you like,' she says, indicating left to turn out of our drive.

I recognise the first few, whimsical beats of 'Days Are Gone'. My mouth turns up in a half-smile. It's amazing the things that my mother logs. I wouldn't have thought she'd registered that this song meant anything to me. I wrinkle my nose, stemming an unexpected tear. She pretends not to see my emotion, humming along and shouting insults at passing drivers. I stare ahead, and listen to the lyrics properly for the first time. They're eerily apt.

Once we're on the M1, it's plain sailing. My mum takes one hand off the steering wheel to make swirly patterns in the air and periodically give me high fives. She skips all the love songs and we play the breakup songs on repeat, shouting at the top of our lungs. At one point, I'm singing along to 'Better Off' and begin to sob hysterically. My mum does not question this, and doesn't tell me to calm down. When the song finishes, she presses the back button to restart it.

'You obviously needed that,' she says, flipping her middle finger at a lorry that's trying to overtake us.

179

Another one of our festive traditions is the secret New Year's resolution swap. We write an intention for the coming year on a piece of card, put it in a sealed envelope, and then hand it to the other person to 'look after'. We've done it since I was a teenager and I started spending New Year's Eves with people who weren't my mum. I have a jewellery box filled with her resolutions. It sits on the bookshelf next to the Raymond Carver collection that Tom used to read to me from.

'Still want to do it?' My mum asks me now, on my sofa. 'Even though we're together this year?'

'Of course,' I say.

'Do you have one ready?' She curls her legs up under her bum, in a position that reminds me of Adele. It's odd to associate my mum with this other woman, who's always belonged to a very separate section of my mind.

'I have plenty,' I say. 'Do you?'

My mum nods.

I rummage through my desk drawer, looking for appropriate stationery.

Holding up a couple of blank postcards, I say, 'What about if this year they're not secret?'

My mum does a funny face.

'What?' I say. 'It was just an idea. They can stay secret, if you want?'

She kneads her eyes with the heels of her palms. 'Oh dear,' she says, quietly.

'What is it?' Armed with my postcards, I join her on the sofa, the material warm where her legs have just been.

'I think there may have been a miscommunication.'

'Right?'

'It's just, I'm not sure why you keep saying the word *secret*,' my mum says.

I can't hide the confusion from my face. I look at her. With my eyes, I ask for a clue. Suddenly, realisation dawns.

'You didn't realise they were secret resolutions?' I say. 'All these years?'

Surely not.

'What on earth would be the point in giving them to each other if it wasn't to share them?'

I do a nervous giggle. 'Are you joking?'

'Not even slightly. I thought it was a bonding exercise.'

'It was!' I say, aghast.

'But they're resolutions,' my mum says. 'Not wishes. It's not like me reading them would stop them coming true. I thought I was meant to be using them as a prompt to guide you through the year?'

I should be annoyed, really, but it does seem like a genuinely innocent mistake. I try to recall what past resolutions might have been. I find that I can't think of a single one.

My mum nods with satisfaction. 'You can't remember any of them, can you? That's why they've been safe with me.'

I reach for a Twiglet, twirl it between my fingers.

'You've had some shit ones,' she says. 'One year it was just, *Wear my jeans less.* Another year was, *Fewer TV dinners.* We've had generic ones too. *Be more patient. Live in the moment.* But do you remember what last year's was?'

I rack my brain, nibbling on the end of the Twiglet. I guess it must be something to do with Tom or the flat or my job. 'Concentrate more on my own life rather than worrying about what everyone else is up to?'

'Nope.'

'Be more ambitious?'

My mum shakes her head.

I feel an acute hot flush, before saying, 'Spend more time with you?'

'Don't be soft,' she says, chucking me under the chin. 'Shall I just show you?'

'You have it with you?'

'Of course. If I've said I'm looking after something, then I'm bloody looking after it.' She reaches under the coffee table for her handbag. From an inside pocket, she extracts a tiny blue envelope. Last year's secret resolution. 'Ready?' she asks, handing it to me.

'Why am I nervous?' I say, accepting it.

My mum shrugs. 'You shouldn't be. It's a nice one.'

I lift the little flap and tug the card out. I find that I'm holding my breath.

In my handwriting, five hastily scribbled words: *Learn how to be alone.*

180

'Did you mean to call me?' I say into my phone.

I hear his laugh. 'Yeah.'

'I thought you might have done it by accident.'

'Oh,' he says. 'That's grim that you would think that.'

I dart across the road. 'Can I call you back?'

'Yeah, sure.'

I wait until I'm inside before dialling his number. Since the breakup, I've found that I prefer to type the digits of his phone number out, rather than finding him in my call list. He's always too far down, and that makes me sad. He picks up on the second ring.

'Sorry about that,' I say. 'I didn't mean to be uncharitable. It was just an unexpected surprise.'

'Well we hadn't spoken for a while – and I saw your Instagram post about the comedy night – so I thought I'd call.'

'No, it's nice, obviously.'

'How was Christmas?'

'Yeah, really relaxing. Just ate and slept, it was good. Had lots of time with my mum. Didn't think about you once.' I say this with a laugh in my voice, hoping that he'll laugh back. 'What about yours?'

'Yeah, good,' he says. A pause. I hear him take a sip of something, and then he does a little sigh. 'On New Year's Eve, I wanted to throw myself off the fucking roof. I was so ready for the year to be over,' he says. He's not even slightly laughing.

'I don't know that you should be making suicide jokes, but yes, I can imagine.'

'It's been a lot,' he says. 'A lot.'

'For me too,' I say. 'It was easily the hardest year of my adult life.'

'So far,' Tom clarifies.

At that, I laugh. 'Well, yes. Of course things can always get dramatically worse very quickly.'

'Speaking of which, how's your colony of moths?'

I shudder. 'Don't remind me. I now have significantly less knitwear and significantly more lavender in my drawers. Dealing with that was worse than the breakup.'

'Mar,' he says, softly. 'I constantly think about how you're doing, but I can't call you every day. You know that?'

'And I wouldn't expect you to,' I say. 'But you know where I am. I'm never going to give you a frosty reception if you do reach out.'

'I'm grateful for that.' He sniffs. It's not tears, his voice sounds as though he's recovering from a cold. 'It's so good to speak to you. I'm glad I called.'

'It's been a long time, Tom.' I don't want to waste this opportunity to ask the thing that's been playing on my mind. 'Are we going to meet up, do you think?'

'I want to.'

'You didn't seem too keen when I last suggested it.'

'What would we even do? High five? Hug? Neck?' He laughs at his own joke. I hear him inhale. 'No, I would like that. I'm actually coming to London in a couple of weeks for Curtis's thirtieth. Maybe we could set something up?'

'Sure,' I say. 'Look at us. Just like Simon and Sinitta.'

181

Jerry finally emerges from his den. I hear the door of his flat opening downstairs and some short, gravelly coughs. The main front door doesn't open, even after a few minutes, so I assume that he's lingering in the hallway, maybe looking at his post. I press my ear up against my own door, in the hope of hearing more.

His phone rings, and he answers immediately.

'Yes, yes. That's it. No, it's past that. You've got the Co-op to your left? No, you're going the right way.'

A long pause. Floorboards creaking, signalling pacing footsteps.

'Tell you what, I'll come out onto the front steps, then you can't miss me.'

The front door does open then.

I pop into the kitchen to grab my cup of tea. When I get back to my listening post, Jerry is speaking to somebody, his tone reverent.

'Thank you for coming out for this. I'm terribly flattered.'

A female voice, young-sounding. 'Please! I couldn't wait to come and see it in real life. This is the highlight of my week.'

'If you'd like to follow me, then, I'm just through here.'

The voices fade, and there's the slam of Jerry's door.

182

Somebody from Bethnal Green Library comes to help out as temporary acting manager. A balding, stooped man called Tony, who I dodge completely for the entirety of his first shift, only sneaking glances at him when his back is turned. Everything he does looks suspicious, even when he's just shelving books. Though I didn't realise until today that I had any interest in the manager role, I find that I feel acutely jealous at the idea that Tony might be trying to take it for himself.

When I hear him laughing good-naturedly with one of my colleagues at the end of the day, I see that he might just be a normal, harmless man, brought in to temporarily act as manager, as his title suggests.

He nods at me, as I put my coat on.

'What was your name, again?' he says. 'I'm terrible with names, I do apologise.'

'Mara,' I say, holding my hand out for him to shake.

'Mara,' he repeats, seemingly to cement it in his mind. 'I wanted to say, I noticed that you have a very natural way with the patrons. They seem to like you.'

'Oh,' I say. I've genuinely never thought about whether the patrons like me or not, excluding the unpleasant case of Starey Man. 'Do you think?'

'Very much so. Especially the children.' He smiles, a wide, warm grin.

I zip up my coat, all the way up to my neck.

'I've been told about the success of the comedy night you set up.'

I nod, slowly.

'An ingenious concept. I love anything that gets people into the library who might not necessarily think the space is for them.'

'I had fun doing it, to be honest. I'd like to make it a regular thing.'

370

'I think that would be excellent.' He rubs at one of his elbows. 'And you like working here?'

I contemplate this, before answering. 'It's not always been a healthy environment,' I say. 'Been much better recently. But yes, I believe very strongly in the importance of libraries. Books have saved me more than once. And I think I'm actually pretty good at what I do.'

'Yes,' he says. 'I think you are too.'

Walking home, in the cold, I get the creeping impression that I've just had an informal job interview.

183

Jerry leaves a handwritten note in my pigeonhole. I'm so pleased to hear from him that I don't hesitate to rip it open. If I'm in trouble, then let me be in trouble.

> *Mara,*
> *I would like to invite you to a private view at mine this evening at 7pm. (I have left a note for Adele too.) I won't go into too much detail, as I don't want to spoil the surprise, but essentially, I've been working on a personal project for a number of years now (thirty, to be precise), which I assumed wouldn't be interesting to anybody but me. In recent weeks, it has been brought to my attention that potentially it is 'art'. News to me!*
>
> *No obligation to come, of course, but it would be nice to have you there. Wine and nibbles will be provided!*
> *All best,*
> *Jerry (ground floor + basement flat)*

Adele and I exchange a few excited texts, and agree to go down together. At 18:59, she knocks for me, and we have a hushed conversation in my doorway. She's holding baby Lila. She named her after her own mum. Tonight, Adele's dressed her in a tiny gingham frock and white tights, ready for the party.

'Hi, beauty,' I say, holding a finger out for Lila to hold.

'I can't tell you how intrigued I am,' Adele whispers.

'Right? What do you think it could be?' I whisper back.

For the last fifteen minutes or so, people have been steadily arriving at the house.

'A collection of emails to the council?' she guesses.

'Do you think he's just been quietly working on his own Sistine

Chapel down there?' I say. 'I can't believe how much I've underestimated him.'

'Come on, I can't take the suspense,' she says, starting to head down the stairs.

Jerry's door is open.

'Hellooo,' Adele calls. 'Can we come in?'

I peer into the entrance. His hallway smells citrusy. There's a completely uncluttered path through the flat, with tall, tottering piles of boxes and books on either side. It appears that he's tidied up.

A woman who I faintly recognise appears from behind one of the stacks. 'Unbelievable,' she mutters, walking past us, and out the door.

I watch her retreating figure, and something about her gait allows me to place her. She's the woman I saw on the day I moved in, the one who was litter-picking on the forecourt. I haven't seen her since. She must be another neighbour, from further down.

Lila starts to wriggle in Adele's arms.

'Shall we go in, baby? Shall we see what the funny man's made?' Adele says, into the little shell of Lila's ear.

I follow mother and baby into the depths of the flat. A hubbub of voices and chatter is coming from lower down. Everyone must be in the basement. We make our way down two flights of wooden stairs. It's unnerving to be in this space that has always been closed off to me, yet somehow familiar.

We arrive in a surprisingly warm and bright space.

'Oh,' we both breathe, as we see what's in front of us.

Jerry turns from the conversation he's having, to welcome us. He's in cords and a suit jacket. His black hair has been freshly dyed and there's a small nick under his nose from where he must have recently shaved.

'You found us,' he says.

Over his shoulder, there are makeshift shelves of varying lengths, stacked with tomes and tomes of books. I can't immediately tell what I'm looking at.

'This is crazy,' Adele says. 'Wow. We never would have known all this was down here.'

Jerry pats the air above Lila's head. 'How do you do, little one?' he says.

'Hello neighbour, hello,' Adele says, jiggling Lila up and down.

Lila offers up a gummy smile.

From what I can tell, each book cover has been whitewashed and adorned with intricate drawings or words. Jerry's canvas is always the same, and his medium seems to mostly be biro.

I am faintly aware of Adele asking Jerry questions, but I step away from them, closer to the shelves, so I can see better. The noise from everyone else fades away, as I focus on one of the books. On it is a hand-drawn likeness of a shop, which looks strikingly like the corner shop where I always run into Jerry. The white paint which makes up the background is cracked and yellowing in parts, but the drawing itself is precise, detailed. He's filled in individual bricks in the façade, the piles of vegetables which spill out onto the pavement. The next book holds a reproduction of a scene from a film: two women, one black, one white, with their arms around each other. In tiny writing at the bottom, Jerry has written, *True Romance, 1982, Hackney*. The next book I zone in on has a drawing of a woman and a child holding hands. It depicts them from the back, and they both have bright red hair. This one makes my heart leap. It's the only colour in the room.

I walk slowly around the space. Some of the books just have hastily scribbled words on them. Names or dates. There are so many faces, some I recognise as local characters. The homeless man with the pug, who sits by the entrance to the Co-op. A barmaid who's served me multiple times in the Adam and Eve. The guy who does tai chi in the middle of the road to get honks from passing cars. And countless buildings and Hackney landmarks. The Rio. Hackney Town Hall, where Adele and Baz got married. Graves in Abney Park. Ridley Road Market. Olympic Park. The Aziziye Mosque.

An image that recurs over and over again is our house. The bones of it are always the same, but little details change. Different figures in the windows. On my floor, there's a family of four, then a man, then a young woman with bobbed hair, and finally, on a low shelf, I spot a version of our house with me in it. He's drawn me with narrowed eyes, my hair loose around my shoulders, and in a hoodie. Tom's Nike hoodie. On the cover of *A Little Life*, painted white, there's our house again, this time with me and Tom in a window each. He hasn't added any features to our faces.

Adele and Lila join me.

'Creepy, right?' Adele says, softly.

I shrug. 'I don't know. I think it's kind of amazing.'

I point at a paperback in front of me. It shows a large outdoor pool, maybe London Fields Lido. Through the white paint I can make out a familiar image.

'Oh no,' Adele says, gazing at my outstretched finger. 'That's *Sons and Lovers*, isn't it?'

I nod, slowly. I can't work out whether I think the drawings are any good. They're certainly sincere. He's an archivist, rather than a straightforward artist, I think, or maybe he's both. Here, in this room, is his personal history of Hackney, a story that he wants to protect at all costs. Lila begins to grasp at the neckline of Adele's jumper.

'She's hungry,' Adele says. 'I might have to go back up. Are you coming?'

'Not yet,' I say. 'I'll be up in a while. We'll do tea and a debrief?' I say.

'Definitely. I've got plenty of thoughts.' She blows me a kiss and Lila blows me a raspberry.

I've just spotted a familiar sticker on the spine of one of the books. It's a Homerton Library book. Withdrawn, I'm sure. I don't picture Jerry as someone who'd steal a library book. Fittingly, the drawing on the cover is of the library itself. I feel seen. Not in a purely positive way. Maybe what I feel is exposed. I definitely feel vulnerable.

I sense Jerry behind me. I look over my right shoulder at him.

'Well,' he says. 'Is it okay?'

This strikes me as an odd thing for him to ask me. I don't say anything, just nod.

'I suppose it's a bit of a compulsion,' he says.

Still, I don't speak.

'An external hard drive, if you will,' he says. 'A way of preserving things.' He leans over me to adjust one of the books. 'You probably think it's very sentimental.'

'No,' I say, finally. 'I don't find it sentimental.'

'You've been here a little while now. I bet you've noticed changes in the area even in that short time. Shops closing, new ones opening, changes of ownership, people coming and going?'

I don't know that I have noticed anything like that. I've been very inward-facing since I've been living in this house. There's been so much happening in my own world that I've felt no need to look much further.

'Do you mind?' he says. 'That I've got you in some of them?'

I've turned, and we're facing each other now, but his eyes aren't looking directly at me. He's looking at a spot just over the top of my head.

Do I mind? I don't think so. It's just an odd realisation that Jerry could have a fully formed impression of me, could have coherent thoughts about my life.

'No,' I say, 'it's okay. I really like your work.' I find that I mean what I say.

'You do?' he says, making eye contact finally. 'And you don't think it's criminal that I've defaced all these books? As a librarian, this must seem like sacrilege to you.'

'I think the outcome cancels out the crime.'

'Well, thank you very much,' he says. 'And have you had a cup of wine? There's a drinks table in the kitchen. I'm asking that people have their refreshments upstairs away from the books. Just in case.'

Though he's not formally sending me away, I take it as an opportune moment to leave. 'Thanks for sharing this with me,' I say. 'And congratulations.'

Upstairs, in Jerry's kitchen, I'm alone. On the table, there's a bottle of red wine, a bottle of white, a bottle of rosé, a stumpy bottle of port, and a line of receptacles. I choose the Leicester City Football Club mug, and pour myself a small measure of white wine. Drink in hand, I look up at the ceiling. Up there is my bedroom, where night after night I've cursed this man for his quotidian noises. The sounds of him simply living his life. Washing his clothes and watching TV and warming up his dinner. I swill the wine around in the cup and down it in one. I cross the kitchen to the clunky black radio, and with one swift movement, I turn it on.

184

Over a Japanese dinner, Tom keeps bringing up happier, shared times.

'Remember when I went to that festival a few days after we first spent the night together?'

I nod, pouring us each a glass of water from a green ceramic jug. I know what he's about to say. It's one of our most well-worn stories.

'And I was panicking, because I had no phone signal and I couldn't check in with you about how you were feeling, and I was just completely terrified that you'd get cold feet.'

'I did get cold feet,' I remind him.

'But then, one night, I was listening to some obscure techno, off my tits, and I just had this epiphany. *It's all going to be fine!* And it was.'

'While it was,' I say.

A waitress places a platter of sushi on the table in between us.

'Do you have everything you need?' she asks.

'Think so, thank you,' I say.

As she makes her way back into the kitchen, I ask Tom, 'So you haven't been on any dates?'

He shrugs. 'No real dates,' he says.

This begs the question, *What kind of dates, then?*

I nod, slowly, recomposing myself.

'I downloaded Tinder for a few days,' he says.

'You did?' I say. I wait a beat, then say, 'I did too.'

'Depressing, isn't it?' he says. 'I deleted it when a girl asked me which Disney prince I most resembled.'

I sip my saké. I pretend it's the most normal thing in the world to hear Tom talking about joining a dating site.

'What are your plans for the rest of your visit, then?' I ask, wanting to talk about anything else.

Tom's face brightens. 'We're going to the Tate in the morning, and then Curtis booked us onto this thing where this forager guy takes you round Hackney Marshes and you pick all this wild produce – mushrooms and leaves and stuff – and then you have a gourmet meal made with all your finds.'

'Sounds fun,' I say.

'I can't wait,' Tom says, leaning back. 'It's actually good here, isn't it? When you know what you're doing.'

Yes, I think, *it really is.*

We eat in silence for a couple of minutes.

There's something I want to say, but I don't know how to bring it up in a natural way. I clear my throat, dab the corner of my mouth with a soy-sauce-stained napkin.

'Was Emma there last night?' I ask. 'At Curtis's party?'

'Yeah, she was.' Tom looks up from his plate, serious. 'She genuinely is just a good friend.'

'Well if it's not her, it'll be someone else,' I say. 'It's going to happen eventually.'

'Another drink?' he asks me, and I nod before he's even finished the question.

185

In the bar next door, after the food, the tone shifts.

'Mara,' he says.

'Yeah?'

He does a half-smile. 'Mara, Mara, Mara,' he says. 'I just love saying your name.'

I start to cry. It's not prompted by him saying my name like that. I just feel tired and overwhelmed. It's a small bar and there are only a handful of other people drinking there. We're both holding whiskies, and I don't know why Tom ordered one, because he doesn't even like whisky.

Next to me, he's quiet, until he says, 'I fucked it all up.'

Though this is the very confession I've needed to hear for the last however-long, it gives me absolutely no satisfaction now.

'Why were you so unhappy?' I ask.

'I never wanted to leave Birmingham.'

'So why did you?' I ask, my voice steady again. 'I wouldn't have broken up with you.'

'I thought it was the right thing to do,' he says.

'For who? For me or for you?'

'For us,' he says, causing fresh tears.

After a long silence, he reaches for me and I fall into him. We hold onto each other for long enough that it becomes inappropriate and we begrudgingly let go.

Wrapping both hands around his whisky glass, he says, 'I took it all for granted.'

At that, he becomes quiet again. That's the problem with him. He can't speak when it matters most.

'What's the matter?' I say.

'It's just sad.'

I can only agree with him. It's the second saddest thing that's ever happened to me.

His phone buzzes in his pocket and he pulls it out to look at it, then, flustered, pushes it back into his jeans. He's not fast enough. I've already seen the Tinder notification. I've clutched my phone to my body whenever I've pulled it out of my own pocket tonight to spare him the same sight.

'Shall we go back?' I say. My kidneys are throbbing. I feel drained. But also at peace and resigned.

'Okay,' he says. 'I'm heading your way, anyway. I'll walk you?'

We link arms, walk together. He puts his arm around me for a few moments at a set of traffic lights.

'You hate me,' he says.

I nod my consent.

'You do. I feel like you hate me and love me at the same time,' he says.

I turn to face him then. 'I do. I do love you and hate you. That's exactly right.'

He pulls such a sad face that I regret agreeing with him. It was a cruel thing to say, and I don't even think that I believe it.

His expression changes, and he looks at me then in a way that says a million things that he'll never say out loud.

It's cold, so we quicken our pace. Perched on a kerb outside a chicken shop, a couple are kissing passionately, clambering one over the other. Tom nudges me.

'They're going to have sex,' he whispers, as we go past them.

'Someone should,' I say, deadpan.

On the corner by the Co-op where we've bought so many dinners to eat together on my sofa, we linger.

'I have to go this way,' Tom says, pointing in the opposite direction to the flat.

'A hug?' I suggest.

He throws his arms open and encases me.

'I just sniffed your hair,' he says, as we pull away. 'Will I see you again before I go?'

I want my bed.

'Tom,' I say. 'You know where I am.' I'm already starting to feel the sadness seeping in.

We hug once more and then I turn to walk to my flat.

I mutter to myself, 'Tom, Tom, Tom.'

For one desperate, unlikely second, I think I hear him coming back towards me, but it's just a stranger on their way home.

EPILOGUE

Spring

186

The baby is screaming, really raising the roof. The noise is other-worldly. As though she's in extreme pain. It's gone from zero to a hundred in seconds. I reach blindly for my phone in the covers. I hear the crash of Adele getting out of bed, her feet hurrying across the room to the corner where the cot is. I squint at my phone screen. 03:02. Adele had a Next2Me crib for a while, which seemed to work fine, but she's trying something new now. They're in a fresh phase.

Usually a pretty quiet baby, this past week, Lila's been irritable. It could be colic, it could be that she's teething. Adele's still learning. She's called Baz many times in the middle of the night since Lila was born, in those nothingy hours before morning, when she's felt desperate and has stopped caring about what it might mean or what Baz might take it to mean or keeping the boundaries firm. Only a handful of times, though, have I heard Adele slapping down the stairs with Lila screaming in her arms, heard the front door open and close, and heard two sets of footsteps coming back up.

He says things like, 'Thank you for calling. You know I'm happy to come any time. Literally whenever.'

And then it sounds like a little family of three. Hushed voices, the baby settling, the gentle pacing back and forth on their landing.

Tonight, the screaming goes on and on, with no sign of Baz. Adele must be trying to handle it on her own. I get out of bed, go to the bathroom, pee. Back under the covers, I push my pillow over my head. I check my phone. 03:16.

There's a text from Adele. *I'm so sorry if we're keeping you awake. I honestly don't know what's wrong with her.*

I don't think about it too much. I just wonder what I'd want if I were in her shoes, and instinctively know the answer. I get up again, put my dressing gown on, tie it at my waist. I glance into my dark living room, smile faintly at the shadowy form of the sunflowers on my dining table. I got them from Columbia Road Market at the weekend, arranging them lovingly in a vintage vase that my mum gave me. Last week I had peonies, the week before that it was tulips. I open my front door, cross the tiny stretch of hallway, and knock.

I have to knock loudly and for a long time before she hears me.

She looks wild in her doorway, eyes bloodshot, her curls piled on top of her head, Lila blue with rage.

'I don't know what to do,' she says. She's frantic. 'I'm sorry. I don't know what to do.'

I lean over and tuck one of Adele's blonde tendrils behind her ear, rest my palm on her hot cheek.

'Adele,' I say. 'Do you want me to take her?'

Acknowledgements

This is first and foremost for Ma. Mara's mum is wonderful, but you're even better. Though thank you will never be enough, I'll say it anyway. You promised to fill the garage with thousands of copies of this book once it came out. Now you actually have to do it!

I'm hugely grateful to everyone at Madeleine Milburn and HarperCollins. My agent, Rachel Yeoh, was one of the easiest yeses of my life. What a thrill it was to hear you talk about this novel and your plans for it that day in Clapham. Lucy Stewart – my first (ever) editor – made the experience of being edited so seamless and collaborative. Your transparency and trust in me was exactly what I needed. Olivia Robertshaw picked up the baton at the eleventh hour, and ran with me towards the finish line. I so appreciate your enthusiasm for this book.

Thank god CWIP exists, and thank god Helen Lederer invented it. (Fiona Brinin-Webb, I still owe you a massive drink for texting me the link to enter!) It's not even a slight exaggeration when I say that winning the Comedy Women in Print Prize changed my life. The 2023 cohort are all thriving, and are a gorgeous font of support and resource-sharing. Women are *so* funny, and one day we will no longer need a separate prize.

I am very grateful for Goldsmiths, a happy space, where I continue to spend many long days, writing. I hope the library – and all libraries – exist forever. Thank you to my Goldsmiths mates, especially Helen Bailey, Mike Carver, Sam Simon and Sam Dixon. You taught me so much about workshopping, and absolutely nothing about networking.

My CBC pals. At a time when I'd lost confidence, you helped me fall back in love with writing. Jane Housham, Sam Elias, Julie Targett and Mima Biddulph were the first readers of *Homesick*, and when they told me I'd written a great book, I believed them.

A special mention to Grace Walker, Veronika Dapunt, and Celia Silvani for all being exceptionally available over text for any existential crisis. Sometimes, all you need in order to feel better is for someone to send you a row of exclamation marks.

For the Saunders clan. Thank you for asking the right amount of questions, but never too many. I have been writing novels for a decade, and you all just sort of assumed I knew what I was doing? That was nice. My gran, in particular, who has been absolutely livid that she had to wait for the book to be published before she could read it. Sorry for the swearing. Thank you for being my extra parent.

Per la mia famiglia Italiana. Sono circondata da dottori, dentisti, avvocati, ingegneri . . . ma mi avete sempre presa sul serio quando vi parlavo dei miei libri. Che gioia poter condividere questo traguardo con voi. Chi mi fa la traduzione?

Rachel Diegnan and Sophie Cliffe, my oldest and favourite friends. We speak non-stop every single day, and I would be a very different woman without you. If I'm any good at writing dialogue, our forever-pinging WhatsApp group has a lot to do with it.

Fabio Miccoli and Daniele Bottillo. You're a big reason why London feels like home. Please never move.

David. You make life so easy and fun, that I have absolutely no excuse to avoid writing. Thank you for talking every endless idea and worry through with me five million times. I promise we can talk about something else now. Ch'amo.

And for my dad, who continues to look after me from afar. You are in everything I am and everything I do.